SHANGHAI TANG

A DAN ROY THRILLER
DAN ROY SERIES, BOOK 4

Mick Bose

ALSO BY MICK BOSE

CHAPTER 1

Jintai West Road
Near East 3rd Ring Road
West Beijing

Lin Yan increased his pace as he walked down the wide Jintai Road. Like most of Beijing's new roads, this avenue was wide, with well-tended grass verges. Tall black buildings dominated the skyline around him. White lights glowed in windows, topped by red circular halogens to ward off incoming aircraft. The habitual cranes that littered Beijing's sky stood like question marks between the buildings.

Lin released the cordless headphones from his ears. They fell back on his neck. Lin dug his hands inside his light summer jacket and looked around him furtively. A woman walking a dog. A man with a child. Two college students, hand in hand. Nothing suspicious.

A yellow haze from the street lamps smeared across the polluted, smog-heavy air. He heard the steady drone of traffic from the Ring Road a couple of hundred meters to his left. He wished it was quieter. He could hear softer sounds, like someone creeping up on him. Or the hum of a car's engine as it slowed behind him. Inside the jacket pocket, his right hand gripped the tiny disk drive.

His passport to freedom. Whatever that meant. He would be getting out, as they had promised. That was more freedom than he had ever had. Funny how freedom meant different things to different people. It all came down to choices. And he had made his.

He was passing underneath a road bridge. Blue signs with white Chinese letters were stuck to the foot of the bridge. A glint of light caught his eyes and he looked up. Towering above him was the weird, two-legged futuristic skyscraper of the China Central Television (CCTV).

"*Da Kucha,*" Lin muttered under his breath. Big Boxer shorts. That was the local name for it. The building had an open center through which Lin could see the dull sparkle of distant light, dimmed by the smog. Two tall towers leaned against each other, connected by a central vestibule. It was completed by the time he finished his studies at the *Beida,* as Peking University was better known. Briefly, Lin's mind went back to his student days at the Wudaokou, the university district in North Western Beijing. The green parks and quiet lakes. The international students, where he had his first conversations with people from outside his country.

Lin shook his head. How time had flown. Back then, he had been a typical Chinese student. Raised in the Party doctrine but questioning his place in the world. A world that changed rapidly in front of his eyes. He had joined the massive production line of graduate students with no jobs. The unemployment figure of ten percent came from the State. Lin, and others of his generation knew the real figure to be closer to one in four.

He had been lucky to find employment with Shaolin Inc. His ease with programming software languages had helped.

It had been his choice to start his own online blog. *Knowledge changes destiny.* Lin closed his eyes briefly. A taste of bitterness came to his mouth. He wanted to spit, like the old Hutong dwellers did in their alley's open drains. He swallowed it back. Nothing would change *his* destiny. Nothing except...

Lin frowned but did not break his step. His thoughts were interrupted by the shadowy figure standing underneath a tree on the other side of Jintai West Road. He cursed. This was no time for nostalgia. No time for regrets. He should have kept a close lookout. How long had that guy been standing there? Lin kept his head bowed but snuck a quick look. There was no doubt. The man was watching him. He wore a dark coat with his hands thrust inside his pockets. The shade of the tree hid his features. He was of average height, tall enough to be a *yangguizi,* a white man.

Lin fought his rising panic and walked on. From the corner of his eyes, he saw the man cross the street. The man fell into step several yards behind Lin. Lin walked faster and realized the man was matching his pace.

Lin broke into a run. He had a plan. He was now approaching Sanlitun, the expensive and fashionable business district. The meeting point had been agreed at Sun Park directly opposite Sanlitun. There was a lake inside the huge park, and Lin knew the place like the back of his hand. But if the man behind him was any indication, Lin knew the meeting point was compromised. He could hear the man running behind him. Going inside the park now would be like signing a death warrant.

Lin had long legs, and he had played basketball at the *Bei Da*. He was fast. He headed straight up the road, past Sun Park and towards the Landmark River. He saw the lights of the bridge ahead of him, and he ran faster. He heard a shout behind him. He ignored it. As he went past the bridge, he could see the well-lit buildings lining both sides of Liangmaqiao Road. He came off the bridge, breath fluttering in his chest.

He ran hard across the road, paying no heed to the beeping of the cars. The bright lights of Dos Kolegas shone in the darkness like a beacon. Beijing's prime alternative rock venue. Lin could see the queues forming already. Kids sporting mohawks and skinheads with chained leather jackets stood smoking, chatting to girls with nose piercings, tight leather miniskirts, and blue-dyed hair. Deep bass music thrummed from inside. Lin vaulted over the steel barricade and ran to the side of the venue, disappearing down a back alley. He knew the back entrance. With any luck, the door would be open for supplies coming in for the night. It used to be when he worked there, only a few months ago.

The stinging blow hit him on the side of his face like a hammer. Pain burst inside his head like an exploding cloud, jangling every nerve in his body. He fell against the wall of the alley, dazed and weak. He sensed a presence next to him. Fingers like steel grabbed the side of his neck, then pushed against his windpipe, making him gag. Lin was tall for a Chinese, and like most tall men, he was not light. Yet his attacker lifted him up by the neck like he was a rag doll.

Lin was slumped, his legs trailing behind him. The dull glow of the streetlight fell against his attacker's face. Through a fog of pain and nausea, Lin blinked. Fear overcame him. The man had spiked blond hair which looked outlandish on his Chinese face. One of his black eyes glittered like a cat's, but the other was covered in a monocle. A look of revulsion lined every inch of the face as the man stared at Lin.

"Where is the information?" the man spoke between clenched teeth. Before Lin could stutter a response, the man shifted his weight. He reached down with one hand, balancing Lin's entire weight with the other. Lin could barely breathe, but his fear-dilated eyes did not miss the glint of steel. A curved sword caught the light as the sharp edge of the blade appeared before his eyes. The ancient sword of a Xia warrior.

"Tell me. Unless you want to die slowly!" The man got his face closer. Lin felt his hot breath on his face.

"I…I don't know," he squeaked out.

The blade pressed against the base of Lin's nose. It cut the flesh, and Lin felt warm blood rolling down the blade onto his lips. He struggled against the wave of panic. The man was literally cutting his nose off. Lin struggled, but the man's strength was immense. It was like bucking against a block of steel.

Lin felt the movement before he saw it. He moved backwards to the wall just as a black shape flew in from the side and collided with his attacker. The blow was heavy enough to blindside a man, but this guy barely felt it. He rocked back on his feet and whirled down to the ground. The sword was removed from Lin's face. Lin grabbed his nose, trying to stem the blood streaming from it. He shuffled back, then ran.

At the end of the alley, he looked back. The sword glinted as it rose high up in the air, then sliced down like a scythe onto the prostate figure below. Lin jumped into the back doors of Dos Kolegas and melted into the crowd.

CHAPTER 2

CIA Museum
Langley, Virginia
8 miles outside Washington DC

Kimberly Smith leaned over towards the glass display, trying to catch every word the museum curator was saying. Bernard DeLillo had a singsong voice that made Kim wonder about the state of his vocal cords. It made the story he was telling sound more enigmatic, she thought. The men and women around her were listening in hushed silence.

DeLillo raised a hand and pointed to the long glass cabinet in front of him. The object inside was a metal reinforcing bar, the type used in buildings to strengthen the bricks and mortar.

"So, ladies and gentlemen, what do you think this is?" DeLillo asked with a hint of a smile on his face.

The object was labelled, but for the purpose of this educational visit for the National Clandestine Service (NCS) employees, a white paper blanked out the information. It was meant to be a fun quiz. And Kim had to admit, she was having fun. Knowing the history of espionage was almost as thrilling as predicting its future. Besides, the CIA museum was out of bounds to the general public. It was a secretive place, run by the CIA, and visited only by CIA employees and their family members who had been "security cleared." Kim felt a certain amount of privilege that she could be here.

"A weapon," one of the agents said.

"A part of an old holding cage," another volunteered. Several turned towards the man, and he shrugged. Giggles were heard.

Kim looked at the now rusty iron structure and thought hard. It was metallic, of course. What properties did metal have? She frowned.

"It's metallic, so it can transmit sound and heat," Kim blurted out. A silence fell over the group. DeLillo turned towards her.

"Interesting," the curator said. "Carry on."

"From the flecks of cement on it, it obviously was inside a building. I mean, it *was* part of a building, right?"

DeLillo nodded.

"This object could, theoretically, accept waves – like sound and radio waves. If it could do that, then it could transmit it as well. If there was a whole system of them…"

"Then you have one of the world's largest listening devices, hidden inside a building," DeLillo finished for her. He smiled broadly at Kim and winked at her. He read her name tag.

"So, Miss Kimberly Smith, where would you find this thing?"

Kim shrugged. "Just guessing here, but inside a U.S. Embassy building abroad?"

"Correct again." DeLillo dropped his voice to a conspiratorial whisper. "In 1982, when the U.S. Embassy in Moscow was being built, the Russkies very helpfully offered to build parts of the building. They gave us these prefabricated cement blocks that would form the outer walls. The State Department accepted their kind offer. It was only when the CIA did X-rays of the building that they found the listening devices. Some of the bugs in this contraption you see were so powerful, they could pick up keystrokes from the IBM computers. In effect, the KGB was turning the entire building into a giant antenna."

Kim opened her mouth to say something, but her pager buzzed silently in her pant pocket. She excused herself from the group and walked to the sunlit door near the exit. She displayed her name badge at the bar code reader and the door swung open silently. She was now in the large lobby, sunlight flooding in from the glass ceiling above. As deputy chief of the East Asia division of the NCS, there wasn't much time she had to call her own.

Kim tucked back a curl of her shoulder-length blonde hair, left loose for once and not tied back, and looked at the screen. The office, as she had surmised. Shaking her head, she walked over to the phone on the wall. Her cell phone was in her locker; no phones were allowed inside the museum. Kim punched the numbers in and leaned against the wall.

"Hal Schumberg," the male voice said at the other end. Hal was her new boss, the sectional chief of South Asia.

"It's me," Kim said. "We still got an hour, right?"

"Wrong. The NSA guys have arrived early. Hot under the collar. It's worse than it looks. For us and them."

Kim gripped the phone. "But they're early."

"They claim we messed up the times."

Kim was going to say something but then thought better of it. She had certainly not messed up the times. The NSA had a habit of wanting to upstage the CIA, especially the NCS. Casting blame would not help anything, especially when they had a job to do.

"On my way," Kim said and hung up.

By the time she reached the conference room on the fourth floor of the New Headquarters, Hal had the large screen on the wall up and running. The large room had an oval-shaped desk in the middle, and a lectern and podium on the left, in front of the screen, facing the desk. People sat around the desk, laptops open. The lights had not been dimmed yet. Hal peeled off from the screen and walked over to Kim as she entered. He nodded and pointed to two of the men sitting at the desk.

"Chuck Dsouza and Rick Everett from the NSA." The two men stood up and shook hands with Kim. Chuck was portly and short, coming up to chest height of Kim's five-foot-nine. Rick looked more interesting, with a square-cut jaw, tousled dark hair and a pair of glasses framing an intelligent face. Easily north of six feet, his figure was trim and athletic, and he carried himself with a certain grace. Mid-thirties, Kim guessed. He held Kim's hand in a warm grip for a fraction longer than necessary.

"A real pleasure. Heard so much about you." Rick's voice was honey and warm, like his handshake. His olive-green eyes danced as they took in her features. Kim cleared her throat, feeling her heart skip a beat as she returned his stare.

How many women do you say that to?

Aloud she said, "Good things, I hope."

Rick smiled. "Maybe we should exchange stories later. See what we know about each other."

Kim removed her hand. He was coming on, and part of her didn't mind it, but the other part was busy on the job at hand.

Is this why you came early? To flirt?

Kim and the others took a seat as Rick walked up to the podium. He clicked on the laptop, and images appeared on the screen. It was of a computer screen with an email displayed.

"The Ghost Faces strike again," Rick read from the screen. His voice was still smooth, but raised an octave. He looked at the audience. "My name is Rick Everett and I am a member of the TAO." Tailored Access Operations was the largest, and most secretive, component of the NSA's Signals Intelligence Division (SID).

Rick continued. "The Ghost Faces have released about ten files loaded with TAO cyber-attack code. These are our implant framework for firewalls, server side utility scripts, and exploit targets. Basically, key tools that we use to hack into foreign banks and government websites.

"This is the third time this has happened. Many of us want to know why, and how." A photo showing the code from the stolen files flashed on the screen.

"Who were the targets?" someone asked from the audience.

"Network security systems of Middle Eastern and Chinese companies. Shaanxi Network Clouds, Emirates Fin Corp, to name a few."

Kim spoke up from the back of the dimmed room. "But the kind of data the Ghost Faces hacked this time – your string codes, binary config scripts – that sort of stuff never leaves the NSA, right? I mean, you stage attacks from the third-party staging servers, never your own. So, this time, the leak could be internal."

There was a murmur of voices inside the room. Rick cleared his throat. "That is correct, Miss Smith. Your eye for detail is unwavering, I see." He smiled wryly, and there was another muted expression of mirth among the guests.

Kim colored in the darkness. "Just stating a fact, that's all." She bit her tongue. That sounded defensive. She should have let it go. It wasn't easy being the only woman in the room, but her hide had thickened a long time ago.

Rick became serious. "And a very important fact. No one here needs to be made aware of the implications." He continued. "Either we have the unthinkable: a mole in the NSA, or what is more likely, the Ghost Faces is an attack force belonging to a foreign government. In fact, the latter seems to be the case, as one of the servers that we have attacked back belongs to the Chinese Ministry of State Security."

Heads nodded in the room. Everyone knew the MSS well, the Chinese version of the NSA and CIA combined.

Rick said, "It is likely that the Ghost Faces launched this attack as a tit for tat of their own recent humiliation. A hacker inside China has breached their firewall, it seems. We don't know if the player is Chinese or another nationality. But we do know that the MSS is deeply embarrassed." Rick clicked on the laptop again and a flurry of images appeared on the screen. Most of them were photos of screens showing bank account details.

"Images of Wells Fargo, First National, and Chase Morgan bank accounts that the MSS hacked into. The source code and the implant binaries definitely belong to the Chinese."

"Who is the hacker?" a voice asked.

Hal Schumberg stood up from the left corner. "We need our senior case officer to answer that question," he said quietly.

Kim stood up and made her way to the lectern. Rick stood to one side to let her pass, a hint of a smile on his face. Kim ignored him.

She plugged in her disk drive to the laptop and brought up the images she had.

"These are satellite images from the National Geospatial Intelligence Agency," Kim said. "China have their own drones over their main cities, so it's not easy deploying our own. The images suffer as a result, but it's the best we have."

The photo showed a tall, young Chinese man on a crowded city street. Kim hit some buttons, and the image cropped up to his face.

"This man," Kim said, "is a 23-year-old Beijing University graduate called

Lin Yan. He is the Chinese hacker in question. What you have seen so far is the tip of an iceberg. Lin asserts that he has downloaded an ultra-secret file from the MSS archives."

Kim looked at the assembled faces, listening to her intently. "This file bears a list of all the agents of the MSS, both active and sleeper."

The crowd stirred, and whispers spread inside the room. A voice raised itself from the back. "I'm sorry, but this is nothing new. We have heard such claims in the past."

"I haven't finished," Kim said. After a pause, she added, "The file also contains the names of undercover MSS agents *inside* the USA."

CHAPTER 3

Dan Roy heard the chorus of human voices, baying like a bloodhound. The roar thundered against the walls, rising and falling in waves as the crowd chanted. The sound was muffled in the basement where he was getting ready. Dressed in silk black fighting shorts with a red border, and nothing else, Dan focused his attention on the column of sandbags hanging from the wall as a makeshift punching bag. He hopped lightly on the balls of his feet in a boxer's stance. He skipped back once, then flung his heavy, muscled right leg towards the sandbags. The shin bone hit the hard sandbags with a dull *thwack*. Immediately Dan hopped back and repeated the kick with his left leg. The aim was to make the shin bone hit the sandbags. Over time, the nerves on the bone got desensitised. A process called cortical remodelling. The shin bones were used extensively in *Muay Thai*, or Thai Style kick boxing. Mainly to block and parry, but in offense as well. A shin kick to the side of the face, or to the side of the ribs, could knock out an opponent.

Dan practiced his kicks till his shins became numb. He stepped in close to the sandbags and did a flurry of punches, elbow hooks, and knee jabs. Sweat poured down his face and back, glistening in the yellow glow of the bulb hanging from the ceiling. With a creaking noise, the door opposite him opened.

Dahai Feng, one of the organizers, came and stood inside. He was several inches shorter than Dan, and older by many years. He bared his yellow teeth.

"Ju-Long," Dahai said, "are you ready?"

Dan stopped punching the bags and stood back. "My name is Dan Roy. Ju-Long is just my fight name. You know that."

Dahai said, "Can you not hear the crowd? Down here you are Ju-Long, the great, gigantic dragon slayer from across seven oceans." He chuckled.

He came forward and picked up the cotton sheets that would go around Dan's hands. Dan stood still with his hands raised, palms facing outward. In the *Kumite,* or Fighting Tournament, any manner of fighting was allowed, from Kung Fu to Western Boxing. The only stipulation in Hong Kong was the wrapping of the cotton sheets on hands. Dan watched as the water-soaked sheets went around his fingers. Then he stretched and flexed his fingers, making them into fists. He nodded at Dahai. The Chinese man went to the corner of the room and picked up an incense stick. The sticky aroma floated over to Dan. Dahai held the incense stick above Dan's head.

Another Kumite tradition. One that Dan had actually gotten used to. He bowed his head and closed his eyes as Dahai moved the incense stick in a circle near his head. These few seconds gave him a focus, channelling his energy towards the fight. He had come to realize it was a form of meditation, a clarity of mind, a blank slate upon which his flashing limbs would soon compose a symphony of violence.

Dan opened his eyes, breathed in, and followed Dahai out the room. A narrow corridor in the disused warehouse led the way to the staircase. The sound hit his ears immediately, reverberating off the walls. The crowd was chanting his name.

"Ju Long, Ju Long!"

As he went up the steps the volume increased till it became a deafening roar as the crowd caught a glimpse of him. This was Dan's first *Kumite* tournament, and already he had gathered a following. Tonight was the semi-final, and Dan had been undefeated so far in twelve fights. The stakes were higher now, and the opponents came from all over mainland China, Taiwan, Japan and Malaysia. Dan was regarded as exotic, as *gwai los* or white men did not often participate in the Kumite. Especially those who lived in Hong Kong as an expat. Out of the corner of his eye, Dan saw Dahai and his men walking around the circle, handing out tickets and grabbing money for bets.

The reason for Dan's popularity was the long odds he had when he first started. No one expected him to win. That changed the first night when people laid eyes on him. The odds shortened but were still nowhere close to that of a local prize fighter. He won his first fight in the first round, a classic roundhouse kick silencing the crowd who had been rooting for his opponent. Over the next few fights, Dan had made a lot of people rich and earned himself a nickname in the process. Ju-Long.

Dan looked to his right and caught a flash of light on the expensive suits of the Triad members sitting in their boxes. The fights were organized by them. The *Sun Yee On*, or New Righteousness and Peace Triads, were the most powerful in Hong Kong. They had ruled Kowloon before it got shut down by the Chinese, the sin city where Kumite had originated. Dan flexed his shoulders. Chinese names sounded weird to his ears, but he knew the Triads were traditionally regarded as the Robin Hoods of their world. In legend, they stole from the rich and gave to the poor. Names like *Sun Yee On* reinforced the notion that they were a movement for the good.

Dan knew better. He caught one of the Triad guys looking at him and he zoned out. He focused on his opponent. Bei-Lo was his name. The man was as tall as Dan and built entirely of muscle. He gave the appearance of being a tree trunk with his bulbous, muscle-ripped legs and toned abs. He was the All Hong Kong champion, the people's favorite. He was also a few years younger than Dan. Dan was still the long shot. Dan met Bei-Lo's cold, unforgiving stare. There was a shout, and the opponents walked out to the middle of the clay circle. Another shout, and the fight had started. The crowd went wild.

Dan circled the man. Bei-Lo was the first to make a move. Impatient to teach the *gwai lo* a lesson. He feinted with a diagonal kick aimed at Dan's torso. Dan lifted up his knee to block it but didn't expect the punch that landed on his chest. The blow was like a sledgehammer, delivered with such speed Dan didn't even see it. Breath exploded from his chest and he stumbled back.

OK, this is a different league.

Bei-Lo took advantage and stepped inside his space. He rotated his hips and went for the roundhouse kick to Dan's head. Through a maze of pain, Dan guessed the move. He covered his face like a boxer and hunched his wide, powerful shoulders together. The blow jarred him still, knocking him sideways. Dan lowered his arms just in time to see the fists coming for him again. He parried two blows and then felt, more than saw, the hook jab.

Bei-Lo's fist was coming up from below, ready to make connection with his chin. Dan executed an elbow block, a defensive move known as "combing your hair from front to back." He grunted as he deflected the jab and reached out to land a couple of quick punches at his opponent. Bei-Lo blocked them easily. They circled around each other, bursting into sudden paroxysms of kicking movements, both blocking and swaying away at the last minute.

The crowd was feverish now, chanting Bei-Lo's name. Dan knew he was an enforcer for the Triads, and this fight was his to win. As if reading his thoughts, Bei-Lo smiled at Dan. He stepped in suddenly, full of the arrogance of a fighter sensing an advantage.

This time, Dan let him come. Bei-Lo rushed in with a side kick, for real this time. Dan flinched back, but he was bluffing. Bei-Lo gave the kick everything he had. Dan raised his right arm and then clamped down as the kick made contact with his ribs. Pain exploded in his chest, but now he had Bei-Lo's right leg firmly under his armpit. Bei-Lo sensed his mistake and tried to move back.

It was Dan's turn to smile. He parried an arm jab and moved inside Bei-Lo's space. He got close, then bent his left elbow and smashed his opponent over the eyebrow. The horizontal elbow cut, as it was known, was one of the deadliest moves in Muay Thai. Bei-Lo's head snapped back, his leg, still held by Dan, suddenly becoming loose. Dan went into a clinch, grabbing his opponent round the neck and lifting his knee up into his face.

Dan's heavy knee smashed into Bei-Lo's nose. Blood and bone fragments flew in the air. But Bei-Lo wasn't done. He pushed Dan back, fell down and rolled over. Eyes wild with hate, he rushed Dan. He kicked and Dan leaned back, missing the blow. Dan stepped in close and hit him with the elbow again, this time an upper cut on the chin. The sound was like a baseball being hit for a home run.

Bei-Lo staggered back, his eyes glazed. Then he stumbled and fell down, unconscious.

For a few seconds, there was a sudden quiet. Dan panted, his breath hot on his lips, a dull roar in his ears.

Then the crowd erupted. Metallic objects hit Dan from the sides. They were throwing coins at him. It was the underground, Hong Kong way of showing respect. Ju Long had lived up to his name.

Dan watched as Dahai and the other organizers ran around, trying to calm the mob. From the corner of his eyes, Dan watched the *Sun Yee On* Triad members stand up and file their way outside. None of them looked at him.

CHAPTER 4

It was late at night when Dan stepped outside the abandoned warehouse. Lights from the skyscrapers across the bay glittered gold and silver, like a forest of giant glow sticks. The air was humid and warm, and the smell of diesel hit his nostrils. A few cars remained in the parking lot, but most of the crowd had dispersed. It was 0300 hours. Dan's body ached, and his head throbbed.

Blood fighting had started as a hobby, then became a way of life for him. He had been in Hong Kong for five months now, and the last two months had been taken over by the *Kumite* tournament.

It had come to him naturally. He had always been a warrior, and this was merely a different expression of it. He trained in Muay Thai at his local gym in Kennedy Town, in the north western district of Hong Kong, where he lived. A number of fighters trained there, and Dan had appreciated the similarity of Muay Thai to hand to hand combat. Something he had excelled in during his years as a Delta operator, and later as a Black Ops specialist with Intercept.

Dan heard a sound and looked behind. Dahai was shutting the door. He hurried up to Dan and reached inside a plastic bag. He pulled out a wad of Hong Kong dollar bills, tied together with rubber bands.

"Your share," Dahai said.

"Thank you," Dan said, pocketing the money. Dahai racked up some phlegm in his throat and spat it out. He pulled out a packet of cigarettes and offered one to Dan, who shook his head. Dahai lit his cigarette, and together they walked towards his parked car. The battered Toyota Camry had seen better days. Dan got in at the passenger side, the leather seats expunging a cloud of dust as he sat in it.

Dan closed his eyes as Dahai drove through the deserted downtown streets of Hong Kong.

"You fought well today," Dahai commented. Dan grunted without saying anything.

"This should pay the bills for a while," Dahai said. "I can send some money back home."

Dahai Feng, like many Chinese workers in Hong Kong, came from the northern Chinese regions of Guangdong and Guanxi. They came to look for jobs, but Hong Kong's real estate prices meant rent was unaffordable for most. His family had remained in a little village near Guangzhou, the largest city of Guangdong. By sheer chance, Dan had met him in the gym where he trained. Dahai worked as the gym's keeper and also happened to live in the high-rise block of apartments where Dan rented.

Dan opened his eyes as they went past the skyscrapers of Soho and the International Finance Centre. These filaments of steel and glass stood so close together, they looked like spines on the back of a hedgehog. To his left, in the distance he could see more dazzling lights of the Mid Level hills, where forests of high-rise residential apartments stood in organized symmetry on the slopes of hills. The whole bay area of Hong Kong was, in fact, reclaimed from the slopes of hills. Forests had been cut down over hundreds of years to make a spatially super-compressed cornucopia of human habitation. The glittering Mid Levels were Hong Kong's idea of a suburb. The sights never ceased to amaze Dan.

They drove past Sheung Wan and Sai Wan, the two fashionable districts close to the bay, and travelled further west. Kennedy Town, situated in the northwest of the island, was less desirable, where dingy clusters of apartment blocks stood huddled close together. Dahai took a turn after the grounds of Hong Kong University and drove down Pok Fu Lam Road. Soon, he was driving through a deserted market street. In a few hours, the hawkers would set up their stalls, and many of the innumerable dumpling shops would open, selling freshly steamed snacks in bamboo baskets.

Dahai stopped the car at the mouth of an alley. Driving in with a car would cause a traffic blockage. Tall apartment blocks crowded either side of the narrow alley, almost blocking out the sky. Clothing hung from washing lines, and the black boxes of air conditioning machines stuck out from every window.

Dan said goodbye to Dahai and took the elevator up to the seventh floor.

The block had twenty floors in total. The elevator creaked and groaned its way up the decades-old building. The light bulb inside fluttered and blinked. The elevator finally arrived on the seventh floor, stopping with a bump. Dan pulled back the collapsible iron gate and stepped out into the hallway. Across a door, he walked into the corridor that housed the apartments. It was dark inside, the only light visible the distant glow from similar tall buildings around. Dan walked down towards his apartment and stopped short.

His door was shut but not locked. He could tell by the way the door was not pulled tight against the frame. The hinges were loose, but when Dan locked the door, it hugged the doorframe. And Dan had locked it before he left.

All of a sudden, his senses were twitching. He whirled around, but the corridor was empty behind him. In the semi darkness ahead of him, he saw no one. Creeping forward carefully, Dan got to his door and put his ears on it. Silence. He did not have a weapon with him. If there was an intruder inside, his bare fists would have to do the job. Which was more than enough, unless they were armed.

He didn't think it was an ordinary burglar. There was nothing in his room worth stealing. Only his clothes, and some books. The alternative was not a palatable one. A flashback from his previous life shot across his mind. Assassinations. Faces of dead targets. The betrayal.

Whoever was inside that room had an agenda. This was how Intercept, the black ops outfit he had worked for, would come one day, he had always known. Someone was sitting there in the darkness, holding a silenced handgun, with a bullet that had his name on it. Or maybe he was thinking too much.

Dan closed his eyes and put his hand on the handle. Whoever it was, he needed to find out. He had never feared death. He was lucky to have lived so long. He would go when his time was up, but till then, he had to do what his conscience told him. Right now, if they had sent someone to kill him, he had to know why.

Why, after all these years? Why, after he had done what had been asked of him. But he also had to protect himself. Dan crouched down on one knee and shifted to the side of the wall. Hand outstretched, he depressed the handle, and pushed the door in hard. Anyone hiding behind the door would be revealed. Dan pressed himself back, away from the door. Nothing. It only aroused his suspicions more. If this was a killer from Intercept, then they wouldn't have fallen for the childish move.

Dan shuffled closer and raised his voice. "Who are you?" Silence. He repeated his question. Then he heard something that surprised him. A Chinese voice.

"*Ni hau, Ju-Long?*" How are you, Ju-Long.

Dan straightened himself. He took a deep breath, and stepped inside the hallway of his small, cramped apartment. A light came on inside the dining room. Dan stood still for a few seconds. Then he shut the door. He walked past his bedroom and the bathroom. To his right, light spilled out of the dining room door, which stood ajar. Dan pushed it open. He blinked. Two men were sitting at the table, dressed in sharp, glossy suits made by the best Hong Kong tailors. Triad men. They looked familiar, perhaps some of the *Sun Yee On* members he had seen at the fight.

Both the men were middle-aged, with slicked-back black hair. The Chinese had an obsession with dyeing their hair. It was hard to find a Honger, as the HK residents called themselves, with greying or white locks. Triad members were no different.

Behind the two seated men stood two younger men, also in suits. These men were thickset, wide like Dan. One of them had a white bandage around his nose. Bei-Lo, his opponent from the fight. Dan stood at the doorway, his wide shoulders filling up the frame. Bei-Lo's eyes glinted with hate as he stared at Dan. Dan ignored him.

"Entertainment is over, guys. What are you here for?" Dan asked in English.

One of the seated men leaned over. "My name is Chow Ying," he said in English, as if that was all the introduction necessary.

"Who the hell are you?" Dan asked. Bei-Lo swore and moved forward. Chow Ying put a hand up.

"No need for that." Ying looked at Dan with narrowed eyes. "I am

Number 426, the Red Pole Enforcer for the New Righteousness and Peace group. Do you know what that means?"

Dan remained impassive. "Even if I did, why should I care?"

Both the standing men swore at Dan in Chinese and reached for their belts. The guy seated next to Ying spoke sharply in Chinese, and they shut up.

Ying smiled. "You got guts, *laowai*. I'll give you that."

Dan did not smile. "I'll give you five minutes to get out of here."

Ying's smile became broader. "And if I don't?"

Dan shrugged. "It's a long way down through the windows, Mr. 426."

Ying leaned back in the chair, smile fixed on his face. His black eyes glittered like hot coal. "I have a message for you."

Dan remained silent. Ying continued. "Our Mountain Master, the Dragon Head of our Clan, wants to employ you. You will become a 49er, or an ordinary member of the *Sun Yee On*."

Dan's face tightened. "I don't work for anyone."

Ying's face lost the smile. He leaned forward. "That was not a request. It was an order. You want to live in Hong Kong, you have to obey the order. No one refuses the Dragon Head."

"There's always a first time."

Abruptly, the two seated men stood up, scraping their chairs back. The room looked crowded all of a sudden. The man next to Ying barked an order, and the two men behind them stepped to the sides with weapons drawn. Both guns pointed towards Dan.

Ying said, "If you want to live till the end of tomorrow, come to the Shanghai Moon Club in SoHo. Otherwise, prepare to die."

CHAPTER 5

CIA HQ
Langley, Virginia

Kimberly Smith curled her fingers around the cappuccino and came out of the Starbucks. She walked down the path that circled around the George Bush Center For Intelligence. She sipped tentatively from the hot cup and realized immediately it was still too hot. She nodded at two of her colleagues as they walked past. Kim walked till she came to the statue of Nathan Hale, the colonial spy who had been hung by the British in New York in 1776.

Standing underneath it was her boss, Hal Schumberg, the head of the National Clandestine Service's South Asia Division. Kim stopped. Hal was staring up at the statue, reading the epithet inscribed on the stone pedestal. He looked up as Kim approached.

"Do you know what Mr. Hale said before he died?" Hal asked Kim conversationally.

Kim shrugged. Hal said, "I only regret I have but one life to lose for my country."

"Great words."

Hal transferred his gaze back to the statue. He sighed and said, "That made me think about the Five Ways situation." Five Ways was the name given to the unfolding Chinese hacking crisis. Lin Yan was still missing, and the MSS were still looking for him. So were CIA assets inside China.

Hal started to walk and Kim fell in step next to him. "What do you mean?" Kim asked.

"I mean, despite mobilizing most of our assets inside China, we still have no word about this guy, right?"

"China's a big place, Hal. Needle in haystack. Remember their internet is censored as well. All the NGO's and Human Rights Groups that used the codename we gave them have seen their websites being hit. Not easy to get information out of China."

"The codename we gave them for Lin Yan?"

"Right. Even if one of our assets knows about him, it's likely they are trying to send us the info without much success."

"Which brings me back to Nathan Hale."

Kim frowned. "What do you mean?"

"That guy only had one life, right? Think what he could have done with another chance."

"Sorry, you lost me."

"The black list."

Kim came to a stop. Hal stopped as well. "You cannot be serious," Kim said.

Hal sighed. "Our diplomat in Beijing has been summoned by the Politburo Standing Committee. State Department is hot under the collar. Tempers are rising, Kim, and it's all to do with this."

"The Politburo have no proof."

"I got a call from the ODNI. The President wants a full report on the situation, including the progress we have made in the last 48 hours. He wants it by tomorrow."

Kim groaned inside but said nothing. Hal said, "ODNI wants names of individuals dealing with this."

This time Kim's groan was audible. "You are kidding me!"

"Nope."

"Who did you say?"

"Well, you and me, obviously. And those guys from the NSA."

Kim wanted to throw her coffee away. "Great," she fumed. "Just great."

"Get the black list," Hal said. "We need to look at the lost ones. See if we can find some in the region."

Kim shook her head. "You know I need clearance for that, Hal. Not that simple."

Hal leaned closer. "And I'm saying you're all set. I made some phone calls. Pentagon is aware. You can access their database."

"Right," said Kim, the frown not leaving her face.

She kicked the chair at her table as she sat down. Bethany, her ginger-haired analyst, leaned over from the side.

"Bad coffee?"

Kim sat down with a huff. "More like a bad smell." Kim told her about her conversation with Hal. Bethany whistled. The black list was a list of former black ops operatives the CIA was not supposed to have. No one knew what had happened to these men, apart from the fact they had taken part in missions that their government would never admit to. Deniable missions. It meant a mountain of work for Kim and her team, having to try and locate someone from that list.

Kim took a sip of her coffee and leaned back in her seat. A space cleared inside her mind. She gripped the handles of her chair, and her eyelids fluttered open.

"If you need anything, call me."

Dan Roy's last words to her. Kim sat up slowly and stared at the black screen of her desktop, her mind working. The memory of his intense, dark eyes and his brooding, pensive personality floated back into her mind. Along with it came the feel of his touch on her skin, the smooth, almost oily hardness of his muscles. A heat spread to her face, and she shook her head.

Dan Roy had meant something to her. What exactly, she did not understand. They had shared death-defying experiences together and managed to come out alive. That created a bond forged in fire, she knew that. But while she had known Dan, she had also found Maya. She flipped out her cell phone. No messages. Maya's curly locks and her wide, expressive eyes stared back at her from the screen lock. Kim traced a finger down the screen. The face reminded her of Sarah, her sister who had died in a terrorist incident.

Kim glanced at her watch. Five minutes to three p.m. Another four hours before she got back home and excused the babysitter who brought Maya back from school. Then it was her time with Maya. The 11-year-old had settled into Virginia life nicely. Kim smiled at the thought. She might never have children of her own, but she would always have Maya. She looked forward to her evenings now, unlike when she lived alone.

Kim slipped the phone back in her purse and leaned back in the chair. Thoughts crowded her mind like a packed subway train.

Dan Roy had been the most lethal killing machine she had ever seen. And Kim had seen many CIA SOG (Special Operations Group) guys, ex-Delta and Navy SEALs. Dan was a cut above. He moved well in foreign cultures. There was something about his dark, tanned looks that allowed him to blend in. She had no doubt that if Dan was put into the Five Ways operation, he would succeed. Or at the very least, achieve more than what she was achieving now.

Then Kim stopped herself. Dan was not operational any more. He had made it abundantly clear to her that he had quit. It would not be fair to drag him into this.

Besides, did she fully understand the angles here? The Five Ways operation was a secret one, and not part of the daily President's Brief prepared by CIA analysts. The White House knew about it obviously, and the political machinery was beginning to stir. That made Kim uneasy as hell.

And the NSA. What was their angle? How had the Ghost Faces hacked into the NSA's mainframes? Her mind went back to the handsome features of Rick Everett. Behind his casual good looks, there was an enigma that she could not fathom. She couldn't deny he was interesting, but a sixth sense told her there was something happening in the NSA that she was not fully aware of. Something that would impact on this operation.

Kim sighed. All of which meant bringing Dan into this was the wrong move. She had last heard from him a month ago. He was in Hong Kong, a place called Kennedy Town. He had called her from inside a gym, where he was training in martial arts. A smile came to her lips. Always a man of action. She wished she could see him again.

CHAPTER 6

Hu Shintao, Number 489, The Mountain Master, The Dragon Head of the *Sun Yee On* Triad, lifted the watermelon knife high above his head.

A mask covered Hu Shintao's face. No one knew his real identity. The Mountain Master was normally a reclusive person, and his name was derived from one of the eight high mountains in China, where the holiest Buddhist temples were situated. The name implied isolation and a purity that could not be sullied by common acquaintance. The Mountain Master, The Dragon Head, only made his identity known to those who deserved it. Legend also said those who saw his face did not live to disclose the truth.

The oval-shaped yellow watermelon was placed between two rungs. Two dignitary guests sat opposite the table, their starched black suits, black ties and white shirts identifying them as Party officials. The men had their eyes fixed on Hu Shintao. A scattering of Triad men stood guarding the doors.

One of the men stepped forward. He was dressed differently than the rest of the Triad men. He wore a grey leather overcoat the came down to his ankles. His hair was spiked and blond in colour. His left eye was covered in a monocle.

Hu Shintao glanced at him. "Hua Dong, my brother," he said in a deep, rumbling voice.

Hua Dong bowed deeply. He took out an incense stick and lit it with a lighter. He put the incense stick inside a hole on top of the watermelon. Fragrant curls of smoke rose up in the air.

Hu Shintao flexed the grip on the machete. The nickname for machetes in Triad society was the watermelon knife, as it was often used in a new recruit's initiation ceremony to slice a watermelon in two. The machete had a jade grip, embroidered with gold. Light shone on the blade and then flashed down like lightning. The watermelon split into two, and small bits of the fruit went flying in the air. There was a smattering of congratulatory noise from the guests.

Hu Shintao remained standing, the machete still in his hands. He focused his attention on the two guests sitting opposite him.

"Comrades," he said, using the standard party name for a colleague, a word that made both men wince.

"May the watermelon slicing bring us luck and good karma. There will be peace and harmony in our community, and death to the traitors. Have we now closed the contract for the land?"

The two officials looked at each other. One of them coughed and rubbed his hands together nervously. In a tremulous voice, he said, "We are almost there, Hu Shintao. Just one more Minister at the Ministry of Environment..."

Hu Shintao stepped forward, his height and bearing imposing. The official stopped speaking immediately and swallowed.

Hu Shintao said, "That is what you said the last time."

Both men were sweating. "I know," the same official continued. "And I plead your forgiveness. There are many licences that need approving in the Ministry. Shangai is growing, as you know, and new developers..."

"You told me you had the ear of the Senior Minister himself. That he wishes to have a villa in the Swiss Alps. I bought the villa for him. He wanted a vacation home in the island of Sardinia, off the Italian coast. I got that as well. Is this how he repays my generosity?"

The official tried to stand up. He spread his hands. "It's just that..."

"Sit down!" The sharp command came from Hua Dong. He bowed to Hu Shintao quickly and stepped forward. "No outsider stands up in front of the Dragon Head." Dong removed his curved Xia sword with a flourish. "Unless you wish to have your nose cut off."

The Party official sat down. Hu Shintao looked at Dong and nodded slightly. Two men appeared by Dong's side immediately. Together, they grabbed the protesting Party official and frogmarched him to where Hu Shintao was standing. The man recoiled as the masked face lowered to his own. The mask was a shiny black, made of hard wood. The eyes were far back behind the mask, but there was no mistaking the intensity of the gaze.

The deep voice rumbled again, "Every tree in the forest must fear the fire.

You will be an example to the others." Shintao glanced at Dong again. "Let the Lingchi commence."

All color faded from the official's face. "No, no, Shintao. I am begging you. Not the Lingchi, please. I beg you…" His voice rose into a scream as the two men dragged him back and out of the room. The door shut and his haunted voice echoed outside in the corridor.

CHAPTER 7

Shanghai, Downtown
Pudong

Xiao Wei-Ling stared out past the towering skyscrapers into the distance. She was standing on the 24th floor of the marble and glass edifice that comprised the Shaolin headquarters. Past the buildings, she could see the vast sprawl of the muddy brown waters of Huang Pu River, bending slightly as it disappeared down to the Yangtze River delta.

Barges and tows bobbed on the water like ducks in a pond, and ferry boats plied up and down across the river, crossing the giant city from west to east. Across the water, hazy in the dusk's diffuse sunlight and traffic smog, she could make out the outline of the Bund, the long promenade of European buildings that made up the Puxi, or eastern side of the city. Lights were beginning to glow on the Bund, and by nightfall the buildings would be lit up a gigantic line of Christmas trees.

Xiao was standing close to the glass panes that formed the western wall of her office, and she realized her breath was fogging up the glass. She stepped back, staring absentmindedly at the circle of fog. Her mind was caught up in other things. She took out her Xiaomi cell phone and thumbed down to the Weixin chat app. The universal method of staying in touch in China. No messages from Lin Yan. She had called and left texts for her colleague, but for the last two days, the guy was as good as gone. Which was not good. With a deadline that was already past, and her boss breathing down her neck about the new app that Shaolin Inc. was bringing to market, her main developer had decided to do a vanishing act.

Her mind went back to the strange phone call Lin made just before he went off grid. He said he was in trouble, and needed help. And that she was the only person he could trust. What did he mean?

Xiao stared at the screen, wondering how ironic it was that she was holding her competitor company's cell phone, hoping to hear from the guy who would make the Weixin chat app obsolete. The Redmi chat app, designed by Shaolin, China's number two mobile phone company, would have built-in features no chat app had in the past. A 3D hologram mode could literally make the person appear in front of the speaker. The Redmi pay service allowed any item to be bought from the supermarket and delivered home within 24 hours. And it had gone one better than the Shake Me feature of the Weixin app. With Shake Me, the customer had to shake their phone to see which one of her friends were nearby. But it also gave her own location away. Redmi hid the location and found out what her contacts had been up to the whole day. Like who they had seen, which locations they had been to, and so on. Xiao had thought *this* feature of Redmi would not be allowed by the Ministry of Communications. Talk about a snooping device.

As it happened, the Ministry loved it.

Xiao heard a knock on her door and turned. "Come in," she said.

She had not expected to see the man who opened the door. She hid her surprise and approached the door quickly. Xiao bowed and said, "Jiang *Xiansheng.*" Mr. Jiang.

Danny, or Dong Quo Jiang, did not bow. He nodded and his lips twitched briefly. He was in his sixties, but like all Chinese men, his hair was dyed glossy black. He wore a black suit and dark tie. His swarthy, flat face was still, his black eyes friendly but always watchful. As CEO and President of Shaolin Inc., Danny Jiang was one of the richest men in China. He had a reputation for being ruthless, and like any wealthy entrepreneur in China, his political connections were impeccable.

"Wei-Ling *Furen,*" said Danny Jiang in a light voice. Miss Wei-Ling.

He ran his eyes over her, and Xiao blushed. She was dressed up for the evening, wearing a black dress that stopped at her bust, leaving her shoulders bare. The dress hugged her shapely, 33-year-old body and came down to her ankles, but in a nod to the traditional Cheongsam dress, the right leg had a split up to her upper thigh. She wore dark tights underneath, preserving her modesty. If it had not been a business meeting, she would have dispensed with the tights and put her high heels on. The thought made her momentarily wistful. When was the last time she had had a night out? Work ruled her life.

"You look as pretty as the evening sky," Danny said, smiling again. "If you don't mind me saying so. Take it as a compliment from an old man."

Xiao had met the old man only once before. That had not been an auspicious occasion. A black cloud of regret suddenly blocked her senses. Then it passed, and she concentrated on the present. She could not dwell on the past.

Danny Jiang had been lenient towards her then. She had wanted to leave, taking her shame with her. But he had seen her worth to the company and made her stay. For that, she owed him. And all he had expected in return was for her to work hard and come up with new, market-busting ideas. Which she hoped she had.

She had heard in the grapevine he was fuming about the delay to the app's marketing phase, and hence called for an urgent meeting. Word had gone out that Party members would also be present, and everyone was to be on their best behavior.

Xiao swallowed and said, "Thank you, Jiang *Xiansheng*."

"Call me Danny, please." Most Chinese women and men had English nicknames.

"OK...Danny *Xiansheng*."

"The cars are waiting downstairs," Danny said. Xiao picked up her purse from the table and walked out into the deeply carpeted corridor with her boss.

"You know, I knew your father," Danny said.

Xiao stiffened. It was true that she had got the job due to her father's name. But that had been many years ago, and she had risen vertically in Shaolin's male-dominated management structure on her own hard graft.

"Oh, I see," Xiao said, trying to keep her voice neutral.

"I lived in Hainan Island," Danny said conversationally.

Xiao stopped and turned, surprised. "You did?" Xiao herself came from Hainan, the tropical island in the South China Sea, to the west of Hong Kong. It was the southernmost part of the PRC, and being on the same latitude as the Caribbean, its weather was similar. Indeed, the island was a hugely popular holiday destination to visitors from the frozen north of the country.

Xiao asked, "Where did you live?" Hainan was a small island, and most of the long-term residents knew each other.

"Haikou," Danny replied. Haikou was the capital of the island. "I was stationed there as a software engineer for five years. I worked in the Party HQ. You were small then. I doubt if you would remember me."

A light was beginning to dawn in Xiao's eyes. Her father worked in the Press Office of the Hainan Party HQ. That must have been where he had met her father.

Danny lowered his tone as they got into the elevator. Xiao recognized the tone of respect. "Hu Wao was a man of principles. Not like other Party members."

Xiao kept silent. Her father, Hu Wao, had been a lifelong Party official. The Press Office was an important posting, even as far out as Hainan. As the South China Sea grew in importance, so did her father's position. She remembered the many attempts local businessmen had made to bribe her father. The gifts often arrived at their modest one-story house. A grand piano had arrived once, from the nearest city of Guangzhou. Her father had sent it back. Xiao had been a keen piano player, and she asked her dad why he didn't keep it.

"If you play cards with the devil," her father had said, "the game never stops." Xiao remembered the words.

"I used to play golf in Hainan," Danny said.

"Which course?"

"The Jack Yongli resort."

"Ah, yes," Xiao said, although she knew virtually nothing about the place. Golf courses were not allowed in China, as they were seen as a sign of imperial decadence. But in Hainan, away from the mainland, it was fair game. As a result, wealthy Chinese flocked to Hainan to play golf.

The elevator pinged, and they walked into the spacious, white marbled lobby, lit up by crystal chandeliers hanging from imposing heights. A bank of glistening black Range Rovers were waiting to take them to the Shanghai Four Seasons Hotel Banquet Room.

Xiao looked at some of her colleagues getting on board. She said, "I better go and join them. Nice to meet…"

"No. Travel with me, Xiao. I wish to speak to you."

Xiao tried not to show the confusion she felt. This was Dong Quo Jiang, the boss of all bosses as far as she was concerned. What did he want from her? One of the uniformed drivers held the door open for her, and Xiao got in. Danny got in next to her. The car in front moved out, and after five seconds, so did they.

"OK," Danny said, looking straight ahead. There was a security guard in the front seat next to the driver, but the back seat was partitioned off from the front of the car.

"I want to know what happened to Lin Yan." He held his hand up. "I have heard the official version. Spare me that. I want to know what you think."

Xiao pressed her lips. In truth, there was not a great deal to say. Lin Yan kept to himself. "He was an introvert. A genius, but an introvert." Lin Yan was in charge of writing the code for the software's app.

"Was there anything bothering him?"

Xiao paused for the briefest of seconds. What Lin Yan had shared with her was a private matter. For now, she would keep it that way. "Not that I could see. He came, did his job, and left. The day he vanished, he simply did not come to work. When the Public Security Bureau Officers came, they took his laptops away. I don't know if they found anything."

"They didn't," Danny said shortly. He glanced at Xiao. "Anything else?"

Xiao knew what Danny was thinking. Getting ahead in the mobile app business was worth billions. In U.S. Dollars, never mind Yuan. The Chinese market was closed to Facebook and Google, therefore competition was fierce between Chinese companies. If Lin Yan had been poached away by a rival software company, he would not be the first one.

Xiao knew the future of the company was at stake as well. Like Alibaba and Baidu, Shaolin could spread its wings to the rest of Asia if this messaging app took off. And from beta testing, Redmi had received consistently high ratings. Xiao herself liked using the app. It was user friendly, and could be easily programmed to find out things about her friends and family no other app could.

She shook her head. "Not as far as I know, no."

"You are his line manager. Nothing has ever come to your attention in the last three years he has been here?"

Xiao thought to herself about the last time Lin had come to see her. He had something important to tell her, and she was the only person he could trust. She remembered his voice, thin and shaking. He was scared.

"No," she said to Danny.

Danny settled back in his seat. They were driving past the forest of skyscrapers that made up Pudong. Xiao watched as the lights of the 88-story Jin Mao building, the tallest structure in Shanghai, reflected on her window. The restless waters of the Huang Pu lay to her right, the waters at the bank lit up red and gold, but the rest of the seething black river was lost in the darkness.

"I fear the worst," Danny said after a while. "The airlines and ports have not found anything either. And in any case, it is easy to jump out of China. If we don't find Lin Yan soon, we might not find him at all."

CHAPTER 8

Kim had a meeting with Rick Everett and Chuck Dsouza in their office at the NSA. She had to admit the NSA offices were plusher than her own. The elevators were a glass box, and she had a stunning view of the Virginia countryside as she glided silently to the apex of the building.

Rick was standing there with a warm smile when she came off the elevator. His handshake was firm and lingered longer than was necessary. He held her eyes as he did so. Kim was the first to look away, but she knew from her skipping heartbeat there was something there.

They settled in Rick's office, and she was glad that Chuck Dsouza was present as well. Rick's office was futuristic, with two-toned pale-colored walls, a legless desk with curved edges that sloped down to the floor, and round, backless seating cushions. Monitors hung on walls.

Kim said, "We have all our assets in mainland China now, looking for Lin Yan."

Rick asked, "Who made contact with him first?"

"He met one of our operatives at a charity dinner. Our op had a cover as a businessman. His story was venture capital funding of an IT start-up. He got Lin interested and talking. Turned out Lin hates his country. His grandparents died in the Great Leap Forward, and his dad was sent to prison for not following Party dictum. He died in a labour camp way up near Mongolia. His mum met someone and had another baby. But the one child policy meant she had to have a forced abortion. She died from complications of her operation."

Rick's face was set in stone. "Shit."

Chuck Dsouza asked, "So what happened?"

Kim said, "Our guy was set to meet him in Beijing. He was followed. Someone attacked Lin and killed our man."

"Any witness?" Rick asked.

"Yes. Reports of a blond guy. Chinese. He was seen running from the scene. No traces. Beijing PSB are being tight lipped as usual."

"And Lin?"

"Vanished. He knows Beijing well, went to college there, at Peking University. But my hunch is he's left already. He's smart enough to know there'll be others looking for him." Kim paused and asked, "Anything on your end?"

Rick looked at Chuck, who shrugged. Rick said, "Nothing as yet. But we put out a tracer on some emails coming out of a software firm in Shenzhen called Zensoft. They are attached to the MSS and provide their back office materials. They deny it of course. Anyway, these emails were sent to a Chinese student in Virginia Tech. The language in the email was coded. We need to break the code. Shall I come over one day if I find anything?" His smile held more than a hint of a suggestion. Kim blushed, then stood up quickly.

"No," she said. "Just call me."

Kim drove out of the parking lot, thinking about what Rick had said. Not much. She wondered if he was holding back. She changed lanes, setting course for the outskirts of McLean, where she lived in an apartment complex. It was then she noticed the grey SUV. The car got closer but stayed three cars behind on the right lane. She had seen it when she left the NSA and joined the highway traffic.

Kim put her foot down on the gas. Her Audi A5 responded smoothly and she left the traffic behind. She did not see the grey SUV anymore. In half an hour, she was home.

She opened the door to her apartment, and before she could shut it, she heard Maya's voice behind her.

"Mommy!" Maya came running towards her and grabbed her around the waist. Kim kissed her forehead.

"How are you, honey?"

Christine, the babysitter, stepped out into the hallway. "She's been really good. Finished all her homework." Christine was blonde, in her twenties, and paying for college by working two jobs on the side. Kim liked her.

"Can I have some ice cream?" Maya asked, her arms still around Kim.

Kim smiled. "Have you had some already?"

Maya pouted, "No. I did ask." She glanced back at Christine, who raised her eyebrows.

"Alright then," Kim said, "Let's get you some."

Christine said goodbye. Kim put her things away and sat there watching Maya eat the ice cream. Her heart melted a little. Just coming back home to hear the M word made her brim over with happiness. She had never thought she would have a child. When she found Maya, she had found a level of contentment that was indescribable. She slid off the stool and stacked some dishes at the kitchen counter. Her eyes fell on the road outside.

On the kerb opposite a grey SUV stood with its windows drawn down.

Kim's breath caught in her chest. She padded silently backwards. A man sat in the driver's seat. The shadow of an oak tree fell on the windscreen, and she could not see his face. But she knew that he could see her apartment. Kim's apartment had a balcony as well, and she had seen cars parked in that same spot in the past.

Kim glanced at Maya, who was slurping at her Ben and Jerry's, oblivious to the world. She went to the front door and put the chain and padlock on. In her bedroom, she punched the four digits in the key safe inside her dresser. The metal door swung out. She picked out her suppressed Glock 22 and slid out the magazine. Full. She snapped it back and made sure the safety was on. She put the gun on her back belt and dropped her shirt over it. Then she went back to the kitchen quickly. Maya had turned the TV on and was lying on the sofa.

Kim looked out the window again. The grey SUV was still there, with its driver. She saw some movement inside the car. There was someone in the back. The windows were tinted, and the back windows were raised. She could not see inside. Light was fading from the April sky too, and darkness had already claimed the horizon.

Panic raised an ugly head from the corners of her mind. Ever since Sarah's death, she had suffered with bouts of anxiety and panic. She fought it down, clenching her fists and setting her jaws. She was leaning against the counter, and the Glock bore into her back. She felt some comfort from the weapon.

The men in that car were a team. In the back, they had surveillance equipment. Kim took out her cell phone. She turned it down and ripped off the battery.

She forced herself to think. She had not seen anything on her way to work this morning. She had only seen the SUV on her way back from NSA. Which meant…no, she could not jump to conclusions.

She looked at the car again. It was a Honda, DC number plates. She sat down at her laptop and looked up the Virginia branch of the DMV, using her Federal password to access their database. The car was listed – and it was rented from Hertz two days ago. The person had paid in cash. Kim stood up.

"Mummy, can we put the lights on?" Maya's voice jolted her.

Kim looked at her and forced a smile. "Are you hungry, sweetheart?"

Maya nodded silently, watching her.

As she put out fajitas and chicken salsa for Maya, Kim thought feverishly. It was dark outside now, and streetlights were coming on. Kim lived just outside McLean, not far from the highway. Her Audi was parked in the basement. If she drove out, she would be followed.

What was the alternative? Wait for them to come upstairs?

She wondered who she could call. Her Facebook and WhatsApp would be under surveillance already, if these guys knew what they were doing. Something told her they did.

But the NCS did have their own remote IM service. It was encrypted, and messages were deleted automatically as soon as they were read by their recipient. Kim wasn't allowed to use it for personal reasons. *To hell with it*, she thought. Besides, why would these guys be following her around, if it wasn't work-related?

She tapped on her laptop and pulled up the site. She fired off a terse message to Schumberg.

"Being tailed. Locked in apartment. With Maya. Tangos downstairs. Need help."

She went to the window and looked out. A cold fear gripped her insides. Two men were coming out of the SUV. They both wore a uniform, to disguise themselves as repair men, she guessed. The driver wore a baseball cap pulled low over his face. He leaned inside the car and pulled out a long leather bag. They shut the doors and crossed the road without looking up.

CHAPTER 9

Kim crossed the kitchen in two strides. She knelt down in front of Maya.

"Honey, you have to listen to Mommy now, OK?"

Maya's eyes were alert. She was a smart girl, and her actions had saved Kim's life in Myanmar. She knew instinctively something was up.

"What's going on, Mommy?"

"We need to get out of here. We're going to get in the car and drive out. Some bad people are trying to catch us."

"Can I take my clothes?"

"No, leave everything."

Kim grabbed Maya's hand, and together, they sprinted for the door. Kim's apartment was on the fourth floor. She peeked out the door hole. Empty outside. They ran out into the hallway. Kim took the Glock out and released the safety catch. Then she shut the apartment door behind her.

"Stay behind me," she hissed at Maya, but Maya was already in position.

One would come up the elevator, Kim thought. The other would take the stairs. She would have done the same. Kim went past the elevator quickly. It was coming up from the first floor. Gun arm elbow ramrod straight, Kim opened the stairwell door with the other hand. She could feel Maya holding her shirt at the back. Her forehead was caked in sweat, and she felt a hot bead trickle down her spine.

She could hear footsteps coming up the stairs. She motioned at Maya to hide herself behind the door. Kim walked across the landing and went to ground. The footsteps were getting louder. Kim stretched out a foot and got to the stairs. She crept down, listening to the footsteps.

Then they stopped.

Kim listened hard. Her heart was pumping against her ribs. She couldn't hear a peep from Maya.

Easy does it. Don't rush this.

Fifteen years of training as a field agent kicked in. Only attack when the element of surprise is in your favor. If not, let the enemy make the first mistake.

She heard the safety catch of a weapon being released. Kim was flat against the wall, watching the stairwell at an angle. In the sudden silence, she could now hear Maya's breathing. She tried to zone it out and focus on what lay below her on the staircase.

She saw the tip of the weapon first. A silvery barrel, coming into the lower level of her visual field. Kim did not waste time. She fired immediately and rolled down the stairs as she heard the dull sound her round made as it hit the gun. A male voice cursed. Kim was up again, this time on one knee, gun outstretched. Now she saw him clearly. Middle-aged, brownish hair, lean and muscular. His baseball cap had fallen off. She did not recognize the face. He was groping for his weapon, and he looked up from the ground just as Kim arrived at the landing.

He scrambled to aim, but it was pointless. The Glock 22 jerked once in Kim's hand, and the man's head disintegrated like a plum being squashed. Kim ran up the stairs. Maya was still cowering beyond the door. Kim grabbed her and they flew down the stairs. Maya shrieked when she saw the dead man. Upstairs, Kim heard another sound. The stairwell door opened.

"Run, Maya," Kim shouted. The man she had killed had the leather bag next to him. Kim picked it up and flung it on her back. She jumped over the body and ran after Maya. Above her, she could hear footsteps running down.

Kim got to the ground floor landing to find Maya opening the door to the basement parking lot. A sudden burst of suppressed gunfire pockmarked the wall above her. They ran out, heading for Kim's car. Kim gave the keys to Maya.

"Open the door and get your head down on the floor!" Kim panted. Maya buzzed the car open on the remote and jumped on the passenger seat, curling down. Kim ran forward, taking cover behind a sedan, and looked at the stairwell door. It moved, and the barrel of a gun poked out.

Kim fired, squeezing off all her rounds. Bullet holes marked the wooden door, smashing the glass panel. The magazine emptied. She refilled and fired just as the barrel of the gun appeared again. This time she didn't empty her magazine. She would need some for later, and she only had one strip left. She tossed the leather bag into the back seat and reversed the Audi out. She heard a sharp crack, and her rear windscreen cracked.

Kim floored the gas, the wheels spun into a banshee wail on the cement floor, then the A5 shot forward like it had been released from a catapult. She drove out into the road. Cars were parked on both sides, but there were no pedestrians at this time of the day. She had narrow country roads to deal with for five miles before she hit the George Washington Pikeway. Kim looked in the rear-view, but she couldn't see headlights.

She gunned the Audi, glancing at Maya, curled up on the floor. When she called, Maya said she was fine.

The road was deserted, dark. For miles around her there was nothing but sage brush and forest land. Kim was beginning to relax when she heard the sound of rotor blades above her. Then she saw the light shining from above, and the helicopter sweeping down behind. Kim pushed the Audi as hard as she could. She bared her teeth as she heard the engine straining against itself.

The Glock was on her lap. She heard the bird get louder, then the whining ricochet of bullets as they hit the road behind her. Kim hit the lights. In the sudden darkness, the road ahead of her became pitch black. Kim wrenched the wheel to the left. She had driven down this road many times. She knew the forest lay about five hundred yards to her ten o clock. She needed to get there before the Audi got shredded with bullets.

Maya screamed as the car came off the road and bounced on the dirt. The helicopter was disorientated momentarily, and by the time it turned to the left, Kim was racing through the brush. She saw the bright yellow glow of the flashlight from the helicopter shining above her like an evil eye, slowly advancing. Kim's eyes were getting used to the dark. She could see the clump of trees ahead of her.

"Maya! Get ready, honey, we need to go!"

The rotor blades were getting loud again. This time the bird was coming down low. The pilot knew of the forest as well, it seemed. They wanted to cut her off before she got to the screen of trees.

With one hand, Kim grabbed the leather bag behind her, driving with the other. She could feel the snout of a heavy weapon inside it. Kim looked ahead, and saw the dark ominous shape of the forest rushing towards her at breakneck speed. She slowed the car down. The sound behind her was deafening now.

Kim brought the car to a shuddering halt and screamed, "Now Maya! Head for the trees. GO!"

Maya opened the door and ran. Kim followed. In a few seconds, Maya was inside the forest. Kim saw the bird zoom down and heard the sharp retort of heavy rounds thudding into the ground. She yanked the door open and ran. A few paces away from the trees, she put the bag on the ground, and unzipped it. She lifted the weapon out. A Heckler and Koch 416. It was loaded. It had a night sight on it. A loud sound burst against her eardrums, and she looked up to see a yellow-orange glow explode where her car had been.

She and Maya could have been in that car. The bird hovered above the car, the light flashing around, looking for survivors. Then it flashed towards the trees. Kim took aim even as the light hit the trees above her, then tracked down to her body. She was crouching on one knee again, adjustable rifle stock against her shoulder, the pilot's cabin firmly in her cross hairs.

No one shoots at my daughter.

Her right index finger squeezed the trigger. A burst of ordnance spat out from the barrel. The pilot's windscreen smashed and she saw the machine suddenly lurch forward. She shifted her aim a fraction to the left and fired again. Then she got up and ran backwards. She heard a droning sound and looked up to see the bird's nose tipping forward. The bird dropped in height till the rotor blades were pointing almost vertically at the sky. In a flash, Kim realized she had hit the pilot. The bird was out of control, and even the strongest pull on the joystick couldn't beat gravity.

Her joy was tempered by the fact that the bird was now rushing towards her like a missile. Kim ran for the trees. She dived in, searching frantically for Maya. The fire from the exploded Audi lit up the forest inside. Several yards inside, from behind a tree, she saw Maya's scared face peeping out.

Kim heard a twisting, moaning sound as the rotor blades hit the ground. The earth shuddered and fissured beneath her feet. Her legs buckled. She screamed at Maya to run, but her words were swallowed up in the gigantic explosion behind her. The bird's fuselage ignited, and the northern Fairfax countryside was suddenly shaken in a cataclysmic detonation of orange-yellow gasoline and fire.

Kim felt her body lifted up in the fireball, and she was hurled against the trunk of an oak tree. She remembered saying Maya's name.

Then she didn't remember anything else.

CHAPTER 10

Dan dipped his spoon into the steaming bowl of congee, swirled it around, and took a mouthful. The rice porridge, mixed with fresh crab, lobster, and everything else from pork giblets to chicken with ginseng, was a staple of Hong Kong diet. The restaurant was packed to the rafters, and the bazaar outside was heaving. Shops selling everything from DVDs, TV, and mobile phones, to ferry tickets to Kowloon and Lamma Island crowded the pavement. The latter place, Lamma Island, was Dan's favorite location to get out of the bustle of HK and go hiking into the hills. Fishing was good there too.

Ho Hung Kee restaurant was located in the back alleys of Westside Market in Kennedy Town. Dan came in the mornings for a bowl of congee and in the afternoons for dim sum. Well, he always came for the dim sum. The place did not need any reservations and was simply a street-side eatery – but it beat many of Hong Kong's numerous Michelin-starred restaurants in freshness and quality.

As he munched, Dan considered his options. He had put down temporary roots in Hong Kong, but he would not be here long. Trouble with the Triads was the last thing he had wanted, but now that it was upon him, he couldn't just make a run for it. It was not his nature. He knew that word would spread that the *Sun Yee On* had tried to recruit him – and failed. That looked like weakness on their part, and Dan knew they would not tolerate it.

His mind went back to his former life. Visions of Myanmar drifted into his consciousness, and with it, Kimberly Smith's face. While they had been together, Dan had known happiness. It had been all too brief, but it had left a tangible mark on him. Maya, the Burmese girl they had saved, was a part of the equation as well. Between them, they had been a weird sort of family, brought together by danger, separated by circumstance. But Maya and Kim had forged a deeply enduring bond, and something distant fluttered in Dan's heart as he remembered it.

Kimberly had softened the edges of his battle-hardened heart. Being with the two of them, even for a little while, had been like a meteor shinning across the desert night sky of his life. He had known warmth, and that had been a novelty.

He wondered what Kim was doing now. He had last called her about a month ago. Dan wiped his lips on a tissue. A waitress came, put down a glass of water on the rough wooden table, and left without a word. Dan considered calling Kim. He might have to leave Hong Kong soon, and he knew that he wanted to stay in touch with her.

Dan got up and left. He spent the rest of the day training in the gym and later doing some shopping in the Central District and SoHo. As night came, he got ready to visit the Shanghai Moon Club. The Club was in the northern part of the island, where Dan lived. But it was in the west, and he lived on the eastern edge.

Dan knocked on Dahai's door, but there was no answer. He had not seen him the whole day. Dan walked out of his apartment and turned down a series of small streets, going deeper into the back alleys of Kennedy Town. Lights still gleamed brightly, but these streets were quieter. He came closer to the derelict leather tanning factory near the Harbor at the end of Sai Ning Street. Street lights lit up the boulevard stretching along the pier, but the old tanning factory stood to one side like a black shadow.

Dan looked around him, then vaulted over the wire fence that cordoned off the suit. He figured in a few years this would become another high-rise apartment complex, given its waterside location, but for now it suited his purpose perfectly. He took out his flashlight and picked his way to the one of the disused laboratories. The door was padlocked and he used his key to open it. The wooden floor complained as he walked into the room. He pushed one of the tables into a corner and pulled away the old tattered rug on the floor. He sat down on his haunches and removed two of the floorboards. A space underneath showed a rectangular metal box with four red digits glowing on it. Dan punched in his code on the keypad. There was a soft click, then the door opened.

One M24 Sniper Weapon System rifle lay inside, detached into components. Dan opened the black box the weapon sat in and checked the barrel, stock, magazines, muzzle brake, suppressor, and the two optical systems that fitted on the picatinny rail. He counted the five ammo boxes. This version of the M24 chambered the 300 Winchester Magnum round, a round he preferred for its heaviness.

He did not take the rifle out but removed one of the two Sig Sauer P226 handguns from its foam holding. The magazine was full, and he sighted along the barrel then put the gun in his back belt. He found his eleven-inch curved KA-BAR U.S.-made kukri knife. The blade glinted in the flashlight, its curved edge only inches from his face. Dan slid the knife back in its brown leather scabbard, then tied it inside his beltline, hidden from casual observers. It felt good to have the knife back on him.

He put the floorboards back in, pulled over the moth-eaten rug, and pushed the table back into position. He walked back into the bustling streets of Kennedy Town and walked to the subway. The Island line train would take him all the way Wan Chai, the area where the night club was situated.

Dan got off at Lockhart Road. It was a long street, traversing the whole of Wan Chai from Central to Causeway Bay. Central was the epicenter of Hong Kong's nightlife, but there had been a time when Wan Chai was pretty famous. Mainly for the "Girly Bars" of colonial times. Now, classy restaurants and gastropubs had converted most of Lockhart Road into a clone of Central, but the older, seedier areas still had the garish lights and beckoning ladies sitting with bright makeup in front of shop stores.

The crowds were gathering around the pubs as Dan walked. The smell of cigarette smoke and perfume hung heavy in the air, relieved by drafts of misty saline air from the harbor. Expats and wealthy Chinese sipped on cocktails and pints of beer. Dan walked along, leaving them behind, till he was at the western edge, near Causeway Bay.

This was the older section, and the Girly Bars appeared with flashing neon lights advertising body massages and dance parlors. Taller and wider-shouldered than most, Dan was called to several times by beautiful Chinese women, their skin luminous in the night, silk dresses rustling in the light breeze. After ten minutes, he saw the sign for the Shanghai Moon Club.

It was a three-story building, with a huge round silver moon hanging suspended at the front of the building. Men lounged against Range Rovers in the front, with the sharp suits and slicked-back hair typical of Triad men. Dan could see the colorful dragon and snake tattoos on those who wore half sleeves.

Several glanced Dan up and down as he climbed up the steps. A young, radiant Chinese woman, shining black hair tied up in a bun, dazzled him with a smile as he came up to reception. Her face was doused in white talcum powder and her cheeks were rouged red.

"I am here for the Mountain Master. Number 489," Dan said. The woman's smile faded. She looked at the wooden panel behind her, which opened almost magically. A short, barrel-chested Chinese man stepped out, followed by another two behind him. They appraised Dan with cold eye, then the front man inclined his head to the left. As Dan came around the counter, the men stopped him. Two stood back with hands on their shoulder holsters while the squat short guy patted Dan down. He removed the Sig and held the knife in his hands for a while, giving Dan a closer look. Dan ignored them. He was pushed across the lobby, heading for a hallway.

Guests were strewn around the opulent jade-green lobby area. Golden statues of Buddha and flying dragons dotted the room. Men in suits lay semi-reclined on deep sofas, most of them talking to alluringly dressed Chinese women. Dan walked past a Caucasian man busy fondling a woman's breast as she laughed in a shrill voice. No one gave him a second glance.

A thick, wide door was held open for Dan and he walked into a room that seemed like a banquet hall without the tables. The windows at the far end looked out over Causeway Bay with its twinkling lights. In the foreground, sofas and tables surrounded a central desk. A seated figure slowly raised itself as Dan walked in. Triad men lined the sides of the room. The air was heavy with incense smoke, and the central figure was wreathed in clouds of the fragrant stuff.

As Dan got closer he realized the man was wearing a long cheongsam dress, colored in red and gold. On his face he had a mask, black with embroidered gold. As the tall figure stood up, the Triad men at the sides lowered their heads. Dan came to a stop ten feet away from the curved desk.

"*Ju-Long*," the man said in a low, gravelly voice. "Or should I say, Dan Roy."

Dan felt a stab of uneasiness. "How do you know my name?"

The man stayed behind the desk. "I am Hu Shintao, the Dragon Head. I know about everything in Hong Kong."

Dan said nothing but the uneasiness was spreading to his limbs, making him restless. "Who are you?" he asked.

"I just told you. No other explanation is necessary."

"Quite a few PSB and Party officials outside. Enjoying themselves with your women. I didn't know prostitution was legal in China."

Shintao snorted. "There is a lot you have to learn, Mr. Roy. I am giving you an opportunity. From tonight, you will be an enforcer. A 45. Do you accept?"

Dan shook his head. "I work for no one."

"I am not anyone."

"Whatever. You heard what I said. Now I want you to leave me alone. Do you understand?"

There was a collective indrawing of breath around Dan. No one spoke to the Mountain Master in that tone of voice. Dan stood still, staring back at Hu Shintao. He felt someone move behind him. Dan looked and found himself staring at a strange face. The features were Chinese, but the hair was short and stood up in blond spikes. A black leather monocle covered one eye. The other eye was dead cold and fixed on him.

"Hua Dong," Hu Shintao said, "Show this idiot what it means to disobey me."

Dan felt the sharp tip of a weapon press into his back. Two of the Triad men stepped forward, hand guns out in the open. They took off safety catches and pointed their weapons at Dan.

"Move," Hua Dong said. They marched Dan out of the sumptuous room. The doors closed behind them and Dan went down a hallway and inside another similar-sized room. The smell hit Dan as soon as he walked in. Stale urine, sweat, and the pervasive odor of fear. His eyes picked up the ghastly sight in one corner. Three men were still standing in front of the figure, whose hands were tied to a board.

Knife marks excoriated the man's torso. The flesh hung out from his ribs. Below the ribs, the bowels had spilled out, and loops of dead, necrotic bowels trailed down to the floor. His face was cut open too, showing bones underneath. Only his eyes remained, and they were closed, mercifully. From the movement of his chest, Dan could tell the man was still alive.

Hua Dong said, "The Lingchi. How the Triads kill. You will end up there next, if you do not obey the Mountain Master."

CHAPTER 11

A distant wail of sirens. Then the graze of something soft on her cheeks. Kim felt the voice more than she heard it. Her eyelids fluttered open. Her head felt heavy, like it was full of water. She tried to sit up but fell back down. She opened her eyes fully and immediately realized Maya's face was hanging over her own.

"Mommy." Maya's face was streaked with tears. Kim opened her mouth to breathe, then gripped Maya's hand, who responded. Kim felt something wet underneath her. She bent her legs and put her hands on the ground. She grabbed Maya and hugged her.

"Are you OK, honey?"

Silently, Maya nodded. The sirens grew louder. Headlights bounced along the uneven ground, getting closer to them. Kim looked at the scene of destruction around her. The burning hulk of the bird, and its charred remains, lay about a hundred yards away from her. The trees around her had been burnt black as well. Kim shuddered, pressing Maya close to her chest. That had been close. The relief was replaced by anger. She gritted her teeth. Whoever had done this, would pay.

The first patrol car screeched to a stop. The headlight beams illuminated Kim and Maya. An officer came up to her and sat down on his haunches. Kim could hear the chatter of radios in the background, and the distant sound of an ambulance as well.

Kim stood up, refusing any help from the state trooper. She checked over Maya once again, and she was fine. They hobbled towards the ambulance, whose tail gate was lowered, and the EMTs were lowering a gurney to the floor.

*****

"Jesus Christ," Hal Schumberg said. Kim was facing him, sitting opposite his desk. Sunlight poured in through the open windows of his office in the fourth floor of the George Bush Center for Intelligence. A rack of books ran from floor to ceiling right behind Hal's leather chair. On either side of it, framed photos of Hal with previous heads of CIA and former Presidents hung on the wall. To their left lay a long oval conference desk with a screen and lectern at the end.

Hal leaned back in his chair. He asked quietly, "Is Maya OK?"

A spasm of pain shot across Kim's chest as she recollected Maya's scared face. She gripped her forehead. "She's OK now, thanks."

Hal said, "This changes everything. I called Rick Everett."

Kim raised her head. "And?"

"No one seems to know who it might be. But someone must know."

"Is it a coincidence that you mentioned my name to the White House..."

Hal cut her off. "I'd be careful about jumping to conclusions, Kim."

"Hell, we need to find them. They attacked my child, damn it!" Kim couldn't help raising her voice.

"And we will," Hal said in a soothing voice. "But not by treading on toes. We need the NSA's help. I also need the Secret Service on board. Let's not piss anyone off right now."

"I am pissed off, Hal."

"So am I, believe me."

Kim said, "We need to find Lin Yan, and fast. This has everything to do with him. What he knows is valuable enough for them to try and kill me."

Hal tapped a finger on his lips. "Did you find anyone from the black list?"

Kim sighed and looked out the window. Low-bellied clouds had moved in over the carpet of greenery that stretched to the horizon. The spring sky was darker than usual.

She had not wanted to do this. But there was only one man she could rely on now. She looked back at Hal.

"Yes, I did," Kim said.

*****

Kim bent over Bethany's shoulder as she zoomed into the image on her screen. Bethany read the names that came up.

"David's Gym, on Nam Kai Lo Street, right? Kennedy Town, northwest Hong Kong."

"Right," Kim said.

"OK. That's where the last phone call traces to. Anything else you have on your cell?"

Kim opened her mail. "He sent me an email. Can we trace that location as well?"

Bethany noted the IP address from the email and traced it. "Right next door." She tapped keys and a satellite image of a tall apartment complex came up with a market behind it. She looked at Kim. "This must be where he lives."

*****

Dan got off the subway and walked back to his apartment. He doubled up on himself twice to make sure he was not being followed. The *Sun Yee On* had returned his weapons. He could feel the kukri pressing against his back and the harder bulge of the Sig. Dan thought as he walked. Hu Shintao, whoever he was, had connections. Dan had travelled out of Myanmar on a false passport. He had taken the ship from Macau to get into Hong Kong, not flown.

But Shintao had still known who he was. The answers were not palatable to Dan. They knew he was here. For some reason, they had leaked the information to the Triads.

Dan crossed the now deserted market place and looked up at his apartment block. He stopped abruptly. A car was parked on the opposite side, and a man dressed in an overcoat was leaning against it, smoking. The man was not Chinese. Before Dan could do anything, the figure straightened.

"Dan Roy?" the man asked in English. American.

Jeez, I am popular today.

Dan asked, "Who wants to know?"

"CIA." The man stepped forward. Dan saw the back door open, and another man stepped out. Together, they approached Dan, who stood very still. His right hand moved slowly but steadily towards the Sig on his belt line.

"No need for that, Mr. Roy. We need your help."

Dan called out, "Stop there." The men were six feet away from him, and they came to a halt. Dan kept his right arm near his weapon. It was useless asking for ID. They could be faked, and Intercept, the black ops organization he had worked for, often posed as CIA agents.

"Who sent you?" Dan asked.

In response, one of the men put his hand inside his coat pocket. In an instant, Dan had the Sig out, pointed at center mass of the man opposite him. From the look on their faces, Dan knew they were surprised at the speed of his movements. They both lifted their arms up.

"Whoa. We just want to give you the cell. The lady needs to speak to you."

The lady? Aloud, Dan said, "Put the phone on the ground and kick it over."

The man did as he was told. Keeping the Sig trained on them, Dan leaned forward to pick the phone up. He put the phone to his ear.

"Dan, is that you?"

His mind lurched at the voice. It was Kim.

Dan sat on the pavement, listening to Kim. He pressed the phone hard against his ear.

"Is Maya OK?" he asked.

"Yes, she's fine, don't worry." Kim told Dan the whole story. When she paused, there was a silence between them, pregnant with knowledge. They both knew what was coming next.

"You have to find this guy, right?"

"Dan, I can't ask you, I know that."

From eight thousand miles away, Dan could see Kim's lowered head, her fingers pressed against her forehead.

"It's alright," he said softly. He wanted to say more. He would do anything to keep her safe. And Maya. But he guessed he didn't have to put it in words. She knew it already.

Dan said, "I need his file. Where was he last seen?"

"Beijing. But he works in Shanghai, and I figure that's the best place to start."

CHAPTER 12

Four Seasons Hotel
Pudong, Shanghai

Xiao looked up as the huge ornate banquet rooms doors glided open soundlessly. She was seated inside the massive room, which stretched needlessly in either directions to almost the length of a football pitch. There was only about a hundred of them in the room, and she figured it could hold a thousand easily. The light of the Bund glimmered across the river, and the chandeliers overhead cast a glow over their dining table. Drinks and starters had just been served to the assembled employees of Shaolin Inc., but their star guest had only just arrived.

The short, heavy-shouldered and fat-jowled man who walked in at the head of his entourage was known to her from TV and magazines. Mayor Cheng Zilou, senior Communist Party member, was in his sixties, had a shock of black hair, and wore a well-pressed black silk Mao suit. He was one of the heads of government in Shanghai, and without his authority not a great deal happened in the city.

Coming up behind him was Director Zhen, the head of the Public Security Bureau, China's answer to the FBI. Xiao knew of him as well. The PSB, although separate from the Communist Party, held high-ranking Party members in its management ranks. They wielded enormous influence in civilian life and worked closely with the Ministry of State Security or MSS, China's version of the CIA.

Mayor Cheng Zilou was highly regarded in political circles, and he was widely expected to become a member of the eight-member Politburo Standing Committee, the body that contained the Premier of the PRC. Shanghai was a recent posting for him. Most of his life, the man had worked around the outskirts of the big cities, building a reputation for himself in the rural areas. He had been a tireless champion of the migrant class – the hundreds of millions of poor workers who flooded to China's big cities for work.

Xiao watched everyone stand up as if on an invisible command. A few stepped forward to shake Zilou's hand. The aura of power surrounding the man was unmistakable. Zilou sat at the center of the table, with Director Zheng and Danny Jiang on either side of him. Xiao was opposite them. She watched the interactions of the men closely. All three laughed and joked, and they appeared to be close friends.

Xiao nodded to herself. It was how business was done in China, and everywhere else, for that matter. But only in China did the proximity to the Party members mean so much. And if you wanted to set up one of the largest software companies in the country, she thought, knowing the Mayor of Shanghai, and a possible future Premier, would definitely do the trick.

Danny caught her looking at them, and he grinned. Xiao looked away quickly, but to her acute embarrassment, Danny had raised his wine glass in a toast. Toasting frequently was a common feature at Chinese banquet tables.

"To the team that developed Redmi," Danny said. Xiao felt like pointing to the rest of the team, but Danny's eyes were fixed on her. As was the custom, everyone lifted up their wine glasses, and waitresses in their pink *qipao* dresses came and filled up their glasses. Everyone downed their glasses with a chorus of "*Ganbei!*"

That was the signal for the waiters to come around and fill up the glasses again. More toasts followed. After her third glass, Xiao could feel her head spinning. The soft Chinese classical music floating in from the speakers sounded dreamy. She closed her eyes, tired. With the launch of the app, endless meetings, the PSB detectives checking her office, and the stress of Lin Yan's disappearance, she was exhausted. She couldn't tolerate more alcohol. Luckily the food arrived soon. Plate after plate of heaped delicacies were put on the revolving roundtable at the center. Xiao went after the whole fried caviar drowned in chilli sauce. The sharp taste was like a slap, waking her up.

Xiao became aware of Danny leaning towards her again. "I have told Mayor Zilou that you are now leading the Redmi team."

Xiao's chopstick froze halfway up from the plate. She was head of marketing. She knew little about technology, or fixing problems. But the offer was an incredibly generous one. She cleared her throat.

"Umm…Danny *Xiangsheng*, surely Fu Lan, our head of technology, is the better pick for the job?" she stammered. Her head was spinning. To go over Fu Lan, the man who had all but led the team from its inception, was downright heresy, Xiao thought. She had no wish to go over him, thereby destroying her *guanxi*, or goodwill, with the rest of the team. She was aware that Fu Lan, at the other end of the table, had pricked his ears up and was listening to their conversation.

Xiao felt her cheeks becoming hot. Part of her was delirious with happiness, the other part was on guard. What the hell was going on here?

To her abject mortification, Mayor Zilou smiled at her gratuitously. "Well, for someone so young to become the team leader is truly an inspiration for China."

If Mayor Zilou, the most powerful man in Shanghai, was congratulating her, could she dare say no?

And that sealed the deal. Xiao looked around the table, and her eyes met Fu Lan's. He was in his forties and had joined the company before her. His nostrils flared, and he shot her a look of pure hatred. Xiao lowered her eyes and looked away. A promotion such as this came once in a lifetime. But this was not how she had envisaged it to happen.

Xiao gave Danny a hard look, but he was oblivious, chatting to Director Zheng. Her mind went back to how Danny had suddenly turned up to her room. It was to surprise her, and also to test her out. She had obviously passed that test, but she didn't know what to make of it.

Danny clinked his glass with a knife, and suddenly the hubbub of conversation died away from the table. All eyes turned to Danny.

"Tonight, we have a missing friend. Someone who has contributed greatly to the genesis of Redmi. To Lin Yan." He raised his glass, and there was another round of toasting, but the celebration were muted.

Director Zheng cleared his throat. "From the PSB, I can report there is no news of the young man. But we are not sparing any effort. Our men are looking all over China. Rest assured, we will find him."

There was silence around the table, then Mayor Zilou said, "I regret to inform you of the death of two Party officials. Unfortunately, they were in the payroll of the Hong Kong Triads. A group called *Sun Yee On*. The Party is trying its hardest to drive out corruption, and I want this somber news to highlight that there is nothing to be gained by drinking from the same cup as the Devil."

Danny said in a thoughtful voice, "Let that be a lesson for all of us." He raised his glass once again. "To virtue." Everyone raised their glasses in response.

*****

Xiao said goodbye to everyone in the lobby, and noticed how Fu Lan ignored her. She felt bad. She would have to take over as team leader now, and the atmosphere at work would be strained. Fu Lan had a wife and two children. Two boys, aged four and ten. He had shown her photos.

Now, the look in his eyes as he went out the doors was pure poison. She knew what he was thinking. *You bitch. You got this job through your connections.*

It has nothing to do with me, Xiao felt like saying. Bile rose up in her throat. A sudden rage gripped her, and she wanted to run after Fu Lan. But she knew that there was no point. Fu Lan knew better than anyone else this was how promotions happened in China. Connections were more important than ability.

Xiao was about to leave when she mentally slapped her forehead. Her laptop. She had left it in the office. She looked around the lobby. The last of her friends were leaving. She sighed. She would have to get back to the office. She had emails that she needed to respond to before she could get to sleep, and she couldn't do them from her cell phone.

"Xiao." She turned at the voice. Danny Jiang walked up to her. There was a look of concern on his face. Two of his aides were behind him, but Xiao couldn't see the Mayor.

Danny said, "I am sorry to drop it into your lap like this. But I wanted to tell you myself, and from tomorrow I will be travelling."

Xiao knew that Danny Jiang was well-known for travelling around the world, raising awareness about his company.

Danny looked deep into her eyes. "Are you sure you can do this? It would be my preference, but if you really cannot…"

Xiao read the subtle undertone very clearly. *If you really cannot then it will be a major loss of mianzi for me. And for you too.* Mianzi was perhaps the most important cultural etiquette among the Chinese. It stood for honor, and to lose it in public meant humiliation and a loss of face. She knew she could not cause Danny Jiang to lose face. It would mean the end of her career.

"Of course not, Danny *Xiangsheng*," Xiao said. She lifted her chin. "I promise you I will not let you down."

Danny smiled with genuine warmth. "Very good. Let your father know as well. I am sure he will be pleased."

This time, Xiao agreed wholeheartedly. "I certainly will." She smiled and bowed, and Danny left with his two aides.

Xiao called an Uber, which arrived within a minute. She settled back in the cab, wondering where life was taking her now.

The black cloud at the back of her mind rose up suddenly, suffocating her. She didn't want to think about it now. But the thoughts assaulted her like a wave, drowning everything else.

It had been four years ago. The names and faces appeared in her mind, making her flinch. Henry Qian was a handsome IT executive who had joined Shaolin from a rival company. He came from a well-endowed family, and his looks, charisma, and charm had swept her off her feet.

The taste of bile rose bitter in Xiao's throat as the memories came back to assault her. She had believed everything he said. A lot of it was true. He did come from a rich, well-known family. Connected to the Party of course, and his father was the Premier's cousins best friend. But Henry had also been good at his job. It had been easy to believe his stories, because he had the biodata to back it up.

She remembered sipping cocktails at Victoria Harbor's finest rooftop bars, seeing the city lit up like heaven on earth around her. One of those nights she spent on his family's yacht. Met his parents. And one of those nights, after making love, she had told him about the secret project Shaolin was working on.

It was a platform to buy everyday goods, and Shaolin, *she,* had worked painstakingly to make sure it was better than their competitors. Just like now, launch was near. And the next morning, Henry Qian, her lover, had stolen the blueprint of the plan and defected back to the rival company.

Xiao remembered walking into the office the next day, and feeling the sudden hush that fell across the room. Everyone looked at her. Everyone knew, apart from her. It was in the morning papers. Henry's former company had announced the launch of an e-commerce platform that had all the advances Shaolin's platform had.

Xiao had resigned, but the management had not accepted her resignation.

That was the first and only time prior to this that she came across Danny Jiang. His words rang out at the back of her mind.

"Make this your greatest lesson. In business, there are no friends. Only enemies."

Xiao closed her eyes. The sense of nausea still remained at the back of her throat. She sat up and lowered the electric window, getting some relief from the humid air rushing in. Danny had been right. She had never trusted anyone since then. But Lin Yan had been different. He was a shy kid, fresh out of Beida or Peking University, the Harvard of China.

She wondered what was happening to him, and what sort of mistakes he had made.

The cab went inside the gated barrier, waved in after Xiao showed the guards her ID. She told the cab to wait, and took the elevator up to her 24th-floor office.

It was pitch-black now. The normal sounds were gone, replaced by an eerie, almost deathly quietness. Xiao saw no one in the building, not even the security guard who was normally at his desk in the lobby.

The elevator pinged, and she came out on the darkened floor. The motion sensor lights flickered into life as she walked down the soft carpeted corridor. She used her ID on the keypad, and the office door swung open into a silent room. She could see the shapes of the screens on the desks, and the glass partition at the end. Her own office lay behind the partition. It was very dim, and she could barely see across the open plan floor.

In the silence, she could hear her own heartbeat. The hair on the back of her neck stood up. She calmed herself. All she needed to do was take her laptop and then get the hell out of there. She stepped into the large office, then stopped, her breath suddenly knocked out of her chest.

A flashlight. It swung around in an arc from behind the glass partition, where her office was. She stood rooted to the spot, her legs quivering. The light moved around and then shone directly at her. A door opened, and a black figure stepped out of her office.

Xiao's mouth was open in a silent scream, but sound was frozen inside her throat. The figure stepped forward, then began to run towards her.

CHAPTER 13

Kennedy Town
Hong Kong

Dan waited until the CIA guys had left. He looked around the street, deserted in the night. The yellow glow of light from above made round, limpid pools of incandescence on the road. He glanced up at the apartment block. He couldn't see his own apartment from here. Dan took a left and walked down the street to Western Market at the back.

As he walked past the now empty livestock stalls, he saw two figures detach themselves from the shadows. Dan walked past them, and they followed. They wore suits and were walking towards him rapidly. Dan increased his pace.

He could see the lights of the Metro station in the distance. He was on a busier road now, with more people around him.

There was a park to his left, the interior shrouded in darkness, but the gates still open. He walked in casually. Trees loomed over him in either direction. He could barely read a sign in white that had red Chinese letters on it, but it said "Duck Pond Ahead" in English, below. A straight road led into the park. It was dark, wet, and silent. Not a soul stirred inside. Dan picked a tree and faded behind its shadow quickly. From his angle, he could see the streetlamp-lit road. Pedestrian passed by hurriedly, some sporting umbrellas, some braving the light drizzle. He saw them within a few seconds.

Two tall men, dressed entirely in black suits. They stopped at the park entrance. They did not confer between themselves. One of them leaned against the railings, while the other slipped inside the gates. He reached inside his shoulder holster and took his gun out. He held it in both hands, elbow extended but pointing down.

Dan reached behind his back and pulled out the knife from its scabbard.

It would not be much use if bullets started flying. But hand to hand combat, or a knife fight, would be a different matter. There was no way he would lose either of those. He could use his Sig, but the noise would alert any cops patrolling the area.

Dan crouched low and stepped back against the trees. The man was diagonally ahead of him, twenty meters away. Dan's foot caught on something, and he slipped backwards. His back landed against a tree trunk, and he rolled off it, falling on his knees. The damage was done. The gunman lifted his head up sharply, the gun pointing in Dan's direction. Dan ran, dodging the trees.

Thwack!

The sound of a suppressed round hitting bark above his head made him dive to the ground. He could not stay here. He stayed low, weaving between the foliage and the trees, hoping the light was dark enough not to allow visibility. He could not see much except dark shapes. Bullets kept slamming into trees and shrubs around him. There was a let-up, and a sound, with a curse. Dan did not look backwards. The man might have fallen. But his friend could have joined him now.

Dan ran fast, coming upon a clearing. The night breeze was cool upon his face. He had found the duck pond. Dan scrambled to the side and eased himself into the water, careful not to make a splash. It was freezing. The pond was shallow and full of moss. Dan waded in, poking just his nose and eyes above water. He saw a bunch of reeds and moved closer to it for cover. His senses were on fire. The wet ground around the pond masked footsteps, but he could still hear faint sounds.

Footsteps approaching. He could see the silhouette. Gun arm raised, treading slow. Dan waited. The reeds were close to the bank, and the shadow moved closer, till it was directly above him. Silently, Dan submerged himself. Amniotic darkness enveloped him. He could not see anything, but sounds were multiplied under water. He heard the ripples as something came into the water, close to him. Staying below, Dan turned slightly. A slim dark shape in front of him, like a human leg. The man was standing with one foot in the water, scanning around him.

Dan waited. The man turned away to go. Dan broke water slowly. He raised his head. His feet were planted firmly on the mud. He rose up behind the man, weed and moss draped around his shoulders. He lifted the knife up, and his left arm reached out to encircle the gun hand. But the man sensed something and he turned around quickly.

But he wasn't as fast as Dan Roy.

He hooked his right arm against the man's waist, jerking him close. The knife rose up like a scythe and buried itself in the man's neck. It sliced upwards through the soft anterior triangle of the neck, cutting the jugular vein and the carotid artery. It smashed into the floor of the skull, breaking the soft bones with a snap.

The man had the gun in his right hand. He fired over his shoulder as Dan had imagined he would. Dan's head was ducked behind him, and the suppressed round flew harmlessly over. Dan pushed the knife in deeper, feeling warm blood pour down his arm. The dying man bucked and thrashed against him, but Dan held him tight and lowered him gently into the dark water.

He chucked his knife into the shallow water next to him and caught the gun hand as quickly as he could. He did not want the chamber to get wet. He pulled the gun off the dead man's hand. It felt familiar, the heavier weight of a Sig Sauer P226, rather than a lighter Glock. The handle was wet. He picked up the knife, wiping it off and sticking it back in the scabbard, and looked around him. Darkness.

The predicted support for his enemy had not arrived. But the man outside would soon start to worry about his friend. Dan did not want to face him with a wet handgun. If the chamber was not waterproof, the damn thing could blow up in his face. Unless, of course, these guys had Sigs with waterproof chambers. Which meant a particular type of operative. The type he was hoping they would not be.

Dan checked the gun's barrel quickly. Not clogged with dirt or mud. He felt for the decocker; it was there. That was what he liked about the Sig. No need for safety, there was always a round in the chamber. He could not dry the gun, he was too wet. Dan cursed and got out of the water, careful not to slip. He gripped the gun tightly, the familiar shape giving him some comfort.

The duck pond was a circle. Dan pressed himself against one of the trees at the edge and looked back the way he had come. More than fifty meters away. Darkness shrouded the entrance, but in the distance, he could see the dull glow of the streetlights.

Movement. Three o'clock. Gentle rustle of leaves. A dark shape, barely above ground. Could be an animal. But he could not take any chances. And if Dan had seen him, chances were…

Thwack!

Splinters of sodden bark flew into his face. He dived into the ground and crawled away as fast as he could. He crouched behind a tree and saw the black shape moving, coming straight for him. Before the shape could duck, Dan fired. He braced himself for the gun not working, but it did. The Sig recoiled against his palm, and the suppressed round flew out of the barrel. Dan heard a grunt up ahead and then a heavy sound as a body hit the ground. He didn't move.

Bullets flayed the trees around him; wild shots. Dan crawled along the ground, out to the duck pond again. Outside the cover of the trees, he spread-eagled himself on the wet ground. He could see the man now. Clutching his shoulder, gun arm raised, behind a tree. Dan aimed and fired at the head. A squelching sound as the round hit the back of the neck, and the figure fell forwards.

Dan stayed on the ground and did a 360-degree SitRep. Nothing from behind the duck pond, and nothing ahead. He waited. After two minutes, he got up and ran forward. It was silent. He frisked the dead body quickly. He did not find anything apart from yuan bills and some loose change. No cell phones. No wallets. He wanted to check for tattoos, but it was dark, and he did not have his flashlight.

He ran back to the duck pond and pulled the other body out. He searched, without expecting to find anything. Expectation fulfilled, he took both men's weapons, stuck them in his front belt, and walked out to the entrance.

CHAPTER 14

Fear paralysed Xiao. She needed to move, but her feet were ice cold, immobile. She saw the flashlight getting bigger, and she suddenly broke free, almost falling backwards as she turned. She slammed against the door behind, and the blow dazed her. She stumbled out, shutting the door. She ran down the carpet, heading for the elevator.

The door opened, and the figure came after her. Xiao glanced back, and her throat became parched at the sight. The figure was dressed entirely in black, with a black mask over his head. From the broad shoulders, she knew it was a man.

This time, the scream left her throat. In a blind panic, she increased her pace, but her shoes were not meant for running. About forty feet away, she saw the elevator. Xiao kept herself fit with daily running and Tai-Chi. She ignored the pain in her feet and pumped her legs as hard as she could with her evening dress hitched up to her knees.

She got to the elevator first. Feverishly, she pressed the buttons for the ground floor. With any luck, the security guy would be in the lobby. Before the doors could close, she heard the running steps reach the doors. Xiao screamed and fell back as the nightmarish, all-black figure jammed his arms into the closing doors. The elevator shook and stalled. Using immense strength, the man started to push the doors apart.

Xiao looked around herself in blind panic, and her eyes fell on the fire extinguisher. She grabbed and pulled it. The object was heavy, but after her second pull, it came off the wall. Just at that moment, the man put a foot into the elevator. Her skin crawled as he reached out a gloved hand, almost scratching her face. Stifling the scream that rose in her throat, Xiao pointed the nozzle of the extinguisher at the man's masked face. She could see his deathly black eyes through the only slits in the mask. Nausea rose up inside her. She pressed the trigger as hard as she could and white foam jetted out from the nozzle at high speed. The man coughed and spit, stumbling backwards. Xiao swung the extinguisher like a bat and threw it at the man as he went back. It him on the side, and he went tumbling on the carpet. He scrambled up to his feet, but the doors were closing again.

Xiao shrank back as the man launched himself at the doors a second time. This time, he was too late. The doors shut with a ping even as his fingertips fought for purchase. With a whooshing sound, the elevator began to descend from the 24th floor. Hand at her throat, Xiao fought for breath. Sweat plastered hair over her forehead. She brushed it back the best she could and thought about her next move. She took off her shoes. She held one of them by the toes and realized that although it didn't have a high heel, the heel was prominent enough to cause damage if someone were hit hard enough on the face. She rolled up her dress to above her knees.

As soon as the elevator opened, she rushed out. The spacious lobby was empty, but to her huge relief, she saw two uniformed security guards sitting at the desk, chatting with their feet up. One of them saw her and stood up immediately.

Xiao ran up to them. "Call the police," she shouted. "A man just attacked me in the office!"

*****

Dan stepped out of the park and immediately saw the black Range Rover parked opposite him. He cursed himself. He should have expected that and left the park by the rear. He thought of retreating back inside but stopped as the door opened and one of the occupants stepped out. It was a Chinese man, dressed in brown cotton shirt and pants. His shoulders were stooped, and bruise marks littered his face. His left eye was swollen and black.

It was Dahai Feng.

Now Dan knew why he had had no contact with Dahai for the whole day. Dahai lifted his face up towards the park, and Dan saw the vacant, lost look in his eyes. The face of a man who had given up on life. More doors opened, and three Triad men stepped out. One of them had an MP5 sub machine gun, finger on trigger. He stood behind Dahai and pushed him forward.

Dan stepped out of the shadows. The Triads cocked their weapons and a gun was placed against Dahai's forehead. A yellow glow from the streetlights fell on them. They were standing across the road.

Dan said, "Let him go. It's me you want."

One of the men spoke in English. "Throw down your weapons."

Dan pulled out the Sig he got from one of the dead guys and put it on the ground.

"And the rest," the man snarled.

Dan took out his own Sig and the kukri knife as well.

"Now come forward, with your hands up," the man ordered.

Dan waited for a few seconds. He knew the Triad men were watching for the same reasons as he was watching them. Scoping out the surroundings, judging the moment.

One man on each side of Dahai. A man behind him, with a gun to his head. Behind them, the black mass of the Range Rover. Dan figured there was a driver inside. That was his biggest problem. But the driver would have to get out and come around. That gave Dan time.

He advanced. His arms were up but bent at the elbow. When he was roughly five feet away, he gave Dahai a barely perceptible nod. Dahai was staring at him, and a look passed in his eyes.

One of the Triad men stepped forward. It was the man with the MP5. Holding the largest and most lethal weapon in the group made him a bit cocky. He swaggered up to Dan, coming up to his chest height. He jabbed the muzzle of the gun against Dan's sternum.

Dan looked behind him and raised his eyebrows at Dahai. It all happened very quickly. Dahai gave a shout and crumpled to the ground. The man behind him frowned and bent over to look. Dan's guy turned his neck a fraction to look, gun still pressed against Dan's chest. His finger was still on the trigger, and he figured he had Dan covered at point blank range.

He figured wrong. Dan's already fast reflexes were honed to razor sharpness with all the Muay Thai training.

Dan exploded into action. With the back of his left hand he slapped the muzzle away, and in the same movement, he bent over and pushed his back into the man's belly. Dan thrust an arm into the man's armpit and pulled him over his back in a *kumite* move, slamming him down in front of him. The finger pressed the trigger, but the rounds fired into the road, chipping up tarmac. The guy landed on his back, and the gun came off in Dan's hand. Dan fired a short burst, and a line of red holes lined up in the man's shirt.

Dan had dropped already and rolled over to the side. He felt the hot burn of bullets whizz past him, then he was firing from the side, lying on the road. He aimed for the man standing next to Dahai. As expected, Dahai was grappling with the man who was standing behind him, having pulled him down to the road.

Dan fired a long burst, MP5 set to semi-automatic mode. Bullets shredded the side of the Range Rover, and the man firing at Dan jerked as the metal ordnance pumped into him. He fell to the road, dead before he hit. The other guy was now on top of Dahai, bringing his weapon to fire. He was distracted by his friend dropping dead, and he moved his head to see. It was the last thing he saw. Dan had flipped the MP5 back to single fire, as he did not want to hit Dahai as well. Two well-aimed rounds pierced the man's frontal skull, and he slammed back against the car.

Dan had moved already, diving for the ground in front, desperately trying to get to the car. If there was a driver, then he had enough time to come out by now. Dan waited, breath hot against the steaming barrel of the gun. No one came. He got up and raised his weapon to the window. No one fired. He raised his face up briefly. Dahai got up and circled around. The car was empty. Dan checked the tires, then ran around to the front.

"Drive, *Ju-Long*," Dahai said, as he jumped on the passenger side. Dan opened the door and stashed his gun inside. He ran back to the road and picked up his Sig and knife. He frisked the men quickly and took their weapons.

He heard the sound of motor and looked up. Headlights, approaching fast.

"Get in!" Dahai screamed from the Range Rover. Dan ran to the car and gunned the engine. A hail of bullets whined and ricocheted on the road. Someone was shooting from the car tearing up behind them. With a squeal of tires, the Range Rover bolted down the road.

CHAPTER 15

Dan drove through red lights, heading up Pok Fu Lam Road, the long road that winds around the west of the island. The car behind them was an SUV. Dan looked in the windscreen as one of the windows opened and the snout of a submachine gun came out. An MP7, he reckoned. The man holding the gun leaned out and fired a long burst towards Dan. He and Dahai ducked. The firing continued, and the rear windscreen shattered into a thousand pieces.

"Go left," Dahai shouted.

"No," Dan said. "That's the way to Center. More traffic and police cars."

"We don't go there," Dahai said. "We go up into Mid Level."

"And then up towards Victoria Peak?"

"Yes."

Dan saw the point. The winding roads up to the shining towers of Mid Level would make chasing more tricky. Cars moved slower up the fork bends of the hills. And once up in Victoria Peak, the highest point in HK, they had the vast sprawl of Victoria Peak Gardens to lose them in.

Rounds smashed into the back of the Range Rover again. Dan ducked and weaved out of the cars in front of him. He held the gas pedal down, driving the car into the traffic bollard separating the two lanes. On this road, they were made of plastic, and they flew into the air as the large car ploughed into them. Cars in the opposite lane honked and screeched, and the side of a sedan smashed against the Range Rover.

Dan felt the Range Rover's fender hit the tailgate of a car in front of them, turning the car around and smashing its front against the sides again. Grimly, he held onto the steering wheel with white knuckles. The car shot across the busy street and into the quieter alley on the left. The alley was narrow and bisected the two main roads heading up to the Mid Level. The road here was uneven, and the car bumped up and down.

Dan glanced into the rear-view to find the SUV right behind him. He accelerated, and the car zipped past bins overflowing with rubbish and entrances to warehouses. A few seconds later, Dan saw bright lights, and a crowd of people partially blocking the narrow alley. It was a nightclub, and people had spilled out into the back to have a smoke.

Dan swore and pressed on the horn as hard as he could. Faces looked around to see the demonic vision of a black Range Rover rushing at them from the darkness like a bat out of hell. Amidst screams and shouts, they tried to plunge back into the narrow entrance of the club's rear entrance.

The car hit a line of tables and they went flying in the air. Dahai had the MP5 in his hand and was leaning out the passenger side, returning fire. In the narrow confines of the alley, the sound was deafening. Dan was forced to slow down as the night revellers in front of him finally cleared out. He drove past them as they looked on, open-mouthed, first at the Range Rover, then the black SUV streaking behind it.

Dan saw the bright lights of the road up ahead and steeled himself. They swung out into traffic, by a miracle not hitting any cars. Several vehicles braked and beeped their horns. They were approaching the Mid Levels now, aiming to go west and then hook around to the top of the hills at Victoria Peak.

"Bad news," Dahai said. Dan looked in the rear-view mirror. They had left traffic behind, but he could now see two identical black SUVs following them. Even as he looked, the car in front speeded up. Dan pressed on the gas as hard as he could. He checked the gauge; the tank was half empty. They still had to go around the curve of the hills; there was no way through them to get to the top. Dan knew he had to get away from traffic. These men would shoot to kill, and he couldn't endanger innocent pedestrians.

They got to Conduit Road and began to snake their way up. Headlights behind them gave away the position of the two SUVs behind them. The bullets still came, but the curving roads, and the angle of the hills, made firing difficult.

"Dahai," Dan said, "I have a plan." He drove fast around the bend and brought the car to a screeching halt. He parked the car diagonally, blocking the road. In the mid-distance, he could see the headlights approaching. Dahai fled up the hill, melting into the darkness of the trees. Below Dan a forest of brightly lit skyscrapers carpeted the valley like the lights of an alien civilization. They stopped where the dark waters of the sea began, then started again on the other side of the island.

Dan hooked the MP5 on his back and jammed the two Sigs in his belt. He took the keys out of the ignition. The headlights died immediately. The car was turned around to face oncoming traffic from below. Dan took the handbrake off and ran to the back of the car as it began sliding down the slope. He pushed with all his might, and the car accelerated.

The first of the two SUVs came around the bend, headlights blazing. Too late, they saw the black hulk of the Range Rover bearing down upon them. The driver screamed and swung desperately to avoid the oncoming goliath, but he was too late. The Rover's front hit the first SUV's front fender with a twisting clash of metal, pushing the car back down the road to collide with the SUV coming up. The Rover rolled forward, stuck on the front of the SUV. The doors opened and the men poured out.

Right where Dan wanted them. He had followed close behind the Rover, and they had not been able to spot him in the darkness. Dan crouched closer, then flattened himself on the road. He had the Sig in his hand and another Sig on the road next to him. They were both half full. He wanted to make sure he used all the rounds carefully. The MP5 was almost empty as well; he guessed about fifteen rounds were left in the 30-cartridge magazine.

Only an amateur ran out of bullets.

Holding the Sig with both hands, Dan aimed and squeezed the trigger. His first shot got the driver between the eyes, and the man behind him. He changed direction and got another three coming out on the other side. The remaining men opened fire, but all they saw ahead of them was a dark road. The rounds flew harmlessly above Dan's head.

Dan got up, bent at the waist till his head was near ground, and ran to the rear of the Range Rover. He had finished with the Sigs now. He unhooked the MP5 from his back and peered over the side. He counted six men, weapons out, coming cautiously up the road, firing sporadically. They looked all around, but couldn't see behind the Rover. And neither were they spread out. Bunched together, easy target.

Dan slipped out the side and, from an angle, sprayed them with bullets. He was only twenty yards away, and the men did not stand a chance. They were mown down like stacked dominoes.

Dan waited, crouched low, listening and watching. The silence of death hung like a pallor over the humid night air. One of the headlights of the rear car was on. The rest had gone off. Dan stepped out and picked up a hand gun from one of the dead men. It had Chinese writing on the side, and he recognized it as a QB7 hand gun. Similar in size and weight to the Sig. Carefully, he picked his way around the scene of carnage.

Battle blood was still pulsing inside his veins. But something puzzled him. Hu Shintao had given him until tomorrow. Dan had to submit to his authority by then. Presumably, Shintao wanted to use Dan. It made sense to keep him alive, then kill him if he did not submit.

Why kill him before? They had ample chance to kill Dan already. Why send a death squad now, when the Mountain Master himself had given him till tomorrow?

Dan went through the dead bodies. When he turned over the last one, slumped half outside the bullet-marked open door of the SUV, his mouth went bone dry. A pressure grew at the back of his eyes, and a cold fear coiled itself like a snake inside the pit of his stomach.

The man was Caucasian. He was the CIA agent who had given him the cell phone, when Dan had spoken to Kim.

CHAPTER 16

Dan felt a movement behind him and quickly turned to look. A shadow was crouching against the slope of the hill, its form barely illuminated in the dull haze of the distant skyscrapers. Dan's weapon was up and pointing instantly, but a split second before he pulled the trigger the shadow cried out and sank to the floor, hands raised.

Dan didn't fire but kept the gun raised. "Who is that?"

"It's me," Dahai shouted.

Dan lowered his weapon. "Don't creep up like that. You should have called." It was something Dan was used to from his Delta days. Operatives returning from a patrol or raid always had a call sign or code. Failing to provide that resulted in a bullet in the head.

Dahai stepped forward, his wide eyes taking in the carnage in front of him. He turned his pale face to Dan. "There was so much noise I didn't know what to do."

"It's OK," Dan said. "Let's get into one of these cars and head out to Shenzhen." He stuck the Sig in his back pocket. "From there we take the bullet train to Shanghai."

Dahai was still looking around. "Who are you?" he asked Dan. A tremor of fear cracked his voice.

Dan was on his knees, searching through the pockets of one of the Caucasians. When he didn't find anything, he pocketed the Glock 22 the man was carrying. Its magazine was full and his Sig had one round left.

Dan said, "I am no one, Dahai. The less you know, the better."

"Why are they after you?"

"The Sun Yee On want me to join them. I refused." Deep inside, Dan knew there was much more to it, and the discovery of the CIA man at his feet had sent shock waves through him. He needed time to think, and to distance between himself and this place. But first, he needed to call Kim. She could be in trouble.

Dan said, "I need to buy a new phone and sim card. A few of them, actually."

Dahai was getting over his initial reaction. He came closer to Dan and peered at him in the darkness. "OK. I know an overnight shop."

"There's always an overnight shop here," Dan muttered.

He put the weapons and the dead bodies inside one of the SUVs. Then Dahai and he pushed it to the edge of the cliff…and beyond. They watched as the car fell into open space, then a loud crash as it hit the trees below. Petrol was dripping out already, and the fuselage ignited in an explosion, lighting up the night in a sudden yellow blaze. Dan ran back to the car, gunned the engine, and they took off with a squeal of tires.

As they sped down from Victoria Peak, Dan couldn't but help glance at the view ahead. The Centre and SoHo was lit up like a giant space ship, its deck crowded with endless antennas of skyscrapers. A myriad of blue red and gold lights shimmered in the night. Beyond that, the dark waters of the bay, with the occasional well-lit cruise ship plowing its way up to Kowloon.

"Head towards Lan Kwai Fong," Dahai said. He racked up a glob of phlegm from his chest, then spat out the window. He took out a packet of cigarettes and lit one, blowing smoke inside the car.

Dan was used to the spitting by now. He glanced at Dahai, managing the contours of the road as he did so. "You sure that's a good idea? Lots of *yangguizi* there." *Yangguizi* meant white devils, and it was a colloquial, if not wholly salubrious expression to refer to white people.

Dahai grimaced. "You are one yourself, *Ju-Long*. What does it matter?" He blew out smoke.

"We don't want bullets flying in the heart of Hong Kong's party town, Dahai," Dan said calmly. He wiped sweat from his forehead. Even up in the hills, the air was humid.

"We head for one of the back streets. It will be quiet there, I promise."

"I hope this place isn't linked to the Triads."

Dahai was thoughtful. "No. I don't think so. My cousin from Guangdong runs it. Lots of *yangguizi* go there too, to get cheap phones."

"How much?"

"100 yuan, maybe less."

Dan grunted. They went underneath a tunnel, the sudden brightness of the white lights blinding. Dahai said, "Where you going from Shenzhen?"

Dan said, "I'll decide when I get there." Dahai had no need to know where he was headed.

*****

They passed the sprawling Hong Kong Catholic Cathedral, and the lights of downtown got closer and more radiant. Dan had gone down Caine Road, and he took a hard right to avoid ending up on a one-way street. Night revellers thronged the street, spilling out of neon-lit bars that lined the pavement. Deep beats of dance music pumped into the crowd of sweaty bodies.

"Left," Dahai directed. They drove down a maze of streets till the lights and music faded in the background. A giant glass and marble structure called the Central Building loomed ahead of them. Dahai led him down a few more turns, then they stopped in a darkened street with a mass of skyscrapers all around them. Dan killed the engine, and the surrounding quietness suddenly flowed inside the car. Dan took out the Glock and released the safety catch. He looked at Dahai.

"Now what?"

Dahai pointed. "Look."

To their right, on the darkened pavement, a door opened, letting out a sliver of white light. A figure slipped out and shut the door. He got into a car and drove off.

"You stay here," Dahai said. "It's safer."

Dan nodded.

Dahai closed the door gently with a soft click. Dan watched him get to the door and knock. He waited for a while, then the door opened and he was let in.

Dan opened the car door and stepped out himself. There was a forest of skyscrapers around him. But on the street, it was eerily silent. Dan stepped to one side of the car, on the pavement. He stood still, pressed against the shadow of an unused doorway. He didn't like this. Inside the car he was a sitting duck, and outside he didn't have much cover.

After an interminable wait, Dahai emerged from the doorway. He hurried down to the car. Dan waited till Dahai was abreast of the car before he stepped up. Dahai jumped back in fright.

"*Ai Ya!*" he exclaimed.

Dan got into the car without a word. Dahai passed him three cell phones and SIM cards. Then he gave Dan a piece of paper as well.

"What's this?" Dan said, looking at the paper. He didn't have a torch on him and turning on the car light would give them away to anyone watching.

"Chinese visa. You going from HK to mainland China, right? You need visa for that."

"This is a forgery. What if I get caught?"

Dahai lit up a cigarette before Dan could stop him. He blew smoke into Dan's face.

"Trust me." Dahai bared his teeth in the dark. "China is full of fake Chinese visas."

"Put the cigarette out," Dan said.

Dahai took a deep drag. "Why?"

The headlights of a car suddenly flooded the darkness of the street. Dan put a hand up to shield his eyes. Car doors slammed, and a group of men in suits ran down the street towards them.

"That's why," Dan said. "This is a Triad car. Someone recognized it…and called them."

Dan reversed fast, doing a turn as he did so. The car swung out to the middle of the street. He put the handbrake on and rotated the wheel viciously, moving ahead. The car shuddered, tires burning rubber. He heard shouts from behind, then the sharp retort of a bullet that smashed into the rear window of the SUV. Glass splintered and Dan slammed his foot down on the gas. Dahai was bent forward, hands over his head.

Dan wrenched the wheel towards the right, heading for the harbor. Behind him, he heard the roar of an engine and then the chatter of more bullets. Dan swerved in and out of tight turns, until Dahai suddenly cried out.

"Pull over."

"What? Why?" Dan shouted.

Dahai gesticulated wildly, pointing at the open mouth of a tall building. The building was dark, and it was undergoing repair work, with a scaffold erected in front. One of the entrance doors had been removed to let in the builder's vans.

Dan turned his lights out and dived into the garage. The car behind them was closing in, running around a corner. They got out quickly from the car.

"Get down," Dan hissed.

The space around them was a makeshift holding place for the large trucks. Tarpaulin covered the sides, and the ground was wet. Dan lay down, feeling moisture seeping in through his already sweat-soaked shirt. He pointed his gun at the road. With a roar, the chasing car drove past the building. Tires shrieked as it took another tight corner and vanished from sight.

Dan was up instantly. "It won't take them long to figure it out. Let's head for the Star Ferry."

Dahai remained in Dan's shadow as they flitted over the dark alleys into the glare of the broad promenades. Dan put his weapon away and walked quickly, trying to mingle with the mainly expatriate tourist crowd. In half an hour, they had reached Victoria Harbor.

Dan said, "You don't have to come any further, Dahai. I can make it from here."

Dahai smiled ruefully. "You think the Triads won't come back to look for me? I am finished in this town, *Ju-Long*."

Dan felt a pang of guilt. He hadn't even asked Dahai how the Triads had grabbed him. He did now.

"They came to the food stall at the market," Dahai said. "I had no chance of escaping."

"What will you do now?" Dan asked.

"What I have always done. Move to another city to look for work."

"You have family in Guangzhou."

Dahai shook his head. "For us villagers, nothing changes. My family will starve in the village if I don't send money. I can only work in construction sites in the big cities. Shenzhen is now the best place for me, or maybe Nanjing."

Dan nodded and got two tickets for the Star Ferry. He looked at his watch as he waited for the ferry to load. Almost an hour since they had left the car. How much longer before the Triads figured out they were trying to get across the island?

Dahai looked back, following Dan's glance. They pressed closer to the steel bulwarks of the massive jetty, getting in between the tourists.

Dan heard a foghorn sound mournfully over the water, and looked out. One of the electric diesel ferry boat was approaching the harbor, belching black smoke. He felt Dahai touch him on the arm. A large SUV had stopped at the border of the promenade leading onto the harbor jetty. As Dan watched, six suited Triad men stepped out and started to move towards them.

Dahai and Dan went to the head of the queue. There were many western tourists, and Dan stood in the middle of the crowd, bending his knees to hide himself. They were the first one to get on the boat. They climbed up to the top floor of the two-floor ferry and watched the jetty below. The suited Triad men had spread out, checking the crowd. Two of them boarded the ferry. When the ticket collector tried to stop them, one of the men simply pushed him back.

Dan pointed to the thick, round chimney funnel in one corner of the deck. It twisted to the right as it came up from below. "Hide in that shadow."

Dahai scurried off. More tourists were making their way up now, eager to see the spectacular sight of the bejeweled shoreline. Dan stepped to the entrance and hid himself behind the open doorway. He took his knife out and held it against his leg. The tourists streaming in couldn't see him. But Dan could see their backs as they went to the sides to stand against railings, or take seats.

The ferry rumbled and shook as the diesel engines fired to life. The boat swayed as it put out to the waters of Kowloon Bay. Dan remained stock-still, holding his breath and watching. There was an exclamation from the crowd. A brilliant radiance of blue strobe lights danced into the boat, lingered for a few seconds, then went out again. From several of the Central skyscrapers the strobe lights continued to flash, changing colors. It had the effect of fireworks, and the sky above downtown, spectacular at the worst of times, was transformed into a dizzying array of lumieres.

Dan ignored it. He had seen it before, the so-called Symphony of Lights. He kept an eye out for Dahai. Wisely, the man had remained underneath the shadow cast by the chimney. Dan stepped out. He walked around the edges of the deck, observing everyone in the light. There was no one resembling the Triads.

He approached the chimney, which was shaking as it worked out the diesel fumes. Dahai stepped out, relieved. They stood against the railing, watching the magical lights of Victoria Harbor. Despite having seen it many times, Dan could not help but be impressed. The carpet of skyscrapers simply tumbled down the steep hills, getting denser and taller as they got to the water's edge.

Dan asked, "When you move to a big city, why don't you take the family with you?"

Dahai frowned. "Too expensive. We live in shacks, far from the center of town. My children cannot go to school there either."

"Why?"

"In China, we have this weird system of registration. It's called *Hukou*. We are classed as either belonging to the city or the villages. It means we cannot use hospitals or schools in the cities."

"Sounds weird all right," Dan said.

Dahai sighed. "I haven't seen my two children for a year, *Ju-Long*. One whole year. You have children?"

"No."

"Then you won't know what it feels like. But I'm not alone. Everyone is in the same boat. There is a whole generation of Chinese kids growing up in villages who never get to see their parents."

Dan looked out at the lights reflected in the choppy waters below. He had never been to the proper mainland. Shenzhen was as far as he had got. Now, for the first time, he would get to see the real China. He knew some of the real people already. People like Dahai.

"Where is your village?" Dan asked.

"Not far from Guangzhou. You want to come and see it?"

Dan shook his head. "Not now. I have too much to do."

He took out one of the phones Dahai had given him. Dan put the SIM card in and powered the phone up. It had been charged already.

CHAPTER 17

Kimberly Smith stood in front of the curved Kryptos statue in the CIA front yard. The 12-foot-high statue curved around in an S-shape, and the words inscribed on the statue formed four encrypted messages. Sunlight fell on the statue and threw a latticework of shadows on the ground.

Kim stretched her arm out to the shadow, watching the pattern on her white shirt. She was deep in thought. She took out her cell phone, but there was no message. She knew that Dan wouldn't keep a phone and she would have to wait for his call. But she had expected a call back from the two agents who had made contact with Dan.

She was about to put her phone back when it buzzed. The sound was different, and there was no caller ID.

She answered, and breathed out in relief when she recognized Dan's voice.

"It's me," Kim said.

"The two agents you sent me, where were they from?"

Kim frowned. She couldn't hear Dan very well; there was a lot of background noise, like wind whistling between his lips and the receiver. She had to make him repeat what he said. His tone was impatient, and she had sense of foreboding.

"I...we pulled two agents based in the Hong Kong Embassy. Why?"

"So, you didn't know them?"

"It's standard procedure, Dan. I can't possibly know all of our field officers spread around the world, can I?" When he remained silent, Kim pushed him. "Enough. What's going on?"

"You need to get out of there."

"What?"

"There's a leak, Kim. Those two agents you sent, they're both dead. They came after me, with the Triads. Somehow, the Triads are on this. I don't know how far this goes, Kim. But you have to be careful."

Kim digested the news in silence. Then she said, "Dan, I just want you to know I had nothing to do with this. I swear to you."

All she could heard was Dan's heavy breathing and the wind whining past the receiver. Wherever Dan was, it was windy, and out in the open.

"Dan?" She closed her eyes, trying to ignore the throbbing headache pulsating behind her eyes. She wanted to ask how he was, and…and what? She didn't know herself. But she wanted some kind of indication from him. She knew he would retreat into his preordained shell of brutal violence and block out the world around him. It was what he was trained to do. But she knew the fire of warmth that glowed inside him. She had felt it herself, and the memory now stung her cheeks.

"Dan?"

"I'm here."

"You know that, right?"

"Yes." The light, icy voice he said it in chilled her to the core. But she believed him; he wasn't a man given to lying.

"I want you to be careful." His voice was stronger now, and carried more force. "Get out of Langley for a while. Take Maya. Do you hear me?"

"I can't right now. Not while this is going on. I need to get to the bottom of this."

He was silent again for a while. Then he said, "What are my instructions?"

This Kim knew, from having prepared already. But she held back her answer. After what Dan had just told her, she needed to double check before she confirmed anything with him.

"Call me back in one hour," she said.

Dan hung up.

Kim clenched her fists and took a deep breath. Leaving the Kryptos statue behind, she stormed up the steps. She didn't bother knocking on Hal's door; she opened it and sailed in.

Hal was on the phone. His hand clamped over the receiver as Kim walked up to his desk and leaned over him.

"What the hell is going on with Five Ways?" Kim said through gritted teeth.

Hal spoke into the phone. "Let me call you back in ten." He looked up at Kim. "What are you talking about?"

Kim couldn't help raising her voice. She was aware her face was warm, and beads of sweat had gathered on her forehead. But she had had enough. Maya was traumatized and she had lost her apartment for all intents and purposes. Now Dan being compromised was the last straw.

She thumped her fist down on Hal's desk. A paperweight jumped up, along with Hal. A pen skittered off the table to the carpet.

"Don't give me that, Hal!" Kim shouted. "It was your idea to send someone from the HK Embassy. Now they're both dead, because they tried to kill Dan!"

Hal's face went pale. "What?" he asked in a strangled voice.

Planting her knuckles on the desk, she told Hal the story.

Hal remained pale-faced. "Jesus."

Looking at his face, Kim realized either he was a very good actor, or he was genuinely surprised. The fight suddenly went out of her, replaced by a weary exhaustion. She was tired by the lack of sleep, getting up to check on Maya every few hours. The search for the men who had attacked her was slow and laborious. She hated her new, and longer, commute to the office. She hated the daily bulletin she was now having to prepare for the White House, and having to take phone calls from the ODNI. Office of the Director of National Intelligence.

Intelligence my ass, she thought to herself.

She remembered, despite everything, how she had enjoyed happier periods when she was a field officer in Asia. She found herself longing to be abroad again, and taking Maya with her.

She slumped down on the chair. "Who were those agents?" she asked Hal quietly.

Hal's eyebrows were knitted together. "They work in the HK Embassy, and they were suggested to me by someone. Hang on, let me get the email."

Hal clicked on the keyboard. After a few seconds, his face lit up, then it clouded over with a frown.

"Who was it?" Kim asked.

"Rick Everett, from the NSA."

*****

Xiao sat with her hands folded on her lap. The April sun was slanting in across the solitary, small window of the stuffy office.

In front of her was a desk, with a man a few years older than her sitting on it, taking notes of what she said. Xiao fidgeted, but the man carried on writing in his notebook, oblivious. She looked out the window.

This was Shanghai's Public Security Bureau Office in Pudong, at 655 Dingxiang Road, of the Pudong New Area. The building took up a street block, a squat, wide, four-story, grey-coloured nondescript office. Only the satellite receivers and antennas at the top gave it away as an official building. That, and the ensign of the PSB in big letters outside.

The man looked at her. She had been introduced and could also read from his name badge. His name was Fong Cui.

Detective Cui asked her, "Miss Wai-Ling, are you sure you couldn't comment on the man's age?"

"I couldn't see his face, no. From the way he moved, he couldn't have been an elderly man. I'm sorry, but I cannot be more precise."

Detective Cui nodded. His black hair was oiled and slicked back. His cheeks were sunken, and his eyes were large and expressive. He was smartly dressed in a suit. He reminded her of Henry Qian. Xiao shook her head and looked away. Now was not the time to be thinking of Henry. In fact, she told herself scathingly, she should not be thinking of him at all.

Cui said, "You know that nothing was stolen from the premises. What do you think the intruder was looking for?"

"Me?" Xiao whispered the word, speaking almost to herself. She shuddered, a sense of nausea filling her.

"We don't know that, Miss Wai-Ling," Cui said in a soothing voice. Xiao looked up at him.

"It is possible that you scared him, and he didn't want to leave someone who might identify him."

Xiao nodded without saying anything.

Detective Cui stood up and handed her a card. "I am the Deputy Director of the Public Offense Division. I will be dealing with your case from now on.

I can assure you no stone will be left unturned."

Cui was holding the card out in the Chinese way, with both hands holding the card from behind, the name and title facing outwards. Xiao took the card and bowed slightly. He bowed back, deeper. For a moment, Xiao thought of mentioning to him that she knew Director Zheng, the overall head of the PSB in Shanghai, but then bit her tongue. She had a feeling the detective had been briefed on that already.

She walked out of the office, its walls painted a light olive-green. There was a larger, open plan office opposite, with many police officers chatting and typing away at their desks. Some of them glanced at her as she walked out of their boss's room, and the chatter fell away. Xiao turned quickly and walked down the corridor to the elevator. She could feel several eyes following her. Xiao had never been inside a police station. There was never any need. Crime was minimal in Shanghai, but it did exist. In comparison to the rest of the country, Shanghai was a veritable den of vice, which Xiao found laughable. She had never met a crime victim in all her years in Shanghai. *Until now*, she thought bitterly.

She decided against taking the metro. Xiao stood on the side of the traffic locked Dingxiang Road and outstretched her hand with the palm flattened, moving it up and down. It was the typical manner of hailing a cab in Shanghai, and after several attempts, a green Qiangsheng taxi screeched to a stop. Its light was on at the top, which meant the cab was empty. Before Xiao could get in, however, she noticed a black limousine hurtling down the road behind the taxi. The limo beeped loudly at the traffic and parked efficiently behind the taxi. The registration number of the cab began with the Chinese sign for X, which meant a private number plate. The driver's door opened, and a uniformed chauffeur jumped out.

"*Nushi* Wai-Ling!" Lady Wai-Ling. It was pronounced New-shay.

Xiao watched the man as he came up to her. Underneath his white cap, his face was red and perspiring.

"Danny *Xiangsheng* is in the car. He requests your company."

Xiao was surprised at the coincidence, but she shrugged. She waved a hand from side to side, palm outwards, which meant a rejection. The cab driver grimaced, annoyed, and drove out into traffic.

Xiao slid into the seat as the chauffeur held the door open for her. Danny had a concerned expression on his face.

"Are you alright?" His fatherly tone brought a quiver of emotion in her, for some unknown reason. Last night's event, a sleepless night, and the interrogation at the PSB office, had shredded her nerves to breaking point. She swallowed and looked down at her hands. She mumbled a reply to Danny.

Danny leaned forward. "Do you want me to do anything?"

Xiao shook her head. "There isn't much you can do."

Danny sat straighter. He paused for a while, looking at the traffic flying past the window. "Take a break. The launch of Redmi can wait. I want to make sure you are alright."

Xiao said in a firm voice. "I am fine. We need to find a replacement for Lin Yan to take care of the bugs that the beta test showed. Then we can proceed to launch."

Danny turned to her. The concern in his voice was genuine. "I want you to take some time off to visit your parents. Come back from Hainan, then we can launch."

Xiao shook her head. "No. I want to get this done." She met Danny's eyes. "I have, we all have, waited for this long enough."

The older man's eyes crinkled, and narrowed slightly, as if he was assessing her. Finally, he nodded. "Only if you can handle the pressure. The media will be after you. I will pull levers, get them to stay away the best I can. But also, we need the publicity."

Xiao nodded. "A lot of our marketing is digital. But I can face the media, don't worry."

The limo had arrived at the gates of Shaolin Inc.'s tower block. Before the car swept inside the gates, Xiao caught sight of a Caucasian man standing on the pavement, staring intently at the limo. His dark hair was tousled, and his similar-coloured eyes were glittery and restless. But what held her attention was his size. He was tall, around six feet, but just as wide, with shoulders that seemed to go on for ever. There was something powerful yet fluent about his movements. He carried his size with ease, and she could sense a coiled tension as he walked on the balls of his feet.

He stopped walking as the limo went past him, and for a second, she could feel his eyes boring into hers. She looked away, suddenly self-conscious.

CHAPTER 18

Xiao walked into her office and checked her emails. Virtually all of them were from the media, and some from government agencies wanting more detail about the new app. Xiao answered them to the best of her ability, then stepped out into the large office floor.

As soon as the office staff saw her emerge out of her room, a hush descended. Fingers stilled over keyboards, heads lifted up from folders. Everyone knew what had happened last night. And everyone wanted to know what was happening now.

Xiao cleared her throat, feeling everyone's attention. "I was interviewed by the PSB today. They are looking for the guizi, don't worry. The security in the office is heavier, and you have nothing to fear."

They waited for her in silence. Xiao continued. "I am fine. We will be fine too. The launch of Redmi is going ahead as planned."

At her last words, a cheer broke out amongst the workers. Xiao felt a flush of pleasure. They had all worked hard for this to become a reality. Now it was within reach.

"Any news of Lin?" one of the programmers asked.

Some of Xiao's enthusiasm waned. "No," she said. "But that makes it much more important for you to step up." She pointed to the programmer who grinned and nodded.

The office returned to its hubbub, and Xiao went back into her office. As she sat down, her eyes fell on a photo of Lin standing with the rest of the team. She felt his absence more than before. He would have been invaluable at this point, using his skills with C++ and Java software languages to get rid of any bugs they had.

A thought struck her. She came out of her office, and walked over to Lin's empty desk. His laptop had been removed by the PSB officers last week. She looked around the desk and found it bare. She went back to her office and clicked on her emails till she got one from Lin. It had his address on it. He had sent it once when he was sick and had needed a lift. Xiao wrote down the address. Lin had written something else in the email, meant only for her. If he was not at the apartment, then Xiao could let herself in via a key that Lin hid in the first floor. He put it inside a light that hung on the main corridor.

Lin Yan lived in a tall apartment complex, in a place called Hongkou, to the northeast of the city. The place was on Xuchang Road, just off Zhoujiazoui Road, a main artery inside the Inner Ring Elevated Road. Several of these elevated roads circled Shanghai, a welcome escape when traffic choked the city streets.

Shanghai was divided into several residential districts both east and west of the Huangpu river, and this place was across the river from Pudong. Xiao thought for a while, then made her mind up. There was still light in the sky, although the gloom was deepening. The threat of rain hung heavy in the air.

Xiao came out of the office and walked the ten minutes to the subway station. She had to get across the river to the Dalian Road stop, on the blue subway routes that traversed the city. The subway was crowded, and she had to stand the twenty minutes it took for her to get there. It was nearly five p.m., and the first batch of the office crowd was heading home to their hideously expensive apartments. Many, Xiao knew, were heading out of the city where housing was much cheaper and the smog was minimal.

She walked, keeping her eyes on the map on her cell phone. She finally got to Xuchang Road, a side road off the main, and overlooking a park. Xiao looked up at the tall building and felt a flutter of nervousness. The nightmare image of the man in black rose up inside her mind. She suppressed it with an effort. When she did that, she found an unexpected ray of courage. *Better to live*, she thought, *than hide in fear.*

She pressed her lips together. She should have done this last week. She had been to his apartment before. She might have found something the PSB officers had not so far.

Xiao took a deep breath, and entered the building.

*****

From across the road, Dan saw the pretty Chinese woman go inside the apartment complex. The place was big, and there was every chance he would lose her when she went in. He waited until she was near the door, then jogged across the lull in traffic.

Kim had checked her sources twice this time and given him the address of a station locker in the Shanghai Hongqiao Railway Station. Dan had alighted from the bullet train after travelling 762 miles, which had taken him all of ten hours. Inside the locker he had found travel documents and money for a reserved hotel near the Bund. He had no time for sightseeing. Kim had told him to check out Lin Yan's workplace. When he had seen the woman in the limo, his sixth sense had told him she was someone important. When she came out on her own, he had followed.

Dan pulled down the baseball cap he was wearing and approached the building. He put on his sunglasses. The woman had slipped inside already, but a man and woman were coming out. Dan noticed them staring at him. He was used to it. In Hong Kong, people did not stare at him as there were so many expats. But when he went inland, he was more of a novelty due to the fewer tourists. In Shanghai, he expected it to be the same.

He smiled briefly at the couple and then walked inside the lobby. The building had an art deco frontage, like many buildings in Shanghai. The lobby had similar influences, with a square reception desk and straight lines carved in the ceiling. The reception counter was empty. Dan looked past the lobby and saw the entrance to the atrium for the elevators. He could not see the woman, but he saw someone who got his attention immediately.

A man his height, wearing a full-length black leather jacket. He was staring up at the elevator floors, watching where the elevator was heading towards. He felt Dan's stare and turned towards the lobby. Dan saw the man was Chinese, but his hair was spiked blond. The left eye was covered with a monocle. The look in the good, right eye was silent, deadly.

Dan knew a killer's eyes when he saw one. The man held Dan's eyes for three seconds, then turned his attention back to the elevators. Dan started to walk towards the elevators when they pinged. A bunch of residents came out from the elevators. There were six elevators in total, and before Dan could move, the man with the monocle had jumped inside one. Dan fought the crowd, trying to get through. It was no use. The man had pressed his buttons, and the doors were closing by the time Dan got to them.

Dan swore to himself and turned around towards the stairwell. He took them three at a time. But the elevators were faster. They zoomed up, and Dan found himself racing up the stairs. He looked at every floor as he went up. At the seventh floor, out of breath, he caught up. He burst across the landing and into the corridor. The carpet was deep, and the walls were covered in crimson wallpaper. Red lantern-shaped lights hung on the ceiling.

The woman was trying to put a key into the door of an apartment. She had turned and was watching the blond man in the black overcoat as he walked towards her, his gait slow and full of menace.

CHAPTER 19

The man was blocking Dan's view of the woman, but he could sense that she had frozen. Dan strode forward quickly, his chest heaving with the effort of running up seven flights of stairs. His body felt hot and tingling with the anticipation of danger.

The blond man felt Dan behind him, and he turned. He recognized Dan from the lobby. In a flash, his hand felt inside his jacket and then thrust forward. Dan had seen the movement, and he ducked, hands over his head. Something zipped past his ears and he heard the clang of metal as it hit the wall above him. He looked to find a semi-circular metallic object with several sharp prongs sticking out from one end. The prongs were embedded in the wall. If that had hit Dan in the head, he wouldn't be getting up.

A dark shadow loomed over Dan, and he moved instinctively, aware he was on his knees, and his opponent had a clear advantage. He tucked his knees in and rolled on the floor, making himself a smaller target. He hurled himself at the man's legs. His attacker had not expected that. First rule of engagement – always do the least expected. It didn't always work, especially if the opponent was good. Dan had faced many good men, but hardly any that were better than him.

Two hundred and twenty pounds of bunched-up muscle slammed into the man's knees. He fought for balance, then toppled over. Instantly, Dan was on his feet, knees bent, ready to straddle the man. He saw the gun as soon as it appeared. The man simply extended his right arm, and a metal rack holding the gun slid out. Dan grabbed the arm as the gun fired, dislodging one of the red lanterns above them. The suppressed gun made a light sound and the lantern shattered, showering them with glass. Dan heard a muffled scream from the woman. He felt a jarring blow to his right flank from the man's other fist. Dan fought to bend the gun arm, and he managed to hit it against the wall. He slammed it several times, and the man screamed as his hand was bruised, but the gun was attached to the railing. It would not dislodge.

The guy's left hand dove inside his jacket and emerged with a knife. Dan parried the thrust and grabbed the knife wrist. Both his arms were occupied now, and he felt a sudden blow to his chest, pushing him back. The man's leg had hit him square, and Dan felt the breath knocked out of him. He fell backwards, and his grip came loose.

The man stood up and fired. The trigger clicked, but nothing happened. Dan had battered the gun so hard it had stopped working. The guy snarled and rushed in with the knife. The knife was like a small curved sword, a type Dan hadn't seen before. Dan stepped inside the blow, cupped his palm, and thrust it savagely up towards the man's chin. With his left arm he slapped the knife away, bent his back, and lifted the man over him, a traditional jiu jitsu move.

The blond man landed on his back, sprawled out. Most men would have stayed that away, but not this guy. With unusual speed, he got to his feet. Dan could shoot, but he wanted the guy alive. Balling his fists, he advanced. The man watched him for a few seconds, then did something Dan didn't expected. He turned around and ran.

He reached the end of the corridor, followed by Dan. He climbed onto the ledge of one of the two windows on the wall. He smashed an elbow into the glass. The glass cracked, and he hit it again. He kicked the pane down and stepped into the outer lip. Before Dan's astonished eyes, the man spread both arms outward, like an eagle about to take flight. There was a clicking sound, and from underneath the armpits of his jacket two sails emerged. The man raised his arms up once, then down. The extensible sails snapped into place, held by plastic rods attached to the underside of his arms.

Before Dan could do anything, the man had leaped out into open air. Dan reached the ledge to see the man dropping down steeply before levelling out into a glide. He had become a human paraglider. He banked and veered left to avoid another tall building and then disappeared from view.

Dan shook his head, then walked back to the woman. She had recovered her composure. As he came abreast of her, he realized how beautiful she was.

Her eyes were large, and drawn out wide, lifting up at the corners. Her nose was small, but her lips were full and crimson. Her skin was luminous, like it had a glow from underneath. A lone blue vein traced across the base of her neck. Exotic was a word that was used loosely, but her face captured the essence of a peculiar Eastern charm. Dan found it hard to take his eyes away.

Xiao was the first to speak. "Who…who are you?"

"I am an American, looking for a friend. His name is Lin Yan. Do you know of him?"

Dan didn't miss the startled look in the woman's eyes. Suspicion replaced surprise rapidly. She frowned and hooked her eyebrows upward, giving her face an enigmatic look.

"What do you want from him?" she asked.

"I take it you know him."

Xiao opened her mouth and closed it, realizing her mistake. Dan looked at the closed door of the apartment. "Is this where he used to live?"

Xiao repeated her question. Dan said, "He is a friend, like I said. And when friends are in trouble, we like to help them out. Only problem is, I can't find him. So, if you know anything, I would appreciate you telling me."

Xiao said, "You didn't answer my question."

Dan looked around him. "This man might not have been alone. If they came as a team, we could be in trouble. I suggest we get out of here soon."

Xiao pressed her hands to her forehead, lowering her face. Dan said, "Look, I am not here to harm you. You just have to trust me."

"How do you know Lin?" Xiao asked.

"I promise I will answer your questions. But not here." Dan indicated the door. "If this is Lin's apartment, I suggest we check, then haul ass."

Confusion appeared on Xiao's face. "Hol what?"

"Nothing, it's just an expression. It means to hurry up."

Dan watched Xiao as she seemed to make her mind up about something. She took out the key and opened the door. The apartment was a modern one. A hallway led into an open plan kitchen and living room. Beyond that, bi-folding doors opened out into a glass balcony. Two bedrooms appeared behind doors on the hallway. One of the bedrooms had an en suite bathroom.

The cleanliness of the place struck Dan. Then he realized the apartment was hardly lived in. Or it had been cleaned out on purpose. On the balcony there was a glass table. There was a half-finished cigarette in an ashtray. Dan picked the cigarette up. It was old and damp. The basin in the kitchen was clean. A stack of CDs stood in the space between the wall-mounted TV and the DVD player underneath.

In the first bedroom, he found a dresser with a suitcase on top. The suitcase was empty. Xiao came into the bedroom as Dan put the suitcase back where it had been.

"Are you sure he lived here?" Dan asked.

"Yes. I came to visit him once. He used to cook his own meals. This place has been cleaned and…"

"And what?"

Xiao said, "I don't know. It just seems he had moved out already."

Dan pointed to the suitcase. "Did he have more than one of these?"

Xiao nodded. "Yes, he had two. And a backpack. Both of them are gone."

"Did he smoke?"

"Yes."

Dan went outside and got the ashtray. He lifted up the cigarette so Xiao could see the brand name at the base. "Did he smoke this brand?"

Xiao thought for a while and said, "Pretty sure, yes. Some of the other guys at work smoke the same brand."

Dan opened the kitchen cabinets. They were empty. So was the fridge. He had already checked the dressers in the two bedrooms. Both empty.

Dan said, "He smoked his last cigarette outside. Then he packed his bags and left. He had planned this. That's why there's no food in the fridge, and no cooking has been done for a while. The place is clean for that reason."

Xiao was lost in thought. Dan said, "Where could he have gone, Miss…"

Xiao looked up at him. "Call me Xiao."

"OK. Call me Dan."

"Da-an," Xiao pronounced his name slowly. She said, "Dan, I don't know where he might have gone. But what you say is true. He had planned this."

Dan glanced at his watch. It was almost 1800 hours. "It's time we left."

CHAPTER 20

Dan left the apartment complex first. Hongkou was close to the river, in the shadow of the International Cruise Terminal. A bank of skyscrapers covered the area before the river, and on either side of the Cruise Terminal, lights had started to glow silver and blue in the tall buildings. Dan reached the traffic crossing and looked back to see Xiao following behind him. He crossed the road and followed the signs for the subway, heading towards the river.

He stopped when he realized that Xiao was walking away from him. He hurried to catch up to her. When he called her name, she slowed down and half turned. There was a look of wariness on her face.

Dan said, "I think I can help you."

"Is that why you followed me here?"

"I did help you right now, didn't I?"

Xiao breathed out in the humid air and looked towards the buildings lit up like glow worms against the dark sky. Across the river, the lights of Pudong were starting to glimmer as well, like it was a contest between the two sides of the Huang Pu river.

Xiao said, "I ask you a question, you refuse to give me a straight answer. You follow me around for no reason. How can I trust you?"

Dan didn't say anything. Xiao turned away. "Stay away from me," she said. She walked off.

Dan pursed his lips, then jogged after her. Traffic whined around them on the broad mantle of Zhoujiazui Road, bisecting two large residential districts from the riverfront.

Dan got close and said, "I know where Lin Yan was last seen."

That stopped her. She turned around again, this time curiosity written all over her face. "Where?"

"In Beijing. Outside a nightclub called Dos Kolegas."

Xiao kept her distance, but she was interested. "And?"

"If you let me buy you a drink, then I will tell you the rest."

Xiao shook her head. "No. First you need to tell me how you know this information. I have asked the Officers at the Public Security Bureau. They know everything. China is not like your country. It is not easy for someone to disappear. Someone, somewhere will know something. They will give the PSB the information when asked. It's how it works here."

Dan stepped closer to make himself heard over the swarm of cars and scooters, beeping and bustling, raising a seething cloud of pollution above them. "Have you thought the PSB might be keeping their knowledge to themselves?"

Dan saw her stiffen, but she didn't change her expression. "If they do," she said, "Then there must be a reason."

"Ask yourself how me, an American, knows more about Lin Yan's whereabouts than the PSB."

Xiao didn't say anything, but Dan could see the indecision etched on her face. He said softly, "Xiao, like I said, I think we can help each other."

Xiao stepped closer to him, her eyes suddenly bright. "You think I'm stupid?"

Dan was taken aback. "What?"

"You spin me some….some bullshit story about Lin, and I'm supposed to believe you?"

There was a redness in her cheeks, and Dan thought she looked prettier than before. Wisely, he kept that thought to himself.

You have baggage, lady. A problem with trust. I almost got myself killed for you just now.

Dan took a step back. He lifted up his hands. "It's up to you. I'm staying at the JinJiang Classiq Hotel, just off the Bund. Room 1304. Call me if you want. Just remember, I need to find Lin Yan. And I'm not giving up." He held her eyes, and eventually she looked away.

He watched her walk up to the traffic bridge crossing the busy road below, and then run across, like she was trying to get away from him.

*****

Xiao got into the packed subway train, barely able to breathe. Her mind was in turmoil. Momentarily, the crowd of the subway was strangely comforting, where she was just one face among millions.

Someone was out to get her. Because she was trying to find out more about Lin Yan. That much was obvious to her now. But she had not counted on seeing that *yangguizi* again. The thought of him made her feel strange. He was obviously a trained fighter. The monocle man had scared the living daylights out of her, and he had subdued him.

The *yangguizi* was also handsome. His tanned skin, the intense look in his eyes...the muscles of his heaving chest. Ever since Henry Qian, she had taken herself off men. She almost laughed in bitterness. She finds a man attractive, in the most dangerous situation imaginable. And that too, a white man. She buried her head in her hands.

Xiao lived in an area called Zhabei, twenty miles inland from the river, near Shanghai Railway Station. Her apartment was opposite Hangzhong Square, in a complex of swanky new apartments, boutiques, and restaurants. She walked down the Square, feeling the first few drops of rain fall. Strains of pop and classical music floated from the open shop stores, in between modern restaurants selling everything from European to Pan Asian food. The restaurants had customers, but for Xiao, nothing beat the busy market streets, with the hundreds of food stalls selling dumplings and craw fish.

She sighed in relief as she entered her apartment. It was small, a one-bedroom with views of the Square below and of the river in the distance. But it was hers, and that was more than any young woman of previous generations could have claimed. She turned the light on in the living room as she shut the door. She had a shower and got changed. She put a pop music station on the radio and made herself a fish noodle soup. She sat down with the bowl, looking down at the moving people and bright lights of the square below. In the distance, across the ring roads, she could see the shining pinnacle of the Pearl TV tower, nested in between the shimmering lights of Pudong. The rain was still falling, spattering against her windowpane, but still the heavy clouds hadn't rolled in, obscuring her vision.

Xiao thought for a while, then decided to do what she had always done when in a dilemma. She picked up the phone, and called her father.

"*Xinxin!*" Hu Wao Wai-Ling's voice was booming. Xiao smiled. Even hearing his voice made her feel better. The word was a nickname for her, and it was a cherished nickname for little girls. The name meant heart and mind, but to millions of Chinese families, the name had become synonymous with "cute little girl."

During China's one child policy, boys had become precious for families, and little girls had become an unfortunate rarity. The sex ratios were badly skewed in China, in favor of men. Xiao parents had differed, like many, and her mother had been content with her only daughter.

"How are you?" Deng asked.

"Fine...I am fine," Xiao said.

"What's the matter, *Xinxin?*"

Xiao sighed and told her dad about Lin's disappearance. She left out the violent details but mentioned the white man, the *laowai,* who knew about Lin.

"So, you don't know if this *laowai* is telling the truth?" Deng had an uncanny habit of hitting the nail on the head.

"Yes."

Hu Wao paused for a while, and Xiao could hear him breathing softly. Then he said, "Imagine you are in a forest, *Xinxin,* riding a horse. If you have lost your way, and a woodcutter offers to help, would you accept?"

"Maybe."

"You can stay on your horse. If the woodcutter has a dark heart, you can always gallop away."

They were silent for a while, Xiao staring at the rain outside her window, thinking.

"Do you know what I am saying, *Xinxin?*"

She nodded. "Yes, *Fuqin,* I do." The word was pronounced Foo-chin. Father.

"Then do as your heart tells you, but don't get off your horse."

Xiao smiled. "*Xie xie, Fuqin.*" Thank you, Father.

"And *Xinxin?*" This time Hu Wao's voice had a harder edge to it.

"Yes?"

"I don't know what's going on here. But remember, if the PSB is involved in this, and so is this *laowai,* then it's complicated. Is this guy American or something else?"

"American."

"Be very careful. You know how twitchy the PSB can be. If they suspect this guy to be a spy, then they will not hesitate to arrest you."

"Like you said, *Fuqin,* I won't get off my horse."

Her father gave a short laugh. " Good girl. *Zai Jian, Xingan.* " Goodbye, Darling.

CHAPTER 21

Dan had woken up early, as was his habit. He went through his yoga routine and then showered. The hotel had a buffet, and he had a hearty breakfast, getting ready for the day.

When he had registered at the hotel, his visa had been scrutinised carefully by the manager. Foreign tourists travelled in groups, and not many had working visas. Dan knew his visa and photo was now at the PSB HQ, being analysed by the Foreign Affairs office. He needed to find more about Lin Yan, and fast.

His mind went back to the woman. He didn't blame her for being careful. But there was more than that. She had layers, and he didn't know if he had the time or desire to go through them. He had to do a job. He felt an unusual jolt of guilt as he thought of Kim. He drained his glass of orange juice and left the breakfast bar, heading back to his room.

In the main counter of the lobby, he saw a woman speaking to the concierge. The man lifted a finger and pointed in Dan's direction. The woman turned, and Dan realized it was Xiao Wai-Ling.

Dan waited as she walked up to him. She was dressed informally, in jeans and a white T-shirt, with a light pink cardigan. She carried an umbrella in her hand. A purse hung from a long leather strap, with the name MiuMiu inscribed on the side. In the clear light of day, Dan was once again struck by her beauty. Her eyes, like her hair, were jet black. But there was a liquidity in her eyes, a quality enhanced by their natural width. Her full breasts strained gently against the fabric of her t-shirt. Dan caught himself staring and coughed gently into his hands. He swallowed, trying to get rid of the sudden flush of desire that had grabbed him unawares.

Xiao said, "You wanted to talk."

Dan nodded. He thought of asking her up to his room but decided against it immediately.

He pointed to the chairs in the lobby. "Shall we sit here?"

She looked around and then back to him. "I know a better place," she said.

They walked down the streets of Shangai's old town, further south from the promenade of the Bund. All of a sudden, Shanghai looked very different. The main street they were walking down was wide, a melting pot of all manner of shops selling everything from shoes, chop sticks, silverware, to even animal hides. Food stalls appeared at regular intervals, with golden whole ducks and legs of lamb hanging from hooks in the front, and fish swimming in aquariums outside.

Dan stopped outside a shop where a small crowd had gathered. He craned his neck to see two men in white aprons and white peaked caps feverishly at work, watched by the crowd. One of the men was smoothing out dough and cutting it into small shapes. The man next to him ladled a paste from one of many jars in front of him, then pressed the white dough into shape. He put the rounded dumpling into a bamboo steamer. A row of such steamers stood, watched keenly by the obviously hungry crowd.

Xiao said, "You want dumplings?"

Dan shook his head. "No, thanks. Though I want to see how Shanghai dumplings are different from Hong Kong's."

One of the chefs said something, and a thin teenaged girl arrived from the back and took off the lids of the steamers. The queue advanced slowly, using tongs to pick up dumplings of their choice, then moving inside to sit at communal round tables.

They walked on. Wires passed between the shops, above their heads. Red lanterns and posters bearing Chinese characters hung from them. Alleys opened up on either side, narrower, still full of shops, and therefore more congested.

Down one alley, Dan saw the entrance to a large temple. The gate was tall and wide, with intricate carvings on the top. Under Chinese letters, in English a sign proclaimed, "City of God Temple."

Xiao said, "Wait here. I'll be back soon." Without any further explanation, she went inside the temple compound. Dan waited for a few minutes, watching people stream in and out of the large courtyard. Everyone was

Chinese. He shrugged and went in. The courtyard was larger than it had seemed from the outside. He spotted Xiao standing in front of a fire burning inside a metallic chamber in the courtyard. She thrust a handful of incense sticks into the fire, lit them, and walked inside the temple at the far end of the courtyard.

Dan followed suit. He grabbed some of the incense sticks and did the same as the Chinese people around him. He held the sticks with both hands and poked them in the fire. He blew on them to douse the fire, then inhaled the sweet, heady fragrance as he climbed up the steps to the main temple.

It was dark inside. He was jostled by bodies but ignored them. Most of the worshippers looked up at the tall *laowai* as he walked towards the huge sitting Buddha statue. Men and women were sitting in the lotus position, some in silence, some chanting softly. Fires were lit in four corners. The Buddha was made of gold, and its shoulders and head gleamed brightly.

Dan stood in one corner. After a while, he spotted Xiao. She was standing still, with her hands clasped together, incense sticks raised. Her head was bowed forward. She straightened and turned around to leave. She hadn't seen Dan, and Dan dropped the incense sticks in the tall, curved earthen bowl of water everyone else was using, then followed her out.

He felt a few specks of rain in his face as he caught up with Xiao.

Dan said, "Are you a Buddhist?"

Xiao shook her head. "No religion in China."

"Then why did you go in there?"

"For good luck."

"Good luck?"

"Yes. If you walk past City of God temple, then light incense stick, it brings you good fortune."

"I could use some of that. Where are we headed now?"

They walked on till the main street opened out into a square. There was a lake, and a red-, white- and brown-tiled building in the middle of the lake, raised on stilts. From each floor of the building, curling eaves pointed up in the air. The black roof was arranged in three portions, each one ending in a sharp spire. Xiao walked onto the bridge that led to this building.

Dan read another sign in English: the Huxinting Tea House. The Tea House was five-sided, and intricate wooden carvings covered all its walls. It looked stunning. Behind the Tea House there was a path with a stone wall forming a perimeter.

Dan frowned as he walked on the bridge. Instead of going in a straight line, the thing zigzagged. He stopped and looked at the water and then the Tea House. He realized he was the only one standing and quickened his pace to catch up with Xiao, who was striding forward without a look in his direction.

Dan asked, "Why the hell is this bridge…"

"Zigzagged?"

"Exactly," Dan said with relief.

"It's called the Zig Zag Bridge. It changes direction eight times to keep away evil spirits. They travel in straight lines."

"Evil spirits travel in straight lines." Dan pursed his lips. "Learn something new every day."

Despite the gloom of the clouds, the beauty of the surrounding lake and gardens was obvious. Yellow- and red-colored leaves hung far over the lake, reflecting their shadows. Rocks abounded on the lake, rising up from the tranquil waters like sign posts. Red and white koi fish were visible darting in the water.

In the distance, Dan could see an ancient building, similar to but larger than the tea house, and more rock walls.

"What is this place?" Dan asked.

"The Yuyuan Rock Gardens. One of the oldest spots in Shanghai," Xiao said. She pointed to the upper floor of the tea house. "We sit there."

They ordered green tea, then sat down on the top floor, gazing out over the lake and gardens. Dan could scarcely believe a few hundred meters away lay the bustle and skyscrapers of a modern metropolis.

Xiao sipped her tea. Dan could feel her eyes on him. Eventually, he tore his eyes off the surroundings and focused on her.

"Tell me about Lin Yan," Xiao said.

"Lin made contact with the U.S. Embassy. We don't know why. He wouldn't tell us anything till he met us. Face to face."

"So, he made contact. Then what?"

"Our guy was supposed to meet him in Beijing. But it went wrong. Lin was followed. Our guy was killed trying to save Lin. Then Lin escaped. That's all I know."

"Then why are you here?"

"Someone I know is trying to find out about Lin Yan. But she is being attacked now. She asked me for help. That's why I'm here."

"You came from Hong Kong?"

Dan remembered what he had said about Hong Kong dumplings and silently cursed himself. Xiao was sharp enough to figure it out.

"Yes."

"What did you do there?"

"Work."

"*Gou pi.*"

"What?"

"Just *gou pi.*"

"Hey listen, I can start swearing in French, and you won't get it either. Wanna start?"

They stared at each other for a while. There was a touch of redness in Xiao's cheeks, and her nostrils flared.

"It means dog fart."

Dan grimaced. "Dog fart? Why?"

"It's our way of saying…how do you say it…Bullshit?"

"Ah, got it. You don't believe that I was working in Hong Kong. You think I was talking bullshit."

"Yes."

Dan shrugged. "Up to you. But I was working." For a moment, his mind went back to Dahai. They had parted in Shenzhen and promised to stay in touch. Dan had his number. He thought of the hundreds of millions of migrant workers in China, a continental mass of human beings, and Dahai's weather-beaten face lost in that multitude. He hoped he was with his family, and that he would meet Dahai again one day.

Xiao had been studying her white polished fingernails. She said, "It doesn't make sense. Lin had a good job. He was quiet by nature, but he seemed happy. Apart from the last time, when he called me. He wanted to speak about something urgent. But that could be anything. I don't understand why he would approach the Americans. And if he has…" Xiao's voice trailed off.

Dan sipped his green tea. He liked the flavor. "He's made himself an enemy of the state."

Xiao looked up at him, color draining from her face. She lowered her voice. "Be careful of what you say." She looked around her furtively.

Dan said, "There must be something about him that you know. Or someone at your work knows. Something the PSB haven't figured out yet, unless the PSB have him already."

"You think that's possible?"

"Yes and no. Yes, the PSB can hide it from the public. But no, because, if they had, then I reckon my friends in USA wouldn't be feeling the heat."

"What do you mean?"

"I mean, Lin Yan knows something that is worth killing for. Killing you, me, everyone."

CHAPTER 22

Dan was getting hungry, and he let Xiao order noodle soup from the bar. A waitress came and put down two steaming wooden bowls in front of them.

Dan said, "There is something you can do. Make copies of his photo. You got that in your database, right? Then we can show them around his apartment complex and ask if anyone remembers him. Worth a try."

Xiao slurped on her soup and sucked a strand of noodle. "OK. I can ask at my *danwei*."

"Your what?"

"*Danwei*. It means my department. Everyone has their *danwei* in China. You report there, every day."

"Sounds like my name," Dan said and had some of his noodle soup. His face changed instantly. A fiery hot stream of liquid blazed across his tongue, burning his throat. Opposite him, Xiao smiled sweetly.

"Like your food?"

Dan was almost choking. He downed a glass of water and gasped. He glared at Xiao. "What the hell have you just ordered for me?"

"Sichuan beef noodle soup. They like spicy food there." Dan had heard of food from the Sichuan province, famed for the extra hot spice they enjoyed.

Xiao raised her hand, and the waitress appeared. She spoke to her briefly, and the waitress looked at Dan and smirked. Dan frowned back. The waitress returned with a glass of white liquid.

"Cold milk," Xiao said. "It will cool your taste buds."

Dan didn't argue. The damn thing felt cool, and as soon as he tasted the milk, he chucked the whole glass down his throat. He wiped his lips on his sleeve. Xiao was right. The fire in his mouth was gone as if by magic.

"Wait till the soap is cold. Blow on it. Then eat."

"Why don't you blow on it." Dan muttered in a low voice, looking down at the reddish soup, spying pieces of beef and vegetable mixed in with the noodle.

"What did you say?"

"Nothing," Dan said. "I said nothing."

But Xiao was right. When the heat went out of the soup, it was still chilly but more bearable. Dan ordered more milk and finished the whole bowl. It was surprisingly tasty, and he found himself wanting more, minus the heat.

"Brave man," Xiao said.

Dan said, "Why don't I see you outside Lin's apartment in Hongkou, in half an hour? Get the photos done."

Xiao nodded. They paid and left, walking back down the Zig Zag Bridge. Dan could feel his tummy gurgling all the way back.

*****

They walked down the busy Fuyou Road towards the Yu Garden Subway station. Before they got on the subway, Xiao said, "We part here. I will see you in Hongkou, outside Lin's apartment. It's best for us not to be seen together near Shaolin Towers."

Dan nodded. It made sense. He watched as Xiao made her way down the steps of the subway. He was at the station gates, and he walked to one side, against the flow of passengers going past him. There was a cement bench in the corner and he sat down. He watched patiently. A couple of western tourists, a sprinkling of Japanese, but mostly Chinese men and women streamed in and out of the station. The migrant labourers with their dusty clothes and worn faces. The preponderance of sharply dressed business men and women, rushing about as they did in Manhattan.

But he did not find what he was looking for. Someone sitting quietly, like him. Reading a newspaper, smoking a cigarette, doing everything they could to avoid his stare. After a while, Dan stood up. If someone was watching him, they were doing a damn good job of hiding. He decided to play it out.

He walked down to the busy main avenue called Renmin Road and turned right. A constant stream of cars flowed down the four-lane road. On the opposite corner, a massive, tall, glass and steel structure called the Shanghai Town Plaza dominated the surroundings. Dan walked down towards the river. The clouds had cleared, and a cool breeze fluttered with the collars of his shirt. Sunlight winked off the skyscrapers in Pudong, across the river.

Dan did not cross to the other side. He turned left and walked down the sumptuous promenade of colonial buildings that was the Bund. Wide and spacious, the Bund was a collection of grand mansions built in stages by the British, and later the Americans, in what became known as the International Concession. The wind was stronger off the river now, and the usual crowd was walking around the paved pathway, or leaning against the railing, looking at the grey, muddy waters of the Huang Pu and the long barges that steamed slowly up and down the river.

Dan stuck to the grass verge that lay closer to the buildings. He stopped frequently, staring at the scenery like any ordinary tourist would. When he had travelled on the bullet train, no one had searched him. He wasn't sure if he would get so lucky now, if stopped by the green uniformed cops of the PSB. Regardless, he had his Sig in the back pocket, and the kukri knife. Dan wasn't worried about the cops. The Triads concerned him more.

He walked past the Neo-Gothic and Romanesque buildings of the China Merchant Bank and several other grandiose Art Deco buildings. Shanghai, for some reason, was full of opulent Art Deco buildings, more than he had seen in any other major city of the world. Zhongsheng Road, on which the Bund was situated, came to an end, and Dan took a left, walking up Waitan Tunnel and crossing a tributary of the river.

To his right, across the waters, history was replaced by futurism in the bevy of skyscrapers around the Pearl TV Tower. The TV tower itself was now dwarfed by the 88-floor Jin Mao building behind it. The rate at which construction was going on in the city, Dan thought there would soon be something taller than that too.

Dan strolled past the International Cruise Terminal and stopped when he was standing opposite the familiar apartment block on Xuchang Road. He looked around, then walked down further. He crossed a traffic bridge and walked back on himself on the opposite side.

If they were following him, they deserved to win. Dan watched an elderly lady walk into the entrance and let herself in. Then he saw a younger woman walking up and, after a while, he recognized Xiao.

She had sunglasses on and kept them on as Dan approached.

"Did you get the photos?" Dan asked.

Xiao nodded and patted her purse. She started to walk towards the apartment block and Dan followed. He pulled his baseball cap down over his head.

"Wait up," he called. When Xiao didn't stop, he reached out and touched her arm. She turned, irritation creasing her face.

"What?"

"Look, I know you don't trust me. It's OK, I get that. For the record, I don't trust most people I meet, either. But you need to tell me what the plan is. We can't just go in there and start knocking on doors. It takes only one phone call for the PSB to come around."

Xiao said, "There's no way out of that. The PSB finds out everything, sooner or later. It's called the Public Security Bureau for a reason."

"So, what do you propose?"

Xiao's command of English was admirable. Dan had been wondering where she had learnt her English from, and he guessed she had spent time abroad, like many Chinese college students.

"In most apartment blocks, there is a Street Committee. Definitely in all State-managed accommodation, but in many private blocks as well. These people are Party members, and they help to look after the apartment. They have a head person, and he or she lives on the ground floor. I want to ask that person."

"You know who that is?"

Xiao nodded. "I looked on the internet."

Dan raised his eyebrows. "Wow."

"What's that supposed to mean?"

"I mean, that information is allowed on the internet. That's great."

Xiao frowned and opened her mouth to say something, then shook her head. She turned and pressed the buzzer. After the second buzz, a croaky voice answered. Xiao spoke to her in brisk Pinyin, the form of Mandarin spoken casually in Shanghai.

The main entrance buzzed, and they walked into the hallway. Motions sensor lights flickered to life above them. Xiao went down to the other end, past the elevator lobby. One door away from the exit door, she stopped and knocked on a wooden door with red Chinese letters. After a wait, the door opened a fraction. Dan heard the quick exchanges again, till they became strained. He heard Xiao repeat the same question three times, and the old woman inside shook her head. Then the door slammed shut, making Xiao step back quickly.

"That went well," Dan observed. Xiao stormed down the corridor, ignoring him. Dan joined her outside. Xiao was sitting on the wall outside, facing the apartment, her chin in her hands. Dan walked up, and sat down next to her.

"What did she say?"

Xiao was not enjoying this. She was beginning to regret looking into Lin's disappearance. She should have left it alone. All the work that needed to be done…she could have done it herself. Then she remembered why she was doing this in the first place. Not for Shaolin, or Redmi, but for Li himself. The gentle, bespectacled young man who had become so troubled, wanted to confide in her, but she had never given him the time.

And now, the street committee lady would tell the PSB, and they would know she was looking into Lin's mystery. Which made her wonder why she cared if the PSB knew. Deep inside her mind, something granite and hard had settled like a mountain of worry. She had the feeling she was getting deeper into something she had no control over. Something that could destroy her.

"Penny for your thoughts," Dan said gently. Xiao came out of her reverie and glanced at Dan. At Yu Gardens, he had finally come clean. Lin was in contact with the Americans. Her instinct told her Dan was using her to get to Lin. She couldn't help the thought circling in her mind like a dog trying to catch its own tail.

Shaolin's competitors in China, *or* a tech company from overseas, would die to get their hands on Redmi.

Two words flashed across her mind. Industrial Espionage.

Did Dan work for one of Shaolin's competitors? For now, she had to use

Dan, just as she suspected Dan was using her. The thought made her uneasy. She wasn't good at playing these games. Besides, she couldn't read Dan well. His mannerisms were dark and brooding, similar to the intense, almost passionate look in his eyes. Every time he looked at her, she felt he was examining her face, looking for some trace of guilt. That unnerved her, and in those moments, she didn't enjoy being next to him. But at other times, like when she brought him the spicy Sichuan soup, his frankness was enjoyable. A rare moment when the cloud slipped across the sun.

"Can I have one of the photos?" Dan asked, leaning across to her.

CHAPTER 23

Xiao looked at him. "What for?"

Dan pointed further down the road, in the direction of the subway. Someone had opened a food stall, next to a bus stop. A tree offered some shade to the tin structure. The stall was open, and they could see some smoke coming out. It looked incongruous, surrounded by traffic, skyscrapers leaning all around it.

Dan stood up. "Lin was a single man. Like most single men, I bet he didn't cook every night and got take-out instead. This stall would have been on his way back from work. Worth asking."

Xiao got up and followed him. As they got closer to the stall, Dan could see a round, black, flat frying pan, the type used for making pancakes. An old woman stood behind it, sweating in the humid heat but wearing a long red frock coat, closed at the collar, and a white cap on her head.

Xiao stepped forward. She peered into the gloom and looked at the poster letters hanging from a string above, denoting the menu. The place sold *jian bing,* a common snack similar to dumplings, but larger in size. The smell of fried onions and eggs hit her nostrils.

Xiao took out the laminated photo of Lin Yan and showed it to the old woman. "Have you seen this person? He might have stopped here in the morning and evening on his way to work."

The elderly woman leaned over and scrutinized the photo. Then her face cleared. "Oh, yes. His name was Lin, right?"

Xiao nodded. The woman said, "He hasn't been here for almost a week now. Must have gone away. He used to come every day."

"When did you last see him?"

"Like I said, a week ago."

"Did he say where he was going?"

Xiao knew from the flat, coarse, sunburnt features of her face that the woman was a peasant. Her accent betrayed the thick vowels of the harsh northern regions. The woman seemed deep in thought for a while. Then she exclaimed loudly, "Yes, I remember, only because the place he mentioned was where one of my friend's father had once lived. Lin Yan had been there to visit and the way he spoke of it, sounded like he had been there a few times."

Xiao leaned forward. "What place?"

"A *shikumen lilong* called Fuxing Zhong Lu. Not far from here. Head southwest." The woman pointed. "Behind the Yu Gardens."

Xiao was thinking. Shikumens were small areas of social housing, characterized by terraces of two- to three-story townhouses separated by alleyways. They were built during the Communist period and comprised whole neighbourhoods across Shanghai.

Now, most of them were being demolished to make way for new apartment complexes. Young Chinese preferred the new blocks, and Xiao thought Lin would belong to that group.

Which begged the question what he was doing there. She asked the old woman.

She shook her grey locks. "That he wouldn't say. Said he had some friends there. I got the impression he went there often."

Then Xiao became aware of Dan standing next to her. She cleared her throat. The old woman saw Dan at the same time and opened her eyes wider. Dan stood like a wide statue, almost blocking the sunlight as the old woman stared up at him.

"He's with me," Xiao said. The old woman looked at Xiao, and she flushed as she read the look on the woman's face. Chinese women having relationships with the *laowai* was not frowned upon as in the old days, but it was still uncommon. This old lady, Xiao imagined, belonged to a time when they were definitely frowned upon. The conviviality between them died down, and for some inexplicable reason, Xiao felt irritable towards Dan for it.

Dan asked, "Any news?"

Xiao ignored him and didn't miss the long sigh that came out of his mouth. She said to the old lady, "You have been very helpful. What's your name?"

"Dol-Mei Cheng."

"*Xie xie*, Dol-Mei."

They walked off, and Dan stopped Xiao again. They were surrounded by the traffic of the eternally busy Zhoujiazui Road. She noticed the hard line of his jaws, teeth bunched together, lips spread thin. He was angry.

"I asked you something."

"And I was going to tell you. When the time was right."

She walked off and Dan followed. He let her walk ahead, and she went down an underpass. Several minutes later she came up on the other side. The path rose up, across a spaghetti junction of roadways into a park. Topiarists had sculpted shrubs and bushes into circular shapes with geometric patterns. Several pathways diverged into the greenery. Dan saw a sign in Chinese, below which the English letters appeared: "North Sichuan Road Park."

Dan looked away and cursed to himself. Xiao's attitude was increasingly beginning to grate on him, and he was getting to the point where he would cut loose and find Lin Yan on his own. Common sense dictated to him that would be well-nigh impossible, given his Mandarin, or Pinyin, was almost negligible, and he stuck out a mile wherever he went. On the other hand, he couldn't go on with the current help he had chosen.

Dan caught up with her and touched her on the elbow. She stopped. Dan said, "You don't like me, do you?"

"For a man, you are very perceptive."

Dan ignored the jibe. "Why?"

Xiao hooked an eyebrow. "Why? OK, let's see," she counted off on her fingers. "Number one. Before the most important job of my career, my main technical guy vanishes. Number two, I get attacked in my office. Number three, I get attacked again, and some American who's looking for my colleague does a James Bond against my attacker." Xiao took her sunglasses off. Her wide, black eyes glittered at Dan. She pointed a well-manicured, long nail at Dan's chest. "Then *you* cook me some rubbish story about Lin being in touch with the American government. I mean, what the hell does that even mean? Is Lin a spy? Are you a spy? Who on earth are you?"

She was breathing heavily, and she could feel her body shaking. *To hell with it,* she thought. She was done with trying to take it easy.

Dan stayed calm and spoke in a soft voice. "You want to know who I am?"

"Yes, I do."

"I kill people," Dan said bluntly. He kept his voice low, barely audible in the relative quiet of the garden. He could see her attention was riveted on him. Her eyes opened slightly wider, and an element of fright came into them.

"I get orders to do things. Things that you don't want to know about. But I have left that life behind. I don't want any part of it. But now I have been dragged into this, against my will. I need to help a friend, who once helped me out."

Xiao looked away, then looked at him again, her eyes full of doubt. Dan didn't look away.

"What do you know about Redmi?"

"What?"

Xiao breathed. "You haven't heard about Redmi?"

"Sounds like a soda drink."

Xiao frowned. "What about Shaolin?"

"I was told by my contact that Lin used to work there. Hence I turned up, and then you saw me."

Xiao was lost in thought. Some pieces of the puzzle was falling into place for her, but they left wider gaps in other spaces. Eventually she said, "If Lin wanted to speak to the Americans, it must mean the CIA is involved."

Dan didn't say anything for a while, but he knew she was smart. She had figured it out; there was no point in keeping a secret from her. "Yes."

"Your contact is the CIA as well."

"Yes. Happy now?"

Xiao had spent most of her pent-up frustration. All of a sudden, she felt calmer. She had suspected Dan had a military background, and he had just admitted that. She wasn't sure if he was lying about Redmi and Shaolin, but when he spoke, there was an honesty, a frankness about him that she had seen before. She believed him. And with that, she realized something about him. He didn't give himself up easily, but when he did, it was easy to figure him out. He wore his heart on his sleeve, but he kept his sleeve wrapped up under a coat of silence.

Right now, she felt he was speaking the truth. He *was* a killer. She looked into those dark, sharp eyes and shivered, as if it was cold all of a sudden.

CHAPTER 24

Xiao said, "Fuxing Zhong Lou is in the south of the city. We can take the subway."

The red subway 1 trains were packed as usual. Dan watched as the usual selection of skinny teenagers with long hair, piercings, and tattoos sat next to the migrant workers from China's vast interior, mixed in with the ubiquitous Shanghai business types. The train was packed, and he was pressed close to Xiao, who did her best to look away and stand apart from him.

The journey took almost half an hour, but for Xiao, it seemed to take longer. Part of her wanted to get off the train, go to the PSB, and tell them everything that had happened so far. She knew that was the wise thing to do. But two facts stopped her. One: The cops had done nothing so far about finding who had attacked her in the office. Her phone calls to them had been politely turned away.

Second: It was Dan who had been there when she was in trouble the second time around. She still harbored suspicions about him, but she also couldn't deny that he was the only one who had cared, so far. Apart from Danny. Briefly she wondered if she should talk to Danny. She dismissed the idea for now. Danny could pull his political connections, but that was the last thing she wanted.

Xiao closed her eyes. What was she getting into? With a *laowai*, of all people...she glanced up at Dan. He was staring forward, head and shoulders above everyone else. She noticed how his eyes moved around, checking people around him. She couldn't ignore the few days' beard stubble on his cheeks, the way his shirt was open at the top buttons revealing a glimpse of his hairy chest, and the ripple of his deltoid muscles, visible through his sweat-soaked shirt.

His eyes settled on her, and she looked away quickly, hiding the rising heat to her face.

They got off at the Shaanxi Road South stop. Fuxing Zhong Lu, like many parts of southwestern Shanghai, was a residential area. They walked down a tree-lined avenue with western-style two-story single-family homes on either side. Two women were sweeping the already spotlessly clean streets. The roads were quiet here, with scooters, bicycles, and the occasional car zipping past them. Dan saw a corner stall selling magazines and pop posters. The posters were displayed on a stand, of Chinese pop stars in various poses. He had seen these stalls on street corners before.

They walked past a few more shopfronts, a bistro, and a bakery that looked remarkably western in design and function. But the scenery changed quickly as they stepped off Shaanxi Road. Older apartment blocks crowded the sides of the road. AC machines stuck out from windows, resting on small cement blocks, covered by a grill. The apartment block reminded Dan of Kennedy Town in Hong Kong. He followed Xiao as she walked down a road called Shaanxi South. They stopped outside a gate that was the entrance to a high-walled compound. Dan guessed the wall was more than fifteen feet high, and he could see the triangular roofs of a terrace of houses inside.

The gate had a grey pediment on top, with elaborate flowers carved on the top. Chinese letters were inscribed in the pediment.

Xiao said, "This is the Chengu Lane *lilong*."

"What's a *lilong*?" Dan asked.

"You'll see," was Xiao's cryptic reply.

An old man was wheeling his scooter out the gate. They walked past him, and the old man gave them a close scrutiny. Dan was used to getting looks, but he did not miss the long hard stare they both got. Inside the gate, the world around them suddenly changed. They were in a narrow alley, with houses on both sides. The houses were all terraced, as Dan had imagined from outside. A group of men sat outside a doorway, with a wooden mah-jongg board. Opposite, a woman washed vegetables on the kitchen sink, keeping an eye on the alley. She met Dan's eyes as they walked past, and then she leaned out, stopping her work. Bicycles were parked outside dwelling, and clothes hung from the second-story windows. Faces peered out from them as well. Dan saw two small hands gripping the railings of a balcony on a floor above him and a chubby-cheeked boy staring at him with avid curiosity. He was no more than five years old. Dan winked at him. The boy gripped the railing harder and opened his mouth, whispering something in Chinese.

Flower pots were planted on windowsills of houses, many of the pots as decrepit as the houses themselves. Plaster was flaking off the outside walls, and wild plants grew at their base. The houses crowded around them, blotting out the sky. Red lanterns hung from hooks outside, and electric wires crisscrossed the space above their heads. The alley stretched ahead, endless, with the rows of residences.

Xiao asked, "Do you know what a *lilong* is now?"

"Communal housing, right?"

"Yes. It's how families used to live in Shanghai. Only in the last thirty years have things started to change."

In the distance, sunlight glinted off the walls of skyscrapers. Dan indicated the tall buildings and said, "Change for the worse?"

Xiao shrugged. "Depends who you ask. For my generation, the comfort of a condo is more preferable. But for older people, these *lilongs* are where they grew up."

They came up to an old man sitting outside on a stool, sunning himself. Xiao stopped in front of him and took out the photo of Lin Yan, showing it to the old man. The man's glance flicked from the photo, to Xiao, and came to a rest on Dan.

Xiao asked the old man a question, but he ignored her. Dan returned the old man's stare, not blinking. The man wore a faded khaki cotton Mao suit, collars creased at the neck. The shirt suit, with its baggy trousers, had seen better days. The man leaned on his wooden stick, his cheeks hanging in folds of flesh. His forehead was broad, with creased skin, and he had a few teeth missing at the front. But his eyes were sharp as flint, and they lit up like embers of fire as he looked Dan up and down.

After a few seconds, he asked in perfect English, "And where might you be from?" There was no trace of accent in his speech.

Xiao looked from the old man to Dan, aware there was a connection between them.

Dan was surprised at the man's flawless English, but he kept his face impassive.

"Here and there," Dan said.

The old man smiled, and his cheeks dimpled. Brown and yellow teeth bared from between chapped lips. "Ah, an American. You know, we have a saying in China. *The pale face of a guest in the morning brings good luck."* He cleared his throat. "I hope you are the purveyor of good fortune, young man."

Dan said nothing. Xiao asked the old man the same question again in Chinese. He stood up and, without a word to them, shuffled inside his *shikumen* house. He left the rickety wooden door open. Xiao shrugged at Dan, and they followed him inside. Dan had to bend his head to get in. The hallway was narrow and confined, with dust on the floor. There was a patch of light ahead, and the old man opened a door at the end of the tight hallway. To their right there was another door, with a flight of stairs going upstairs.

They followed the old man to the room he had entered. It was a lounge room, with an old red leather sofa set in one corner, and a writing desk in the other. Posters of Chinese alphabets hung on the wall, white letters on a red background. Papers and books were stacked in a floor to ceiling shelf that took up the far wall. Newspapers were strewn on the floor. Below the writing desk there was a stack of children's toys. On the desk, Dan saw a pack of Dunhill cigarettes.

There were also some framed photos on the wall. Dan frowned as he recognized a face on one of the photos.

Dan said, "That's President Nixon, right?"

The old man was stooped low, and he shuffled forward on his walking stick. "Your memory serves you correct."

Dan pointed to the photo. "And that's you next to him, many years ago." Flags of the USA and the PRC stood on each side of the two men. Both men were smiling and wore suits. "This is an official photo, taken at a meeting when Nixon visited China." He turned to the older man. "Are you a Party member?"

The man's eyes twinkled. "Isn't everyone a Party member in China?" He guffawed at his own joke. He coughed at the end of his laughter, a wheezy, rheumatic sound. Then he extended his hand. "Fushong Lee. Glad to make your acquaintance."

Dan watched the man for a few seconds, then extended his hand. The man's grip was soft, warm. Dan knew a pen pusher's hand when he shook it.

"Dan Roy," he said.

"Mr. Roy, you asked me if I was a Party member. Let me tell you something. In USA you have Jesus Christ and churches built for him. In China we have Mao Zedong and buildings built for the Party he brought to life."

"Hardly the same thing."

Mr. Lee raised a finger. "Ah, but to deny it is foolish. To quote Marx, religion is the opium for the masses. But the Communist Party is like a religion in China. No heresy is allowed. Or at least, it wasn't in my day."

Mr. Lee walked slowly over to his desk and sat down. "The answer to your question is yes, I was a Party member. Now I am old, and they have no need of me."

"What was your role?" asked Xiao in English.

"A translator. I translated for Nixon when he came for his visit."

"You went abroad to study?" Xiao asked.

"Yes." Mr. Lee turned to Dan. "I studied at Peking University, then went to University of California, in Berkeley, to do a Masters in English Literature."

"I graduated from Beida too," Xiao said.

Mr. Lee swung his head back to Xiao. He nodded slowly. "You did well to gain admission. I hear it's becoming harder. Everyone wants to study there."

"Knowledge changes destiny," Xiao said. It was a common Chinese saying, and the children were indoctrinated in it during their school years.

Mr. Lee turned his lips. "Yes, as long as it's the right knowledge."

Xiao took the photo out again. She held it in front of Mr. Lee.

Dan said, "You know who that is, right? That's why you came inside. You have something to tell us."

Mr. Lee said, "Your powers of observation are admirable. To be honest, I realized you are not a tourist." His voice took an edge. "Trouble follows you around, does it not, Mr. Roy?"

The two men looked at each other. Mr. Lee looked away and said, "Yes, I have seen that boy." He paused for a while. "He used to come to Number 667. A few doors down. The Jiang Sheng family used to live there. A long time ago. They have all moved out, apart from the father, Jiang, and his wife, Wuxi."

"Are they in, now?"

Mr. Lee shook his head. "I haven't seen them for one week. About the time this boy came to visit them."

Dan asked, "Has he been to see them before?"

"Yes, a few times."

"Why did you have to come inside to tell us this?"

"Young man, this is a close neighborhood. We all know each other. For generations. No one likes strangers coming in, asking questions."

Dan said, "Especially Americans."

Mr. Lee smiled. "I guess it would be the same if I went to a small town in USA. Right?"

Dan shrugged. "I don't think so. Depends where you go."

Xiao said, "Thank you. We should go now."

Before they turned, Dan looked at a photo on the table. It was of a young woman and a child. The photo was recent.

"Your daughter?" he asked.

A shadow passed over Mr. Lee's face. His eyes became bleak, and his jaws bunched together tight.

"Yes," he said tightly. He did not elaborate any further.

"*Xie xie*, and *Zai Jian*." Dan said. Thank you and Goodbye. It did not draw any response from Mr. Lee. He sat still, staring ahead, as Xiao and Dan walked out into the narrow corridor, leaving the old man in the dusty room, nursing his memories.

CHAPTER 25

The sunlight outside was blinding. Dan blinked, yellow dust motes swirling in the air around him. When he looked up, a woman was standing in the doorway opposite, staring at him. She was elderly, and she looked at Dan with avid curiosity. The she smiled, the tanned creases on her face stretching. She said something to Dan in Chinese.

Dan didn't understand a word. He looked at Xiao. She said, "She said, Welcome to our *lilong*."

Dan bowed his head. "*Xie xie.*"

Xiao walked up to the woman and showed her Li's photo. The woman frowned in recollection, then pointed further down the alley.

Xiao said, "She mentioned the same apartment number."

Number 667 appeared derelict. Weeds grew on the doorstep, and the ground-floor windows had their wooden shutters closed. A heavy padlock hung on the door. Contrary to the rest of the building, the padlock was shining and new. Dan pulled on it, making the door rattle. A man with a bicycle trotted past them.

Xiao said, "Whoa, take it easy." She glanced around herself. In the houses opposite and around, not a soul stirred.

Dan stepped back and raised himself up on tiptoes. The doors and windows of the upper floors were similarly locked. He said, "No one's living here. Is it the same family on each floor?"

Xiao said, "Sometimes, depends who owns them. When the landlords rent them out, it can be to a different family on each floor."

Dan walked over to the doorframe and sat down on his haunches. He ran his hand along the base of the doorframe. He got up, went to the closed window, and ran his hands down the sill. He looked at his fingers. Then he poked the wooden shutters and gently ran his finger tip along the edges.

"What are you doing?" asked Xiao.

"Looking for the film of dust. When furniture is not used for weeks or months, the surfaces collect dust. The longer they are not used, the thicker the film. These windows and door have been used recently. There is hardly any dust on them."

"So, maybe closed for a week. About the time when Lin disappeared."

"Right."

Dan said, "We need to have a look inside. But first, we need to find out more about the Sheng family."

They walked back along the alley. Fushong Lee was sitting outside again, leaning back against his wicker armchair, legs spread out in front. He shielded his hand against the sun as he saw the two of them appear.

His earlier ebullience seemed to have returned. "Ah, the return of the prodigal native," he said, smiling at his own joke.

Dan said, "What can you tell us about the Jiang Sheng family?"

"For someone who has just walked into our *lilong*, you ask a lot of questions, Mr. Roy. Or is that an American habit?"

Dan bent his knees and sat down. Old Man Lee stood up stiffly. "No, no, that will not do. You must forgive my manners. I need to get you a chair, and one for the lady, of course."

Dan said, "If you tell us where they are, we can get them."

Mr. Lee looked uncertain for a second. Then he said, "Let's go back inside. You can sit down, and I can make you some green tea."

Dan said, "No. I don't want to impose on you. We should be on our way."

Mr. Lee put his gnarled hand up. "Please, it's no problem. Ever since my wife died, I have a lack of visitors. Especially one as illustrious as you."

Dan smiled for the first time. "I wouldn't call myself illustrious."

"Ah, just the opposite then. Dark as the night. I think you prefer that. Like the moon, you keep yourself in the dark until light falls on you."

Xiao said, "I can make the green tea, if you like."

Mr. Lee nodded. "Thank you, my child."

Xiao and Dan went inside to get the chair. Xiao looked around in the kitchen, which was basic. On a cement board, holes had been made for the stove and hobs, with a gas cylinder underneath. Pots and pans were arranged in shelves above. She found the jar of tea leaves and put some water on the boil. Dan went to the lounge and sat down opposite Mr. Lee.

He asked, "Who is the young man whose photo you showed me?"

Dan told him who Lin Yan was, and why Xiao was looking for him. Mr. Lee said, "And your reason is purely altruistic?"

"I have my reasons," Dan said shortly.

"When a man helps a woman, there is always a reason."

"It's not what you think."

"How do you know what I am thinking?"

Dan didn't say anything. Mr. Lee said, "You know, Mr. Roy, there was a time in my country when you could be sent to the prison camps for what you think."

Xiao came back with a pot of steaming green tea and three cups. She put them on the table, poured the tea, and handed them out to everyone. She sat down on a stool, away from Dan.

Dan pointed to the books, "You must have done a lot of thinking."

"Ah," Mr. Lee's eyes twinkled. He got up and traced his hands along the bookshelf. He picked up a thin volume and shuffled back to his seat. He handed it to Xiao. She looked at the title and the writer's name. She looked up in astonishment. "You wrote this?"

"Yes."

Xiao said to Dan, "The book's title is: Alternatives to One Child Policy – Strategies for Population Control." She handed the book to Dan. He looked at the yellow cover, and then leafed through the white pages, the writing on them still clear. It was all in Chinese. He handed the book back to Mr. Lee.

Mr. Lee said, "When this book was published by the printing press in Chengyu Lane, the authorities were not happy."

"Wait," Xiao said. "There was a printing press in this *lilong*?"

"Yes. In fact, the first translated Chinese copies of Karl Marx's book, *The Communist Manifesto,* was printed in that press, just the other side of this alley. In 1920."

Mr. Lee felt inside his pocket and took out a piece of paper. He unfolded it and gave it to Xiao.

She read it out loud. "Notice for the replacement of families living in Chengyu Lane Shikumen…." She glanced down the rest of the paper and frowned. "They're breaking this place down, to make apartments?"

Mr. Lee nodded in grim silence. Xiao said, "And it's signed by the Mayor of Shanghai." She thought back to the squat, powerful form of Mayor Zilou sitting opposite her in the Four Seasons Hotel. It had only been two nights ago, but it felt like a lifetime.

Mr. Lee said, "We are resisting obviously. I have written a petition. We have an important piece of Chinese history here, and they can't just tear it down. But I have a reputation, albeit an old one." He smiled ruefully. "I might do more damage than harm."

"What do you mean?" Xiao asked.

"It's to do with the book in your hand. When I wrote it, the book was considered revolutionary. I had just come back from California. It was 1964, and the contraceptive pill had arrived. In that book, I advised the widespread use of the pill and to make it compulsory. That, I said, was much better than an enforced One Child Policy. As I was a Party Member, and had access to the printing press, the book sold quickly. Very soon, people wanted to read it all over China. More editions were released. It was what you call in the West a bestseller."

"Bet that went down a storm," Dan said drily.

Mr. Lee chuckled. "As they used to say in Berkeley, you bet! The Party banned the book and burned all the existing copies. I was branded a heretic, a decadent imperialist pansy, a sell-out who had betrayed our glorious nation."

He became quiet all of a sudden. A moment settled around them, in which the old man suddenly seemed to grow out of himself and become the flesh and blood youth who had lived through those days and nights so many years ago.

"I was arrested and sent to labor camps all over Heilongjiang."

Xiao said, "The frozen northeast deserts, near Mongolia. Way north of Beijing. Winters are horrible there."

"And they last almost all the year through. We ate what we could raise from the ground, which was not much. The camps were made of writers, journalists, scientists – anyone who criticized the Party. Most of them died."

Dan said, "But you lived."

"In spirit, yes. My body died several times over. When I left my wife was pregnant. When I came back five years later, my little girl didn't recognize me."

Dan looked at the man. Deep skin creases carved up his face, like the lines of a worn-out map. He wondered what this man had seen...and lived through. He himself had lived through hell on earth, but he figured this man had been through worse.

Dan said, "That didn't make you bitter?"

"After I came back I led a very restricted life, as you can imagine. I lived in the hope for a better future. It kept me going. I learnt that in the labor camps. It is important to carry on, despite everything. We have a saying in China, *Where there is life, there is hope.*"

He looked at Dan, his old eyes shining like black jade stones. "As long as I was alive, I could hope. Do you know what I mean?"

Dan nodded. "No bullet can kill a spirit."

"And you have killed, have you not, Mr. Roy? There is a hardness in your eyes I have only seen in the eyes of violent men."

Dan didn't answer. He sipped his green tea. When he looked up, Xiao was staring at him. Dan returned his attention to the teacup.

Xiao asked, "So, you don't agree with the one child policy?"

Mr. Lee sighed. "It's a difficult situation, as you know. We Chinese love our extended families, and having seven, even ten children in one family was not unusual. The Party had a choice to make. To let population growth go unchecked would have resulted in economic ruin. I agreed with that. What I didn't agree with was the means they employed. As society changed, women would want to work and have less children. Contraceptives would have been ideal."

"And the present proves you correct."

"Yes. But one cannot live in the past." Mr. Lee picked up his tea and sipped noisily. It had gone cold.

CHAPTER 26

Mr. Lee said, "The Shengs have lived here all their lives. I have been here from the late sixties, after I came back from the labor camps. They have been here at least that long."

Xiao and Dan waited.

"They had a daughter…and a grandchild. A little girl. After the daughter got married, she used to leave the grandchild with them when she went to work."

Xiao nodded. It was the tradition in Chinese families. Grandparents looked after the children, often moving in with the family to do so.

"This young man, Lin Yan, he used to come and see them, but I don't know why."

"How often did he come?" Xiao asked.

"Once a week, maybe more. I noticed him only recently, about six months ago. Before that, I had not seen him."

Dan said, "Did Mr. Sheng, the father, ever mention him to you?"

"He kept to himself, old Sheng. Never saw him much."

"And his daughter?" Xiao asked.

"Never saw her much either. She never used to come. I think Mrs. Sheng looked after the grandchild."

"Have you never seen the daughter?"

"In the beginning, yes. She dropped off the child and picked her up. But then Mrs. Sheng started doing that. Of late, I think the granddaughter just stays with them."

Xiao frowned. "So where is the daughter? And her husband?"

Mr. Lee spread his hands. "I couldn't tell you." He passed a hand over his head. "This is all I know."

Xiao got to her feet. "We will leave you alone now, Mr. Lee. Thank you very much."

Dan stepped forward and shook his hand. Mr. Lee looked at him, a vacant look on his face. He looked right through Dan, as if he was staring into another world.

*****

Xiao came out of the Fuxing Zhong Lu *lilong* and turned left onto Shaanxi South Road. Dan walked beside her. After their earlier exchange, the air between them was still tense. Going into the *lilong* and speaking to Old Man Lee had got her into a more relaxed mood, but she still knew next to nothing about Dan.

Once again, the incredulity of the situation hit her. *What was she doing?*

More to the point, what was she supposed to do? Seeing Mayor Zilou's signature on the eviction notice for the *lilong* residents had unsettled her. Part of her wondered if she should try and get in touch, but she rejected the idea as soon as it arrived. The Mayor was a powerful figure in the male-dominated Shanghai political circle. He would refuse to see her, and she would suffer with a loss of *mianzi*, or face. The PSB were of no help, either.

Which left Dan. She sighed. She was days away from the biggest launch of her life. The launch that could catapult Shaolin to one of the biggest software companies in China. Yet…her attitude towards Shaolin was changing. Danny was protective of her. But no one apart from her seemed bothered about Lin. And she felt responsible. Lin had tried to tell her something important. Something that affected her life as well. And without finding that out, she could not get on with her job at Shaolin.

Her cell phone beeped, and the Weixin Chat app made its familiar buzzing sound. She picked it up to see pages full of messages from work. She groaned audibly.

"Which way are we going?" Dan asked.

She turned towards Dan, still going through the messages on her phone. She put her phone away and faced him.

"We need to talk," she said. "You need my help, and I need yours. But first I need to know more about you."

Dan was silent for a few seconds. Then he nodded. Xiao pointed across the road. There was a white, oval structure that looked like a smaller replica of the 2008 Beijing Olympic Stadium. It was entirely white, shining in the sun.

"Shanghai Culture Square," Xiao said. "We can sit in one of the cafés."

They walked into the huge opening that housed the stadium-like building. There was an opera house inside, and The Phantom of the Opera was the current show. Dan shielded his eyes against the sun. He followed Xiao to a café with a canopy roof and seats outside. A few people sat outside, and they chose a table away from everyone.

Over coffee, Dan told her about his life. The few years of his childhood in the mountains of Nepal, his days as a Ranger, then as a Delta operative. He touched on his years in Black Ops with Intercept, leaving out operational details.

"The rest you know," he said, sipping his cappuccino.

Xiao was wearing sunglasses, and he could see his face reflected in them. She appeared to be in deep thought.

He said, "The families who live in the *lilong* stay forever, right? It's weird that the Sheng family moved out so suddenly."

"With the grandchild, and no one knows what happened to their daughter, or her husband."

"Right. That's what we need to find out. We also need to have a look inside their house."

Xiao caught his look. "How? It's locked."

Dan sat back in his chair.

"No, you can't," she said. "It's against the law. If you get caught…"

"I won't get caught, and it's our best chance to find information." Then he said, "We need to make enquiries with the police about the Shengs, but I doubt we're gonna get anywhere."

Xiao said, "I can do that." Her cell beeped again. "Right now, I need to get back into work." Even the thought was giving her a headache. "What will you do?"

"I need the keys of Lin's apartment again. Then I'm going back to Fuxing Zhong Lu."

Xiao walked off towards the subway, and Dan walked in the opposite direction. Dusk had arrived, and evening wasn't far off. A mass of clouds had rolled in, making it darker than the 1800 hours Dan had on his watch. As he walked, he thought. Lin had planned this. That's why his apartment was empty.

Dan stopped walking. Being in Shanghai must have distracted him, for he had overlooked the most obvious of leads. Lin had been in Beijing. No one knew how he got there, but it had to be either train or flight. Dan had not yet asked around in the bullet train station, or at the two airports. The Pudong International Airport or Hongqiao. The latter was closer to him.

Would Lin have been carrying something? Would he have wanted to go through airport security? Dan thought to himself. It made sense to check out the train station first. Dan went down the stairs of the nearest subway station. On the wall map, he plotted his route to Maglev Station, the bullet train station for Shanghai. Maglev was not that far from the center of the city, just north of the People's Square. Dan got there in fifteen minutes. As he walked closer, he saw the elevated train tracks, rising up on huge columns above the road. He went inside the dome-shaped, futuristic fiberglass building that glowed white at night. Light streamed in from the transparent ceiling. Large displays on the sides showed photos and maps of the trains and their pathways. Dan walked over to the ticket booth, which was not crowded.

He showed the woman at the counter Lin's photo. He cleared his throat. "This is a good friend of mine who has gone missing. Can you remember if you saw this man on the 2nd of April?" That was exactly a week ago, and the day before Lin had been seen.

The woman could speak English. She looked carefully at the photo, then shook her head. "But you can ask my colleagues." She pointed to the three other booths next to her. Dan thanked her and joined the queue for the other booths. He hit pay dirt at the last booth.

The woman at the counter frowned and asked Dan to slide the photo under the counter. She held it close and then nodded. "Yes, I remember," she said. "Only because he was a young man with a child. He seemed too young to be her father."

Dan went still for a second. "He had a child with him?"

"Yes. A little girl, about five years old."

"Can you tell me where they got tickets for?"

The woman flipped back pages on her tablet screen. "He got tickets to Beijing. But only one adult ticket."

CHAPTER 27

It was almost eight p.m. by the time Dan got to the narrow alleys and bright lights of the Old Town. Endless stalls lined the alley, meat cooking in huge frying pans by the roadside, the smell of soy and hoi sin sauce and ginger mixing in the close night air. Dan sat in a wooden bench and ordered spring onions, noodles, and barbecued meat. After he had eaten, he took the subway back to Fuxing Zhong Lu *lilong*.

The bistros and cafes had opened up, and the lights were on in the balconies of the western-style houses. He slipped past and stood opposite the walls of the *lilong* compound. The gates were open, and yellow bulbs hung from the wires over the alleyways. Red paper lanterns hung against doors, glowing in the dark.

Dan watched as some residents walked in and out. Most were old or middle-aged. A teenager, back hunched and head bobbing up and down to music from his headphones, walked past him, paying him no attention. Dan left his spot and walked around the block. He sat down at a park bench and looked at his cell phone. He had a missed call from Kim. He would have to call her later.

He got up and walked back to the *lilong*. The gate was now shut, and some of the alley lights had turned off. Dan crossed the road and walked down the side of the building. There was a recess in the wall, and a metal door was fixed into it. Maybe an old entrance that had been bricked up on the other side. Probably used by the workers who made the *lilong* in the first place, back in the day when most people in Shanghai lived in these communal houses.

The door was solid and wouldn't budge. It had a handle that was fixed. Dan felt above the door. He could feel between the bricks. Old cement brushed off and fell on him. Dan took a last look around him. Then he felt for a fingerhold on the bricks above him and put his right foot on the iron handle of the door. He lifted himself up. With his left hand, he found more gaps on the brickwork. He climbed, then stood on top of the door. The parapet of the wall was above him. By standing on his tiptoes, he could reach the top of the wall.

A splash of light from the road fell against the wall. Dan went motionless as he heard a car roll past him. It did not stop. But he was at his most vulnerable right now. Anyone could spot him, and if attacked, his defenses were limited. He grabbed the lip of the parapet with both hands. He pulled, nothing came off the old wall. He pulled harder; then, using the power of his shoulders, lifted himself up, his feet feeling against the bricks for a toehold. There was none.

As soon as his shoulders were level against the parapet, he hooked his right elbow over, then his left, and pulled himself up more. Panting, he straddled the parapet, which was wide enough for him to sit on. He was on eye level with the second-floor window of a house opposite him. A light was on, as it was on several windows of the houses.

Terraces of houses stretched out in front of him, endless rows of them. The place was big, and Dan thought of the time when Shanghai was full of such compounds, and what life must have been like. There was an alleyway right underneath him. Wires crossed below his feet, and he shuffled along till he found a space wide enough for him to either climb or jump down.

The height was more than ten feet. He was considering climbing down when he saw an old woman come out of the house opposite. She emptied the contents of a pan into a garbage can, then went back inside but left the door open.

That did it. He had to jump down and take cover. The last thing he wanted was some old Chinese woman screaming at the *yangguizi* hanging from the walls of their *lilong*. Dan grimaced and, grabbing hold of the parapet, he slid down. He let himself swing for a few seconds, then bent his knees and let go.

He fell on his feet and felt a sharp, wincing pain up his ankles. He rolled over quickly and scurried underneath the window of a house that was dark. No one came out of the open doorway, now about three houses away from him. Light spilled out from it. Dan stood up and casually walked past it.

Running attracted the wrong kind of attention.

He went to the end of the alley, and the main gate was just ahead of him. He hooked a left and walked down towards the area he had been to in the morning. Windows were open, and voices floated out of windows, with the sound of oil splattering. Steam rose from the chimneys above. A round white moon played tag with the floating clouds. Dan picked his way silently to the Shengs' residence. He passed by Fushong Lee's house. It was silent, and the lights were off.

Dan crept forward, flattening himself against the wall now, but taking care not to dislodge the plants on the first-floor windowsills. He climbed up the Sheng house the way he had climbed up the boundary wall. This time, his fingers reached the upper floor window when he stood on the windowsill. He climbed up, then jumped gently on the balcony. The wooden door to the balcony was shut, but there was a glass window. He took out his knife and scraped off the putty at the corners of the window frame. Carefully, he took out the window panes, held together by a crossed timber panel. When the glass was out, he gave the timber panel a hard wrench, and it came off with a splintering sound.

Dan put his hand inside the window. Walls around it. Beyond, it was pitch-black. His eyes had become used to it, but he still couldn't make anything out. Gingerly, he put his head in through the window. A dank, musty smell hit his nostrils. No animal waste. Just old furniture. He took his head out, then put one leg in, feeling for the floor. Then he let himself inside.

He stood still, listening to the silence. Only his own breathing. He felt for the curtains to the window but found blinds. He lowered them, working slowly. He groped his way along the walls, taking small steps like a blind man. When his foot hit something, he bent down and touched it. Something soft. It was a bed, large enough for one adult. Next to it, he found a cot. He felt his way around a desk against the wall, and then he was at the door. The door creaked as he pushed it open.

He was out in a hallway. He guessed this was the upper floor landing. Below him, he could make out the staircase. To his right, another door. The joints protested, but the door opened. Dan felt along the walls. He found a light switch. He didn't switch it on but went inside the room. This room was smaller. Light from a *lilong* opposite fell inside, through the cracks of the closed window shutters.

Dan could see another desk, and a bookcase stuck on the wall. Red posters of Chinese letters hung on the wall. He knew the Chinese had a habit of leaving good fortune messages on the walls to bring them luck. He closed the door and switched the light on. No one from the alleyway would be able to see, but they might from the back. He had to take that chance.

He worked his way through the bookcase. They were all in Chinese. He pulled out the desk drawers. They were empty, but he found a small bill in Chinese letters. He didn't know what it was, but he put it in his back pocket.

He closed the drawers and stood up. That's when he heard the noise from downstairs.

CHAPTER 28

The padlock was being moved. He heard a scratching sound, metal against metal. Then a sharp crack. Sounded like bolt cutters being used to snap the padlock – exactly what he would have used. Then the creaking of the front door opening. Dan had already turned the light off. He opened the door a fraction and stepped out quickly. He went to the floor as the beam of flashlights hit the ceiling. He counted two lights, and two whispering voices.

This was not old Mr. Sheng coming back. He wouldn't have to snap the padlock of his own house. Dan slipped inside the bedroom. In the opposite house, a light was on, and there was also a streetlight on now. He would be seen if he climbed out the window. Dan looked outside. The alley was deserted. *For now*, he thought. If two had come inside, they should have someone outside.

He heard the squeak of stairs as shoes stepped on them. The beam of the flashlight danced against the bedroom door. Two voices whispered to each other in Chinese. Dan recognized the lilt of the Hong Kong accent.

The study door creaked open and then shut. It was a small room, and a quick glance had been enough. Dan took the kukri out and put it in his belt line. He couldn't use the Sig; the noise would wake up the neighbours.

The bedroom door creaked open. Dan was crouched behind it. The lights strobed in, the two men standing at the doorway, flashing the beams around. Then they came in. As soon as the second man was in, Dan kicked the door shut. He grabbed the collar of the man closest to him and pulled him back, slamming him against the closed door. The man bounced off the door, snarling. Dan already had his left elbow bent, and it exploded against the man's nose, rupturing it instantly.

He sank to the floor, clutching his face. Dan lifted his foot and kicked viciously, snapping the man's head back. His torchlight fell on the floor. Less than three seconds had passed since the men had entered the room.

The other guy flew at Dan with an oath. The snout of a compact handgun gleamed in the flashlight. Dan knew very well it wasn't easy to hold a flashlight in one hand and fire with the other. Many crossed one wrist across the other, but coordination was still compromised.

And he had the benefit of surprise. There would not be any escape.

Dan stepped over the fallen man and grabbed the gun wrist, his eyes better trained in the dark, his reflexes like lightning. The weapon fired, and the sound of a suppressed round zipped above his head. Then the kukri was in his hand, and he aimed below the head, at the soft of the neck. The blade came down in a clawing motion, ripping into the anterior triangle of the neck, cutting through the internal carotid artery and the external jugular vein. Warm blood pulsed over Dan's hand. He kept the pressure down hard, and the blade slid down behind the collar bone, puncturing the top of the lungs which project just above the collar bone. His attacker made a choking, gurgling sound, and his knees became weak.

He was losing blood rapidly, and the lung injury had given him a pneumothorax. He was holding the gun still, Dan's fingers wrapped around his. He fell to his knees, and the gun came away in Dan's hand. Dan left the knife in the man's throat, and he was on his knees instantly, scanning around for threats.

No rounds flew at him. All he could hear was a soft moaning from the fallen man who was still alive. Dan listened for five seconds. Then he went into the landing and did a quick SitRep. No sounds from downstairs. He slid back into the bedroom and checked the guy who was still alive.

He trained the flashlight on the man's face. He was wearing a suit. Tattoos came up his neck. Dan ripped his shirt open. More tattoos. Red and green dragons, Tao demons with tridents. He frisked the man quickly. Nothing, as expected.

Then he turned his attention to the guy on the floor. He was lying face down, and Dan turned him over. He blinked, and the breath caught in his chest. He knew the face. Bei-Lo. His competitor at the Hong Kong Kumite tournament. The man he had beaten in the semi-final.

Dan got up and went slowly down the stairs in the darkness. The kitchen and lounge areas were empty. He glanced outside. The lights in the house opposite had gone off. Dan sneaked out the door. The alley was empty. He ran down the way he had come. He skidded to a halt at the gates. They were shut, and they raised higher above the ten-foot wall. But he could climb the gate easily, on the decorative panels that were carved on it. He climbed quickly, silently. When he came to the level of the parapet, he balanced himself and slid along the wall.

Just at that moment, he saw a car's headlights around the corner of the road. Dan jumped. He fell and slipped, hurting his lower back. He ignored the sharp pain and ran across the road. He stayed beyond a tree trunk as the black SUV screeched to a halt outside the *lilong* gates.

Men poured out of the SUV. One of them had keys to the gate, and they rushed in, semiautomatic weapons in their hands. He recognized them as QB7-92s, 30-magazine weapons similar to Heckler and Koch's MP5s.

Dan memorized the SUV licence plate, then ran off before he could be spotted. He did not take the subway. His hands were caked in blood, and his clothes were stained. He walked through the massive park where the Shanghai Culture Square glowed like a diamond in the middle. In the rush of traffic across the main roads, most pedestrians ignored the *laowai* who walked past them quickly.

There was a bathroom in the lobby, and he stepped into it. He washed the dried blood off his hands and scrubbed his face clean. Taking his keys from the concierge, he took the elevator up to his room. A hot shower later, he was beginning to feel human again. He got dressed and went out immediately.

From a phone booth, he called Xiao. She answered on the first ring. Dan told her what had happened. She did not speak when he finished.

"Are you still there?" Dan asked.

She cleared her throat. "Yes, I am."

"I need you to check this licence plate for me." He read it out to her. "Can you do it?"

"I have a friend who works at the Transport Ministry. I could ask him."

Dan said, "Did you find anything about the Sheng family?"

"No, I didn't have time. I will try tomorrow."

"When can you get me the car details? All I want is a name and address."

"Let me call her. She might be able to do it from home."

Dan hung up and called back in thirty minutes. Xiao had the details. "What will you do?"

"Pay them a visit, tomorrow."

"I'm coming."

"No, you're not."

"You don't know where it is."

"I can find out."

"I rented a car today."

This was news to Dan. Having a car would make his life a lot easier, especially if he had a driver. He said, "Can I borrow your car? Promise to bring it back in one piece."

He heard her snort of derision. "I'm coming, and that's the end of it."

They were both silent for a second, then Xiao said, "We need to find out more about the Sheng family. But you cannot go back to the *lilong* now."

Dan thought to himself. He was starting to get a feel of how mainland China operated. People talked. If the authorities came calling, there was no such thing as personal information. The fear of retribution was greater. The PSB had eyes everywhere. More disturbingly, so did the Triads. If he went back to the *lilong* in broad daylight, word would spread quickly. He could only maybe visit again under the cover of darkness.

The Triads were bothering him. Had it been a coincidence they arrived the same time as him? Triads tended to be territorial. Hong Kong gangs would not be in Shanghai without a reason.

He said to Xiao, "I think you are right." Not for the first time, Dan wondered if someone was tracking him. Maybe he was followed all the way to the *lilong*, despite his best measures. The thought was unsettling.

Xiao said, "I'll call you tomorrow."

"Goodnight," Dan said and hung up.

CHAPTER 29

Virginia, USA

Kim's driver was a former Marine Recon NCO called Marly Hopper. He was in his fifties, and after he picked Kim up from her new apartment in Sleepy Hollow, they chatted all the way to the suburb in Arlington. Marly parked out of view of the two-story home across the street from them. He gave a pair of binoculars to Kim.

It was 0900 hours, and the sun was bright in the sky. As their intelligence had suggested, Rick Everett was still at home. He came into the porch, locked the door, and got into his Honda Civic in the drive.

Marly let him get a head start, then eased the Chevrolet out behind him. Kim knew Marly wouldn't lose his mark. He had worked for the Secret Service in the past, and as a driver for the FBI's Hostage Rescue Team. The car was armored, and both of them were armed. Two more units were on standby if they needed help.

Kim's cell beeped, and she glanced at the screen. It was Dan. "Hello?" Kim answered immediately.

She listened without interrupting. "Who is the girl?" Kim finally asked.

"I told you," Dan said. "She works in Shaolin, and our guy tried to tell her something before he left. She knew him, but only as a colleague."

"That's not what I asked you. *Who* is she? Have you done any background checks?"

"I'm in China, Kim. I can just about order food. Can you give me a contact that you trust? Then I can run checks on her. If not, for now, her help is all we have."

There was a tense silence between them. Dan said, "How is Maya?"

"She's fine. Call me back later with a more detailed SitRep."

"Roger that."

Kim hung up and tapped the phone against her palm. Dan was right. In the absence of any other sources she could trust, it was best to leave Dan to his devices.

Marly glanced at her in the rear-view mirror. They had crossed the Roosevelt Bridge while Kim had been on the phone.

"Approaching Foggy Bottom Campus of George Washington University," Marly said.

"Thanks, Marly," Kim said, her attention on the Honda Civic four cars ahead of them. The traffic was worsening, and the frequently changing lights did not help. The Honda drove up to the GWU campus gates. Rick Everett showed the guards a pass, and the barrier rose. Marly drove past, then banked a left, going past the GWU Hospital. The University campus sprawled over three blocks horizontally, and its upper portion was shaped into a wedge by the Pennsylvania Avenue NW.

"We need to get in there," Kim said. "We can't lose him."

"As you please," Marly said and conducted a high-speed turn onto H Street NW, by the Foggy Bottom Metro. Cars behind him bleated in annoyance, but he ignored them. They were stopped at the barrier by the campus guards. Kim showed them her ID.

"CIA, National Clandestine Service. This is a matter of national security. We have reason to believe an individual who is a threat is inside the campus."

The guard took Kim's ID and jogged over to his booth. He came jogging back after a minute. Kim fumed at the delay.

She asked, "Can you locate this car on your campus?" She gave the guard the Honda Civic's licence plate. She could see the bank of video screens inside the guard booth. The guard spoke to his partner on the radio.

"Parked in front of Monroe Hall, at the south of the campus." The guard gave Marly directions.

Kim breathed a sigh of relief. She thanked the guard and wound up her window as Marly breezed in through the gates. She took out her Glock 22, checked the mag, and slapped it back. She put the weapon in her shoulder holster.

Marly parked discreetly, a hundred yards away from the Monroe Hall building, under an oak tree. "Miss," he began, "you shouldn't go there on your own."

But Kim was already out and shutting the door. She crossed over to the other side and walked towards the Hall. She could see the car parked ahead. She stopped and walked over to the grass verge, sitting down with a group of students.

She sat there, waiting. The students were joined by their friends, and Kim was well-hidden within the group. She could see Marly inside the car, watching her. After fifteen minutes, she was getting anxious. She was about to stand up when she saw Rick. He was walking down the steps, deep in conversation with a young man. He had a small backpack and looked like a student.

Kim flipped open her cell and called Melanie, her analyst. Melanie was waiting for her call at the National Geospatial Intelligence Agency, or NGA, in Maryland. Melanie was coordinating a team that had a combination of drone feeds and satellite images on Kim's position. The position was fed through the GPS on Kim's cell phone.

"Melanie," Kim said, "you got eyes on me?"

Melanie said, "The coffee is rubbish here, did I ever tell you that? Total rubbish. I mean, I hear they're better funded than us. They could try some real coffee. And let's face it, the DoD is red-faced about asking for billions when Google maps gives us better images, right?"

Kim closed her eyes. "Melanie, not now, OK?"

"Sure. But you know I'm right about Google maps."

Kim had to concede that to her junior analyst. Commercial satellites had proven so much more effective to troops in real time, than anything so-called military satellites had provided. And yes, federal budgets for satellites had been trimmed considerably.

"Eyes, Melanie, I need eyes."

"Yes I got them. Whoa."

"What?"

"Cute guy next to you. Ginger beard. Can you get his number?"

"Shut up. Can you see our tango at the bottom of the steps? He's with a student, I'm pretty sure. Looks the right age."

There was a pause, then Melanie said, "Yes, I got him."

"I need a positive ID on the student. Run it on the GWU student database. If not, widen your search."

Another longer pause, followed by clicking on buttons. Kim watched as Rick and the student went around the building and started to disappear from view. She got up and started to walk. Melanie's voice crackled on the headphone receiver.

"Thelma calling Louise, do you copy?"

"Just give me his damn name."

"His name is Bohai Zilou, a Chinese overseas student. Here for a masters in Chemistry."

Kim frowned.

Melanie said, "Whoa."

"What now?"

"You'll never believe who his dad is."

"This better not be a joke."

"This one ain't. His father is Deng Zilou, the Mayor of Shanghai."

CHAPTER 30

Xiao was dozing on the subway. She had not slept well the night before. Her head felt heavy, and she was leaning against the glass partition at the end of her seat. The rhythmic movement of the train was hypnotic, and as she slipped in and out of consciousness, the vision of the man in the black mask suddenly appeared in front of her. He was sitting opposite her in the train, dressed entirely in tight black Lycra, like he had been that night. Strangely, no one else in the train seemed to pay any attention. Like they knew who he was. If anything, it was *she* who was getting strange glances. One of the passengers leaned over and spoke to the man next to her, pointing to Xiao.

The man in the black mask stood up. Xiao's mind froze in shock. She opened her mouth to scream and felt her head bump against something soft. She jerked awake and sat forward.

It was a dream. She was in the train, and it was full. She focused on the man sitting opposite her. He was an old man, and he was staring forward without looking at anyone. Xiao rubbed her neck and looked around her. No one was paying her any attention. Just another daily commute to work, when nine million Shanghainese took to the street and subway.

Xiao sighed. The dream had been reminiscent of last night's. They were becoming more frequent. She had dealt with emails until late last night, taken calls and delayed already stretched deadlines even further. It was three weeks now to Redmi's launch. There was still no sign of Lin Yan. She thought of what happened to Dan last night. There was obviously something about the Fengs that someone wanted to keep hidden. A sudden flush of determination seized her. She looked down at her small, pale hands, and made them into fists on her lap. She hadn't asked for any of this. Yet she was being chased, hunted. Well, she would take the fight back to them.

She wondered if she should inform the PSB. It was what everyone did. China was a safe country, without violent street crimes like in the west, because of the PSB monitoring everything. Unless when, she thought bitterly, the PSB sanctioned the crimes themselves. She knew very well of corruption in the ranks of the policemen. More than anything else, it was her inability to suddenly trust the PSB that was unsettling her. She frowned. Surely that was more reason she should look deeper into what was going on here.

A voice in Chinese and English announced her stop. "Thank you travelling the Red Line today," the female voice said in English. "We hope to see you again." It was the Mayor's new push, to make the city friendlier to foreigners. Xiao didn't see the need. Shanghai already had a sizeable expat community, albeit less than Hong Kong's. In mainland, her city had the reputation of being the most open to other cultures.

Xiao walked up to the gates of Shaolin, like she normally did, and showed Security her badge. They knew her, but there was extra caution following her incident. When she walked into her office, heads turned and hands raised in greeting. Xiao nodded back, glad to see the team was busy at work. She spent the rest of the morning in a whirlwind of meetings and interviews. Thankfully the media was staying away for now, but in another week they would be snapping at her heels.

When she had a moment to herself, she typed in Lin Yan's name on the search button of Shaolin's website. She frowned. The page that came up was blank. But Lin, as far as she knew, was still an employee. She picked up the phone and rang Human Resources. The department, or *danwei,* was tiny, with only two young women as full-time staff. Most of the employees in Shaolin were recruited by micro resumes posted in blog sites like Weibo and WeChat. Somehow, Chinese graduates were able to fit their education and work experience into 140 characters. The system worked. There were too many graduates in China to go through, Xiao thought, and the micro resumes were a useful way to eliminate candidates.

No one picked up her call. Xiao took the elevator and went downstairs. Biyu, one of the ladies in the office, looked up as Xiao walked in. She was in her mid-twenties, fresh out of university, and typical of the hundreds of millions of Chinese graduates.

After greeting her, Xiao asked, "Biyu, I need to see the details of Lin Yan, one of our employees."

Biyu wrote down the request on her desktop keyboard, then opened the page. Xiao stood behind her. Lin's photo flashed on the screen, with his details.

"Scroll down," Xiao said. She bent closer to look at the screen. "Stop."

The cursor hovered over the closest relative icon. Biyu pressed it and a name came up on the screen. Chunhua Lee. Sister. Xiao wrote it down and then looked for the rest of Lin's family. There was no photo or address. She thanked Biyu and went upstairs.

By late afternoon, Xiao had managed to deal with most urgent matters and push others back to the next day. She called Dan and made plans to meet him in the Old City.

Dan was waiting for her outside the metro stop for the French Concession. He was wearing jeans, T-shirt, and a light jacket, a useful precaution against the temperamental Shanghai rain.

She felt an odd sense of reassurance when she spotted his tall, wide frame leaning against the side wall, next to the shadow of a tree. She hadn't spotted him easily, and when she did find him it occurred to her his effort to remain inconspicuous was deliberate. His clothes were dark, and he was wearing sunglasses, although it wasn't particularly sunny. The glasses effectively hid his eyes. She strolled up to him.

"I need some green tea," she said.

"I'll let you lead the way," he said, keeping his glasses on.

They walked away from Yu Gardens and into the narrow, cloistered charm of the old French Concession. Small shops and cafes crowded both sides of the stone-paved alleys. They went past some well-maintained old European hotels, going deeper into the labyrinth of streets. Xiao stopped outside a food stall. Skewers of lamb were being cooked in an open-air grill. The middle-aged chef wiped sweat off his brow and turned the skewers. Large pots of tea bubbled behind him, and two young girls were serving a few people sitting in outdoor tables.

They sat down. Dan watched the chef, and the waitresses, who looked different from the Chinese. His skin was more tanned, the nose broader, and he looked Central Asian as opposed to the usual Han Chinese. The women looked similar. Xiao spotted him looking.

"If you are wondering about the owner, he's an Uighur, from Xin Jiang."

"That's in the northeast, right?"

Xiao gave him an appraising glance. "You know about them?"

Dan shrugged. "I can look at a map."

"You will see Uighur shops all around. They know how to cook meat, and their lamb skewers are yummy."

Xiao had placed the order before she sat down, and soon their food arrived. Green tea, lamb skewers, and minced fish dumplings. Xiao picked up a dumpling with her chopstick, dipped it in a sauce of soy and green chilli, then popped it in her mouth. Dan did the same.

He reached inside his pocket and took out the bill he had picked up from the Sheng household. He smoothed the crumpled piece of paper on the table and passed it to Xiao. She looked at it while sipping her green tea. Then she put her finger on the red Chinese letters at the top of the bill.

"Double Happiness Laundry," she read. "It's a laundromat. Not far from here, a few stops on the subway."

Dan told her about what he had found at the Maglev Station.

"He had a child with him?" Xiao frowned.

"Yes."

Xiao told him about Chunhua Lee, Lin's sister.

Dan said, "Can we find her?"

"I searched in the WeChat and Weixin apps, and send friend pokes to the Chunhuas in Shanghai. There's a lot of them, and we might never find the right one."

"If she still lives in Shanghai."

"Exactly."

Dan drained his glass. They left and wandered back out through the maze of streets. In front of the roaring traffic of the elevated Yan'an Road, they took the subway and headed west towards Fuxing Zhong Lou. They got off two stops before and headed down a similar rabbit warren of streets till they got to the right address. An elderly Chinese man, his cheeks pinched and sallow, looked up at them with hazy black eyes when they appeared in front of his store. The sign above his head was rusty, with paint peeling. It was all in Chinese. Clothes hung in racks arranged in rows inside the small shop.

Xiao showed the man Lin's photo, but he shook his head. When he saw the bill, he became more animated. He got up, went to the side of the shop, leaned out and spat on the narrow drain that ran down the side of the street. He raised his voice and shook his finger, pointing it upwards.

Xiao glanced at Dan. "Mr. Sheng did not pay the last bill," she said. Then she turned back to the man and spoke in rapid Pinyin, the Chinese dialect that was spoken in Shanghai. The old man walked slowly to the back of his shop and fumbled through items of washed clothing. He came back to the counter and opened a dog-eared notebook. He wrote something down on a piece of paper and gave it to Xiao with both hands.

Xiao accepted it in similar fashion, her thumbs holding the piece of paper, and she bowed slightly to the older man. Then she turned, and Dan followed.

Xiao said, "This is the address of the man who used to pick up their clothes and deliver it to the *lilong* house."

"Who was he?"

"He doesn't know. Some kind of relative. Never said much apparently. He takes down people's addresses in case they don't pay."

"Where did he live?" Dan looked at the Chinese letters on the paper.

"On the Pudong side. We need to cross the river."

They walked out of the narrow streets into the broad, traffic-filled avenue of Zhaojiabang Road, heading for the subway stop.

CHAPTER 31

"Where did you learn to speak English so well?" Dan asked.

"I spent a year at State University New York in Stony Brook, as a foreign exchange student."

Dan nodded. That accounted for her almost native English speech. "Did you like America?"

"That's like me asking if you like China."

"I guess. Good and bad, right?"

"You could say that."

Dan detected a coldness in her tone. He left it alone. After a while, Xiao said, "I got lonely out there. Far from home, you know."

"Uh-huh."

"And everybody has an opinion."

"That's not just in USA. Everyone in entitled to an opinion."

"I meant everyone has an opinion about China. Like they know what China is like."

"What do you mean?"

"All the bad things you see in the media. Lack of free speech, corruption, and so on."

Dan said, "You know better than me that all of that exists." He added, "We have similar things back home. Our politicians are corrupt as hell, the big companies make life difficult for the man on the street. Often, the corporations and politicians ride with each other. But we are open about it. Here, you're not allowed to talk about stuff like that."

Xiao shot him a glance filled with venom. "Now you sound like my American college friends."

"Isn't it true?"

"No, Dan it's not true. In fact, we are very vocal about corruption within politicians, and the kickbacks they get from big companies. The Party knows about it, and they get rid of corrupt politicians."

Dan didn't say anything. They walked in silence and soon got sight of the river. The subway stop was a few blocks ahead. Xiao said, "Look, all I'm saying is that people judge according to what they hear. Yes, we do have problems. But I also think the system, for all its faults, works quite well."

Dan nodded. "Sure looks like it around here."

They were at the station and joined the usual rush of people. The ride was longer than Dan had expected, a half hour by his watch. Dan blinked when they got out in the bright sunlight on the other side.

It looked very different. The usual throng of people and hubbub of chatter was replaced by a quietness. Tall buildings stood all around them, and they looked like residential apartment blocks. The metal and glass skyscrapers of downtown were gone, replaced by these buildings that looked uniform in shape, size, and color. A handful of cars plied the wide avenue in front of them. They were in the outskirts of Shanghai.

People filed out of the station and walked down the road. These passengers did not wear the sharp suits of Shanghai's business commuters. Their old coats, torn and repaired in places, and their features distinguished them as migrant workers from China's vast interior. Dan also noticed a large number of young men, some wearing cheap suits from online shops, others wearing labourer clothes that marked them as building site workers, like most of the migrants.

Xiao turned right, and Dan followed. The buildings were regularly spaced and rose up tall and grey into an overcast sky. A couple of street stalls stood on the pavement. But gone was the bustle and chatter of city life, the kinetic palpation of energy that touched Dan's skin every time he walked on Shangai's bustling, warm, humid streets.

He watched as the legion of workers walked with their heads bowed. One by one, they crossed the street and entered the bowels of the tall buildings that served as their homes. None of them gave him the customary curious glance. Once they disappeared inside the buildings, the streets became deserted. A wind blew an old newspaper across the street. Dan felt he was in a Chinese equivalent of a deprived small town, far out in the country, steeped in lethargy and disillusion.

"This where the ant tribes live," Xiao said softly.

"What's the ant tribe?"

"It's an expression we have. The people who work in the city but cannot afford to live there. Every day the ants move in and out, like an army."

Dan looked around him. For the first time, the reality of life in China hit him. These were the teeming millions, the ones who made up the country. What he had seen so far were the privileged few.

Xiao stopped outside a building complex. On the wall surrounding the tall apartment buildings, characters written in red paint were flaking off. Above the wall, red banners hung with slogans on them.

"What do those letters say?" Dan asked Xiao.

She read them. "*Peace and contemplation. Loving and kind, hearty and warm. Good deeds bring good fortune.*" Xiao looked at Dan and said, "You'll see these inside many homes as well. These letters are hung on walls as good luck charms."

"And the slogans?" Dan wanted to know if he was heading inside a Party building.

"*Safety in unity. Be considerate to your neighbour,*" Xiao read.

There was a gate, but it had blown open in the wind. No guards were visible. They went inside. The large courtyard had a garden that was weedy and overgrown. At the mouth of the gates, a couple were selling skinned pineapples from a hand cart. A man was haggling with them. The woman weighed up some fruit on a scale and spoke to her customer. Xiao approached them when the man had gone. She gestured to Dan, and they walked towards the building, followed by the stare of the fruiterers.

Four tall apartment buildings stood in the corners of the long courtyard. They walked to the nearest one and then headed towards a small brick building to one side, which had a tunnel-like entrance that led downstairs.

Dan touched Xiao on the arm. "Hold it. Are we going into the basement?"

Xiao nodded. "That's what the woman said. The man who lives at this address lives in one of the basement rooms."

Dan frowned. "Why the basement?"

"Because it's even cheaper than living aboveground. They're still living in Shanghai, right?"

"This is the real cost of the real estate boom, isn't it?"

Xiao nodded. "What is that term, something to do with cotton? You know, like when you understand something."

"You mean cottoning on."

"That's it. Rents in Shanghai are so high that it drives people underground."

"The ant tribe." He looked at her and raised his eyebrows. "Guess I'm cottoning on."

The door to the ground-floor building was locked, and Xiao had to knock loudly several times before there was a jangle of keys. A broad-faced, flat-nosed woman squinted at them. Xiao spoke to her, and she glared at them for a while, then spoke to Xiao again. Eventually, she stood to one side, suspicion in her eyes as they flitted from Dan to Xiao.

There was an office ahead of them, used by the woman with the keys. She stood at the top of the stairs as they went down. The air was suddenly musty and thick. Dan had to bend down to avoid his head hitting the ceiling. One flight down, they arrived at a corridor that looked like a college dormitory.

"Number 479," Xiao said. They walked down. 479 was locked. Xiao knocked, but there was no response. After a few knocks, they walked down to the end of the corridor. There was a communal toilet and washroom, and a basin to wash clothes in. Dan looked around him, at the numerous tiny rooms that had been carved out underground.

"There's another floor below this," Xiao said. "Seventy rooms in the floor, and fifty below. That's what the woman said."

Dan shook his head. He took a deep breath, but the air was dank, and it smelt old, heavy. He couldn't live in a place like this and felt sorry for the people who did.

Xiao wrote something on a piece of paper and slid it under the doorway of 479. Then they climbed back up to the ground level. The woman glared at them in silence, and opened the door to let them out. She stayed at the door, watching them walk down the large courtyard.

CHAPTER 32

The sky was overcast and a stiff breeze blew across the overgrown grass of the courtyard. The four tall buildings stood like lonely sentinels at the corners.

Dan asked, "What did you write on that paper you slid under his door?"

"My cell number. I called myself Mei. And don't worry, it's a new cell that I brought yesterday. Once he calls me, I'm destroying the SIM."

Dan gave Xiao an appraising glance. "Good. Let's hope he calls back."

"If he doesn't?" Xiao asked.

"Then I come back here tonight. Stake the place out."

Xiao's voice was uncertain. "Are you sure?"

Dan said, "Done it many times." Visions from the past rose up in his mind like dark shadows. The butt of his H&K 416 rifle still against his shoulder, target's head and shoulder in the viewfinder. The barely perceptible recoil of the rifle as it jerked in his hands. Target's head blown up like a watermelon.

He transferred his attention back to Xiao. "This time will be no different. Don't worry."

As they neared the gates, Dan saw a man speaking to the fruiterers. He was about a hundred yards away. The man looked up as he sensed movement and saw them approaching. The fruiterer turned to look, then turned back to the man and said something. Dan had increased his pace, and Xiao was struggling to keep up. She broke into a jog. The guy suddenly turned and ran back the way he came, in the direction of the subway.

Dan exploded into a sprint. He heard Xiao shout at him, but he didn't look back. He went past the gates and saw the man run across the road. Dan waited for two cars to pass, then followed. He could hear Xiao behind him. The man had a head start, and Dan saw him run inside the subway station. He looked behind and saw that Xiao had broken into a sprint as well, and had almost caught up with him. She held her shoes in her hand and was running barefoot. Dan turned and increased his pace, reaching the roughly five to six hundred yards to the station in no time.

He was panting with the effort by the time he ran into the station, and his shirt was sticking to his back. He ran up to the turnstiles and put his Century subway transport card in the slot. He rushed downstairs. He heard Xiao call his name again and looked back. He waved to her from the stairs, then rushed down them. A train was pulling up at the station as he jumped down the last five steps. Landing on the balls of his feet, he ran forward.

A few people scattered as he brushed past them. Desperately, Dan looked around. Women and women looked at this tall, sweating *yangguizi* with avid curiosity. There was an announcement on the PA, and passengers streamed inside the train. Dan heard Xiao shout his name, and he raised his hand, but did not look back. Then he saw his man. The doors were closing, and the man darted forward from behind a pillar. He wore a light summer vest with a hoodie, and his face was covered. He pushed past a knot of people and boarded the train.

Dan ran forward, but the doors were almost closed. He had to make a split second run for the carriage closest to him, one behind his target's. With a shudder and whistle, the rubber gaskets of the doors closed. Dan thrust his right arm forward and, with his fingertips, prised the door open. The train began to move. Dan pushed the gates open further, putting both his shoulders inside. Xiao had arrived right behind him, breathless. Dan jumped on board, keeping his legs akimbo to keep the doors open for her. Xiao got across him and came on board as the train began to pick up speed and pull out of the platform. Dan let go of the doors, and they closed with a snap. He stumbled forward and stopped himself from falling by holding on to railing above.

Xiao's face was on fire, and she was fighting for breath. Dan pointed to the carriage ahead of them. "Our man is in there," he said. He started to walk towards the vestibule that separated the carriages. He lowered the glass and felt for the handle on the other side. He pushed it down and the door opened. Both of them walked across. Dan felt a hand on his back and turned.

"What's he wearing?" Xiao asked.

"A cream summer top with a rain hoodie." Dan saw the sweat-plastered hair on her forehead and the color on her cheeks. "You should stay here. I'll call you when this is over."

Xiao shook her head. Dan was getting to know the determined, inflexible side of her personality. He turned and head down the carriage slowly, looking around. The man was not there. They went on the next carriage, carefully looking at every face. Dan felt the train beginning to decelerate. Xiao shifted to a window looking at the platform as the train pulled in, and Dan walked over to the door. He stepped out on the platform but stayed close to the door.

"There," Xiao cried from behind him. Dan saw a figure run out of the carriage ahead of him, heading for the stairs. A crowd of people were pushing to get on the train. Dan pushed past them, but they were in downtown now, and the crowd was thicker. The bodies hemmed him in, and Dan didn't want to use brute force against innocent civilians. By the time he had pushed his way into the open, he couldn't see the guy on the platform.

Dan ran up the stairs, taking three at a time. He vaulted over the turnstiles and came out into the open. Traffic roared on roads on either side of the station. A flash of movement caught his eye. There was only one figure running hard. He was on the pedestrian bridge that crossed the wide road on the right, his body framed as a moving dot against the sunlight winking on the skyscrapers. Dan sprinted for the bridge. People swerved away from him. As Dan ran down the stairs of the bridge, he noticed a car pull up at the base, tires screeching.

Dan didn't have time to stop. He saw his target vanish across the side of a building up ahead. He carried on running, aware that Xiao had given up the chase now. He was in a pavement with boutique shops on one side, and he cut a strange figure, running past the strolling shoppers. Dan went around the building and found himself in a narrow alley that ran along the back of several skyscrapers. He saw the man far up ahead and resumed his chase.

The man reached a chained gate and climbed up, then dropped on the other side. For a few seconds, he stood there, looking at Dan. It was too far for Dan to see his features, and he had pulled his hood back on. Then he turned and ran. Dan reached the gate and clambered up it. He jumped from the top, landing on his feet and rolling over on his back. He was up in the same movement and running again.

He was going past alleys that forked out left and right. He glanced at them as he went past. At the second one, he caught sight of a figure slumped on the ground and he stopped. He heard car doors slam and he looked up. At the mouth of the alley, a car stood with one door open. The others had slammed shut.

A figure stood in front of the open back door. He was dressed in black, and Dan could see his spiky blond hair and the black monocle over his left eye. They stared at each other for a few seconds. Then Dan saw him reach inside his coat. In a blur of movement, the Sig was in Dan's hand and he had fired, aiming for the figure. His shot struck the body of the car, and he noticed the way the round flew off. Armored. The guy in black did not get to fire. He ducked and disappeared inside, and the car took with a screech of rubber on asphalt.

Dan ran to the figure on the ground. The man was in his thirties. The hood had fallen from his face, and Dan could see the pallor that comes with heavy blood loss. He was still breathing, and his eyes fixed on Dan's face. His chest rose up and down rapidly. Dan looked down his body and saw two gunshot wounds. One at the left chest, the other in the abdomen. He turned the man over. No exit wounds. Bad news.

The man was trying to say something. Dan turned him over, watching the face turning blue. Blood-tinged sputum frothed at the man's lips. His eyes were bloodshot and tears squeezed out the sides. His hands came up, trying to touch Dan. Dan grabbed his hands and held them. *Jeez, man,* he thought, *all I wanted to do was talk. Why did you have to run?*

Deep down, Dan knew the answer. This man had been running for a while. The poor guy was terrified, and now he was going to die.

"Sheng," Dan said. He pointed to himself. "Me look for Mr. Sheng. Who are you?"

The man mumbled again and gripped Dan's hand harder. He blinked through his tears. Dan put his ears to the man's lips.

"*Jinjing...Jinjing Sheng.*"

"Jinjing Sheng?" Dan asked. The man's eyes rolled backwards. Dan picked up his head in the crook of his head and shook him till the man opened his eyes. His glazed eyes remained unfocused but his lips moved.

"*Wo...wo de taitai. Jinjing wo de taitai.*"

Dan memorised the words, feeling helpless. The man's eyes closed for the last time, and then his chest stopped moving. Dan put his head back on the ground. He gritted his teeth and smacked his fist into his thigh.

"Damn it!" he shouted.

His cell phone beeped. He picked it up and saw the Weixin Chat app blinking. He pressed on it. Xiao's urgent voice came on the phone.

"I can see you on the phone," Xiao panted. "I'm coming."

Dan got to his feet. "No. Stop there. Go inside a busy shop and stay surrounded by people. I can see you on the app too. I'm on my way."

Dan hung up and took several photos of the dead man. He frisked his pockets quickly and found a wallet with an ID card. He put the wallet in his pocket and ran out on the street, where the sound of sirens was getting louder.

CHAPTER 33

Washington DC

Kim jogged around the university building. Students had formed a knot outside a playing field, cheering on a practicing team. She ran past them, looking around desperately. Her eyes fell on a parking lot to her left. She saw the flash of sunlight as the door of a car opened. It was Rick Everett. Kim pulled the cap lower on her head and walked quickly to the bank of trees in front of the parking lot. She could see Rick and the Chinese man next to him in the passenger seat. Rick began to reverse the car. Kim pressed on her earpiece quickly and called Marly. He picked up on the first ring.

"Where are you?"

"We are at the back of the building. There's a parking lot. He's heading out. Can you cut him off?"

"You mean stop him?"

"Hell no. We need to follow." There was a silence as Marly fiddled with the buttons of his sat nav.

Kim saw the car disappearing out of the car park. She burst into a run, heading back to the car. She called Marly on her headphones while she ran. "Forget it. I'm coming back." She hung up and called Melanie.

"Yo," Melanie said.

Kim kept herself fit, and the tremor in her voice was not due to running fast. "Tango headed out on from the parking lot. Keep track of him and feed it back to me. We are following."

Marly had pulled away from the curb already and was waiting when she arrived. He beeped his horn gently at some students and drove around the bend, heading for the parking lot.

Melanie's voice cracked on Kim's earpiece. "I got visual. He's headed out towards Virginia Avenue Northwest." Melanie took her earpiece off and matched it to the car's Bluetooth. The speaker came on. Melanie repeated her instruction, and Marly swung the car out to the south exit.

"Route 66 now, looks like he's heading for the TR bridge."

Marly said, "Crossing over to Arlington." A row of cars lined up in front of him, all waiting for the lights to change. "Shall we put the siren on?" he asked.

"No." Kim knew she couldn't arrest anyone. But she did have the right to investigate. Putting the lights and sirens on would do nothing but warn Rick. The lights changed and Marly sped up, honking and swerving to get ahead. He got some beeps and shouts back but the hard-nosed former Marine ignored them with a curl of his lips.

Soon, they caught sight of Rick's car. They were coming off Theodore Roosevelt Bridge, and the car was heading left onto GW Memorial Parkway. Marley followed, driving expertly, staying on the same lane, three to four cars behind.

Kim called Melanie on her cell phone. "I need the low-down on Mayor Zilou."

"How low?"

"The lowest it gets. I doubt you'll find much though, as the PRC polices the cyberspace effectively. But see what you come up with."

"And then his son?"

"Yup."

Melanie rang back in ten minutes.

"Shoot," Kim said.

"Long-time Party faithful. Used to be a child cadre, then at college became full time Party member. Finished his degree though, in political science at Peking College in Beijing. Age sixty-two. Got posted around the country and known for his campaigning for villagers' welfare. Good friend of Deng Xiaoping."

Kim interrupted. "That's the guy who started the economic reforms in 1979, after Mao died, right?"

"Right. Don't stop me, I'm on a flow."

"You're just reading off a screen."

"It's not any screen. It's the CIA clandestine records…"

"Alright, I get it. Hurry up."

"Just so you know. Like his mentor, he shares a peasant background and a thing for open markets. Also keen on adopting Western social policies like a free press and judiciary. He thinks it will reduce corruption and give people a voice. But he wants it done the Chinese way, of course. Whatever that means. Wants to stop the one child policy, saying it's harming China now. Also, friendly with the Taiwanese."

Kim was thoughtful. "He sounds like a good guy. Any dirt?"

"None on our records. Got a wife, and one son, Bohai, who's here right now."

"Right, let's get on to Bohai."

"I got some photos of him, but I'm keeping an eye on the car as well, like the good analyst I am. When do I get a promotion?"

"Melanie, this is serious."

"So am I. Anyway, Bohai is the opposite of his dad. Had a privileged upbringing in Beijing and went to college at his dad's alma mater. He's a playboy, with flashy cars and a string of girlfriends. Nice photos. Did I ever tell you I had a thing for Asian men?"

Kim sighed. "Melanie, you have a thing for all men."

Marly turned to glance at Kim. She caught his eyes and raised her eyebrows. He grimaced and got his eyes back on the road.

"And by the way, can I remind you, that you are on official duty right now. So, cut it out."

"Hmm, Grumpy. OK, Bohai is here doing a one year master's degree in International Politics. Been here since last September but has visited the U.S. before with his family."

"Did we ever try to contact him? Develop him as an asset?"

Melanie said, "Not that I can see on his files."

Kim knew she would have to look into this deeper when she got back to the office. Things were suddenly getting interesting.

"Did his father ever do a state visit?"

"No. But, he might do in the future. Mayor Zilou is a shoo in for the

Politburo Standing Committee next year."

"The eight-man group that decides China's future."

"Correct."

Kim looked at the buildings on either side of the road. The April sun was bright, and Arlington Boulevard hummed with traffic. Marley gripped the wheels, eagle eyes on their target. The car moved steadily.

She said, "What if someone wanted to stop Zilou from getting to the Politburo? I mean, he's good for us. Open to Western policies."

"Who would want to stop him?"

Thoughts were jostling around in Kim's head. She needed time to think, and that time wasn't right now. She got the feeling she was circling round something big, and if she could connect the dots, she might just get there. She thought about the implications and got a sudden chill.

She said to Melanie, "Keep your eyes on the car. See you back at the office." She hung up.

Marley said, "He's turning off." They followed the car into the exit that led to a traffic junction.

"Do you think he's seen us?" Kim asked.

"If he has, he's not showing any signs yet."

The roads got smaller, and warehouses, abandoned factories sprouted on either side of the road. They were going through an industrial estate. Pedestrians were few and far between. Sounds of traffic had died down. Marly sped up as Rick's car accelerated.

Kim said, "He's spotted us now."

"Uh-huh. Had to happen sometime."

Kim saw it a split second before Marly did. A black transit van rushed out from one of the side roads. It smashed into the hood on Marley's side, spinning the car around to hit the side of the van. With a twisting clash of metal the two cars collided, and Kim's head banged against the window glass. The Glock was in her hand, but she was too dazed to do anything. Gears crunched as Marly revved the engine and reversed the car. With a squeal of tires, the Honda came off the van.

Two men leaped out of the back door of the van. Their faces were covered in ski masks, and they held what looked like MP5 sub machine guns.

"Get down," Kim shouted. They bent under the dashboard as a hail of bullets few at them. Rounds splattered against the hood, denting metal, whining off the front fenders. The windscreen fractured in a spreading spider web and finally exploded in a shower of glass fragments that rained down on them. Marly was still driving. With one hand, he held the steering wheel and kept it on reverse, foot on gas. The bullets came still, and Kim could tell the men were running forward.

"Hold on," Marly shouted. Lifting his head above the dashboard, he turned the handbrake on, simultaneously wrenching the wheel as hard as he could to the left. Tires squealed, leaving black marks on the road, and the smell of burning rubber hit Kim's nose. The Honda spun round in a circle, flinging Kim against the door. Marly managed to straighten the car and take the handbrake off. The gunfire now came from behind them, but Marly had managed to put distance behind them and the car.

The Honda shot forward, heading for the exit they had come off earlier. Kim looked behind her, aiming with the Glock. The two men with guns had piled back in the van, and the vehicle was turning around.

She called Melanie. "Did you see what happened?"

"I'm on it," Melanie said in a terse voice. "Two SAD MSVs on their way to you." Special Activities Division, Mobile Support Vehicles.

"What about Rick?"

"He went inside a warehouse and then an SUV came out, heading west. We're on him."

"Good." Kim could barely speak. Glass particles were still coming off the shattered windscreen. Marly indicated and pulled over, hazard light flashing.

Kim got out and kicked the side of the car, fuming. "Damn it." She put her ear piece on and got Melanie back on the airwave. In the distance, the sound of sirens were getting louder.

"I want everything on Rick Everett. Who he talks to, who he sleeps with, what he eats. Ditto on Bohai. Get me his yearbook photos from college, bank accounts details, his personal life in the U.S. I want it all."

"Roger that," Melanie said.

CHAPTER 34

Shanghai, Pudong
Lujiazui District

Hu Shintao looked around the suite room. He was resplendent in a dark maroon silk cape with a silver dragon engraved on it. The dragon had its claws out, and white fire emanated from its mouth. Tied to his belt was the long, curved sword of the *Sun Yee On* Triads. The Dragon Head had his customary black leather mask attached to his face, showing only the dark crevices of his eyes.

The penthouse presidential suite of the Chenguang Towers in eastern Pudong was the size of half a football field. It had a banquet room, jacuzzi and sauna, an office and two luxury bedrooms. The ceiling was triangular and made entirely of glass, and the building sent off a halo of light that rose up in the night sky like a beacon. In the jungle of skyscrapers that was the Lujiazui district, its distinctive rooftop was envied by many.

Shintao was seated at the head of the table, in the only highbacked chair. His seat was close to the main exit door. He looked to his right, towards a floor to ceiling tapestry image of *Wusheng Laomu*, the Eternal Goddess Mother. She sat on a lotus throne, surrounded by golden light. By her feet her two children sat in smaller thrones. Yin, the daughter, and Yang, the son. There was no father, as The Eternal Mother conceived from herself. Shintao closed his eyes and murmured a prayer his mother had taught him as a young boy. He needed *Wusheng Laomu's* guidance tonight.

Twenty-four guests sat around him, right under the apex of the triangular roof. Each one of the guests were heads of Shanghai's Triad families. Waitresses streamed in, carrying red crystal flutes of champagne. Once everyone's glasses were full, Hu Shintao stood up and raised his.

"To the Mountain Spirit," he said. As the Mountain Master, it was his duty to invoke the name of the deathless spirit that resided in the holy mountains.

Everyone echoed the toast, then downed their drinks. The glasses were drained, and Hu Shintao said immediately, "*Ganbei!*" This was the cue to another toast, and to have their glasses filled again.

"To peace and fortune." Shintao remained seated this time but raised his glass up. Everyone downed their glasses.

Deng Cuo, the head of the 14K family in Shanghai said, "*Ganbei*," in a soft voice. Deng Cuo was a gently spoken man, but his stature was unmistakable. 14K was a powerful triad group originating from Kowloon, the island just north of Hong Kong. Their influence was vast, and it was rumoured many officers of the PSB were in their payroll. They had a virtual monopoly on the nightclubs that dotted the riverside south of the Bund. Some of them were "singing parlours" reminiscent of the old Shanghai, where glamorous musicians and film stars cavorted with wealthy businessmen and government officials.

Deng Cuo said, "To new business opportunities." A murmur of voices echoed his toast.

Cuo said again, "Hu Shintao, it is a pleasure to have you with us." He looked around the table with his puffy, beady eyes. "I know I speak for everyone when I say, thank you for inviting us." Another chorus of agreements rose around the table. "The first rain that arrives at the end of summer, feeds the parched earth. You too, must be here for a reason. After all, you and your brothers are doing well in Hong Kong." Cuo paused, and a pregnant silence filled the space.

Shintao waited for several seconds before replying. "The rain falls because clouds darken the sky, Brother Cuo."

There was an intake of breath at the word Brother. Most Triad families only called their own members by that pre-fix. By calling Deng Cuo a Brother, Shintao had indicated he was already on business terms with him. The bosses looked at each other around the table. This was news to them.

Shintao continued. "The *yangguizi* might have gone from Hong Kong, but many of their friends remain. It is not easy doing business with them.

They do not understand *guanxi*." Pronounced *gwan-shee,* the word stood for respect and looking out for one another. If one had *guanxi* in the right places, the world was his oyster.

"Whereas in the mainland, it is not two country and one rule. It's one country, one rule." Shintao spread his arms, lifting up the sides of his cape. "You benefit from that. A little *guanxi* goes a long way here."

A man known as Sheizian, the head of the Lazy Boys clan, cleared his throat from the end of the table. "That *guanxi* took a long time to develop, Shintao. How do you see our connections helping you here?"

There was a low murmur of voices. Shintao took a deep breath and tried to control his rising anger. He would show these lowly dogs not to speak that way to him. That time would come soon. Aloud he said, "Sheizian, we know of your karaoke bars, and the brisk business you do. I am not saying I want to tread on your toes." He looked around the table, looking at everyone. "All I am saying is you give me the space to develop my own connections."

Another man said, "But by doing that, Shintao, you deprive us of our connections. Our guanxi diminishes. We know how big the *Sun Yee On* is. If you move in here…"

Deng Cuo cut him off by raising his voice. "What our Brother here is trying to say, Shintao, is that we need some assurance from you."

Shintao was bristling. It was good they could not see the anger on his face, he thought. "What kind of assurance, Brother Cuo?"

"Assurance that you will not open…businesses close to ours."

"Brother Cuo. Pudong and the Bund, Fuzhou, Maoming Road, all the prime spots are taken by you. I respect that. But I also need to start from somewhere. I suggest that I begin south of the Yu Gardens and the French Concession."

The chorus of voices became louder this time. Deng Cuo raised his hand. "Shintao, please be reasonable. What you suggest is the prime location of our Taiwanese brothers. You know that. If we allow you to begin operations there, it will lead to a turf war with them. Nobody wants that."

Shintao was quiet for several seconds. Then unexpectedly, he said, "How is your *Huashan Bao Mi* running these days, Brother Cuo?" *Bao Mi* stood for secret club, on Huashan Road.

Cuo narrowed his eyes. "Fine. Why do you ask?"

Shintao raised his hand and snapped his fingers. The man with spiky blond hair, Hua Deng, arrived with a cell phone in his hand. Shintao picked up the phone and listened, then slid it down the table towards Cuo. "It's for you," he said.

Cuo's flat, broad face was like a storm. He curled his lips, then picked up the phone, his stare fixed on Shintao. His face changed when he heard the frantic voice on the phone. His face contorted in a deep frown

"What…how…put him on the phone…do you know who you are dealing with?" Cuo listened for a while, then stared at the phone as the line cut off. He looked at the stunned faces surrounding him.

"The PSB Vice Squad just shut down the *Huashan Bao Mi*. Said they had orders from above."

One of the bosses stood up, scraping his chair back. "Tell them who you know in the PSB. This is impossible!"

Cuo said, "I did tell them." He turned on Shintao, who was sitting there calmly. He wagged a finger at Shintao. "You. Shintao. You cannot do this. You call me Brother, and on the other hand…" Cuo screamed a curse and threw the phone at the opposite wall. It hit the painting of *Washeng Luomu*.

"Watch the Mother Goddess," Shintao shouted.

"*Cao ni ma*!" Cuo said, his voice quivering with rage. "You want a war between our tribes? Shanghai will drown in blood!"

Shintao stood up, his attitude conciliatory. He put his hands up. "Alright. I apologize. I shall leave you alone now. I will move our operations away and not open them on your doorstep."

Without another word, he got up and turned to leave the room. His entourage left with him. Hua Deng was the last one to leave, closing the door of the banquet room with a soft click.

The Triad bosses looked at each other. They all spoke at once, preparing to leave the room. A distant tremor passed along the walls of the banquet hall. There was a sudden gust of ice cold wind and a loud scraping sound above them. They turned their heads up to see a fantastical sight – the glass roof of the Chenguang Towers was sliding back, opening up the room to the wind and night air. White flecks of distant stars were visible in the black sky.

The tremor increased, and a guttural, deep sound spread along the floor and the walls, making the room shake. The sound increased till it became a booming sound, desiccated by a repetitive, chopping beat. They saw the spotlight first, falling on them with blinding intensity, then the rotors of the massive helicopter that rose up in the night air above them like a dragon rising above its prey.

They screamed and ran for the door, but it was locked. Wooden walls had slid down from the ceiling, and the only way out was through the glass above. They were trapped.

The 50-cal. machine gun started spitting its heavy rounds with accuracy. The bullets streaked across the wood, lifting large chunks, blowing up the upholstery of the chairs. The bodies shook and trembled as round after round of ordnance pumped into them. The helicopter did a circle, firing till the table split apart in the middle, and then two grenades were lobbed in. No one was left alive.

Washeng Lumou was hit in the face and eye, then her entire painting collapsed on the floor, draping over the bloodied, lifeless body of Cuo Deng.

CHAPTER 35

"*Wo...wo de taitai. Jinjing wo de taitai.*"

"What does that mean?" Dan asked Xiao. They had taken a blue cab from the southeast of the city towards the Bund, sticking to the main roads. Now they sat on the main promenade of Zhongshan East 1ˢᵗ Road, close to the elaborate stucco building of the old East China Commercial Bank. Across the choppy waters of the Huang Pu, the towers of Pudong glistened in the sun. But neither of them were watching the scenery.

Xiao said, "It means my wife. He was trying to say that Jinjing was his wife."

Dan thought for a while. "This guy collected the laundry for the Sheng family, right? He probably did more than that, and he could be related to the family."

Xiao said, "He won't be a son, as the old man said they didn't have one. They only had a daughter."

"So this guy was the son-in-law."

Xiao nodded. Dan took out the wallet. It was made of faded brown faux leather, with cuffed edges. Inside, there was a few yuan notes and a photo ID. Dan memorised the face. All the letters were in Chinese. The man was in his thirties, with black hair. His face was that of a Han Chinese man, with no distinguishing features. He gave the card to Xiao.

Xiao read the card, then said, "It's a KTV bar, somewhere downtown. He worked there as a doorman."

Dan nodded. KTV bars were common all over China. He said, "There's one person who will know who this man was. Old Man Lee, back at the *lilong.*"

"*Fuxing Zhu Long.* But you can't go in there."

"I might have to."

Xiao sighed. "No. It's safer if I go and you keep watch."

Dan pondered about it. "Tell you what. Let's go to keep watch outside. With any luck he'll come out for a walk. He does his own shopping, right?"

Xiao shrugged. They walked down the Bund and got into the subway, heading back down to the south of the city. As they approached the *lilong*, Dan saw a crowd of people. They had placards, and two of them in the front held a red banner with large white Chinese alphabets. Xiao read for Dan. "Save our Shikumen. Protect our history."

They watched as the crowd walked down the road. Traffic had stopped, and drivers beeped their horns. Dan stepped out to join them. With Xiao he weaved inside the throng as they chanted slogans and waved their placards. Eventually, near the front, Dan found Mr. Lee, wearing his khaki-colored Mao coat, buttoned up to his neck. Dan tapped him on the shoulder. Mr. Lee was holding a placard, and when he saw Dan, a look of astonishment spread across his face. Then it was replaced by a wry smile.

"Mr. Roy. Have you come to join the march of the unhappy citizens?"

Dan took out the photo ID card and showed it to Mr. Lee, holding it up in front of his face. Mr. Lee's face creased in recognition.

"Baoshan Yang." Dan lowered the photo. Mr. Lee said, "He was the son-in-law of Mr. Sheng."

Dan asked, "Was Sheng's daughter called Jinjing?"

Lee nodded. A voice at the front chanted a slogan and the crowd took it up, shouting it back. The old man turned his attention back. Xiao stepped forward and asked, "Where is the march headed to?"

"The Mayor's office," Mr. Lee had to raise his voice to be heard. "We are being relocated to different parts of greater Shanghai, with hardly any compensation. The land is being sold to the developers for million, and we get hardly a few thousand per family. It's a disgrace."

"What do you hope to achieve?" Dan asked.

Mr. Lee said, "This might surprise you, Mr. Roy, but we look to the State for guidance in such matters. Confucius said, the relationship between the State and the citizen is like parent and child. It is the state's duty to look after us. In this case, I believe it needs a reminder."

Xiao had already made her mind up. She admired the old world charm of the shikumen *lilongs,* and while she understood the need for development, she also hated the destruction of the city's heritage. "I'll march with you," she said. She looked at Dan. "You don't have to come."

Dan was caught in a bind. He was wary of marching in a crowd where someone might have seen him the night before. On the other hand, his instincts were telling him it wasn't safe to leave Xiao on her own. He wanted to walk her back to her office, or home.

"I'll come," Dan said. As they walked on, he said, "You still have the address that car is registered to?"

"The car that came to the lilong last night? Yes I do."

"That's the place I need to check out tonight, and the KTV bar."

They marched, slogans from the crowd echoing in their ears. Dan didn't understand a word of it, but he noticed people stop and watch the parade. On the main roads, they stuck to the pavements, and a police van loaded with deep-green uniformed officers unloaded in front of them. The officers stayed at the front and back, shepherding them towards the Mayor's office downtown.

Dan kept his head low and used the placards around him to remain inconspicuous. He said to Xiao, "Lin Yan brought a ticket to Beijing. When he purchased the ticket, he was with a little girl, about five years old."

Xiao told Dan about Lin's next of kin, his sister. Dan asked, "He didn't have parents?"

"Not as next of kin, no. Might be dead. Or they live somewhere else."

Plates were spinning in Dan's mind, all in the air. The Sheng family had a little child as well. They had disappeared, with the child. So, apparently, had Lin Yan. He wondered if Lin had ever been to the *lilong* with the child, or with his sister. He searched for Old Man Lee, but couldn't see him in the closely pressed throng of bodies.

The Mayor's office was behind the Bund, halfway down, heading south. As they got closer, Dan realized he was close to his hotel. The buildings were all old colonials, Victorian and Edwardian office blocks built during the last years of the International Concession. These, along with the Bund, had once been the commercial hub of southeast Asia.

The procession came to a halt outside the broad flight of steps that led to the seven pillars of the Mayor's office. To Dan's mind, the building was an exact replica of the New York Stock Exchange. He saw some men in suits come down the steps, and the crowd surged forward. One of the men stood at the foot of the stairs and read out a statement. As he was going past, Dan noticed Xiao reach out and grab his sleeve. The man turned, annoyed, but his expression changed when Xiao spoke to him. Dan moved forward.

"What's going on?" Dan asked.

"I wanted to know if the Mayor was coming down. He said yes."

They waited another ten minutes, then saw a squat short figure, flanked by men in suits on either sides, coming hurriedly down the hill. The TV reporters with the their long overhead microphones rushed forward. A media scrum began, with cameramen jostling for space with hand-held cameras, pushing in behind the reporters. The Mayor came to a stop five steps above the crowd. He lifted up both hands, and they finally quietened down, but the placards waved.

Whatever the Mayor said, it did not please the crowd. He had barely spoken three sentences when there was a grumbling dissent, rising like a black cloud. The Mayor raised his voice, and his guards tightened their cordon around him. Dan looked down to find Xiao had disappeared. He craned his neck and saw her up front. Somehow, she had wriggled her way forward and was now standing behind a reporter, who was leaning forward with her microphone trying to catch the Mayor's attention.

As soon as the Mayor and his entourage turned to go back up the steps, Xiao leaped forward. She was up the flight of steps very quickly.

"Mayor Zilou!" she shouted. "I am Danny Dong Quo's friend."

That stopped the Mayor, who turned with a frown on his face. The frown did not leave his face when he saw Xiao's petite form. One of his aides, the man Xiao had spoken to earlier, leaned forward and whispered in the Mayor's ears. He narrowed his eyes and squinted at Xiao.

Xiao said, "We met at the Four Season's banquet hall, remember? You were there for the Shaolin meeting."

The confusion lifted from the Mayor's face, but an uneasy expression remained. He squared his shoulders. "I am late for another meeting," he said brusquely. "Can you talk while we walk?" He turned and started to climb up the stairs. Xiao hurried after him. She had just approached one of the most powerful men in Shanghai, and she could feel butterflies in her stomach.

"The *lilong* residents have a valid complaint, Mayor Zilou. They are being forcibly evicted, and their relocation costs are meagre."

"Miss…"

"Wei-ling."

"Miss Wei-ling, I would advise you not to meddle in affairs of the state. The people are getting a good deal, which does not end with their relocation. They will be given new employment, and their families will also be compensated. The State does not have an endless bank account."

"The State might not, but the Party will." The words were out of her mouth before she could stop herself. She regretted it as soon as she uttered them.

The Mayor stopped abruptly. His aides had heard the remark and they leaned forward, their expressions hard and fixed.

"What do you mean, Miss Wei-Ling?"

Xiao took a deep breath. She kept her voice steady with an effort. "The Party needs to know what is happening here. The developer who is buying the land is paying tens of millions. How much of that benefits the people who lose their homes?"

The Mayor stepped forward. Xiao swallowed, feeling a trickle of sweat steal down her neck. Her heart hammered in her chest. The Mayor bushy eyebrows were knit together, and his small black eyes were like glittering gems.

Then unexpectedly, he smiled. "Well, I never. Danny was right about you. You do have guts." He scratched his cheek. "By all means, write to the Party. Address the letter to Comrade Deng Zilou, who is the head of Government in Shanghai as of last week. Let's see what he says."

He turned and jogged up the stairs, his group following him. A bewildered Xiao stared after them.

CHAPTER 36

Kim was sat in the back of the armored Chevrolet SUV as it sped through Route 613. Marly was in front next to the driver, and an armed SAD guy was next to her. His name was Mike, and he wore a bulletproof vest, his finger on the trigger of his MP7. The driver, whose name Kim had not identified as yet, was similarly armed.

Kim was busy looking through the IPAD screen that was inside the SUV. She held it in her hand and swiped left, looking at images that Melanie had sent her. She wiped the perspiration off her forehead. The radio cackled in the front, giving them the latest location of their target.

Bohai Zilou's college photos, which Melanie had gotten a hacker to download from Peking University's website came on the screen. Kim focused on a group photo, where Bohai's face was circled in the back row. A tall, handsome Chinese man, with floppy hair falling over his face. Kim looked carefully at the faces next to him.

Suddenly the breath caught in her chest. She couldn't breathe. Fighting a wave of excitement, she took her cell phone out and flipped through photos till she got to Lin Yan's image. She held it next to Bohai's group photo. The face to the right of Bohai was identical to that of Lin Yan.

Kim fell back on the seat, her mouth open. *But that meant...*

She was about to call Melanie when the radio burst into a cackle, getting her attention.

"Tango lost, I repeat, Tango lost."

Kim leaned forward. "What the hell was that?"

The radio came alive again. "Four identical cars. We followed the wrong one. Sorry. We got a family of four coming off the SUV we followed."

Frustration and anger boiled up inside Kim. She slammed her phone down on the seat. "Damn it!" Rick had known they would have eyes on him. He had had other cars to give him cover. She put a hand to her warm forehead. She needed to get a grip.

She called Melanie on her earpiece and told her about Bohai and Lin Yan. "They stood next to each other in a group photo. Chances are they knew each other."

"I'm looking into it. But I got news about Rick Everett," Melanie said. "He's got a fake name of Rupert Chiltern. Mr. Chiltern's name comes up in linked bank accounts. He's got a passport in that name too. He's grown a beard and wears glasses. But it's definitely Rick Everett."

"What does he do with the fake identity?"

"His name comes up in a lot of company filings. Looks like he's on the board of companies that are onions."

Kim nodded. "Can you peel the layers off?"

"Very hard. The companies are all off shore, based in Bahamas, Belize, you name it. They have boards of trustees we can contact. They can stonewall us and that's the slow way. The faster way is to hack into one of their websites."

"And?"

"The companies are just blank shells that accept money coming from all over. I traced the IBAN codes; the bank sending them money are all in Singapore and Hong Kong."

"Chinese money."

"Looks like it. But it gets better. The money's being used to buy luxury villas in Florida, So Cal, and nice parts of Europe. South of France, Spanish Balearic Islands."

"Gotta be dirty money being laundered clean. And Rick Everett's fake name is in all the company filings?"

"Front and center. Looks like he's doing all the transactions."

Kim said, "Good work, Melanie. Keep me updated."

"I got that promotion, right?"

"Sure thing. See you in ten," Kim said and hung up.

*****

Deng Zilou stood in his office on the Bund and looked out the window. People were strolling on the Bund promenade, enjoying the sun and the cluster of grand old buildings. A warm breeze came off the Huang Pu River, fluttering the curtains of his long sash windows. The room had tasteful dark brown oak panelling on the walls. Sporting two giant mahogany tables covered in green leather, and a cluster of leather sofas, the room was big enough to hold a conference. It was a far cry, Deng thought, from the cramped Ministry offices he had worked from his whole life. In recognition of his post's importance, the Party had moved his office and the whole of Shanghai's civic administration to the colossal Neo-Victorian mansion, which used to be the HQ of an English merchant bank two hundred years ago.

Deng watched a couple holding hands, and his mind went back to his son, Bohai. He permitted himself a smile. Bohai was exuberant, even foolish at times. He had much to learn, but learn he would. Deng already had plans for him to be sent to remote parts of the country when he returned. To the Xinjiang province in the frozen deserts of the northeast. A few months there, immersed in the hard life of the villages, would make him more responsible. A maturity that Bohai would need, if he was to follow in his footsteps.

China was changing, and so was the Communist Party. People were educated, read the papers, and sniffed out a corruption scandal easily. They wouldn't tolerate seediness within the Party, and rightly so, Deng thought. On his shoulders rested many things, but above all, the integrity of the Government.

The red phone on his desk rang, interrupting his thoughts. The phone was third in a row, and it was the secure line. Deng was between appointments, and his whole day would be taken up in meetings about the modernisation of a shikumen *lilong*. A controversial project he would have to navigate carefully. But he wasn't expecting a call now, and certainly not on the secure line.

He crossed over and picked up the receiver, expecting to hear his female secretary's voice. Instead, he heard silence and the hissing of static.

"Who is this?" Deng asked in an irritated voice.

"Deng Zilou." The voice spoke in Mandarin. The sound was distorted and metallic, and the voice was not human. Deng's frown deepened.

"Who is this?" he repeated.

"You must do as we tell you. We have your son in our possession." Deng felt the hair rise on the back of his neck. He gripped the receiver tightly, his palms suddenly sweaty.

"What? Who are you?" Deng asked.

"Like I said, we have your son. If you wish to see him alive again, then do as we say."

Despite the rising panic, Deng called their bluff. "You're lying. You don't have my son."

There was a fumble on the other side, and a sharp cry. "Daddy."

An ice-cold fear spread through Deng's body, rooting his legs to the spot. His tongue wouldn't move, and a sickening feeling was rising up in his throat. He felt his heart hammer against his chest.

"Bohai? Is that you?"

"Yes, Daddy, it's me. These people..." Bohai's faint voice was abruptly cut off.

"Bohai! Bohai!" Deng shouted, gripping the phone.

"Stop shouting," the weird, metallic voice was back on the phone.

"You don't know who you are dealing with. Release my son immediately..."

"Or what? Who you going to call, the U.S. State Department? Your son dies if you make one phone call. Your only son. We'll send you different parts of his body every day of the week. Starting with his fingers. How does that sound?"

Deng's face was white as a sheet. He slumped down in his chair. "What do you want?" he whispered.

"Listen very carefully," the voice said.

CHAPTER 37

It was evening when Xiao left her apartment. Dan had escorted her back, despite her protests. She wouldn't admit it, but after the recent events, she felt glad Dan was around. He had returned to his hotel to get ready, and she was going to pick him up. She locked her door and took the elevator down to the underground parking lot. Her VW Santana was one of the few cars remaining; most people had driven out of the city for the weekend. Within minutes, she had joined the downtown rush.

Xiao knocked on the door of Room 1306 of the Jin Jiang Classiq Hotel room. After a pause, Dan opened the door. He was wearing his bathrobe and had a shaving razor in his hand. He leaned out and checked the hallway, then let Xiao in.

"Two minutes," he said, and went inside the bathroom. Xiao heard the tap running. She stood near the window, watching the traffic far below moving illuminated toys on a play track. The striking promenade of the Bund lay a few hundred meters in front, and beyond that the dark waters of the Huang Pu. Barges and passenger ferries bobbed up and down on the small waves, light twinkling.

Xiao turned her attention to the room. Dan had left his jeans on the armchair. She saw the bloodstains and realized it was meant for the laundry. On the table below the mirror, she saw his wallet and cell phone. Some loose change had spilled out of the wallet, and it was open. On the inside flap, she saw a photo of two middle-aged people. It was an old photo, and the paper was greying. She guessed it was his parents. She turned her attention to the bed. It looked like it had not been slept in. She noticed a stack of books on the bedside table.

She was in two minds whether to check the books, but her dilemma was resolved as she glanced up at the bathroom door. Her mouth went completely dry. The door was half open, and from the reflection of a mirror, she could see Dan.

His bathrobe had fallen off, and she could see his naked back. It was broad and muscular, tapering down to a strong waist. She had not expected the number of scars and cuts on either side of the deep groove of his spine. His legs were stout like tree trunks, and hairy. His attention was focused on the mirror, and he hadn't realized the door was partially open. Xiao breathed heavily, and despite a small voice in her head saying no, she took a step forward.

Dan caught her in the mirror. Their eyes met for a brief second. His razor was at his cheek, cutting through white foam. For a second, their eyes held, and she saw something inscrutable pass in his eyes. Then it was gone, just as quickly as it came. He kicked the door with his heel, and it shut with a soft click.

Feeling foolish at being caught, Xiao walked back to the window and leaned against it. She licked her lips and tried to control her breathing. Dan appeared in a minute, dressed in jeans and T-shirt. His manner gave no indication to what had just happened.

"So, where is the car registered?" Dan asked, pulling his socks on. Xiao flipped her phone open and scanned.

"Not far from the airport," she said. "A place called Hongqiang. It's a half-hour drive from here."

Dan reached under his pillow and took out his Sig. He slid out the magazine, made sure it was full, then put two extra mags in his side pocket. Xiao watched wide-eyed. Dan put the kukri and scabbard in his back-belt line, letting his T-shirt fall over it. He turned slowly to face Xiao.

"You don't have to come. Give me the car keys."

Xiao shook her head. "I don't know what's going on here, Dan." She looked at him, and Dan found fear in her eyes, but also something else. Her wide, normally demure eyes were alive with possibility, a touch of excitement. He looked at their almond shape, and the different shades of brown and black in them. He found it hard to swallow all of a sudden. He broke off eye contact and put his pillows back, patting them unnecessarily.

Xiao said, "But I need to find out. Because I think what is happening is more than the disappearance of Lin Yan."

179

When Dan straightened, she had moved close to him. He was against the bedside table, with nowhere to go. He could smell the light but intoxicating perfume she was wearing and feel the heat of her body. The swell of her breasts was clearly visible beneath the blue summer dress she was wearing.

"You were right when you said we needed each other's help," she said.

Dan felt something stir inside him, a slow fixation of desire that had lain dormant for many months. He took a deep breath and stepped out into the middle of the room.

His fists were bunched, and he released them quickly. "We should get going," he said without looking back.

Xiao picked up her purse, slung it on her shoulder, and walked past him to the door. In the parking lot, Dan got in the passenger side of the VW Santana.

"Sure you don't want me to drive?" he offered.

Xiao shot him a look. "Have you driven in Shangai before?"

"Can't say I have."

Xiao raised her eyebrows without saying anything. Dan realized what she meant when they hit the road. The 40 km/hr speed limit was for show only. Xiao drove sensibly, but cars sped around her. A VW Santana taxi blared its horn behind them, then swung out to overtake. It must have been doing 60 km/hr, Dan figured. And it wasn't the only one. He saw several cabs driving recklessly, passengers swaying in the backseats like rag dolls.

"Why the hell do they drive like that?" Dan asked.

Xiao smiled. "Because they make their money per trip. More trips they can get in one shift, the better. There's a saying in Shanghai – once you get into a VW Santana, keep your eyes closed till you get to your destination."

Dan watched a car almost ram a bicycle as it took a corner. It missed by inches. They were driving through a shopping district, marble pavements and glossy shop fronts everywhere. They came to a halt at a crossroads. Boutique shops and Western-style bars lined the road.

"This is Xintiandi," Xiao said. "Shanghai's most expensive shopping district."

Dan looked at the pretty people, all Chinese, with their Prada and LV handbags. "So much for decadent imperialist habits, right?"

He had meant it as a joke, but when he looked at Xiao her white fingers were gripping the steering wheel tightly. "This is just for show. It's not the real China," she said, her voice suddenly stiff.

Dan sensed a defensiveness in her attitude. He should have left it alone, but part of him could not resist. "What is the real China?"

"China is many things, Dan. What is happening to China now is just a chain in the link that goes back five thousand years. These bright lights and skyscrapers only mean we do business in a different way to the seventies. The future might hold something very different."

"You might become a democracy, if you're lucky."

"Lucky?" The tone of incredulity was sharp. "You mean lucky like you? You elect politicians who are corrupt and waste tax payer funds on useless wars. A quarter of your country does not have health insurance. Is that what you mean by lucky?"

Dan took a deep breath. "I am lucky I live in a country where we have a free press and the rule of law. We allow a diversity of opinions, but we still have a consensus. When I see some parts of the world, where a man is tortured when he speaks his mind, I definitely call that lucky."

Xiao said, "The Communist Party has put roofs over everyone's head, and food on their plates. Go to a village or small town and ask anyone what life was like in the seventies and eighties. People starved. Now they have a good quality of life. Look at the other countries of Asia, like India, where Western powers have meddled for centuries. We remained closed, and look what we have achieved. You think this would be possible with a democracy?"

Xiao exhaled, heat touching her face. Dan had his own opinions on the matter, which he seldom divulged. But now he did.

"Millions in China now want democracy. Mostly in your generation. You know why? Because they are tired of not having a voice."

"You've been to China for a few days and suddenly you're an expert? We live for the collective here, not for the individual. What one person wants is never as important as what his community needs."

"You're gonna tell me next there's a saying for this in China."

"As a matter of fact, there is. *An upright nail gets hammered down.* You know what that means?" Xiao answered her own question. "It means you live for the people."

Dan said, "Your argument makes no sense. There are hundreds of billionaires in China. You even work for one of them. Look at the way the *lilongs* are being destroyed to make land available for greedy property developers, and making poor people homeless. You call that living for the people? I call it the opposite. It's the worst of capitalism."

They had stopped at a traffic light, and Xiao turned to face him. She waved her hands in front of his face. "That's the market, Dan. When Deng Xiaoping liberalised the economy in 1978, we knew this would happen one day. Demand and supply, nothing else. Don't take examples of the market and equate that to democracy."

"I wasn't."

The lights changed and they moved forward. "You see, Dan, democracy would cause chaos in China. This is what you people don't understand. China has so many people, there would be so many voices, parties, the whole country would grind to a halt. Then the fighting would start. Like it always has. The Communist Party has given China the stability it so desperately needed. That stability has ushered in economic growth. You want us to leave all that and start a democracy? You have no idea."

Dan was quiet. Xiao had speeded up, overtaking cars. Now she slowed down. Her voice was softer. "I don't want to give you a history lesson. The British fought us in the Opium Wars. The Japanese invaded us in the thirties."

Dan nodded. Even in Hong Kong, not part of mainland China, the anti-Japan rhetoric was evident. Songs and slogans abounded about the evil Japs, some of it translated into English.

"I know how much you guys hate them. But look, it's history, right?"

"I know, but you wouldn't be saying that if Canada or Mexico invaded USA, would you?"

Dan was silent.

"Even after the Communist Party was formed, in 1949, we had the madness of the Cultural Revolution. When students were given the power to override their teachers."

Dan said, "Death of the Four Olds."

Xiao sneaked a look at him, impressed. "You know?"

"Some of it. Schools and colleges shut down, professors were sent to prison, even parents were told to shut up and listen to teenagers."

Xiao's voice was a whisper as she remembered her father's sad stories from those dark days. "It was the worst of times."

They were both quiet for a while. Xiao suddenly felt ashamed. She had a quick temper. Dan was just trying to make conversation, and she shouldn't have snapped at him.

She said, "In many ways, China and USA are similar. They have a complex, violent history, and yet managed to be very successful."

Dan nodded. "You got that right. It's just two different civilizations, and different ways of looking at life. In the end, we all want the same thing."

"Yes."

CHAPTER 38

Xiao took a turning off the Yan'an Elevated Road five kilometers away from the Hongqiao International Airport. They went down a few roads till they came upon a road of squat, one-level industrial buildings. Most of them had tall iron fencing out front, guards at the gates, and security cameras. Xiao drove past a building with its forecourt full of cars, then came to a stop more than a hundred yards away.

Dan looked behind him. Xiao asked, "Do you remember what type of car it was?"

"A black Buick GL8." Dan hopped out and stood by the passenger side door. He motioned at Xiao to stay inside. The road in front was empty. The security guards were further away, and he caught the sight of one, smoking and chatting on his cell phone. Dan kept to the pavement and walked down till he was abreast of the forecourt. He spotted the Buick SUV immediately. It stood out among the VWs and Chinese models. A Triad man, with a gangster on each side, came out of the building's entrance. One of the men held the back door open for him, and he got in.

The man was older, dressed impeccably in a suit, and Dan had the feeling he had seen the man before. The driver got inside the Buick. Dan turned and walked quickly back to the car. Xiao had already done a K-turn, and the car was facing the right direction.

Dan jumped in and, without a word, pointed to the Buick coming out of the gates. Xiao waited till the Buick reached the end of the road and then turned around a bend. She gunned the engine and picked up speed.

They followed the Buick back up to the elevated Yan'an Road, one of the main arteries carrying traffic back to downtown Shanghai. Skyscrapers towered around them, giant red and blue neon signs of electronic companies and banks glowing in the dark. Xiao followed three cars behind at a steady pace.

They left the elevated road to enter the neighborhood close to Fuxing Zhu Lou, the *lilong* area. Dan recognized some of the buildings. Xiao followed well as traffic grew. They went past a metro station, and Dan read the name Dapuqiao in white English letters underneath red Chinese alphabets.

"We are in the south, right?" Dan asked.

Xiao nodded. "Close to the river."

The Buick stopped in front of a wide three-story building that had the letters KTV inscribed in huge blue neon. Xiao had pulled up by the roadside and was going through her phone.

She said, "Do you have Baoshan's ID? The man who got killed."

Dan nodded and took the ID out of his wallet. Xiao glanced at it, then back at Dan. She whispered something to herself in Chinese.

"What?"

"This is the place where Baoshan used to work." She held Dan's eyes for a second before Dan looked away, towards the large KTV building.

The road was clearly a shopping area, with glass-fronted stores replete with dressed mannequins. Dan watched the Buick drive into a parking lot. A valet came out and opened the doors. There was an entrance gate at the front, with a portico over it. But the men went to the side and into a lift that was colored gold and shone in the blue neon light from above. The lift went up to the second floor, to a golden door that opened, releasing a shaft of bright yellow light into the night air. The men went through the door. The driver and one Triad member stayed in the car.

Guests went in and out of the main entrance. Xiao said, "Do you know what KTV is?"

"Can't have a party in China without Karaoke, right?"

"Right."

For some reason that Dan didn't understand, hiring a private room and singing drunken Karaoke songs was the pinnacle of entertainment in China. Everything else came second to it. He knew the Chinese had a natural love of music, especially the glitter of the pop variety. He guessed that pretending to be pop stars for a few hours fed into an escapist fantasy that nothing else could provide.

KTV was one of the biggest chains around. Dan had seen several other chains, and Dahai had even asked him to be a bouncer at a karaoke bar in HK. But Dan knew what happened inside the plush private rooms. He would never be a part of that.

They parked the car close to the side entrance of the bar. At the main entrance, the doors slid open into a brightly lit foyer of glossy cream marble-tiled floor, reflecting the lights above. In the middle there was a sculpture of a bronze horse, its middle hollowed. The horse had its head bent and was charging forwards, frozen in motion. Full-length gilt mirrors lined the four walls, and low chandeliers hung from the ceiling. Everything about the place said bling in big capital letters.

There was a counter next to a faux rock waterfall at the far end of the foyer. Two receptionists with snow-white grins greeted them. They wore black skirt dress suits and white shirts undone at the top to show a generous cleavage. They paid special attention to Dan, cocking their heads and leaning forward to him.

"Welcome to the Xanadu Pleasure Dome. Your wish is our command."

Dan gave Xiao a glance, but she was looking around her, ignoring the receptionists like they were ignoring her. He said, "We need a room for two hours."

"No problem, sir. All our rooms have microphones, speakers, a fridge bar, Beluga Caviar, sofa sets, and TV. Will you be having any food?

Dan shook his head, then smiled. "Can we have a room upstairs?"

The two women looked at each other, then had a hushed conversation. One of them smiled sweetly and picked up the phone. She spoke quickly, then turned back to them.

"I am sorry, sir…"

Xiao interrupted. "We came to this branch of KTV from Xintiandi because it was recommended as being more exclusive." She looked at Dan and shrugged. "No point in bringing Brian here. It's the same as the others. Come on, let's go."

She grabbed Dan's hand in an easy, confident gesture. Dan felt an electric jolt as the warmth of his hands found the softness of hers. His fingers closed over hers, and he suddenly realized his mouth was bone dry.

"Excuse me, sir." One of the girls was leaning forward. Her smile was fixed and strained. Her colleague was hanging up the phone.

"We can get you a room upstairs, sir, no problem."

"Make sure no one disturbs us for the next two hours," Dan said gruffly.

"Thank you, sir. That will be two thousand yuan for two hours."

Dan paid in cash from his bundle of notes.

The girl smiled and pressed a buzzer. Another girl, who could have passed as a relation to the two behind the counter, arrived, bowed to them, and led them to the elevators. The elevator rose smoothly to the second floor, where their guide led them through a maze of corridors. The walls were covered with fake paintings of European masters.

Xiao pointed to one and said, "Why did the Europeans have such an obsession with painting naked people?"

Dan shrugged. "Don't know. Why were the Mings so crazy about vases?"

"That was a golden age of porcelain craftmanship."

"Guess the Europeans had their golden age of painting nudes."

The carpet was deep enough for their feet to sink into. Dan noticed the walls were soundproof. They passed an alcove with a shrine to an angry god. His face was red, his eyes were bulging, and his lips were open in a snarl. His toes were like claws, gripping the wooden base of the shrine. Chocolates and flowers were laid at the foot of the shrine, along with notes and coins.

Dan asked the usher, "A close friend of mine, Mr. Cheng, is here today. He came in a black Buick GL8, with three of his friends. Have you seen them?"

The girl looked uncertain, and Xiao translated. Dan pulled out a roll of notes and gave the girl two hundred yuan bills. She bit her lower lip and looked at them. She took the money quickly and put it in her pocket. She leaned closer and whispered something to Xiao. They had arrived in front of a soundproof door. The girl opened the door with a key and waved them inside.

Dan shut the door securely behind him. The rooms reflected the kitsch glitz they had seen downstairs. The leather sofas were plush and bright red, the tables were marble-topped and more fake European-style paintings of naked people adorned the walls. There was a platter of caviar, sliced watermelon, and cherry tomatoes with an open bottle of Champagne on the table.

Dan said, "What did the girl tell you?"

"Go to the end of the corridor, take a right, then straight on. You come into the back portion of the building. Where only special guests are allowed. You might see guards."

Dan thought for a while. He couldn't get into a firefight in a building full of gangsters. If more Triads arrived, there was no way he was getting out alive. Then an idea came to him. He explained to Xiao, and she nodded.

They left the room and walked towards the back section. When they turned right, they saw two guards immediately. The suited men were standing outside a doorway. Dan had his arm around Xiao's waist, and she was nestled against his chest. They were both laughing loudly at a joke, weaving around the corridor like they were drunk. Dan's head was hanging forward, and he stumbled, barely keeping his balance.

The two Triad men were watching them dispassionately. Xiao and Dan arrived at the doorway and stood for a second, weaving in front of the man on the left. Xiao peeled off Dan's right arm and fell backwards along the wall. The man facing Dan didn't even see Dan's fist rising up like an uncoiled spring. The upper cut exploded against the man's chin, a blow so hard it almost lifted him off his feet. His head hit the wall behind him, and his body shook as it went down, out for the count.

The other guy rushed Dan, reaching inside for his shoulder holster. Dan cannoned into him, forcing him against the wall, jamming his hand inside the coat. He bent his right knee in a well-practiced Muay Thai move and slammed it deep inside the man's abdomen. But the guy was stout, and strong. He came off the wall and gripped Dan around the midriff. He pushed Dan back, and he stumbled. Dan planted his left foot on the carpet and bent his right elbow. Like a hook, the elbow swung around, smashing into the man's face. The blow spun his head back, and before he could look again, Dan rammed his elbow straight into his face for the second time. The face turned into a bloody pulp, and the body sagged to the floor.

Panting, Dan looked around him. Xiao was a few feet away, crouched against the wall. She looked up at him with fear in her face. Dan wiped his forehead and nodded. She nodded back, scampered up and ran down the corridor.

CHAPTER 39

Dan pressed gently on the door handle. Four men had entered this room. Two were knocked out. One was the boss. That left one soldier. The door was locked, as Dan expected. He knocked on the door lightly, and whispered, "*Ni ho ma?*" How are you.

The door opened slightly and a cautious face appeared. Dan kicked the door viciously, knocking the man backwards. He was straddling the man's chest in an instant, and the butt of the Sig Sauer P226 slammed twice into the man's forehead. The head lolled back on the carpet. Dan kicked the door shut with his heel.

In the middle of the room, there was a four-poster bed. The Triad boss, wearing only his boxer shorts, was scrambling out of bed. Two naked women were sitting on the bed, trying to cover themselves with bedsheets. Dan saw the flash of light on the barrel of a gun. The man had lifted his hand gun to aim at Dan. He was too late. Dan fired from his sitting position, the unsuppressed round making a shattering sound as the Sig kicked backed against his rock-hard palm. The unerring bullet hit the man's weapon hand and, with a scream of pain, he dropped his weapon. The bullet had only grazed the hand, and Dan noticed he could use his fingers. But the man was howling like someone had hacked his hand off with a saw.

In three strides, Dan was towering over the man. When he looked up, Dan recognized him.

Dan grabbed the man by the throat and sat him on the bed. He trained the gun on the man's forehead.

"Chow Ying. Number 426. The Red Pole Enforcer. Far from home, aren't you?"

The man who had come to recruit him after his fight in Hong Kong. One of the senior Triads of the *Sun Yee On*, the Peace and Righteousness Brothers.

Ying said, "*Ju-Long*, you are a dead man. You can't get out of here alive."

Dan glanced at the girls, who were cowering in fright. Both beautiful, with smooth, pale creamy skin, and both terrified. He turned his attention back to Ying. He grabbed the man by the throat and pulled him to his feet. Ying made a choking sound, his hands clawing at his throat, where Dan held him in a vice-like grip. Dan dragged the man over to the armchair where his clothes lay. He threw Ying on the floor ,and keeping the Sig trained on him, quickly searched for a weapon. Then he threw the clothes down.

"Get dressed," Dan said. "Or get ready to die."

When Ying was dressed, Dan went behind him and pushed the barrel of his Sig deep into the man's back, pressing on his left kidney. Ying squirmed in pain.

"One shot. That's all its going to take, dickhead. And I'll do it too, so just try me."

Ying grunted as Dan frogmarched him to the door, left hand holding his collar, right hand on the gun. He gasped as he saw his men on the floor. Every one of them still out cold.

"We're going down on the external elevator, slow as you like. In the parking lot, you'll see a VW Santana, near the elevator. Get into the back seat with me. You make one false move..." Dan pushed the barrel in again, making him whine.

"OK, I get the message," Ying gasped.

They went down the corridor and into the elevator. From the glass window, Dan could see Xiao waiting, engine running. The two suits at the gate looked up as Dan came out of the elevator first, his arm around Ying's shoulder. He opened the door and put Ying inside, then climbed in quickly.

"Drive," he told Xiao.

She knew the destination already. They crossed the river at the Fuxing East Road Tunnel, and the fiery lights of the Lujiazui District gleamed on their left like a giant spaceship. The rest of Pudong stretched out in front of them. Xiao navigated the streets expertly, and they were soon on the outskirts, heading south from the right lights. Dan used two ties he had ripped off the men to tie Ying's hands, then blindfold him.

They drove past the apartment complex where Baoshan had lived, and from where Dan had chased the poor man to his death. He shook his head, staring at the four apartment blocks, their yellow window lights gleaming. Baoshan had held the key to this whole puzzle. Dan set his jaw and glanced at Ying, who was sitting still. He had another key right here.

Xiao stopped outside a darkened building that was being constructed. Dan got out and found the workman's entrance door. He found a loose piece of timber, then held it like a club and smashed it on the padlock around the door. The timber broke, and the padlock remained steadfast. Dan took four steps back, then rushed forward and kicked the door with the flat of his boot. After two kicks, the door sagged on its hinges, then came off the frame. He looked around him. Another similar construction site lay behind him, the south of Pudong being extended to make more homes for the "ant tribe." Apart from building sites around him, there wasn't much else. The noise was unavoidable, but it was one hell of a lot quieter than the unsuppressed Sig he had.

Xiao was waiting outside the car. Dan grabbed Ying and pulled him out. He fell on the ground, raising dust and swearing. The went inside, Xiao using a flashlight she had in the car. They came into a vast atrium that was empty, still having the finishing touches. The elevators were brand new, unpainted.

Dan shook his head. He didn't know if the elevators were connected at the higher floors. They walked around to the back, picking their way up on the newly laid lawn turf and surrounding residues from the construction. Dan found the workman's elevator. Before they went in, Xiao looked around till she found a length of rope. It was a heavy coil of coired rope, and Dan had to lift it on his shoulder. Ying was pushed down on the floor, face down, Xiao holding the gun on his neck. Once the rope was inside the lift, Dan hauled Ying up and pushed him inside. He pressed the red button on the outside, and the grilled elevator rose along the open corner shaft of the building.

Higher they went, and the air changed from humid to fresher, cooler. Soon it was cold, and through the grilled slats of the open elevator a strong breeze flowed in. Unconsciously, Xiao stepped behind Dan, using his bulk to block out the wind.

Dan had counted the floors. They were at the fourteenth level. He could see a huge dark mass above him, but no lights. He had no idea how high this thing went. At the next floor up, he slammed the red button again and the makeshift elevator came to a shuddering halt.

"Move." Dan pushed the gun into Ying's back. He pushed him to his knees, then had a look around with the flashlight. He found what he was looking for at the far edge, wind whipping up the tarpaulin covering the building equipment that lay in stacks on the floor. A pulley, with a hook and a long line of nylon rope. He pulled on it, and the rope moved. It slid further up, and he could see it lifting up in a long black line from the floor below.

He grabbed Ying by the neck and pulled him to the edge. Ying felt the sharp wind on his face, and his voice broke. "What...what are you doing?"

Dan didn't say anything. Silence increased anxiety. He tied the nylon rope around Ying's ankles, hitting him on the knees once, hard, to stop him from trying to move. When the rope was fixed, Dan turned to Xiao.

"You don't have to see this. You should go."

In the semi-darkness, lit by an odd glimmer that was reflected off the distant buildings, Xiao's eyes were wide. "What will you do?"

"Field interrogation techniques."

"What?"

"Like I said, maybe best if you don't see."

Xiao swallowed, then said, "No. I'll stay."

Dan shrugged, then walked back to Ying's prostate form. He pulled Ying right to the edge of the fifteenth floor. Ying screamed and thrashed around, realizing he was in trouble.

"Let me go, you *yangguizi,* and I swear to you, I'll let you live."

"Wrong statement, Ying," Dan said. He grabbed one end of the nylon with one hand and tied it around an upright steel beam than ran vertically through the building. Then without ceremony, he grabbed Ying by the belt line and threw him over the side of the building. Ying screamed as he went flying into the cold night air, and the sound mingled with the scream coming from Xiao.

The nylon rope jerked taut like a fishing line, and there was another bloodcurdling scream as Ying smacked against the side of the building with a dull thud. Xiao grabbed Dan's arm.

"What in the name of the sky are you doing?"

Dan was utterly calm, unruffled. "Is that a Chinese saying?"

"What is?"

"Name of the sky."

Xiao face contorted. "This guy will die! What are you doing?"

"Nothing he wouldn't do to us." Dan unhooked the rope around the steel beam, feeling the pressure grow as he took Ying's weight. Ying screamed again, his voice cracked and wild with fear. He slid down further as Dan grabbed the rope with both hands.

Xiao ran to the edge of the building. Her hands were on her head. She turned to Dan and saw him pulling on the rope slowly, his feet against the steel beam. He pulled, bending his back, his breath heavy, as Ying was not a light man. The rope burned in his hand. When Ying was dangling upside down with his face level with Xiao's, Dan stopped. He tied the rope tightly around the steel beam again. He stepped forward to the edge.

"Well, Mr. Enforcer, do you feel like talking now?"

"*Shabi*! You will die for this!"

Dan shrugged and walked back to the steel beam. He put his hands on the rope and tugged.

"No!" Ying screamed. "No, please don't."

Dan walked back. He grabbed Ying's collar and pushed his face close to his. The smell of urine hit him. The man had peed himself.

"We have all the time in the world, Ying," Dan said. "I'll keep you hanging till your head swells up like a watermelon, and when you can't bear it anymore, I'll cut the rope. By then, you'll be begging me to stop."

"What...what do you want?"

"Everything. Why you came to my apartment in Kennedy Town, in Hong Kong. Why you tried to kill me when I didn't join you. And why the hell you are here."

"I follow orders. I was told to recruit, and if failed, then kill you."

"Who was Baoshan?"

"Who?"

"The man who was killed. Your cute blond hit man did it."

"I don't know anything about that."

Dan reached forward and slapped the man across the face, then dug two fingers into his eyes, holding the collar. Ying screamed and thrashed. Dan let go, then slapped him again, twice.

"Not much of an Enforcer, are you?"

Ying was gasping, tears streaming out of his eyes. "Like I said, I had orders. Honest...the honest truth."

"What about Jinjing Sheng, the girl who worked at the KTV bar?"

Ying stopped moving. Dan sensed he knew something. He grabbed Ying's collar and pulled his face closer again. "You wanna hang for longer, amigo? Tell me."

The man's voice was a wretched whisper. "This is...it's deep. They'll kill me. You don't understand what you are dealing with here."

"Understand that I will kill you if they don't. Now tell me. Who was she?"

Ying shook his head around and made a strange, whimpering sound from his throat. Dan realized he was sobbing.

"She was one of the girls....one of the girls we get. Her husband joined the KTV bar, we didn't know. When we found out, we chased after him. He escaped."

"Where did the girls come from?"

Ying was crying again. Dan took out his Sig and crammed the barrel inside Ying's mouth.

"Tell me now or this is it," he whispered menacingly. The whites of Ying's eyes were wide with fear, close to Dan's face. Silently, the man nodded.

CHAPTER 40

Dan got Ying down and used his KA-BAR kukri to cut pieces of the rope to tie his hands and feet. He gagged him with the tie and dragged him inside the elevator. Xiao watched Dan in silence. Dan pressed the red button and the elevator jerked into a downward movement.

Ying had already given Xiao the address. Dan put Ying in the trunk and slammed the lid down. He got into the front and sat next to Xiao for a while. The engine was running, but the headlights were still off. An uneasiness had appeared between them. After their suspicion of each other, and the outbursts, they had become friendlier. Now, Dan detected a wariness. He didn't blame her. He knew it could be a shock to see what was often necessary in the line of duty.

"Are you OK?" Dan asked.

Xiao did not answer for a while. Dan said, "I'm sorry you had to see that." Inside, he was relieved he didn't have to go much further with the torture. So-called advanced techniques. Ying had split the beans just in time and saved himself a lot of pain.

Xiao said, "You don't have to explain."

The uncomfortable silence fell between them again. Dan didn't know how to break it. Maybe he didn't have to. In any case, he needed to move on with the mission.

"Can you drive us to the place?"

Xiao nodded. "It's not far from the Bund." She flicked the headlights on and did a K-turn on the road. Soon the bright lights of Lujiazui appeared again, and they were driving across the road tunnel under the Huang Pu. Xiao took the Yan'an Elevated Road and headed westwards, cutting across the city from right to left. They came off the elevated road into a wide avenue that was dotted around with brightly lit apartment complexes.

Numerous shops and malls were open on the sidewalks, as well as street markets. The glitz and glamour of downtown Shanghai was absent here, but the streets were busy with people despite the late hour. They went past a well-lit park, and inside Dan saw a group of older women practicing Tai'ichi.

He read the sign in English. "Putuo?" he asked Xiao.

"Yes. It's a residential area. Quite big, but we are going to a smaller part of it called Caoyang."

Soon, Xiao had parked the car next to an empty, silent park. Lights were on inside the perimeter, but not a soul stirred inside. Next to the park there was a row of one- and two-story houses. Xiao looked at the address she had written down on the palm of her hand. Only one house had its lights on. She pointed. "That one."

Dan said, "Kill the headlights."

They stayed inside, observing for a while. They could see the house clearly, across a small slice of pavement that divided the road into two. Trees grew in the middle of the garden section of the pavement, giving them some cover.

A series of muffled groans came from the boot. "What will you do about him?" Xiao asked.

"Keep him for future use. It depends on what we find here."

They sat still for a while longer. Then Dan saw some movement. A light flickered in the dark, and someone at the gates lit a cigarette. Soon, there was a pair of cigarette lights. A headlight glowed behind them. Dan grabbed Xiao's neck and pulled her down.

The car drove past them on the opposite side of the pavement. Dan stayed down and took his Sig out. He peeked above the dashboard. Two men in suits got out of the car, with a woman between them. The guards obviously knew them. They exchanged a few greetings, then went inside.

"What is this place?"

"Where they kept girls like Jinjing."

"But why? Jinjing had a husband and child. Why would she want to be a whore for the Triads?"

Dan was thinking the same thing. "Someone in there knows." He jerked his thumb backwards. "I think this guy knows as well. He's just too scared to talk."

"So what do we do now?"

Dan wasn't listening. He was peering intently at one of the guards who had wandered into the halo of the streetlight. Even from a distance, his olive-green uniform and the red epaulettes on his shirt were clearly visible. Dan patted Xiao on the arm.

"It's a cop from the PSB," Xiao said, her voice unsteady. Dan nodded, deep in thought. Part of Dan wanted to get Ying out of the trunk and give him a thrashing to the end of his life, just to get the truth out of him. But he didn't get the chance. The two men came out with the woman and got into the car. One of the men held the woman by the arm. After they went past, Xiao reversed and followed. The car was another Buick GL8. It stuck to the back roads. Dan told Xiao, "Speed up and overtake it. Then push it to the pavement. Can you do that?"

Xiao asked, "Why?"

"He'll see us soon. While the roads remain quiet, let's pull him over." He looked at her. "But then you stay in the car, OK? Let me handle this."

She nodded in silence, her face a sudden mask of concentration. She gripped the steering wheel and floored the gas. The Santana leaped forward. The Buick saw them coming and accelerated. Dan knew if the powerful Buick got going, they wouldn't be able to stop it.

"Keep going," he shouted to Xiao. He leaned out the window, Sig gripped in both hands. He was on the same side as the Buick. He aimed, allowing for the car's speed, then fired at the tires. After two shots, he got lucky. With a blast, one of the rear tires exploded. The heavy car skidded, its tail jutting out. Dan fired again but missed. The Buick spun across the road and slammed into a tree, its windows shattering with the impact.

Xiao had braked, and Dan was out, a fresh magazine in the Sig. Crouching, he approached the Buick from behind. The driver opened his door, weapon in hand. He saw Dan and aimed, but Dan had him in the center as soon as he stepped out the door. Two of the Sig rounds tore into the man's chest. He collapsed to his knees, gun skittering on the road. Dan sensed a movement to the other side of the Buick. He didn't wait. He sprawled on the road, rolling over to his front. The move saved his life. Two louds shots rang out, flying where he had just been. Dan stayed on the road, spread-eagled, and aimed for the source of movement.

All I need now is a car to come up behind me, he thought. His only hope was Xiao would somehow block the road.

The man peeked around the back of the car, and Dan fired, smashing the rear windscreen. The man ducked and retreated, and Dan fired again. Then he got up and ran hard but stealthily towards the Buick, dropping to the ground just as he reached the rear tires. Dan didn't want to risk another medium-range shot. If his aim was off, he could hit the woman inside the car.

The man hadn't heard him coming. He had gone around the front, peering over the hood. He couldn't see Dan crouching, and he took a step out, weapon first. That was all the opening Dan needed. His first shot macerated the man's hand, and he dropped the weapon with a scream. The second round ripped into his throat, cutting the cervical spinal cord into two. He slumped to the floor, dead before he hit it.

Dan yanked the passenger seat and took cover against the side. He pointed his weapon inside.

"Come out," he shouted. "I'm not going to hurt you."

He glanced towards the VW at the back. He could see Xiao. She was now sitting up in the driver's seat. Dan waved at her. She fired the engine up and drove closer.

"You are safe now," Dan told the woman inside. "Come out. Are you there?" He closed his eyes briefly. He hoped like hell a stray bullet hadn't killed the woman.

There was a scuffling sound, and a pale, frightened face peeked out the door. She gasped when she saw Dan and fell backwards. Dan put his gun away. He motioned at Xiao to come and join him.

Xiao came over and spoke to the woman. She finally emerged, shivering, although it was a humid night. The dampness of rain was in the air. Xiao put an arm around her shoulder and took her back to the car. Dan took the keys off her.

"I'll drive" he said. "Ask her where she lives. She's more likely to speak to us if we take her home."

CHAPTER 41

Kim opened the door to her new apartment in Langley and breathed a sigh of relief. It had been a bruising day. Melanie and the team had worked nonstop all day to get data on the Zilou family and Rick Everett. There was still no sign of Rick, or Bohai, and Kim was trying her best not to stress herself. The whole thing was now intricately mixed with Lin Yan and what he had to show them. The connection between Bohai and Lin was not clear yet, and that was another loose thread she needed to clear up. She had a seven a.m. meeting with Hal Schumberg tomorrow, and the ODNI would be close on her heels. Her head ached.

She said goodbye to the babysitter and pressed the door shut. This apartment complex was for CIA employees, and the federally funded building was only used for special purposes. Security was state of the art, and the patrolling guards were hand-picked and subject to extreme vetting.

She stopped in front of Maya's room. The time was 2100, her bedtime. She was in bed, but Kim still stopped to listen if she was asleep.

"Mummy," Maya called out, like she could see Kim through the open door. Kim smiled and went in. Maya turned the table lamp on. Her curly black hair fell on her face as she lay to the side. The blanket was tucked under her chin, and she clutched an orange lion plushie with a striped tail.

Kim sat down and ran a hand over her face, then kissed her. "You should be asleep, honey."

"Are we in trouble, Mummy?"

Kim sighed. She was worried Maya would have nightmares about her experience, and she had been right. The unknown quantity was the amount of psychological distress the poor child had suffered. Considerable, Kim thought with bitterness. Anger surged inside her suddenly, a rage at the bastards who had done this to her, and to her child.

She stroked Maya's face, and hugged her. The ten-year old's next question took her unawares.

"Can't you call Dan to help you?"

Kim slowly sat up. "Why do you say that, honey?"

"Because he helped you before, maybe he can help you again. He likes you. And I know you like him."

Kim smiled to herself and, for some reason, felt strangely emotional. She blinked back the rising tears in her eyes. Children had an unerring sixth sense. Maya could see through her effortlessly. She told Maya the truth.

"I *have* called him, honey. And he is going to help. Don't worry, it's all going to be alright, I promise. Now go to sleep." She turned the bedside lamp off and rose to leave. Her cell phone beeped inside her pocket. She waited till she was outside the room before she took it out.

Speak of the devil.

She put the phone to her ear and hurried to the lounge, turning off all the lights in the hallway.

"Dan, is that you?"

"Yes." She could hear him breathing heavily, but his voice was calm as steel. Sounded like the Dan she knew.

Kim said, "Tell me what's happening."

She listened in silence, digesting the information. It sounded convoluted to her, like Dan was on the trail of something, but the target was still eluding him. She explained to him what had been happening her end.

Dan said, "This thing goes higher. Who does Rick report to at the NSA?"

"The head of the TAO. He's been checked out. Seems clean, but we're still looking."

"Be careful what you wish for," Dan said softly. "It might come true."

Kim massaged the back of her neck. It felt good to hear Dan's voice. "I know. Maya and me are protected now, don't worry." She added, "You better be careful too."

A female voice called Dan's name. Kim felt herself stiffen. Dan said, "I better go."

"Who is that?"

Dan paused for a second before replying. "Xiao. She's in this as much as I am now."

"Bye."

Kim hung up and tossed her phone on the sofa. She sat in the darkness of the lounge, watching the compound lights slant in through the blinds. An odd feeling of frustration and anxiety came over her. She wandered into the kitchen to fix herself a whiskey and soda.

*****

Kim was at work early next morning. She hurried past the Kryptos sculpture and almost into Hal Schumberg, who emerged from the other side.

"Good morning," Hal said. "Heard about yesterday."

"It's under control."

They walked up the stairs together and into the lobby. Hal lowered his voice. "This college kid is definitely the Shanghai Mayor's son, right?"

"Yes." They crossed the atrium quickly and got into the elevator. They were alone inside.

Hal said, "You can imagine the political pressure on this one. Although there's nothing from China as yet. Kinda odd that, but I'll take it for now."

Kim glanced at him. "Can't we keep this to ourselves for the time being? We haven't told the FBI anything. Strictly speaking, the ODNI don't have to know."

They got off at Hal's floor and walked down the corridor to his office. He said, "What about the daily brief?"

"It can wait one day, right? Sure the DNI has lots of briefs to look at."

Hal stopped outside his office, fingers on the handle. He said, "You got 24 hours. Then we have to share the news. Potentially, this is a time bomb, Kim. Heads can roll at the fallout from this."

Kim hardened her jaws at the veiled threat but didn't say anything. She matched Hal's stare. "24 hours," she said, then turned and left. She went to her level and stalked across the floor into her open plan office. She had needed a start like that like a hole in the head. But at least she had 24 hours. That was better than nothing. And Hal was right about something. The political fallout from this could be messy. If a blame game started between China and her country, heads would *definitely* roll.

Kim got busy answering her emails and making calls. The floor behind her office was slowly filling up. Melanie knocked on her door and poker her head in. She noted the look on Kim's face.

"Coffee?" Melanie asked.

"You bet," Kim said. Melanie returned with two steaming paper cups and set one down on Kim's desk. She said, "The State Troopers want to know a reason for the BOLO." Be On The Lookout Orders had long replaced an All Points Bulletin.

"Fugitive, national security, I don't know. Whatever."

Melanie took a sip. "They're not buying it. I got a call from their chief last night."

"This one stays between us, you got that? We got one day to get this tied up." Kim's tone was sharper than she intended. She softened her voice. "Any leads so far?"

Melanie shrugged. "We got a list of registration plates. The DMV will do a screen for us. Apart from that…"

"We need to check out his house today. I want to go through all the stuff you found out. His fake name is Rupert Chiltern, right?"

"Right. I checked with the MI5 in London, and the French *Surete*. Waiting to hear from Interpol, and Canada. Sounds like a Brit name, right?"

Kim nodded. She glanced at her watch. 0730 already. "Let's check his files, then hit the house."

She went over to Melanie's table, and they pored over the company filings Melanie had found. As Kim went from page to page, Melanie said, "He needs a safe house."

Kim stopped, and looked at her. "Safe house."

Melanie stared at her boss like she was stupid. "You just repeated what I said."

"Safe house."

"Again?"

A light was gleaming in Kim's eyes. She tapped the screen. "With all this money, he goes around buying exclusive properties, right?"

Melanie understood. She took over and clicked on a spreadsheet. "I made a list of them. You wanna know if they have any in the U.S., right?"

"Yup." The women leaned over the page, checking the names. "One in Malibu," Melanie said.

Kim shook her head. "No. Too far. He couldn't have flown. He drove."

"Key West…Virgin Islands… oh shit!"

Kim saw it the same time as her. "East Hampton!"

Melanie brought up the map. She pointed at the screen. "Right there, 5670 Ronbrook Drive." The image of the house came up on Google Maps. A Neo-Edwardian mansion with acres of land surrounding it, its white picket fences giving way to wavy sandy dunes that merged into the sea.

Kim said, "We need a drone up there. I'll get clearance from Hal. You call Marly and get a team ready."

She was on her feet and rushing off when Melanie called out, "There's an airport in East Hampton." Kim gave her a thumbs up.

An hour later, they were scrutinizing the images from a drone feed from high above Long Island. Kim spoke to the operator on her headphone. "Closer in. Hold it."

A moving black dot, trailed by a plume of dust, got bigger as the image magnified. A black SUV, rushing up the dirt track to the house. On the drone visual, the house looked in need of renovation. Parts of the eaves had broken off, and the gardens were overgrown. The SUV pulled inside the gates and stopped.

"Closer," Kim snapped. "We need an ID." The man who emerged from the vehicle was bald, and he had something strapped to his back in a case. Two more men alighted from the car. They opened the trunk and pulled out three large holdalls. A door opened in the main house and a man stepped out.

"I need that face," Kim said urgently. The image blurred out of focus, then got clearer after it zoomed in. Although she could see the top of the man's head, she recognized him immediately.

"Rick Everett," Kim whispered. She sprang up and tore the headphones off her head. "Move it!" she shouted, running for the elevators.

*****

East Hampton Airport was a hive of activity. The two Black Hawk helicopters landed almost simultaneously. Kim jumped out after the four SAD men who had flown with them. She bent her head and ran towards the waiting armored Range Rovers. Marly was in the driver's seat already. As the doors slammed shut and the car pulled off the tarmac, Kim was on her phone.

"I need two RIBs," she said. Hal had given her clearance to call the Coast Guards. It was too short notice to get the Navy, and Kim didn't think the sea was a viable escape route. But she wanted to cover all bases. Rigid Inflatable Boats might come in handy. These guys had enough money to get a diesel submarine in the waters off Long Island.

As they sped down the road, Melanie said, "I never got why they call it Long Island?"

Kim was looking at the screen attached to the back of the seat. The drone feed was displaying, and there was an almost total lack of activity all of a sudden. The black SUV sat still in the courtyard.

She looked up and frowned. "What?"

"I mean, it's wide, right? Flat and wide. Why call it Long?"

Kim shook her head and transferred her attention back to the screen.

CHAPTER 42

Dan opened the trunk and peeked inside. Ying's face was caked in sweat, but he took the time to glare at Dan's face.

"You're a dead man, *Ju-Long*. Whatever you do from here on, you're a dead man."

Dan took out the Sig and pointed it at Ying's head. The Triad man glared back at him defiantly. "Go on. Pull the trigger."

"The night you came to my apartment in Hong Kong. Who told you about me?"

Ying smiled but didn't say anything.

"You didn't just know my name. You know who I was, what I did. Only a handful of people have that sort of security clearance, and they're not in China." Dan leaned forwards. "I know who you work for. Question is, do the Triads know?"

Ying's smiled faded, slowly replaced by a sneer. "Think you are so clever, Mr. Dan Roy? Well, I'll tell you what. You let me go, and I'll tell the Triads you're already dead. How about that?"

"I bet any money the Triads would love to know you work for the CIA. Or is it the NSA?"

This time, a look of fear flashed across Ying's face. Dan said, "I want a name. Someone told you about me, and that I might be looking for Lin Yan. When you couldn't buy me, you sent your goons to kill me."

The cockiness was returning to Ying's face. "You'll never find out."

Dan persisted. "Someone in the NCS black list recruited you as an asset. Maybe the NSA, but they don't come this far out. And this is what Lin Yan found out, right? Who you guys are."

Ying remained silent. Dan leaned over, grabbed his collar, and hauled the man out with one hand. He threw him on the tarmac and aimed the Sig at him. A thought had occurred to Dan. Ying was not the boss. It was possible he didn't know a great deal and was just following orders. The real boss kept secrets from Ying.

"Not much use to me, are you?"

"Dan?" Xiao's voice called him from the car, and her tone was urgent. For a fraction of a second, Dan's attention wavered. For a man who had been lying cramped for so long, Ying moved fast. With lightning speed, he latched onto the gun arm with one hand, while the other felt along Dan's belt line where the knife was. The move was too quick for Dan to block, and he fell backwards, jarring his spine on the rear bumper of the car. Ying fell on top of him, bending the gun arm backwards, lifting his knee into Dan's face. The blow hit Dan on the chin, and pain exploded inside his head. His vision dimmed, but he did not let go of the gun. He heard a rushing sound and bent his body sideways, lifting his arm. The blow aimed for his chin landed on his shoulder.

Chow Ying was a fast, lethal fighter. He pummelled Dan's body with his fists, and Dan covered his head, curling himself up. He could feel Ying's fingers closing on the butt of the gun. Sweat and pain was making Dan's fingers loose. He had to do something, or they were all dead.

Using the car as support, he rolled off it, cannoning into Ying. He grabbed Ying's shirt and they scrambled backwards. Dan grabbed Ying's waist and pulled the man towards him, bracing his neck back at the same time. He headbutted Ying on the chest and got some purchase as the man gasped. Dan was standing straighter now, and he held Ying close and headbutted him harder this time, right in the face. Ying staggered back, blood flowing from a broken nose. His fingers came loose and he let go of the gun.

Dan pointed the gun at him, shaking his head to rid himself of the dizziness. He spread his feet wider, balancing himself.

"All I want is a name," he said.

In the dim streetlight, Dan couldn't see his face, but he sensed the man was smirking at him.

Dan's heart beat against his ribs. "Does the name McBride mean anything to you?"

The look of momentary confusion that flitted across Ying's face was enough for Dan to know the truth. It wasn't his handler from Intercept. No one had survived an Intercept hunt down. No one. Dan breathed a small sigh of relief.

"What about Rick Everett?"

Ying frowned and shrugged. Then he said, "You forgot something." He smiled. In his hand, he was holding a small paging device. Dan cursed himself. It must have been hidden in his shoes. "I just called for reinforcements."

Ying suddenly threw the paging device at Dan and charged towards him. Dan didn't hesitate. He fired, aiming for center mass, but the head was closer. Ying's skull disintegrated into a hundred fragments of blood and bone. Dan picked up the pager. The thing was turned on, but he couldn't read the Chines letters flashing on the screen.

He crushed the device under his heel and kicked the remnants off the road. He turned to see Xiao waiting for him anxiously at the driver's door.

"I heard," she said. "We need to get moving."

Xiao took the keys from Dan, and he was glad. She knew the roads, and if the Triads turned up behind them, like he expected them to, she would know the back routes. As she drove, Dan kept his eyes peeled. After a while, he glanced at the woman in the back seat. She was sitting bolt upright, eyes large with fear.

"What's your name?" Dan asked.

Xiao translated for him. "She doesn't speak English well," she said. "Her name is Biyu Guo."

Dan asked, "Where we going?"

"Suzhou."

"Is that where she lives?"

Xiao nodded. They had come down the elevated ring road that circled South Shanghai and were now speeding down a highway. Cars zipped past them on the opposite lane. There was a railway line on a slope above, about five hundred yards away. There was a sudden blast of air and a blur of movement, and Dan felt, more than saw, a tubular shape streaking through the night. Then it was gone.

"Was that the bullet train?" Dan asked. Xiao nodded. They drove on in silence, Dan holding the Sig in his right hand. His neck felt stiff, and he needed a drink.

An hour passed, and Dan felt his eyes beginning to close, the car's rhythmic movements having an almost hypnotic effect. He forced his eyes open. He turned to Xiao. "My turn to drive," he said. Xiao's face was haggard and drawn, her cheeks pale.

"We need to stop," she said. "I need a drink."

Dan shook his head. "No. They're behind us. They'll be expecting us to stop and rest. We need more distance."

They pulled up on the road side and he got into the driver's seat. He slapped his cheeks and pulled on his hair, getting more circulation in his scalp. Then something strange happened. He felt soft fingers on his left temple, pressing on a spot that was at once excruciatingly painful and almost unbearably relaxing. Xiao put both hands on his head and began pressing lightly on either side of his temples.

Dan closed his eyes; he couldn't help it. A dilated space opened in the blackness of his eyes, turning them to light. His head felt light, floating, and his shoulders relaxed. Xiao's fingers rubbed the two spots gently in a circular motion. It only lasted a few seconds. When Dan opened his eyes, his vision had more clarity, and he felt more focused. He fired up the engine and pushed his foot down.

"What was that?" he asked Xiao.

"Chinese medicine. The body has nerve centres which control the mind. Your body was telling your mind you were exhausted. I overrode that."

"By pressing on my temples?"

"Tell me you didn't like it."

Dan shrugged. "Hey, I liked it." He let out a sigh. "For real, I feel much better." He glanced at her. "Thank you. By the way, you ever fired a gun?"

Her silence was enough answer for Dan. He took the Sig from his lap and gave it to her, butt first. "Aim for the middle. Don't try to shoot the head. Got that?"

Xiao nodded in silence, looking at the Sig that suddenly looked big and menacing in her little hands. Her fingers closed around the butt slowly. Dan glanced at the back. The woman was curled up in a ball on the seat, asleep.

"Get some shut eye," Dan told Xiao. He changed lanes and sped up.

CHAPTER 43

East Hampton
Long Island, New York

The two SUVs stopped one mile out from the mansion, by the shadow of a sand dune. Kim jumped out and strapped on the bulletproof vest one of the SAD men gave her. From the hood, she chose her weapon, a Heckler and Koch 416 rifle. She checked the magazine of her Glock 22 and slipped it into the right thigh holster. Around her, the others were going through the same motions. Melanie and one of the drivers would remain in the car. Marly could have stayed behind if he wished, but the promise of excitement was too much to bear for the grizzled fifty-two-year-old veteran. Wild horses couldn't hold him back.

One of the men said, "Comms check."

Kim pressed on her ear phone and made sure she was on the same wavelength as the others. Dusk was falling over the roaring blue sea, and the sky was turning from crimson to a dark shade of blue. The first stars were bright in the April sky.

David, the man leading the SAD team, gathered his men around. "OK, listen up. We don't know what sort of welcome to expect, but be prepared for the worst. We shoot to kill, but for the real POI, we aim to capture." He looked to Kim for guidance. She stepped up to the ring of six men.

"There's one man and a hostage. The rest are the hired muscle. I have only seen two men so far on the drone feed, but it's more than likely there's more inside. We need Rick and the Chinese man alive. In any circumstance, we cannot harm the Chinese guy. Is that clear?"

The men nodded, their faces invisible in the darkness that was falling rapidly. David said, "One mile to target. Ten minutes ETA. Let's move."

Melanie gave Kim a thumbs up, and she nodded back. The march to the mansion was brisk, and Marly kept up pace with Kim and the others without breaking sweat.

"Doing well, Marly," Kim said. The older man frowned, making Kim smile.

"You think I'm an old fogey? I can still do this with a 30-pounder on my back."

David, who was at the lead, raised his hand when the building came into view. The men scattered, aiming to surround the building from high positions. Kim stayed with David. They sprawled on top of a sand dune, listening to the surf pounding behind them. Two black shadows darted towards the white picket fence from either side of the road.

Kim didn't like it. The house was quiet, silent. It was a big place, but she didn't believe they would keep the front unguarded. But the SAD men had circled the place and cleared the surroundings. They should be good to go. She just hoped they weren't walking into a trap.

The car was still in the drive. The garage was shut and it was big enough to hold another five. She wondered what transport they had inside. The two men approaching the house lay very still on the ground, and they had become invisible unless someone knew they were present. One of the men raised himself silently. He slithered to the fence and climbed over it. There was a sound like air escaping a bicycle tire at high speed, with the flash of muzzle fire from one of the windows facing the sea, and the man fell backwards. He didn't move.

The roar of gunfire suddenly split the night wide open. It came from the side of the house, and Kim saw the blast of gunfire from a window. Her radio crackled to life.

"They're moving at the rear. We need to cut them off." It was one of the men who had circled around the back. Kim got up and set off at a sprint, following David and Marly. T

hey had to stay under cover to avoid the sniper inside the house. A firefight had started in earnest now, the SAD men returning fire for their fallen comrade, and regular bursts of gunfire punctured the silence of the night. There was a sudden explosion at the rear of the house, and the roar of an engine. Kim came around the bend just in time to see a Range Rover hurtling out of the garage and race down the side of the garden. Bullets followed the car, but they ricocheted off the armored body. Kim aimed her rifle, but the car had swept past her as she squeezed the trigger.

They ran after it. "Where the hell is it going?" she panted on the radio. Melanie was hooked up to their comms channel, and her voice came in Kim's ear.

"It's going down a dirt track that leads down to a jetty. There's a boat waiting for them."

"Damn it. Call the RIBs."

"On their way," Melanie said.

Leaving the house behind, Kim, Marly, and David rushed down the dirt track. Melanie guided them with visuals from the drone feed, and they left the track to slide down a sandy slope that led into the beach. They ran to the left. For a while, nothing was visible. Kim knew the first person to turn a light on risked a bullet.

In the distance, they heard the screech of brakes as the Range Rover came to a stop. They ran harder and eventually made out the outline of the car and the jetty. A speedboat, no longer than ten meters, bobbed up and down on the water, barely visible.

"Get down," David screamed and pushed Kim down to the sand. Seconds later, the loud staccato burst of unsuppressed rounds filled the air. They flew over their heads. Kim shook the sand out of her eyes and aimed her weapon, then gritted her teeth. She couldn't fire. The enemy knew that. She tried to get up, but David pushed her back down. She saw the logic. If they were loading up on the boat, someone was standing guard, firing on them.

She watched in frustrated silence as dim shadows moved towards the boat. She counted three men, clearly pushing another figure in the middle. In a while, she heard the welcome sound. The sound of the RIB engines parting the waters behind them, approaching the jetty. With a roar, the speedboat came to life. More bullets flew at them, passing over their heads, and this time David fired back. There was a grunt and the thud of a body hitting the wood of the jetty. The speedboat took off into the dark waters of the Atlantic.

They stood up and ran towards the RIBs pulling up. The wounded man on the jetty had been hit in the neck. Kim bent down and flashed a light on him. She didn't recognize the face. She turned the body over. The bullet was lodged inside the cervical spine. This man didn't have long to live.

David helped her onto the RIB, and the nose lifted up in the air as they sped after their target. Kim wondered where on earth the boat was headed to. She could feel the salt spray on her face, and the smell of the sea deepened. In a short while, she had her answer. A single light twinkled in the distance, above the waves. It had to be a larger boat.

Kim said, "This ship could take them further out, maybe to make rendezvous with a submarine."

David said, "They're headed north. Could end up in Canadian waters, and then we have no jurisdiction."

The RIB's engine was going full tilt. Kim got on the phone to Melanie. "We need backup. Call Hal. We need Coast Guard, Navy, anyone, to stop this boat."

There was a flash in the darkness ahead of them, and bullets streaked over the water. Kim leaped forward for cover, grunting as her chest hit the boat's base. She fired back, aiming for the dark shape they were catching up with. The other RIB had circled around, and they had caught the speedboat in a pincer movement. Gunfire erupted around them, despite Kim screaming at them to stop.

No one paid her any attention. But after a few volleys of fire, there was a sudden quietness, broken only by the buzz of the RIB engines. The speedboat was silent.

David looked back from the front, the muzzle of his weapon smoking. "Their engine's stopped. Time we boarded."

"Be careful," Marly said from next to Kim. "This could be a trap."

The RIBs cut their engines, drifting up silently to the speedboat. Kim's heart was in her mouth. The stock of the rifle was steady against her shoulder, ready to shoot. The boats rose up and down in the swell of the rising tide, water splashing against the sides. As they got closer, a ghost-like figure raised itself up.

"Don't shoot!" Kim screamed.

"Hold your fire," David shouted. "Put your hands up."

The figure looked at the approaching RIBs and lifted his arms slowly up in the air. Hooks were launched from the boats, and they clattered against the side of the speedboat. Kim saw the distant flash of white light and heard the sound of a siren. She looked up to see the large hulk of a Marine Protector Class Boat splicing the waves, heading for the bigger boat.

David was the first person on the speedboat. The three men were dead. Two of the bodies lay slumped against the sides, covered in blood. Another one was on the floor, not moving. Kim transferred her attention to the man standing. She turned her light on him, and he held his hands up to the beam, blinking. He was a young Chinese man. His jeans were torn, and his dark jacket had ripped at the front.

"Bohai Zilou," Kim said softly, trying her best to stay upright as the boat moved in the sea waves. Surprised at the mention of his name, the young man lowered his hands.

David appeared by her side. "There's no sign of your man."

Kim nodded and checked the dead bodies. Rick Everett was not among them.

CHAPTER 44

The white halogens glowed bright over the highway, but Dan could see the remaining countryside was now a blanket of darkness. Clusters of light appeared in the distance, shining dimly like yellow stars. But the glittering skyscrapers had gone, and with them, the traffic. He wound his window down. The humidity was gone too, and the air smelt fresher, clearer.

Then he saw the headlights. Bearing down from a distance, but still approaching fast. Dan pressed the speedometer up to 110 mph. He looked at the gas tank indicator. Leaning on red. Xiao had fallen asleep, and he nudged her. Her eyelids snapped open, and she sat up with an exclamation.

"Time to wake Biyu up. Our friends have arrived."

Xiao looked behind them and saw the headlights. She leaned to the back and shook Biyu. The two women had a rapid conversation. Dan watched as the cars approached. Three of them, all SUVs. The lead car was closing the gap fast. Dan had pushed the Buick as fast as it could go. The engine was making a whining noise now, and the body rattled.

He figured the rear car was doing 130. Dan looked around the highway. There was a turn coming up, but there was no sign on it. He heard a sudden cracking sound and the sharp ricochet of a heavy round.

"Get down," he yelled. Another bullet came in, closer this time, and the rear windscreen erupted in a shower of glass fragments. Biyu screamed in the back.

Xiao shouted as Dan swerved from one lane to the other, trying to confuse the marksman. *Amateurs*, he thought. The first thing he would have done was to shoot the tires out.

Xiao was trying to tell him something. Over the roar of the engine, he heard her. "Take the turning. Take the turning!"

Dan wrenched the wheel without slowing down. The car bucked and fought under him, tires squealing on the road. A road sign appeared above, and it said "Suzhou" in English. "Straight ahead." But the turning he was taking had no sign, just a white arrow. They were hurtling towards it, the lead car less than a hundred meters behind them now. Dan turned his headlights off.

"You sure this is the right way?" Dan yelled.

"Yes," Xiao responded. "Keep going."

They took the turning in a rush, and Dan had to turn the headlights on briefly. The exit looked like a workman's road, with no marking, but wide enough for two cars to pass. Trees leaned on either side, forming a dark space lit up by the headlights. Beyond the trees Dan couldn't see much. The road bent to the left, and he followed it, turning the headlights off.

Biyu said something from the back, and Xiao translated. "Pull over."

"What here?"

"Yes."

Dan didn't have much time to think. He figured the woman knew what she was doing. It was possible there was cover behind the trees. He flicked the lights on for an instant and found a gap in the foliage. He heard the growl of engines behind him. They had fallen further back; the sharp turn had slowed them down. Dan braked, swerved, and crashed into a jumble of overhanging branches. Xiao had ducked. Dan stayed upright and drove in further. A heavy branch thudded loudly against the windscreen, and he heard the crack as the screen split.

All of a sudden, there was silence around them, broken only by the sound of engines on the road. Headlights cut through the barnacles of twisted foliage. Xiao and Biyu were out already. Biyu was picking her way assuredly over the tumbling shrubs. Dan followed, pushing leaves away from his face. He let the women go ahead. He took out his weapon and turned back briefly. The light beams were strong, and he heard a car screech to a stop. No more time to waste. He plunged into the undergrowth.

Dan tried to walk light, wary of giving his position away by snapping twigs. He didn't manage it, and he knew his heavy boots were getting in the way. In contrast, he could barely hear the two women. The moon shone out from behind a bank of clouds, and the landscape in front of him was sudden washed in silvery light. The forest tumbled down into a river, and he could see a dense bunch of traditional Chinese houses, made of bamboo and wood, with curling eaves. The houses lined both sides of the narrow river banks.

Dan figured Biyu knew a way through the thick foliage. They came upon a path and followed it down to the river bank. The rustle of water and the sound of wind filtering through reeds came to his ears. There was a damp, musty smell. His feet squelched in mud. The moon had vanished behind clouds again. In the starlit darkness, Biyu stole her way to a wooden jetty. Xiao kept looking back to ensure Dan was following.

A narrow, long boat, reminiscent of a Venetian gondola, was tied to the jetty. Dan whispered, "I can row."

Xiao said to him, "That's fine, but Biyu wants to know if you have ever held a long oar."

"There's always a first time."

Before Dan got in, he took his boots off and tied them around his neck with the laces. He rolled up his trousers and ran up the bank. With his kukri, he cut out a branch from the foliage. He went back over their tracks, sweeping the mud with the branch. It wasn't ideal, but it was the best he could do to cover their tracks.

Xiao got in first. Biyu grabbed the handle of the single oar that was tied upright to the boat. She handed it to Dan and said something in Chinese. Then she made a downwards, pushing movement with her hands. Dan understood from her gestures. He was meant to push the oar down as far as possible and use it to steer, as well as row.

Well, he thought, *it sure as hell beats getting a bullet in the back.*

Above him, there was a flash of a light beam, and the distant sound of voices carried to them in the stillness of the night. Urgently, Biyu got on the boat, and both women huddled in the middle. Dan got into the boat carefully and perched on the edge. He remained seated, grabbed the oar, and used it to push off the jetty. There was a current in the river, and they were borne down gently. Dan dug the oar in deep and was surprised when he hit the bottom. He lifted the oar up quickly and steered the boat to the near side, close to the banks. The houses were all dark. The moon came out again, playing hide and seek. Some of the houses were made of cement and bricks, with wooden balconies on the upper floor.

The throng of houses meant a dense community lived here. Clothes dried on the balconies. At regular intervals, there were steps going up from the river, to the pavement on both sides. They came across a bridge, and the boat passed beneath. Dan had to crouch slightly, but the bridge was wide enough to allow the passage of several rivercraft. The river wound its way to the left, and Dan followed. He became aware that he was in a small town built on waterways. Jetties and mooring places for similar boats to his abounded, including some motorized ones. Water alleys branched off the main river, some spacious with houses on either side, others only wide enough to allow a single boat.

The strange beauty of the place, ephemerally lit up by moonlight, was absorbing. But Dan didn't have the luxury of time. He kept an ear back for sounds. Sooner or later, their attackers would figure out they had gone in the river. As he listened, he heard the splash of water on oars. They were coming, and coming fast.

He whispered to Xiao, "We need to hide. I say we ditch the boat and head inside."

Biyu indicated a row of steps on the bank nearby. Two rows on each side, going up a small cement path back to the pavement. Dan tied the boat up and was about to alight when he saw the flash of lights coming around the river bend. He hurried after the women, hoping he hadn't been seen.

There was no gap between the houses for them to hide in. The sounds of the gliding boats, voices and the lights came closer. Dan felt the hair rising on the back of his neck. The Sig was in his hand, but without cover, it wouldn't be any use against superior firepower. He ran after the two women. Several of the houses were dark, and he wondered if any of the ground floor doors would be open.

The sounds were getting closer, and Dan reached out to grab Xiao's hand. "We need to…"

"This way," Xiao whispered quickly. Dan looked up to see Biyu melting into the shadows of a front porch. Xiao followed, pushing open the wooden door. There was a smell of wood and old furniture inside, mingled with the familiar smell of frying chillies and oil.

A sudden, sharp beam of light pierced the darkness outside. It spilled in through the windows, falling on them. Xiao lifted her hand to the glare, and Dan pulled her down. Biyu was on the floor already. "Stay down," Dan whispered. He crawled to the open door and shut it gently. He reached for the wooden bar above that fell across the door on a latch to make an old-fashioned door lock.

The light was gone, but it was flashing around the other houses, looking for movement. Whispered voices and sharp orders rang out in the silence. Dan held the Sig loose in his hand, aware his palms were sweaty. This was someone's home. Women and children were sleeping in the houses around him. This was the worst place ever to have a firefight. He closed his eyes and clenched his jaws. Nightmare visions of previous operations rose without warning in the back of his mind. The ravages of war were like claw marks in the soul. He shook his head, dispelling the images. He would attack first and let them shoot him. It might buy the women some time to escape down the back.

He whispered to Xiao, "If they get too close, I'll hold them. You two go out the back."

She gripped his forearm and dug her fingers in. Her nails were sharp. "No!" she hissed. "No way." But Dan had made his mind up.

The light beams danced around, and the voices came closer. Dan heard a rattling sound and realized they were trying out the doors. He crouched closer to the front. The light became brighter, and several beams shone inside the room, filtering in through the iron bars of an open window. Whispered voices came closer.

Xiao could feel her heart beating in her mouth. Biyu and she were hidden beside a wooden sideboard, close to the window. A beam of light cut across the top of her head and lit up the floor in front of her. Bamboo chairs and a small wooden table stood at the side of the room. Red posters with Chinese letters were fastened to the wall. A fat Tao God with a long, flowing white beard had a shrine in one corner. The light danced from one corner to the other. She could see Dan, crouched very still. The light beam fell on the wall he was hiding behind.

Then it swung back and lit up the sideboard again. She felt Biyu stiffen beside her. They were huddled up into the tightest balls possible. A male voice above them said, "Something here, boss."

Sweat broke out on Xiao's head. Her knuckles were white. She held her breath. Footsteps outside, and more lights flowed around the room, picking out all the shadows and furniture.

"Let's open the door and have a look inside," the same voice urged. There was a shuffling sound, and then another voice. "Hundreds of houses on this street, you *shabi*. Can't look at all of them. This is too close. They must have moved further on. Let's go."

"No boss, I saw something, I swear."

A sound of swearing, then the door rattled. Xiao saw Dan stand up, bent at the knees. Her breath became gasps, and her clenched fists were ice cold. A panic seized her. She couldn't let him die like this. She simply couldn't. Xiao turned and got ready to move towards Dan.

The male voice outside said, "The door is shut, *cao ni ma*. All those drugs you take has gone to your head, you fool." More swearing, then the voices dissipated. Footsteps faded, and the darkness flowed back. Xiao fell back against Biyu. She took great gulps of air, feeling like she had just cheated death.

CHAPTER 45

Dan crawled over to the two women. "Where are we?" he whispered.

Xiao said, "This is Biyu's parents' house. They are sleeping upstairs."

The women spoke in hushed tones. Xiao said, "Biyu wants to go upstairs."

"Go with her," Dan said. "I'll stay down here." He looked at his watch. It was 0100 hours. "Come down in three hours."

Xiao nodded, and although Dan couldn't see her face well in the darkness, it seemed as if she wanted to say something to him. Biyu rose and padded to the hallway behind the room. She went up the stairs.

Xiao remained, on her knees, staring silently at Dan. He said, "What?"

In response, Xiao reached out a hand and touched the side of his cheek. Her fingers were cold, and they trembled. Dan put his hand over hers. He kept it there for a few seconds, then lowered it gently. He could feel her proximity, the warmth radiating off her, and the smell of sweat on both their bodies. Something stirred inside him, and he was aware he was holding her hand tightly. He let go, and she lifted her hand and caressed his cheek again. It was deeply comforting, and he closed his eyes, feeling the soft brush of her hands.

Then it was gone. Dan opened his eyes to see Xiao had padded out to the hallway. She went up the stairs, and Dan was left alone, wondering if he had dreamt it all.

*****

On the edges of his consciousness, the smallest of sounds. Like the sound of a single raindrop on glass. More felt than heard. The faintest disturbance in the thin veil of sleep that had overcome him. A primitive, inchoate reflex had him rolling over, holding out the Sig, rock steady in his outstretched right hand. He was barely awake, but he was ready to shoot.

He blinked as there was a scream, and the sudden crash of something falling on the floor. Daylight, bright and effusive, streamed into the room. There was an old woman in front of him, wearing a vest and long skirt. A bowl of noodles was on the floor, liquid pouring out of it. The woman's mouth was open in shock. Dan lowered the weapon quickly and tucked it on his back beltline. He scrambled to his feet.

"I'm so sorry," he said. From behind the woman's skirt, a little hand appeared, then a round, cherubic face with red cheeks. It was a little girl, and her hair was tied up in two pretty bunches on either side of her head. She stayed behind her guardian but gazed at Dan with wide, astonished eyes.

Xiao came running down the stairs, with Biyu behind her. Dan said, "Please tell her I'm sorry."

As Biyu bent down to help the woman clean up the mass, Dan noticed another child who had come down the stairs. Both were small, and he guessed they were similar in age.

Xiao said, "This is Biyu's mother." The old woman had stood up. Her face was lined and wrinkled from the sun. Deep creases lined her forehead, and her eyelids, like her cheeks, sagged downward. There was a sharpness in her eyes as she looked Dan up and down with curiosity. She said something to Xiao.

Xiao grinned and said, "She said you move very fast. Like a coiled snake."

Dan said, "Sorry to alarm her. Is there a place where I can wash up?"

The bathroom was at the back, behind the small kitchen which was steaming hot. As Dan splashed water on his face from a bucket, he looked at the alley of water behind the house and the bank of houses behind it. Rows of houses stretched on an intricate pattern of waterways, crossed by frequent bridges.

When he was back at the living room, Biyu scraped back a chair for him at the table. The Tao God was seated, his eyes closed and the white beard spilling over his protruding belly. The shrine had flowers and coins at his feet to keep him appeased. Another bowl of noodles arrived, the steam and sharp, spicy smell invigorating. Dan suddenly realized he hadn't eaten for almost a day. The noodles were thick, and the soup was a thick, meaty broth. Food had never tasted so good.

As he ate, the two children came up to the table, feeling braver. They stood close to each other, gaping at Dan. He wiggled his eyebrows at them as he slurped with his chopsticks. He finished and drained the bowl of soup. He wiped his hands on his sleeve. Both the children were dressed alike, and he realized they were two girls. Pretty pink bands held up their hair. Their eyes were very large and shiny. They stared at him with infinite curiosity, like he was some crazy big doll that moved, talked, and ate noodles.

Dan leaned slightly forward and said, "*Ni ho ma?*" How are you.

The two girls screamed and ran away as fast they could.

*****

Xiao came into the room, followed by Biyu. They sat down in the bamboo chairs in front of Dan. The door was shut still, and curtains were drawn against the window that had been open last night.

Biyu looked at Xiao and nodded. Dan could see Biyu properly now. Her skin was alabaster, and above her high cheekbones she had a pair of wide, tapering eyes. She was very pretty, even though she appeared tired and withdrawn.

Xiao said, "Those are Biyu's two children."

Dan nodded, "I got that."

Xiao shook her head and gave Dan a meaningful glance. Something had passed between them last night, and he felt closer to her. He read the reproach in her eyes and was initially confused. Then like a flashbulb, the realization hit him.

Two children. In a country with a one child policy.

Xiao did the talking. "When Biyu was pregnant with the second child, the Sterilisation Committee came around. They fined her because she had removed the copper T coil from her womb. Every woman around here has to wear the copper coil after their first child, and they need a scan every year to ensure it's in place."

"Biyu paid the fine, but there was more to come. They wanted her to have an abortion. If she did, then she would get to keep her *hukou*, and not pay any more fines."

"What's a *houkou*?"

"It's the permit to own land, housing, schooling, and health care. *Hukou* are very important in China. A citizen gets a *houkou* where they are born. But when they move to another place to work, they don't get *houkou* there. Hence they have to leave their families behind."

"Their kids get schooling and healthcare in the villages or the city where they come from. Right?"

"Yes, right. This is one of the reasons why there are so many migrant workers in China. People don't have the right to own houses in big cities if they come from villages. They have to pay for schools and healthcare too, which are normally free in China."

"But what if you are born in a city, like Shanghai?"

"Then you are lucky. A city *hukou* is very hard to get. Either you are born there, or know someone in the Party who can get you one."

Dan was beginning to see. "Kind of a divide between city and country."

Xiao frowned. "Big divide. We have a classless society, apparently, but the real gap in China is between the elite in the cities and the poor, uneducated in the villages. Our laws make it very hard for villagers to make it in the city – even when they work there and earn good money."

"Anyway," she continued. "Biyu wanted to keep her baby. She was born in the outskirts of Shanghai, so she was lucky to have a Shanghai *hukou*. The Sterilisation Committee kept up the pressure, and she had to escape when she started to show. She came down here. But she couldn't hide for long. The Sterilisation Committee has eyes everywhere. When Guoguo, her second daughter was born, she lost her *hukou* and was slapped with a heavy fine."

"How much?"

Xiao spoke to Biyu and said, "Fifty thousand yuan."

Dan whistled.

"She didn't have that sort of money. Her husband had to get another job, further away. Things got worse. Government officers came down and told her they would take Guoguo away if she couldn't pay the fine. She had lost her healthcare and housing, and now this."

Dan shook his head. "Sounds barbaric."

Xiao looked unhappy. "I know. But then something happened." She glanced at Biyu, who nodded again.

"A man came to see her one day. She was taken to his car, and they had a private conversation. If she came to work for him in a KTV Bar, she would get to keep her new baby, and she didn't have to pay the fine. She would also get her precious Shanghai *hukou* back."

Xiao gave Dan a stare, and Dan knew what was coming next. It sounded unbelievable but it had to be true. "She sold herself."

Dan glanced at Biyu, whose head was bent, her fists knotted deep into her lap, like she was holding a secret inside them.

"Biyu is not the only one. There's a whole tribe of them. Women who lie to their husbands and families. Don't tell them what they have to do for a living. Otherwise, they lose their children, everything."

Xiao looked out the window. "All for having a second child."

Dan didn't say anything. He heard a sniffing sound and looked towards Biyu. Her head was still bent, and she wiped a tear off her cheek. Her eyes remained downcast.

"Where's her husband?" Dan asked.

"Away with work. He doesn't know, but she told her mother. She sees her children rarely. They are raised by the grandmother. Her father is dead."

"What's with that house where she was staying? Why were the PSB guards there?"

Xiao leaned forward and spoke to Biyu softly. "She doesn't know. Some important people come there, with government cars and guards. The girls have to sleep with them."

"So that place is a brothel for the big cheese, right?"

Xiao nodded. Dan said, "Ask her about Jinjing Sheng."

"I already have. Jinjing worked in the KTV bar with her. The one we went to."

"She used her real name?"

Xiao shook her head. "Good point, and no, she didn't. They all have English names. Jinjing was called Christine. She remembers Jinjing because of her husband who worked there. He wasn't supposed to. But he found out where Jinjing was working, because he was suspicious. Jinjing begged him to leave, but he wouldn't."

"But then he made a run for it. Maybe they threatened him, or he got scared he would lose the children." Dan closed his eyes. That poor fucker had now lost everything. This was turning out to be a bigger mess than he had imagined. He opened his eyes.

"And what about Jinjing?"

Xiao asked Biyu and shook her head. "She disappeared from the house and the KTV bar one day. No one has seen her since."

CHAPTER 46

Dan stood up and walked around the room, bare footed. He stared at the gaps between the horizontal wooden planks. He asked Xiao, "Someone must have known about Jinjing?"

Xiao translated. Biyu's face was ashen, and she spoke in a low voice, like it was difficult for her to speak. "She says Jinjing was not the first girl to disappear."

Dan and Xiao looked at each other, and he could see a shiver pass through Xiao.

He asked, "Where was she being taken last night?"

"She doesn't know. But she had just been with someone important. She's seen his face in the papers and knew who it was."

"They were moving her out to a village where she couldn't talk to the press."

"Maybe."

Dan said, "Or worse. Jinjing might have...." He stopped suddenly, rooted to the spot. A flash popped in his brain, setting off a chain reaction of brain cells firing their synapses, making connections.

"Wait."

"What is it?" Xiao asked.

Dan said urgently, "You said Lin Yan's next of kin was his sister, right?"

Xiao nodded. Her eyes widened, and she saw Dan's angle immediately.

"Her name is Chunhua."

"Ask Biyu about Lin's sister," Dan urged. "Do we have a photo?"

His question was ignored. The two women were engrossed in conversation. Xiao looked at Dan and shook her head. "I don't have a photo, and she doesn't know anyone with that name. Also, if Chunhua was there, she would have used an English name. Why do you think Chunhua would be there?"

"I went to the train station, right? Showed them Lin's photo. One of the ticket ladies remembered him. Guess why?"

"Why?"

"Because he had a child with him. He bought one ticket for Beijing. That's where he was last seen. When our agent was killed, but Lin managed to escape."

Xiao's face was a mask of concentration. "Hang on," she said slowly. "What are you saying?"

"This is a stretch, but think about it. Lin went to the *lilong* to see the Shengs often, right?"

Xiao nodded.

"We know that Jinjing Sheng used to work in the KTV bar. There had to be a reason why Lin went to see them. Maybe Jinjing knew about his sister. Maybe they worked together."

Xiao was catching on. "And if they did, chances are Lin's sister, Chunhua, was in the same boat as Jinjing. She had a second child and sold herself to make sure she could keep the baby."

"Correct."

"So, the child that Lin was seen with in the station, that could be one of Chunhua's children?"

"Affirmative. Lin never told you about any of this?"

Xiao thought back to the last panicked phone call from Lin. He was desperate to tell her something. That moment never came. She shook her head slowly. "He didn't, no."

Dan patted his back pockets and found it. A folded and creased image of Lin Yan. He opened it up and held it out. Xiao took it and placed it on Biyu's lap. Biyu stared at the photo for a long time, lost in thought. She was frowning heavily. Her head suddenly jerked upright. There was a light in her eyes, and she turned her wild gaze to Xiao.

"Julie!" she exclaimed. The two women had a frenzied chat, words tumbling out of a suddenly energized Biyu.

Xiao said, "She saw this man twice. He came and spoke to one of the new girls she didn't know very well. Her English name was Julie. Julie used to smoke. She met this guy when she went out for a cigarette."

"She sure it was him?"

"Yes. She remembers him because he was dressed like a college kid. Not one of the suits who came to the KTV private rooms, or back to the house. She wondered why Julie was talking to him."

"Did she ask her?"

"No. She didn't know her well enough, but she does remember where she was from. A place called Hangzhou. She also said she was going back there, soon."

"Where is that?"

"South from here, not far. It's a big city by the coast. Big port there as well."

A space was opening up in Dan's head. He could suddenly see things with a crystal-clear clarity.

"Julie must have been Chunhua." A light was dancing in Dan's eyes. He knelt in front of the two women. "Xiao, I want you to ask her this very carefully. She needs to think. This could be our answer to everything. Does she remember the brand of cigarettes Julie smoked?"

Xiao shot him a quizzical look. "The brand of cigarettes?"

"Yes," Dan said forcefully. "The brand. Like Marlboro, Lucky Strike."

Xiao translated.

Biyu got up and strolled over to the Tao shrine. She bent her head and murmured a prayer. She stood still for a while, then turned to Dan. In English, she said, "Dunhill."

Dan stood up and clenched his fists. "Yes," he whispered. He sat down on the chair and hung his head in his hands. "Shit. I have been so stupid."

Xiao was intrigued. "What?"

Dan said, "Get ready. We are going back to Shanghai. Just pray we get there in time."

CHAPTER 47

The tall metallic gate to Fuxing Zhou Lou was closed. Dan stood under the tree and stared at the paint flaking off the metal. Parts of rusty iron was exposed, and the arrows on top had rusty tips. The heat of the afternoon was palpable, and it was humid again, making him sweat. He looked down the Shaanxi South road, to the row of shops at the end. Xiao was seated in her VW Santana. Dan looked around him. No other cars, for now. No PSB guards on duty outside the *lilong*. He waited.

After half an hour, his patience was rewarded. A pedestrian opening carved into the gate opened and a suitcase was pushed out. Dan was about to cross the road, when he froze. This was better than he had hoped for. The head that protruded out of the gate was bald, and the body that straightened after was that of an old man. It had been difficult for him to extract himself out of that small gate and his face was pained. He arched his back and reached for the suitcase.

It was Mr. Fushong Lee.

Mr. Lee dragged the suitcase along the ground, walking away from Dan. He signalled to Xiao and crossed the road quickly. He walked around to face Mr. Lee, stopping the old man in his tracks. He looked up, and confusion clouded his face. Then he recognized Dan. Fear and uncertainty spasmed across his eyes. Then he smiled wryly.

"Greetings to you, Mr. Roy. If you hadn't noticed already, I am departing on a journey."

Xiao braked to a stop next to them. Mr. Lee looked at the car, then back at Dan, who stepped across and opened the rear passenger door.

"If you are going somewhere, then let us drop you off to the station."

"That is quite all right. This old body needs some exercise, you know."

Dan said, "This is no longer a game, Fushong Lee. Get in the damn car right now, or I'll make you."

Mr. Lee looked from Dan to the car and then down at his feet. He looked up and said, "Do I have a choice?"

"No."

Mr. Lee got in the car. Dan grabbed the suitcase, which was heavy. Mr. Lee was going on a long journey. He tossed the suitcase in the trunk, slammed it shut, and got into the front passenger seat. Xiao drove off. They drove in silence till they got close to Shanghai South Railway Station, one of the four rail stations in the city. Xiao stopped near a park, under the shade of a tree. The park was deserted, and so was the street.

Dan got into the back seat, opposite Fushong Lee. Xiao clicked all the doors shut and remained in the driver's seat.

Dan looked at the old man, who stared back at him. His eyes were hooded. His look was that of a defeated, broken man.

Dan said, "Lin Yan was your son, wasn't he, Fushong Lee?"

Mr. Lee closed his eyes, and a vortex of unbearable pain played across his features. He breathed out, and his head sank down. Then he looked up at Dan. "How did you know?"

"When we first came to your house, there was a photo of a woman and child on the writing desk. There were also children's toys under the table, and a packet of Dunhill cigarettes on it. You don't smoke, I can tell from your teeth, and your nails, which are not nicotine-stained. So, those Dunhill cigarettes belonged to your daughter, Chunhua. It's her photo on the desk as well, right?"

Mr. Lee looked down again, his eyebrows knotted. The look of anguish was back on his face. He nodded in silence.

"Your wife had died, so Chunhua left her second child, the baby, with the Sheng family, at Number 667. That's why Lin used to see them. And he came to see you too. When you talked about him, you looked away from me. I could tell you were lying. When I asked you about your daughter, you didn't answer."

"Don't," Mr. Lee said. "Don't do this."

Dan's voice was gentle. "I'm sorry. I think I know what you have been through. But let me get this straight. You had a second child. I'm guessing your wife was on the contraceptive pill, because it was you who wrote the books on them. Your second child was a son, Lin Lee. I can only imagine what your wife had to live through to give birth to the second son. She went away to the country, didn't she?"

Mr. Lee nodded, sighing deeply. His eyes were closed, and his jaws clenched, like he was reliving a nightmare inside his head.

"To protect the new baby, and yourselves, you gave him a different name. Shan. Your wife lived in the village with Lin, and you stayed in Shanghai with Chunhua. Having that second child broke your family apart. But you had no choice. You were still working for the Party, and if they knew you had a second child, your penalty would be even greater. You might even have gone to jail. Right?"

Again, Mr. Lee nodded in silence. Then he cleared his throat. His voice was a whisper. "There are millions of families like mine, Mr. Roy. And millions of children who don't know their parents, or who their siblings are. Many babies have been abandoned in orphanages. I was determined that would not happen to my son. He was raised by my wife's parents. I couldn't even see him till he was five years old. Too risky. A man in the village pretended to be my wife's husband. I had to pay him."

Dan shook his head. "That's crazy."

All three of them were silent for a while, each bound within a sphere of their own musings.

Dan broke the silence. "It happened again. When your daughter was older, she had a son, the child whose photo I saw on your desk. But then she got pregnant again, right?"

"Yes."

"She lost her *hukou,* and the only way she could survive was working in the KTV bar. The Sheng family, you, and Lin looked after the baby. I think the Shengs looked after the older child as well. The boy who was seen at the station with Lin. He didn't go to Beijing with Lin, and Lin lived alone. So I guess the Shengs helped to look after the boy as well, didn't they?"

Mr. Lee mumbled, "Yes."

"Lin and you planned his disappearance. You are now going to meet Lin, aren't you? And I bet you, the Shengs are there as well. With your two grandchildren, and their own. And," Dan continued, "you are heading down to Hangzhou."

Mr. Lee looked up at Dan sharply. The question was evident in his eyes. Before Dan could explain, Xiao explained in rapid Pinyin about Biyu and last night's events.

Mr. Lee rocked in his seat. His hands were tight fists, knuckles pale. A dark cloud of rage filled his face. "Those bastards. This racket has gone on for long enough."

"Who's behind it?" Xiao asked in English.

"I don't know," Mr. Lee said. "I know the Mayor has tried to shut that KTV bar down several times. But he has been stopped, each time."

Xiao said, "The Mayor?"

The old man nodded. "Despite what is happening with the *lilong,* Mayor Zilou is a good man. He is stamping out corruption within the Party. He is aware of this terrible racket. Using poor women who cannot pay for a second child as…as…" His voice broke finally and he covered his head in his hands. Sobs shook his body. He suddenly seemed a fragile, lonely old man, who had seen enough of life's ugliness and brutality, enough to know it wasn't worth living anymore.

Dan felt peculiar all of a sudden, an emotion searing through him. He wasn't prone to emotions. He blocked everything with a heart of stone. But seeing the old man finally pour out his tears brought a lump to his own throat. His throat was constricted and he found it hard to speak. He swallowed, hard, and put a hand on Mr. Lee's back.

Mr. Lee whimpered, "My child…Chunhua…"

Xiao asked in English, "Where is she, Mr. Lee?

Mr. Lee sobbed harder and stamped his foot down with sudden anger and frustration, making the car shake. He mumbled something in Chinese, not raising his head.

Xiao looked at Dan, her face ashen. "He says they killed her. She had threatened to speak to a foreign press about the whole thing."

CHAPTER 48

Mr. Lee had composed himself. His eyes were vacant, hollow, and he stared at Dan like he was looking right through him.

"Lin used to write this blog." Dan looked at Xiao, who nodded. Mr. Lee continued. "But the blog got taken down shortly after Chunhua vanished. It's like they knew Lin would write about it."

Xiao said, "Lin's blog was popular. Not big enough for the State to notice, but his following was growing." She looked at Mr. Lee, who didn't meet her eyes. "He took after you."

Dan said, "Do you know where Lin is now?"

Mr. Lee shook his head. "No. But he knows where we are supposed to meet in Hangzhou."

"And then you escape."

Mr. Lee kept his silence.

"Let me guess," Dan said. "I looked at a map while we drove down. Hangzhou sits on the Grand Canal that opens out into Hangzhou Bay, and then the East China Sea. Your plan is to get on a boat to sail across the sea to Japan, or travel south down to Taiwan. Taking a plane to fly out of the country means you'll get found out. I figure you intend to head down to Taiwan, as you don't like the Japanese, and Japan is further across the sea. But you can drop to Taiwan easily, and then present to the U.S. Embassy there."

Dan stopped, waiting for a response.

Eventually, Mr. Lee said, "I love my country, Mr. Roy. Do you love yours?"

"Yes."

"I can see it on your face. And I have given my life to my country. But I also love my children. And I shouldn't have to choose between my children and my country."

"I don't have children," Dan said, "But you are right. I am sorry."

"Don't be. The fault is not yours. The fault is no one's except the bad people who are holding my country to ransom."

"You are not betraying your country, Mr. Lee. You shouldn't feel bad."

Mr. Lee shook his head. "I don't feel bad about that. I know what I have to do. But it still makes me sad."

Xiao asked, "When does your boat leave Hangzhou?"

"Tonight. At 2200 hours."

Xiao and Dan glanced at each other. Xiao said, "It's 10:30 now. That doesn't give us much time."

Dan sat back in his seat, then realized he needed some fresh air. He got out of the car and shut the door. The park opposite had seen better days. Weeds grew all over the railings. He could see a large glasshouse in the middle, with lakes around it. Dan went inside, sat down on the grass, and pulled at the weeds. He thought of how he had met Xiao. Trying to enter Lin's apartment. Why was she doing that? Her story of Lin asking her for help, and being of critical help in the launch of the new app, had always rung hollow to Dan. Xiao had not stopped him from making contact with Mr. Lee. But she had been the only person to know that Dan would visit the *lilong* the night Dan was attacked inside the Sheng household.

Unless...unless the Triads were following them all along. Looking to see if they could lead to Lin. Kill two birds with one stone. Dan rubbed his forehead. Someone could also have been keeping an eye on the Sheng house. They had seen Dan enter.

If Xiao was crooked, then why would she put herself into harm's way? She had almost killed herself in the car chase to Suzhou. Those bullets could easily have hit her. Without her help, he would never have got Ying, the *Sun Yee On* Enforcer.

Xiao sat in the car and watched Dan sit on the grass inside the park, clearly lost in thought. She wondered what he was doing. She heard a beeping sound and looked behind her. Mr. Lee had his eyes closed. A cell phone was ringing on Dan's seat. He might have taken it out from his pocket to make a call and then left it. Xiao was about to pick the phone up when it died. After five seconds, it started to beep again. Mr. Lee opened his eyes. He reached for the phone and, without a word, handed it to Xiao. She hesitated, then took it. Caller ID was barred. The phone kept ringing. Xiao looked to where Dan was sat, immobile, staring straight ahead like he was looking at something.

She answered the phone.

"Hello, Dan?" It was a female voice, the accent American. Xiao didn't answer, and the voice repeated the question. Then a note of caution came into the voice

"Dan...can you reply?"

Xiao cleared her throat and said, "Dan's not here."

The sudden silence at the other end was deafening. It lasted for a while. Xiao could hear her heart beating. Then the female voice said, "Who is this?"

"Xiao Wei-ling. Who...who are you?"

"Kimberly Smith. I, uh, work with Dan. Where is he?"

"He's here. Do you need to speak to him?" Xiao felt stupid as soon as she asked the question. Why would this woman ring otherwise?

"Yes, I do." The voice was flat, cold. "Get him for me." The last sentence sounded like an order, and Xiao didn't like it. She didn't reply back and tossed the phone on the leather seat. She went outside and called Dan. He turned at her voice and strolled over. He caught the look on her face as he came closer.

"What is it?"

"Call for you. Some woman called Kimberly Smith."

She saw the change in Dan's features, and she knew. A pang of jealousy echoed through her, and it came unexpected. She didn't know when she had started to develop feelings for Dan; it had crept upon her slowly. She had come close to kissing him that warm night in Suzhou, but she had told herself there was no point. What would it lead to? Her life was here, and sooner or later, she knew Dan would leave. They didn't have a future together. Her head was shouting at her to be careful. But her heart was saying something else.

Dan hurried to open the car door. He searched in the back seat, and Xiao let him. He turned to her. "Where's my phone?" She didn't reply. She was seized with an irrational insecurity and an anger aimed at no one in particular.

She watched as Dan fumbled around in the front seat and finally got the phone. She closed her eyes, feeling foolish, then got into the driver's seat.

Dan walked away from the car. "Hello?" he said on the phone.

Kim gave an irritated sigh on the other end. "Jeez, Dan, what the hell is going on?"

"I didn't know you called. Xiao just told me."

"Oh, she did now, did she? After making me hang on the phone for an hour."

Dan was silent. Kim's voice became business-like. "We found the Mayor's son. Rick Everett is gone, and the search is under way. He won't get far."

"Has the son talked?"

"Not as yet. Anything at your end?"

Dan told her. Kim listened without interrupting. Then she informed Dan of Bohai Zilou and Lin Yan being friends at college. "Lin might even have known Deng Zilou, Shanghai's Mayor. You gotta be careful now, Dan. This thing is deeper than I imagined."

"Don't worry." Dan hung up. He got into the front seat of the car and noticed Xiao was staring forward, ignoring him. "We better get to Hangzhou," he said. He looked back at Mr. Lee, who nodded slightly.

"Drop me off at the station," the old man said.

Dan said, "I guess we're all getting on the train."

Without a word or look in his direction, Xiao fired the engine up and drove out.

CHAPTER 49

Hu Shintao stood on the raised floor at the end of the banquet room in the Presidential Suite of Chenguang Towers. The usual leather mask covered his eyes and nose, exposing his thin lips. Casually, he flicked the hem of his cape, revealing the long ceremonial, curved *Xia* sword strapped to his waistband. The men standing on the floor below him stood with their heads bowed.

Shintao raised his hands and lifted his eyes upward. He caught *Wusheng Lamou*, the Mother Goddess, staring at him from her perch on the wall. He closed his eyes and bowed his head momentarily. Destiny was in his favor. The Mother Goddess had aligned the stars for him.

He opened his eyes and looked at the men, who dared not look him in the eye.

"Brothers. From tonight there will be no fighting between us. No more bloodshed. I can promise you that, if I have your word of peace in return."

The men, who were the remaining Triad Bosses of Shanghai, nodded and murmured their assent.

Shintao made a sweeping gesture with his hands. "The kingdom of the Peace and Righteousness Brothers will stretch from Hong Kong to Shanghai. And I, as the Dragon Head, will rule. You will come to pay your respects. Together, we will annihilate all our enemies. Do you agree?"

The men murmured again, and one by one, they filed out of the room. Hua Dong closed the door to the banquet room and strode up to Shintao.

"Mountain Master, our Enforcer, Ying Chow, is dead."

"How?"

"We don't know. But there are reports of a *yangguizi* taking him out of the KTV bar in downtown Shanghai." Hua Dong told him the whole story. Shintao listened, chin resting on the handrest of his golden lion throne.

"Is this the same *yangguizi* who attacked you in the apartment?"

"Yes Master, I think so. We lost them in Suzhou, but then we found the girl who had helped them escape. Her parents live in Suzhou."

"And?"

"She spilled the beans. They are on their way to Hangzhou."

Shintao stood up and walked over to the glass wall that looked over the glittering night scape of downtown Pudong.

"We find him, Brother Dong, then we find everything else. I can feel it. It is destiny." He turned around. "Do not fail this time, Brother Dong. I am counting on you."

Dong bowed deeply, then grimaced and clenched his jaws. "I swear on my forefathers' graves, Master. If they are in Hangzhou, that town will be their grave."

"Take every Brother in Shanghai if you have to. Bring me their bodies."

*****

The drive to Hongqiao Train Station, adjacent to the airport, was short and tense. A bullet train was the most convenient way to travel from Shanghai to Hangzhou. Dan had the map spread on his lap and with his index finger traced the line of the highway that went down in almost a straight line to the coastal city. The place was big, and he figured it was just as well they had Fushong Lee with them. He snaked a look towards Xiao. Her face was like a storm, her jaw set in a tight line. He noticed how hard she gripped the steering wheel, the creamy skin of her hands stretched tight, with the blue veins visible underneath.

He didn't understand what he had done. He thought something might have occurred when she had spoken to Kim, but he had no idea what it might be. In his own mind, Dan was conflicted. It was in his nature not to accept things without questioning them. After thinking about every step he had taken with Xiao, he now knew he could trust her. But there was also an undeniable attraction. It was the liquid quality of her eyes, the small and endearing nose, and the fullness of her lips. Then he thought of Kim, and a spasm of uneasiness ran through him.

It wasn't guilt. He didn't owe Kim anything. In Myanmar, after the whole ordeal, they had come together as lovers. While they were together, it had been the most joyous time of his life. A time when her loving hands had molded the hard corners of his battle-weary heart into something softer, more pliable. And caring for the little girl, Maya, had added a dimension to it that he couldn't fathom. He doubted he would ever be a father; even the thought was laughable. He couldn't get himself a stable home, never mind care for someone else. Especially a child.

But despite everything, while he had been with Kim and Maya, a part of him had felt like he belonged. He had felt the same way in his early days in the Army. When he was a proud Bat Boy, a U.S. Ranger. That sense of belonging, that youthful idealism, had been lost slowly as his career progressed and he became more cynical. He was what he was. A man of violence. He always would be. It was too late for him to become something else. He wasn't even sure if he *wanted* to be something else.

That didn't mean he was incapable of love. Kim had shown him that. For that alone, he would always be grateful to her. They had parted as friends, and he had known there was every chance they wouldn't meet again. The thought had made him sad. But he knew he couldn't go back to his old life. An assassin for hire. Neither could he get himself a job and settle down to a nine-to-five life. When neither path was the right one, he had to strike out by himself. And yet, not being with Kim made him realize what he had lost when he let go of her. She had seen a part of him that he never knew existed. She had switched on the light, when he had groped like a blind man all his life. She had shown him what love was.

Dan made his hands into fists. Kim wasn't here. She had her own life, and she had always made it clear what she wanted. Whatever Dan owed her, he also needed to live his own life. He thought back to the last few days. He had arrived in mainland China without any knowledge of the country. If it hadn't been for Xiao, he would have left the same way. She had opened the country up for him like a map to a lost continent. He looked at the Chinese in a different light now. For that, he owed Xiao too. He glanced at her again, and saw her look at the rear-view mirror. He checked the traffic quickly, thicker now that they were approaching Hongqiao and joining the airport rush. He kept his eyes on Xiao for longer, then looked away.

For the first time, he understood what Asia had become for him, a place that was so different, so brand new, that he wasn't afraid to be himself. Becoming an underground street fighter had come to him naturally. No one judged him. No one asked him to get a regular job. He didn't have to fill forms and check boxes.

That didn't mean he missed home. He remembered hiking in the Blue Ridge mountains with his parents, when he graduated from high school. The endless beauty of those rolling hills, with the clouds caught between their peaks. Now, it made him think of Kim. He breathed out again. He still had a job to do.

He saw a side road before the train station and told Xiao, "Pull in here?"

She still wouldn't look at him. Gone was the easy warmth between them, replaced by something cold and frosty. "Why?" she asked.

"It's possible they will be looking for us. I can't hide. They might spot you too. I think we should let Mr. Lee have a look, then report back to us."

Mr. Lee leaned forward and, for the first time, the old man had a twinkle in his eyes. "And if I don't come back?"

"You will," Dan said. "We can help you. If Lin's in trouble, you won't be able to save him on your own."

"That makes sense, but I didn't have you down as the trusting type," Mr. Lee said.

Dan didn't say anything. Mr. Lee opened the door. He left his suitcase and slowly shuffled off towards the busy concourse across the road, his back bent, leaning forward. Then he joined the mass of people walking towards the station, and he was lost in the crowd.

"How do you know her?" Xiao said. Dan jerked his face back to her, surprised.

"Know who?"

"The woman on the phone."

"Kim?"

"If that's her name, then yes."

Dan could tell by the coiled tension in her body, and the way she averted her face from him, that she didn't like this conversation.

241

"I have worked with her and…"

"She's more than your friend, isn't she?"

Once again, Dan was taken aback by the directness of the question. It seemed Xiao wanted to get something off her chest. He shrugged mentally. He had no problem with that.

"Yes. She was."

"And is."

Dan wound the window down. The hot dusty air of the Shanghai afternoon, mingled with the sounds of honking taxis and traffic, floated inside the car.

He said, "I don't really know. Why do you ask?" It was his turn for some answers. She didn't reply for a while. He saw her tap the window frame with a long nail, the pink nail polish flaking off. She turned to face him, and he found in her eyes the softness with which she had touched his face that night in Suzhou. He felt something melt and disentangle inside him, and the sudden stirring of a desire rumbled inside.

When she spoke, her voice was husky. "I don't really know, either." She looked away.

CHAPTER 50

Dan watched as Mr. Lee walked slowly back to the car. Xiao started the engine and reversed the car. With a grunt, the old man hoisted himself back in the vehicle.

"Too many policemen," he wheezed. "I have never seen anything like it. And also a lot of Triad men. I can tell from their suits and the tattoos on their necks."

Dan looked at Xiao. "That leaves us with one option only."

Xiao nodded. "Before we do that, I need supplies. I haven't changed clothes in more than a day. We have to stop by my place."

"No. Your apartment and my hotel are being watched as we speak. Those are the first places they'll expect to see us. Can't we stop by at a shopping center?"

She thought for a while. Then she seemed to make her mind up about it. She asked Mr. Lee, "You know where to go?"

"I have the address to our old home. We lived there before moving to Hong Kong."

"Is that where the Shengs are living, with the children?"

"Yes."

Dan took the wheel after Xiao had navigated the suicidal taxi drivers and lax traffic rules of Shanghai. Hangzhou was a popular tourist destination, and a load of buses were plying on the four-lane highway, slowing the cars down. After half an hour, Dan managed to get himself free from the back of a bus belching acrid black fumes.

He sighed in relief and stepped on the gas. The tank was full, and they had munched on cold rice balls and shredded lamb, washed down with bottles of green tea. Xiao had changed in the shopping center bathroom, and they had taken turns to go in. He knew the lookout would be for a couple, and they stuck out like a sore thumb. He bought himself a baseball cap and change of clothes, but what he needed more than anything was more ammo. He had the feeling he would be needing it soon.

The green countryside flashed past them. Green hills undulated in the distance, and pastel and brick towns nestled within their folds. Rivers like silver necklaces snaked around them, all joining the mighty Quintiang River, emptying into the wide mouth of Hangzhou Bay.

In two hours, tall marble and steel towers came into view, with signs in Chinese and English proclaiming Hangzhou, the capital of Zheijian Province.

He awoke Xiao, and Mr. Lee directed him the rest of the way. The city was smaller than Shanghai, and they crossed the river again, heading for the east of the town. Xiao was now driving.

Dan asked Mr. Lee, "Where is Lin going to meet you?"

"At one of the smaller docks down the river. Ten miles from here."

"How do you know that?"

"We left comments on his blog, using a code we had used before. But then they took his blog down. The arrangement still stands."

"So, Lin has arranged the boat?"

Mr. Lee nodded. Dan didn't say anything, but a sense of foreboding was filling him. The plan was riven with holes. First off, if Lin had been captured, the boat was a trap, and same for the house. He tried not to think what they could do to the Sheng family and the children. Faced with that, he had no doubt Lin would give up his secrets.

Secondly, the Triads might have already figured out which was the best place to look for. In which case, they were still walking into a potential trap.

They were driving through a residential district. From what Dan had seen so far, the buildings were much more traditional that in Shanghai. Eaves curled gracefully into the air from every house. The vast majority were one- or two-storied, with balconies on the second floor. The crowdedness and cosy feeling of the *lilongs* was absent here, and the buildings were more spacious as land was less of a premium.

Dan asked, "How far?"

Mr. Lee said, "About three blocks away."

Dan put his hand up. "Stop. We pull over here and wait till dark. Then I check the house out by myself. Got that?"

"You must have a reputation for not leaving anything to chance, Mr. Roy," Fushong Lee said.

"It's how I stay alive," Dan muttered.

*****

The street on which they had stopped was lined on either side by a row of *shikumen lilongs*. White characters had been painted on the side of the walls, circled with red paint. Dan knew that meant the buildings had been marked for destruction. However, life seemed to go on. A group of men had put a table outside, and along with cigarettes and green tea, a lively game of mah-jongg was in progress. Children played on the pavement, rolling a bicycle tire down the road with a stick.

Xiao got off the driver's seat and walked past the groups of neighbors standing around and gossiping. Dan and Mr. Lee remained in the car. She couldn't bring herself to talk to Dan about Henry Qian. Those bitter memories had faded, but the mistrust remained. It had taken her a long time to trust another man. She wondered if it would have been different if she hadn't lived through the mad events of the last three days with him. She thought back to when they first met. How she had walked away from him, and he had come running to talk to her. How they had sat and spoken to Mr. Lee the first time, inside a *lilong* much like the one she was now walking past.

And although it seemed strange, the face that he was an outsider, a *laowai*, who knew nothing about her past, or her life, made getting closer to him easier for her. It was her father who had originally told her to trust him, and she suddenly wished she could speak to her parents, especially her dad. But she dared not. She wanted to keep them out of this as much as possible.

She kicked a small stone with her shoe, watching it skitter into the road. She smiled ruefully. Yes, she had found a man she liked. Someone who would be gone soon, perhaps back to the arms of the woman who was waiting for him in America. Maybe that was just as well, she thought, fighting down the pang of jealousy that shot through her. She needed to find Lin Yan and get her own career and life back on track.

That was what she wanted. Then why did it sound like she was trying to convince herself?

Xiao gave up. Everything around her was a mess, and she didn't have time to sort out the mess in her head. It could wait. She went around the corner and headed back to the car.

CHAPTER 51

Dan watched as lights came up in the *shikumen* buildings alongside the road. There seemed to be an impromptu street party going on. Red lanterns had been lit on the walls, right above the white letters which signified their imminent destruction. People strolled in with wicker baskets in their hands and put trays of food out from them on the table. Dan could see a TV set on a table, playing what appeared to be a Chinese serial. People sat around it, chins on their hands, listening to every word.

Mr. Lee was watching Dan. "The Chinese like social activities."

Dan said, "You see it in Honkers as well, in the old neighborhoods, away from the coast."

"Yes, but not very much. Here, we love it. Sitting around on the street and chatting to friends."

Dan was used to seeing these gatherings. Soon, he guessed, there would be singing and ballroom dancing right here on the street, accompanied by Chinese classical music. He mentioned it to Mr. Lee.

The old man grinned. "You ever been to Beijing?"

"No."

"If you had gone say 20 years ago, you would see Beijing full of *hutongs*, long alleys of courtyard houses. People sit outside their houses and chat, like here."

"*Siheyuans*," Dan said.

"Correct. The *shikumens* and *lilongs* of South China are our answer to *hutongs*. There's more of them left here. In Beijing the old houses are almost gone. It's a shame, but it also true that our young workers need more housing in the cities."

"Like America in the nineteenth century."

"Yes." Mr. Lee glanced at Dan, who was still looking at the people outside. They were occupied with themselves and weren't paying the VW Santana parked under a tree any attention.

"Our two countries are more similar than people realize," Mr. Lee said.

Dan nodded. He looked at the dome of the night sky above them and could see the first stars appearing. He felt for the Sig in his back belt. He took it out and slid open the magazine. Five rounds left. He felt for the other weapon he had put inside the glove compartment. A QSZ-92 Chinese handgun. He slid open the breech and looked at the rotating barrel lock. The rounds were smaller than in the Sig; they looked like 9x19mm Parabellums. The 15-cartridge magazine was full, but he wished he had another box. Above all, he wanted a longer-range rifle. He took out the curved sleven-inch KA-BAR kukri from his belt line. This would have to do when he was out of ammo.

He felt eyes on him and turned his head. Mr. Lee was gazing at him with interest.

"I might have something for you, Mr. Roy," the old man said. At his request, Dan got out and waited, taking a long look around. It was dark under the shade of the tree. He couldn't see anyone observing them. A few parked cars were the only objects of interest, but he had watched them for long enough to know they were empty. He saw a movement near the cars and stiffened, then relaxed. It was Xiao, coming back from her visit to the bathroom.

He popped the trunk open. Mr. Lee appeared next to him. He opened his suitcase and rummaged around, then pulled out a worn brown leather holster. He gave it to Dan.

"A memento of my old days," Mr. Lee said.

Dan took out the gun and held it. "This is an old Soviet weapon. I have seen them in Afghanistan; the Taliban still use them. It's a Tokarev semi-automatic, right?"

"Your knowledge of weapons is excellent. Yes, this is a model based on the Tokarev, but the Russians supplied the parts, and we gave it a new name: Type 54."

"So that's the Chinese name for it."

"Yes."

Dan looked up as Xiao approached. Her face was impassive.

"You OK?" Dan asked.

She nodded without replying. "What's the plan?"

"I will walk down and check out the house. If I'm not back in one hour, I want you two to head out to the harbor where Lin is supposed to meet you."

He saw something flash in Xiao's large, limpid eyes. A sudden animation, tinged with regret. She knew what he was saying. He knew it too, but for him, that had always been the way.

Dan said, "When all of you are on the boat, I want you to set off immediately."

She asked, "What about you?"

Dan shook his head. "Mr. Sheng will have the children. You cannot take any chances." He was about to turn away, but the look in her eyes held him. She seemed to be on the verge of saying something, but then looked down. Dan blinked. There was nothing to say, he knew, because there was too much to say. He knew what he felt for her was real. But they were caught up in a restless, violent world, and their confused emotions needed time and peace to resolve.

Regrets. Wasted chances. False beginnings, premature ends. He had had his fair share of them in life. Every time, his brutal, ruthless existence had chipped away at any chance of happiness. He was what he was. He couldn't change it if he tried.

Xiao was staring at him, and Dan looked away, unable to meet her eyes. She wanted the truth, and he couldn't give it to her. It was easier to seek refuge in the urgency of the situation. He wanted to hold her, tell her it would be all right. Instead, he just spoke.

"Don't worry. You'll be fine." His words sounded hollow to him. He took the Type 54 pistol out of its holster and slammed the trunk down. Xiao took up her vigil at the driver's seat. As he was leaving, he heard footsteps behind him and looked. Xiao was running up to him.

She stopped, panting slightly. "I just wanted to say…" She broke off mid-sentence, leaned over, and kissed him lightly on the lips. Dan closed his eyes. He had dreamed of kissing her coral pink lips, and the soft touch of them sent electric showers shooting down his body. He responded, and she stepped closer, holding his face with both her hands, standing on tiptoe.

They came up for air, and Dan lowered her hands gently.

"This isn't goodbye," he said.

She blinked, and a sudden sadness engulfed him when he saw the tears in her eyes. He reached out a thumb and wiped them. She gave him a last peck on the cheek, then turned on her heels and ran back to the car.

CHAPTER 52

Dan kept to the shadows and walked at a measured pace. The four-lane road zipped with traffic on either side. Some pedestrians walked past him, and he kept his head low, face averted. He followed Mr. Lee's directions and took the third left. The road was quieter, and as he walked down, the street lights became fewer, leaving large black shadows between them. He was the only one on the road after a while, and hair prickled at the back of his neck.

After fifteen minutes of walking, he saw the red posts that marked out the house. The houses were set apart on this road, each with their own walled courtyards. In the dim glow of a street lamp, Dan could see the curling eaves of the first, second, and third floors, the balconies of each floor becoming smaller as they went upwards.

He waited and watched for five minutes. The house was silent as a graveyard, no lights inside. The houses on either side were more than a hundred yards apart, and it seemed to Dan he had entered an expensive neighborhood. He had not seen such large, exclusive properties in the parts of China he had visited. Mr. Lee must have done well for himself at some stage of his life.

A shrub fence formed a perimeter around the house. It came up to his shoulder, and he crouched, then ran along the side to the back of the house. He felt a coolness in the air and stopped. When his pupils dilated wider in the darkness, he could see. A lake glimmered in the faint moonlight ahead of him. Dan pressed on, and soon he was near the back of the house.

The rear was as wide as the front. He could not see the far end of the garden. But he could make out long patio doors that opened to the outside. The two upper floors loomed high above him. Dan pressed himself against the wall.

It was dead quiet. He didn't like it. Either someone inside was being almighty quiet, or the place was empty. Before he stepped in through the shrubs, he looked carefully to make sure he wasn't tripping alarms. Underneath the eaves he couldn't see red lights which would have implied infra-red beams that would pick him up and set alarms off.

Above him he could see two windows, side by side. He watched for a while, but no one came to them.

He looked around him, then saw the tree. An old oak tree, with thick sturdy branches that he could walk on. One of those fat branches got close to one of the windows on the first floor. Dan got to the tree, jammed the Sig back into his belt, and started to climb. He got to the branch. It was indeed wide enough for him to balance on two feet. The ground was more than five meters down. A fall would probably break his ankle, and if that happened, he was done for.

Dan stretched his arms out and stepped into the branch gingerly. One step first. He was heavy, and even a thick branch would snap under him. He pressed down. It did not give way. Dan got to the end quickly. He looked at the open window, less than two meters away now. Dan crouched on the branch. It tipped forward. He stepped back quickly and revised his plan.

He walked back to the wider portion of the branch. This took his weight better. He walked all the way to the end. He steadied himself, then broke into a sprint. He accelerated, pumping his thigh muscles. As he got to the thinner edge of the branch he bent down, then hurled himself full tilt at the windowsill. He flew through the air and smacked against the wall, his fingers clawing desperately at the windowsill. His palms found purchase. He gripped the old wooden timber sill tightly.

His boots felt for the ledge beneath him. One foot, then the other. Then he stopped and listened for a while.

Voices. At the front of the house. A flashlight beam searched around the bush where he had been hiding.

With both hands, he grabbed the windowsill above him. He gritted his teeth and raised himself. He hooked an elbow over the sill as soon as he could and raised himself up. He stopped for a fraction, looking inside. Granite darkness. The voices below him were getting louder. The flashlight came again, lighting up the ground below him. Two Chinese men were asking each other questions as they patrolled the ground. Any second now, the flashlight would flick upwards and catch him framed against the wall.

Dan went through the window. He crouched against the wall inside and took his Sig out, pointing it ahead. If there was someone in here, then they were keeping very quiet. His eyes got used to the dark. The room was spacious. Dark shapes stood in one corner. He felt a creaky floorboard underneath him.

The voices below him got louder. The flashlight beam got brighter. Dan tiptoed away from the wall. The voices stopped underneath the window. The beam pointed upwards, spilling light inside the room.

The two men were having a heated conversation.

Dan did not wait to hear it. If the men were debating something, like why was the window open, action would be taken. He needed to get out of the room. He now saw the long table with chairs around it and a door next to it. The flashlight moved away, and the room was sunk in darkness again.

Dan moved towards the door. He tried the handle; it moved down. He opened a crack and peered outside. Darkness, as he had expected. He came out and stayed low. He was in a hallway and it circled around a grand staircase. Still, not a soul stirred in the place. Dan closed his eyes momentarily and cursed himself.

He had made a mistake. He should not have come here to check for Sheng and the family. He should have known they would be at the meeting point, waiting for the boat. But he had come to confirm his worst nightmare. They had been found and killed in the house. If that was the case, he had to know.

Dan crept forward. He could see doors leading off the hallway. He had taken a few steps when he sensed it before he heard it. A faint creak of a floorboard. He scurried forwards, reaching for one of the door handles. It was locked. He heard a rattle behind him and glanced down.

An oblong object had landed less than a meter from his feet. One glance told him what it was. A flashbang. Stun grenade. He ran, but the air around him morphed into a million shards of light, totally blinding him. His senses were overpowered by the smell of the exploding mercury and magnesium gas, and when he breathed it felt like he was pulling knives into his chest. The explosion threw him against the wall. He felt his head crack, his eyes went black, and he slumped to the floor.

CHAPTER 53

A muffled ringing sound that seemed to be coming from a distance. Persistent, demanding. Layers and layers of darkness lay in his eyes, a deep density that allowed no visibility.

More sounds. Mumbles, like voices in distorted microphones. Dan felt his head move, then fall, and move again.

Then suddenly, like a slap from the devil, a cold and wet sensation on his face. His eyes opened. It was blurry. Redness rimmed his visual field. He had a headache and felt sick. The ringing sound in his ears was louder. He blinked and found himself looking at something. A bucket. Half full of water. As he stared, the bucket drew back, then splashed water onto his face again. He did not have the strength to avert his face.

Fingers gripped his cheeks and pointed his face up to a white light. Dan blinked and was forced to open his eyes. Two men stood around him, both wearing suits, one taller than the other. He didn't recognize either of them.

The blackness returned, and his head slipped forward on his chest. He wanted to be sick again. Water splashed on his face again, forcing him to take a deep breath and look upwards at the light. He squeezed his eyes shut, then opened them.

The tall guy leaned forward and seemed to ask him something again. He was speaking in English.

"…hear me?"

Dan shook his head. Some of the mist was clearing from his head. He saw the smaller guy watching him closely. The tall guy bent forward again. This time Dan heard him, but his voice still came from a long way off.

"Can you hear me?"

Dan did not reply. He tried to move. He felt a pain in his shoulders. His arms were pinned back. He moved his wrists, then realized they were tied together behind the chair. Dan sat up. The ringing was fading from his ears, but he still felt dizzy as hell. It was almost ironic, he thought. Every time he had been exposed to a flashbang, he had a protective mask with a respirator on. Except this time. When he was alone, with no backup.

The tall guy leaned forward again and repeated the question. This time Dan looked up and met his dark eyes. Then he spat on the floor.

"Fuck you," Dan whispered.

The blow took him by surprise. There was someone behind him. A heavy fist slammed into the right side of his neck, making him wince. Stars appeared bright in a sudden darkness, then faded.

Dan swallowed, then breathed in and out. He shook his head to get rid of the mist of pain, then looked up. He still could not hear properly, and his own voice sounded dull, distant.

He said, "That the best you got?"

Both men in front of him smiled and moved back. They looked behind him. Dan steeled himself. It came from the left this time, an iron fist plunging into his left cheek like a sledgehammer. The pain mushroomed like an exploding red ball in his head, and he slumped forward. He felt his jaw crack. His mouth hung open and blood, mucus, and fragments of a broken tooth dripped out of it. The blackness came back, inky and absolute.

Dan shook his head again and straightened himself. He opened his eyes. The two men in front of him swam around for a while, hazy. Then his sight steadied. Dan cleared his throat and spat out the broken tooth and blood inside his mouth.

Dan said, "You two pansies are just gonna stand there and watch? You faggots." He smiled through the pain, baring his teeth, feeling warm blood pour down his split lips.

The tall guy snarled something, and moved forward. So did the other Triad guy, and Dan saw him removed something from his pocket. The flash of a blade was unmistakable.

"That's enough," a voice rang out behind them. The two men stopped, and the heavy hands that had gripped Dan's throat from behind stayed there, but relaxed their grip.

Dan looked as the two men stepped aside. To the right of him, in an old brown leather armchair, a man sat wearing a black overcoat, despite the humid weather outside. His hair was spiked blond, and he wore a black monocle over his left eye. Dan recognized it was the man he had fought with outside Lin's apartment. The man who had come to kill Xiao.

Hua Dong spoke to everyone in the room, but kept his eyes fixed on Dan.

"He cannot hear us well," Dong said, raising his voice for Dan's benefit. He looked above Dan's head. "Chen, get him some water."

Dan felt the ground move, and a shadow seemed to lift off him.

Dong said, "You are the man they call *Ju-Long.*" He smiled without mirth. "Look at you now. Not much of a dragon slayer, are you?"

A huge, ham-like fist that gripped a ridiculously small glass appeared in front of Dan's eyes. Dan opened his stiff mouth. His jaw hurt like mad. The glass was thrust into his mouth. He retched but swallowed his bile down with the blood-stained water. He breathed heavily.

Hua Dong stood up. "Where are they, Mr. Dan Roy?"

Dan wasn't surprised he knew his name. Seemed like all the Triads did. He said, "I should be asking you that question, blondie."

Dong frowned and said, "My name is Dong. Hua Dong."

"Whatever. Where are the Shengs?"

"Do you really think you are in a position to ask questions? Soon, you will die. *How* you die depends on you. Tell me where Lin Yan and the woman is, and you get a bullet in the head. If not..."

"If not then you got a big problem on your hands. Your boss has to explain to whoever told him about me that Lin Yan is still gone with the disk drive. He's probably sitting pretty inside a U.S. Embassy right now, and the contents of the drive are being uploaded onto the CIA database. The names of all your covert agents. Imagine your loss of *mianzi* when that comes out."

Hua Dong's black eyes glittered like burning coal. "I should have killed you when I had the chance. But this time, we will make it more special." He looked above Dan's head. "Remember Bei-Lo?"

Dan frowned. He felt the large fists close round his neck again, and the pressure steadily increased. Dong said, "This is Chen, Bei-Lo's baby brother. He knows you killed his brother. He's been very anxious to meet you."

Dong took out a semi-automatic handgun from his shoulder holster. "Take him downstairs. Let's see how long he can resist."

Dan felt his hands being untied. Dong was facing him, the handgun pointed at his chest from an angle. The angle ensured the bullet would not emerge from Dan's body and hit Chen behind him. But it would still kill Dan. He had no chance of fighting back. Chen forced Dan to his feet, lifting him up by grabbing his collar. The metal of another gun muzzle poked Dan in the neck.

Dan exchanged one last look with the three men in the room. He considered his options. The distances. The force of impact. He glanced at the window.

Dong was one step ahead. He said, "I know what you are thinking. But there are others in this house, Mr. Roy. They'll come after you."

Chen said something behind him, the universal expression for *get a move on, you asshole.*

Shirt collar chafing his neck, Dan stumbled forward. Dong opened the door for them and turned around to face them. Then he went down the stairs rapidly. He stopped at the landing, pointed the gun at Dan, and nodded.

Chen pushed Dan again. The duo moved slowly down the stairs. Dan could feel Dong's eyes on him, sweeping from his feet to his untied arms. Any false movement, Dan knew, and that heavy .45 slug would tear into his chest.

CHAPTER 54

They reached the ground floor. Dan saw a spacious hallway, with the main door in front of him. Heavy, tall oak door with black iron bracings. He noticed the two cameras on the ceiling and heard a humming sound. They moved towards a side door and, as before, Dong went through it, then turned to point the gun at Dan.

They walked through the doorway into another landing. The humming was louder, and Dan looked to his left. An electric generator thrummed away in the corner. Dong stepped down another flight of stairs, going down into the basement. At the bottom, a hallway opened up into three doors leading off it.

The steel door was like a prison cell, with a visual grill at the top. They walked in. Two men were in there already. They were stout and wide, shorter than Chen but barrel-chested. Both wore suits, with bulges under their shoulders.

The door shut behind them with a clang.

Dan looked around the room. It was big. There was discarded furniture in the far corners. There was a wooden board against a wall with a pair of handcuffs. Next to it, a machine with a dial, and a set of wires. A human electrifier. Crude, but effective. Used widely in military prisons of Eastern Europe and the former Russian states.

In the middle, for some reason, there was an old pool table. It had not been used for years. The green felt on top was worn out. An old cue stick lay on it.

Chen pushed Dan, who stumbled and fell to his knees. The two men at the far side looked on, arms hanging loose at their sides. Dan noticed that they moved close, flanking him. Chen walked to the front and faced Dan.

"You killed my brother," Chen said. Dan looked up at him. Dong stood a few paces back, watching.

"Inside the *lilong*. It was you with the knife." Dan didn't have to feel for his weapons to know they were all gone. He saw his knife in Chen's hand.

The big man tossed the knife on the floor behind him. One of the men stepped forward and handed him a golf-stick-sized steel pipe. Solid steel. Light shone on the dull surface. It was marked with flecks of blackened, old blood. Chen picked up the pipe and swung it like a baseball bat. The weapon passed inches from Dan's face and he leaned back. Behind Chen, Dan heard Dong chuckle. Dan remained on his knees, looking up at Chen's swarthy, sweaty face, pasty-colored in the yellow light from the bulb.

"Ha ha." Chen smirked. "Now you feel real pain, bastard."

Chen swung the pipe in a wide arc, aiming for Dan's head. Aiming for the killer blow. He raised it high and brought it down with a flourish. In that instant, Dan moved forward. He used the lean, thick muscles of his thighs to propel himself forward and into Chen. Into the blow that was destined to end his life and make mincemeat of his head.

The move took Chen by surprise, but he was too far into it to stop. Dan stepped inside the big guy's space, turning his back to him. With his right hand, Dan caught the hand gripping the steel pipe as it swung down to where he had been a second ago. Grabbing Chen's wrist, Dan bent at the waist, lifting the man over his shoulder and dropping him in a heap on the ground.

It was a basic Ju Jitsu move, using the attacker's strength against himself.

Even as Chen fell, Dan was over him, reaching for the steel pipe that had fallen from his hand. Chen scrambled, out of breath, and caught Dan by the trouser leg. Dan smashed to the floor, but his fingers curled around the steel pipe. He twisted around just as Chen was on all fours, trying to lever himself.

This time it was Dan's turn to swing. The blow made solid contact with Chen's jaw, smashing the temporomandibular joint into smithereens, ripping the right eyeball out of its socket. The broken jaw dropped loose, and blood spurted from the torn optical artery inside the eye. A moan like a wounded beast arose from Chen's throat. His head lolled to one side, but he did not fall down. He made another strangling sound and somehow got to his feet. From the corner of his eyes, Dan saw that guns had appeared in the hands of the two men, and they were pointing in his direction.

Dan reversed his arms and, like a tennis player doing a backstroke with both hands, hit the other side of Chen's face. The jaw snapped again, and this time the face caved in. Like a zombie, Chen lurched forward, eyeball hanging out, face a mess of blood and bone. But he did not fall to the ground. Dan grabbed onto him and, using him as a shield, drove him backwards, into Dong, who was trying to get a clear shot at Dan.

The men behind him could shoot, but they might hit Chen.

The three of them went sprawling on the ground. As Dan fell, he saw his knife on the floor. In a flash, it was in Dan's hand.

Dong was trapped below Chen and tried to move his gun hand, but Dan's knife found his wrist. The blade slashed the man's wrist, cutting through the bone with a sharp crack. The radial artery exploded in a spurt of red blood, and the gun went sprawling on the floor. The man screamed and tried to get out from under Chen's.

A shot was fired from behind, but Dan had already rolled over. The bullet kicked up dust above his head, but he had found the gun from Dong's almost severed wrist. Using Chen's body as cover, Dan fired in quick succession, aiming for the centers of the two men aiming at him. Rounds whined past his shoulder and he ducked, but his bullets had found their mark. He had never missed from this range. The two men stopped as if they had hit a barrier and slumped to the floor in slow motion.

Dan turned around quickly. Dong was screaming still, but he had dragged himself clear. He shouted an oath and raised his good hand. Dan saw a snub-nosed 9mm pistol. Dan fired even as he saw Dong press the trigger, falling back as he did so. His evasive action was worth it, as another round shot inches past his right ear, burning the few tufts of hair sticking out. From the floor, Dan grabbed the weapon with both hands, his palms slippery with sweat. Dong had lurched to his feet, right wrist half-ripped off, blood dripping off it. His monocle had fallen off, and for the first time Dan saw a hollow socket of white bone. Next to his normal black eye, and his blonde hair covered in blood, the empty hole looked hideous, grotesque. Dong opened his mouth and showed his fangs like a wild animal, saliva dripping from his teeth. His weapon was pointed towards Dan on the floor. Dan fired and rolled away, then fired again from a lying position.

His first bullet missed, but with the second one he saw Dong stumble. He fired again, this time aiming not for center mass but the H-zone of the head, the killer shot. The man's head mushroomed in a mist of red blood. He hung oddly suspended for a second, left wrist dangling in a morass of blood, head all but obliterated, then he crashed to the floor.

Dan was already moving. Neutralizing the enemy was not enough. Taking cover from further fire was paramount. He dived for the pool table, shielding against its side. The gun shots would alert their brothers. They would come running. Dan held the weapon tight in his hand. He put the knife in his back belt. He strained to listen above the sound of his breathing.

Silence. Only the humming of the generator, felt more in its vibration on the floor above. After twenty seconds, Dan moved out cautiously. He frisked Chen and found a heavier gun that reminded him of a Colt Anaconda. He took that as well. With two guns in his belt, along with the knife, and the handgun on his right arm, Dan slowly paced out of the room.

He opened the door a crack. A yellow light gleamed in the hallway. Silence. Dan stepped out, pointing his gun along both sides of the hallway. It was illuminated by a naked bulb hanging from a single wire. He listened, then stole up the staircase.

The landing was empty. The house was silent as before, as if nothing had happened since he had entered. But he could smell the cordite and blood in his nostrils and feel the rush of hot blood in his veins. Heart thudding and nostrils flaring, he padded up the steps at a crouch, ready to dive down and fire at the same time.

Nothing happened. He did a SitRep around the whole house. The place was clear.

CHAPTER 55

Xiao was clenching the steering wheel tightly, her face a mask of concentration. For the umpteenth time, she checked her cell phone. Dan would give her a missed call when he was done. If he was done. Almost an hour had passed since he had left. A deep sense of foreboding was filling her. The party was still going on in the street ahead of her. But with Dan gone, she felt a renewed sense of helplessness. She checked the mirrors all around her. The dense black shadows at the ends of the road suddenly looked ominous. Mr. Lee sat patiently in the backseat, giving no indication that he was stressed.

Xiao started the engine. Mr. Lee said, "Whoa, he said wait, right?"

"Something's happened, I can feel it." Thoughts raced through her mind. There was only one thing to do. "Give me your address," she snapped. Mr. Lee reeled it out. Xiao swung out onto the road. She felt like a sitting duck waiting here. If they had captured Dan, they would guess he had backup. They would start looking…Xiao thought of what happened to Jinjing and Chunhua, and she shuddered. Then she thought of the children, and hairs stood up on her arms. A sob came up in her chest, but she suppressed it.

Dan might be hurt. She could take him to a hospital, but she still had to get Mr. Lee to the meeting point. Bottom line—she needed help. She thought of who she could call, and apart from her parents who were too far away, only one person stood out. Danny Dongquo. One of the most powerful men in China, and one who looked upon her with almost paternal benevolence. She mentally smacked her forehead. She should have called him already. She flicked open her phone and speed dialled Danny. He picked up on the second ring.

"Danny Xiansheng, it's me."

"Xiao, is that you?"

"Yes it is." She fought to keep the panic out of her voice. "Listen, I will tell you everything later. But I think I know where Lin Yan is. I have a friend who might be hurt. I need help, and I need it right now."

Xiao heard his voice change. "Where are you?" She told him where she was headed.

"I'm sending a helicopter down there right now and calling the Hangzhou PSB Serious Crimes Division. The Deputy General is a friend of mine."

Xiao felt relief flood through her. She said goodbye to Danny and hung up.

Xiao drove down the darkened, deserted road, watching the well-spaced houses with interest. She saw a sign and frowned. She glanced at Mr. Lee in the rear view. "This is Hangzhou's ministerial district. You lived here?"

Mr. Lee said, "There was a time when I was an influential man in the Party. I had the ears of Politburo members." He lapsed into silence.

Xiao switched her attention back to the road. She was coming up to the three-story house, and she slowed down abruptly as she saw a movement. A dark figure had stepped out, then withdrawn swiftly inside the bush fence that surrounded the house. Headlights on, Xiao pressed closer, heart beating inside her mouth. The figure stepped out, and she recognized Dan. He had two rifles strapped to his back, and he wore a vest with more weapons attached to it. She figured he had got them inside the house. He jogged across the road, and when he got into the car, she gasped. His face was covered in blood, and so were his hands. In fact, it seemed to be all over him. Bruises marked his face, one almost obscuring his left eye.

Dan said, "There's no one there anymore. I reckon they are at the meeting point already." He checked his watch. "2150 hours. How long will it take us to get there?"

Mr. Lee said, "Ten minutes at least. We have to be there by 2200."

"Let's step on it," Dan said. The engine growled as Xiao moved out into the traffic at speed, cars honking at her. They approached the bright lights of Hangzhou Port, sprawling at the mouth of the Hangzhou Bay, the last port before the Quintiang River merged into the East China Sea. They drove past the Port at speed, following Mr. Lee's direction. Xiao banked a hard left, and they entered a bumpy country track with no lights. It stretched out endlessly, and then lights appeared like at the end of a tunnel. Xiao was driving down a hill, and she soon saw the lights were large transporter vehicles, moving slowly over a clearing, lit up dimly by feeble streetlights over it. In the distance, she could see light falling over the dark, restless waters of the Bay.

"Slow down," Mr. Lee said. Xiao did, and pulled over. Mr. Lee said, "From here we go on foot."

Xiao rolled the car down a slope and killed the engine. They got out, and Mr. Lee took his suitcase. Dan offered to pull it for him but the old man refused. This smaller port had a wire fence all around, and there weren't any guards. The forklift trucks and transporters moved lazily around, travelling to and from the warehouses to the three ships tied up at the docks.

Dan stopped at the gates. He said, "I'll see the two of you inside."

Xiao was going to say something but Dan cut her off. "Don't ask why. When you get the signal, take cover."

"What signal?"

"You'll know when it happens."

"This way," Mr. Lee said, moving towards one of the warehouses. The place was quiet when the whine of the engines faded, replaced by a cool, fresh wind from the waters. As they approached the clearing in front of the warehouse, with Chinese letters printed in red above the huge doors, Xiao stopped. She had seen movement from the sides of the warehouse. The others had stopped too. She looked around her and saw more men forming a circle around them.

Xiao looked at the sky feverishly. She hoped to hear the rotor blades of a helicopter, or the siren of a PSB car. So far, she had heard nothing.

The ring of men grew tighter around them, and they had no choice but to press forwards. In the center, she noticed a group of people sitting on the tarmac. Next to them was a strange sight. A man stood wearing what looked like a cape and mask. Flanking him on either side stood two heavily armed men in suits. As she got closer, Xiao saw an old man and woman kneeling on the tarmac, hands tied behind their backs. Mr. Lee made a noise in his throat, and then he raised his voice.

"Sheng!"

At his voice, the old man looked up. He muttered something, and his wife looked up as well. Xiao now looked carefully at the theatrically dressed man. His cape was long and black, with a silver dragon painted on it. The dragon gleamed. The man's eyes and nose were covered by a black leather mask. He smiled.

"Welcome, Miss Mei-Ling, welcome." He spoke in Mandarin, not the Pinyin favored in Shanghai. There was no trace of accent in his voice.

"Who are you?" she asked.

"I am many things to many people, but tonight I am only The Dragon Head, The Mountain Master of the *Sun Yee On* Triad." He smiled at Xiao again.

Mr. Lee asked, "Where are my grandchildren?"

"On the ship."

"And my son?"

"Ah." The smile vanished. "I was hoping you could tell us that."

Mr. Lee said, "You are Hu Shintao."

"Correct."

Shintao's eyes moved from Xiao's face to Mr. Lee's. His voice had a taut edge to it. "One of you know where Lin Yan is. Tell me now, or these two oldies will be killed. And then, regrettably, I have to bring the children out. I will have no choice."

Mr. Lee shook his head helplessly. "I wish I knew."

Shintao indicated to one of his men, and he pulled out his gun and pushed it against the back of Mrs. Sheng's neck. She whimpered. Xiao said, "We told you the truth."

Shintao wasn't smiling anymore. He said, "One last chance." He raised his hand. "When my hand comes down, he shoots. One last time. Where is Lin Yan?"

"I told you, we don't know..." Xiao raised her voice in desperation. But another voice cut through hers, rising above every other.

"I am here," a male voice said. Heads turned to look. A thin young man, dressed in T-shirt and baggy jeans, with four weeks' stubble on his cheeks, stepped out of the darkness.

"Lin Yan," Xiao gasped.

CHAPTER 56

Lin Yan looked haggard, like he had been sleeping rough. He stopped way behind them, and the men stepped away, making a gap in the ring.

"Let them go," Lin said. "And then you get what you want."

"You have the disk drive?" Shintao asked.

"Yes."

"Then give it to me, or the old man dies."

"Let them go first. Put them on a cab and let them drive off. I can't go anywhere, can I?"

'And then find out you were bluffing all along? No. Give me the disk now. Enough talk."

Lin raised his voice. "No."

Casually, Shintao said, "Shoot the old man." He indicated Mr. Sheng, on the ground. The Triad man raised his gun and pressed the trigger. The sound of the unsuppressed weapon was like a cannon ball. Mr. Sheng collapsed on the tarmac head first, blood seeping out from the wound where his head had been.

Xiao was not aware that she was screaming. But she was, screaming, raving, she was running towards the man they called Shintao. Mr. Lee couldn't hold her back. Xiao snarled and tried to jump at the man, but she was plucked out of the air by a pair of his bodyguards. They wrestled her down to the ground.

Xiao spat at Shintao. "Help is on its way. The PSB have been informed. You can kill all of us if you want to, but you won't get out of here yourself."

Shintao sighed theatrically. "So, you told your good friend Mr. Danny to send help, did you?"

Xiao gaped at him, a fist of cold fear slithering into her belly. "What have you done to him? And how do you know?"

In answer, Shintao slowly removed the mask from his face. He crouched down on the floor to get closer to Xiao. She could only stare, transfixed. The earth was slowly slipping away under her feet, and she could feel herself become dizzy with pain and confusion. She couldn't speak, and her numb brain felt like it had become a block of ice.

Her mouth opened in shock. "No," she said in a trembling voice. "It's not possible."

*****

Dan darted to the left, heading for the warehouse. He stayed under the cover of trees as long as he could, but eventually he had to cross the road. Dan crouched and ran. When he was fifty metres from the site, he went to ground. The dark shape of the warehouse was in front of him now, and he could see the ring of men in the forecourt. He found a part of the wire fence that was loose in the ground where animals had dug in. Using his hands like paws, he made a hole big enough for him to squeeze through.

He shuffled on his elbows till he got to the back of the timber structure of the warehouse. He prised the sharp tip of his knife into between two slats of old timber. They were both damp, and the nails holding them together snapped easily. He repeated the procedure till a part of the wall was removed- big enough for his head and shoulders to get through.

He could see the front grill of a fork lift tractor in front of him as he crawled in. Gasoline stank out the air inside. A smell he liked, for the reason he had planned. He crawled straight underneath the vehicle. With his flashlight, he found the fuel pipe after some rummaging. He came out, and looked around. He only shone his flashlight when he needed to, cupping the mouth, and pointing it to ground. The warehouse door was locked, but it could be opened any moment. He found a ball of cotton and cut it into a long strip.

He crawled back underneath the vehicle. He found the fuel pipe again, and used the knife to make a hole in it. Drops of petrol leaked out, making a puddle on the ground. Dan used the cotton strip to soak it up. He left petrol to leak out, and stretched the cotton strip out. He came to the door of the warehouse, holding the cloth in his hand. It was wet with petrol. It would have to do as a rough made detention cord.

He opened the warehouse door a fraction and peeked outside. The gangsters were forming a ring around the figures in the center. Dan heard a single gun shot ring out, then the scream of a female. His nerves tightened. It was Xiao's voice.

He flipped out his zippo lighter, and lit the end of the petrol soaked cotton strip. Twenty seconds to explosion was his rough estimation. Staying low, he ran out of the warehouse, around the back of the people in front, and flattened himself fifty meters away. He pointed the MP7 sub machine gun at angle, so that he didn't hit the group in the middle.

The explosion shattered the ground floor windows nearby, and lifted the small warehouse roof high in the air. A sharp, sudden cataclysm ripped through the air, the boom deafening Dan's ears. Glass and other debris smashed against the wall and fell around him.

*****

Dan lifted his head from the ground. The diversion had worked. The Triad men were running like ants whose house had just been stamped on. Dan stepped out, and aimed the MP7 at the men. None of them had seen him. Easy pickings. Dan mowed them down, blasting fire in an arc, moving from left to right. Many of them understood what was happening and tried to fire back, but they were caught unawares. Dan ran in, and dived to the ground, firing while he did so. The disorientated gangsters did not stand a chance. They fell like flies.

The muzzle grew hot, and smoke came out from it. Dan stopped firing, feeling a sudden silence fall over the place. Fire crackled inside the warehouse, and pieces of corrugated fell from the roof with the occasional smash. Dan inched forward. Then he called out, "Xiao."

He turned at the sound of a woman's voice. An arm lifted from the ground, trapped under a man's body. Dan ran over. Mr Lee lay over Xiao, and he wasn't moving. Dan pulled him, and the old man grimaced. He was still alive, Dan thought with a surge of relief. He picked Xiao up, resting her arms on her shoulder. She grabbed him and pulled herself to him. Tears sprang in her eyes. She wiped them, chin on the back of his shoulder. She opened her eyes, and what she saw froze her heart.

The man known as Hu Shintao was standing up. He was unsteady on his feet, and his eyes were full of hate. Blood poured down one side of his face, lit up by the yellow flames, giving him a ghastly appearance. He had a gun in his hand, and it was pointed directly at Dan's back.

Xiao knew instantly they were both dead. There was no time for her to release Dan, for him to turn, aim and fire. Her limbs were like iron, she couldn't move. She whimpered, and somehow, willed herself to do something. She pushed herself off Dan.

But it was too late. Shintao smiled, and fired his gun. The sound of the bullet exploded in the night air, and Xiao flinched, closing her eyes. She was aware that Dan had pushed her to the floor, and he was turning, moving. It happened in a blur. With a spasm of pain, she realized Dan was going to die.

She opened her eyes. Shintao was still standing, and there was bright red hole in the center of his forehead, dripping with blood. To her right, stood the wiry figure of Lin Yan, right arm extended, smoke emanating from the barrel of a gun in his hand.

Shintao stood for an impossibly long time, his hands hanging useless by his sides. A disbelieving look on his face. Then his knees buckled, and he toppled forward.

Dan stood up, and strode over to the fallen figure. He put a hand on the carotid pulse. It was absent. The mask was off, and he could see the face now, which looked vaguely familiar. Xiao and Lin came to stand behind him.

He looked up at them, and Xiao said in a whisper, "That is Danny Jiang. The owner of Shaolin Inc, and my boss."

Dan raised his eyebrows as the full impact of the revelation hit him. He shook his head slowly, then stood up. He nodded to himself. "It figures, right? Only he could have known your whereabouts all along."

Xiao agreed in silence, looking away from the morbid scene on the ground.

Dan looked at Lin. "You fired that gun well."

Lin said in English, "I was a cadet at the youth PLA Brigade." PLA – People's Liberation Army.

"Ok," Dan said. "Come with me, and don't hesitate to shoot if you see anyone alive. Got that?"

Dan looked at the worn face of the young man who had suffered in the last few weeks, and grown older, quickly. He had once been like that too, after his first combat tour. He asked, "Can you do that, Lin?"

Lin Yan nodded. They left Xiao to look after Mr Lee and picked their way among the dead and wounded. In the distance, Dan heard sirens. He walked back towards Xiao as police vans streamed into the dockyard. They screeched to a stop, and PSB officers in their lime green uniforms piled out, aiming their weapons at Dan. They shouted orders in Chinese.

Xiao was standing up shouting back at them. It went on for a while. Dan stood in front of Xiao and Lin, covering them. His weapon was ready to fire, but he was not pointing it at the cops. He kept the muzzle to the ground, but his finger on the trigger, his dark, restless eyes watchful.

Another siren sound came from the road. A cavalcade of limousines swept into the yard, lights flashing, with cops in motorbikes riding up front. The soldiers who poured out of the cars this time weren't ordinary PSB officers. Dan recognized special ops men when he saw them. These guys had ski masks on, and an assortment of weapons that he used during his years in Delta.

A short, broad man in his early sixties, wearing a suit and carrying the unmistakeable swagger of authority, picked his way over the dead bodies. Xiao stepped out to meet him. She bowed and shook his hand.

"Mayor Zilou," she said. She explained to the Mayor what had happened.

The Mayor listened, then asked, "Do you know about my son? How is he?" He looked from Dan to Xiao.

Dan said, "Sir, I can guarantee you that your son is safe. He is in the custody of the US Government, but he will be returned to you any time you want."

Mayor Zilou stepped forward. "Who are you?"

"My name is Dan Roy."

"Are you sure about my son?" Mayor Zilou's voice cracked with emotion.

"Yes, I am sure" Dan said.

The Mayor reached out, and shook Dan's hand. "Thank you, Mr Roy. Thank you so much."

CHAPTER 57

The Mayor's private guards led the way into the ship, followed by Dan, Lin and Mr Lee. Xiao had her arm around Mrs Sheng, comforting her. It was a hopeless task, Xiao knew. Her husband had just been shot dead in cold blood, in front of her. Someone she had shared a life with. How can you comfort someone after that?

Dan had his Sig out, and he watched the men ahead train their rifles inside each room of the single decked boat. He had a horrible feeling in the back of his mind, and it made him nauseous. Shintao, or Mr "Danny" Dongquo Jiang, had said the children were on board. He hoped they were alive.

As they went from room to room, the anxiety grew. Dan could see it in Lin's face, his haunted eyes searching every nook and corner carefully. Every door they opened was empty. The final room in the corridor had a steel ring, and it looked like an old fashioned safe inside a bank vault. It had a lock, and a few bursts of automatic fire from a rifle snapped it. The door opened with a slow groan.

Lin and Mr Lee were the first ones in after the guards. Xiao stepped in after, and in the dim light, she saw four children huddled in one corner. Lin cried out, and ran towards them. Two children recognized him and stood up. They went into a hug, joined by Mr Lee. Mrs Sheng approached the other two with Xiao and they too jumped up, and embraced each other. Tears flowed freely, and the adults clung to the children, desperate to allay their fears, their own hearts broken over the loss of their children. An ambulance crew boarded the ship and took the children and women downstairs. Lin Yan and the Mayor came up to Dan. Lin shook Dan's hand, then hugged him.

"Thank you for everything."

Dan was fighting his own emotions. Seeing the children united with their families, knowing their parents were dead, had unsettled him. After a pause he said, "I didn't do much."

Mayor Zilou and Lin looked at each other. Lin said, "I'm glad Bohai's safe," in Mandarin. Dan didn't understand a word, but he realized Lin and the Mayor had a connection.

He asked, "Did you and Bohai know each other?"

Lin nodded. "Both of us were activists against the one child policy. I blogged about it, taking off where my father had left off, in a way. It got worse after my sister had a second child. When she was killed, I knew I had to do something."

"Is it true that you hacked into the MSS and got the names of the agents?"

"Yes. But while I did it, I realized I was being watched at work. I knew there was a ring of corrupt politicians who had a racket going. They sold women who couldn't afford to pay for a second child into prostitution. I never knew the head of my company was the main instigator. After they killed my sister, I had to go into hiding. I went to Beijng to meet with a covert CIA agent, but you know what happened there."

"So, hacking into the MSS archives was your way of taking revenge for your sister's death?"

"Yes. And also the realization that the government wasn't going to do anything."

Mayor Zilou coughed and said, "That's not strictly true."

Zilou said, "The Party will not tolerate this type of corruption. We had to stamp it out. But it was very hard to get proof. I supported Lin, but couldn't do it publicly, for fear of what might happen to Bohai. That's why they kidnapped him."

"How did Danny have contact with Rick Everett?"

Zilou said, "We don't know. But it seems he had connections inside USA."

Dan asked Lin, "Do you have the disk drive?" Lin nodded. "Then we need to send it off."

Lin took out his cell phone. "This phone is brand new, and I can email it." Dan gave him Kim's personal email address, hosted by an encrypted app. Lin sent it, then gave Dan the phone to scroll through the names.

Dan looked at it for a while, then gave the phone back to Lin. He went outside, and took out his cell phone. Kim picked up without delay. Dan told her what had happened.

"Jesus," Kim sighed when Dan had finished. "Well, tell the Mayor his son is safe and sound. Also eager to get back to his family."

"Any sign of Rick Everett?"

After a pause, Kim said, "No. He's gone off the grid. He had some help, for sure."

"What did you think of the list?"

"I haven't looked at the whole of it, but already there are some bombshells. Everett's name's there, along with his alias, Rupert." Kim dropped her voice to a whisper. "I don't know how high this goes, Dan. There's going to be a fallout from this. But for now, it ends here."

"Yes, it does," Dan said. There was a silence, and they both knew what each other was thinking. Kim asked it finally.

"What will you do now, Dan?"

Dan closed his eyes, and thought of Kim and Maya, and how for a few days, he had known true happiness in his life. He thought of her smile, and the day he had said goodbye to her. Then he thought of Xiao, and a shadow passed over his soul like the wind moaning over Hangzhou Bay.

He said, "I don't know."

"Are you OK?"

"Yes." His breath was hot on the phone. The fire burning in his veins was slowly cooling down. This was his life, but what sort of a life was this? There were many things he wanted to say to Kim. He wanted to…he gripped the phone harder. There was so much to say, he didn't know where to start. If he *could* even start. If he could bare his heart one day, it would always be to Kim. The one person he had shown his true self to. Then, why was it so difficult to tell her how he felt?

He knew then that he had to move on. To where, and how, he didn't know. He needed space, somewhere to cool his fevered brow. Movement was his life, and he could feel it moving in his arteries, calling out to him.

Kim's voice was a whisper. "Stay in touch, Dan. You know I'm here."

"I know," he said. "And I will."

He put the phone back in his pocket, and stood for while on the deck, looking out over the dark restive waters that merged into the East China Sea. Somewhere out there, where the starlight fell over waves that rolled for eternity, lay his own destiny. Somehow, someday, he would find it.

THE END

Also by Mick Bose:

THE DAN ROY SERIES:
HIDDEN AGENDA (Dan Roy Series 1)
DARK WATER (Dan Roy Series 2)
THE TONKIN PROTOCOL (Dan Roy Series 3)
SHANGHAI TANG (Dan Roy Series 4)
SCOPRION RISING (Dan Roy Series 5)
DEEP DECEPTION (Dan Roy Series 6)

STANDALONE THRILLERS

ENEMY WITHIN – A thrilling manhunt set in USA during WW1.
LIE FOR ME – A complex psychological thriller.
DON'T SAY IT – A stunning suspense thriller.

90189382R00157

Made in the USA
Middletown, DE
21 September 2018